Crumbling Alliances

Rebirth of the Fallen | Book Seven

JR Konkol

Black Rose Writing | Texas

This is a work of fiction. Names, characters, businesses, places, events, and incidents are either the products of the author's imagination or used in a fictitious manner. Any resemblance to actual persons, living or dead, or actual events is purely coincidental.

ISBN: 978-1-68513-570-6
PUBLISHED BY BLACK ROSE WRITING
www.blackrosewriting.com

Printed in the United States of America
Suggested Retail Price (SRP) $23.95

Crumbling Alliances is printed in Georgia Pro

*As a planet-friendly publisher, Black Rose Writing does its best to eliminate unnecessary waste to reduce paper usage and energy costs, while never compromising the reading experience. As a result, the final word count vs. page count may not meet common expectations.

For Kelly

You can find summaries of the previous books
in this series at my website:
WWW.JRKONKOL.COM

Crumbling Alliances

1
Raelyn

Raelyn cocked her head to the side and leaned in, letting her exquisite chandelier earrings swing to the forefront. She built intricate illusions into each of them. Raelyn hated spending the power necessary to craft them, but Barrister Valargus assured her it would increase sales, and he wasn't wrong. With how often she was a guest on the Netten and Naga show, ignoring a golden advertising opportunity would have been foolish.

Valargus was pressuring her to craft a necklace next, but Raelyn didn't think she could spare the power. She was trying to sell him on simpler things, like small bracelets for her horns. Initially, he rejected her offer, but she was gradually swaying him to her position.

Between healing Alahn, healing Attia, crafting permanent illusions, running the House of Healing, preparing for her first Court, and her frequent appearances on the Netten and Naga show, Raelyn was utterly exhausted. As much as she loved her new life in Derregain, part of her longed for less complicated times. She missed the simplicity of living in a rundown village in a remote corner of the Netherworld.

"I know I've said it before, but those earrings are absolutely gorgeous," said Naga. As usual, she was resting in a pile of colorful pillows, surrounded by a small army of hookahs and waterpipes.

"I'm glad you like them," said Raelyn. She turned her head, setting many facets of her earrings into motion. She spent hours practicing in front of a mirror, studying how subtle differences in her movements made her earrings react differently. It was all part of the marketing plan.

"And tell us, do you plan on crafting any more pieces for your little imp friend?" asked Netten. His necks extended, bringing his trio of heads closer to the camera. "Justinivious made it all the way to the semifinals. With a few more pieces of your jewelry, maybe he'll win it all next year."

"We'll see." Raelyn didn't think Justin planned on competing next year. She expected him to be insufferable after doing so well in the Imp of the Year contest, but he was surprisingly humble about it. "Right now, I think he's focusing on his job. Given my new position, he has many additional responsibilities. I've been keeping him busy."

Naga collected several colorful hoses from nearby hookahs, carefully arranging them in her mouth before inhaling. A moment later, she exhaled a vibrant rainbow of smoke. "Talk to us about that," she said between coughs. "We were all surprised when Chariden promoted you."

"So was I," said Raelyn, only partially lying. She earned the position by orchestrating Lamenica's death, but she half-expected Chariden to back out of the deal.

"I'd like to think we had something to do with it," said Netten, his voices speaking in perfect harmony. "Rumor has it she watches our show."

"Of course, she does. Everyone watches the Netten and Naga show!" cheered Naga.

Raelyn was supposed to join in, shamelessly praising the show. Barrister Valargus made her rehearse her lines endlessly prior to her appearance today, but Raelyn wasn't feeling up to it. "I think you're right, Netten," she said after a long pause. "I think she watched that interview, the one where I defended her."

"That was one of my finest interviews, if I do say so myself," gurgled the flesh demon.

Raelyn found the rapid shift from perfect harmony to guttural gurgles disturbing. It reminded her that Netten wasn't much different from the flesh demon that nearly killed her in the House of Healing. "It was a great interview. Honestly, I think you drew that reaction out of me. I came on the show intending to defend myself, not Chariden." Raelyn paused and smiled. It was something Barrister Valargus coached her to do. "Your questions made me see things differently. They made me understand that Chariden and I weren't all that different from one another, and if I was hurting inside, she probably was too."

"And tonight, you're holding your first Demonic Court as her viceroy over Derregain. Are you nervous?" asked Naga. The concern in her voice was palpable. Raelyn knew it was all an act, but damn, Naga was good.

"I'm hearing it will be quite the event," said Netten. "All of Derregain's demons should be there, gathering to pay tribute to you."

Raelyn was doing her best not to think about it. Lamenica did little to control Derregain's demonic population during her rule, and it got worse after her death. Most demons expected Raelyn to immediately impose population controls. Many took advantage of the time leading up to Raelyn's first official Court to summon friends and allies. "Of course, I'm nervous, but I think it will go well," said Raelyn. She was lying. She expected it to go horribly.

"At least the Queen sent Cinderhorn to help you," said Naga. "Even the orneriest of demons will think twice about crossing you with him there."

"I'm grateful for his presence, but I can't rely on him too heavily. Cinderhorn has his own duties to attend to," said Raelyn. She only spoke with the Guardian a few times since he arrived. They were both terribly busy. "I'll succeed or fail on my own merits."

"Of course, sweetheart," cooed Naga. "I was just pointing out that he's a powerful ally. A girl could do worse than having a Guardian demon at her side. If you're challenged, will he fight in your place? Is he willing to be your champion?"

Raelyn nodded. "He already offered, and I'm thankful for it, especially for this first meeting." During Court, demons could issue formal challenges. They weren't binding, so Raelyn could always refuse to fight, but doing so would make her look horribly weak. Another option at her disposal was to name a champion to fight in her place. Raelyn suspected the mere threat of Cinderhorn fighting on her behalf would prevent most demons from challenging her.

"We can't wait to watch," said Netten, his voices harmonizing once again.

Raelyn shook her head, confused. "What do you mean, watch?"

Naga sprung up from her ocean of pillows. "That's right, loyal viewers, join us tonight for an exclusive look at Raelyn's first Demonic Court. After the show, stay tuned for a special broadcast, where we'll break down all the action."

Raelyn bit her lip to stop from screaming. How dare they! No one breathed a word about this to her. She was already terrified about hosting her first Court, and now it was going to be broadcast across the entire Netherworld! "Why wasn't I told?" asked Raelyn.

"We weren't sure we could pull it off," said Netten. Only one of his heads spoke. The other two were leering at her with smug smiles plastered across their fleshy faces. "We didn't want to get your hopes up."

Raelyn wanted to argue, but she knew it wouldn't get her anywhere. "Of course, that makes perfect sense," she said. Forcing a smile on her lips, Raelyn gazed into the camera, or at least the part of the holographic image she thought of as the camera. "Join me tonight for my first Demonic Court. I expect you all to watch." She ran the tip of her tongue across her upper lip seductively, another move she practiced in the mirror. "Don't you dare disappoint me."

Raelyn pressed a small crystal disc into one of the channels carved into her worktable, interrupting the unbroken stream of blood. The image of the Netten and Naga show sputtered and faded, leaving her alone in her workroom. She took several deep breaths, hoping to calm her shaking hands. When that didn't work, she screamed at the top of her lungs.

She wasn't sure she could do it. Up to this point, stubborn pride was the only thing keeping her from canceling Court. In all the time Raelyn lived in Derregain, Lamenica never hosted a single Demonic Court. Sure, she hosted a few parties, but those were no substitute. The Traditions often spoke of the importance of such gatherings. Unfortunately, they didn't expressly require them.

But thanks to the Netten and Naga show, Raelyn couldn't postpone or cancel her first Demonic Court. The entire Netherworld was invited to watch her fumble and stumble her way through it. It was a no-win situation. Doing a good job would likely paint an even bigger target on her back. Doing poorly would damage Chariden's already tarnished reputation.

Her hands still shaking, Raelyn climbed to her feet. She didn't have time to feel sorry for herself. There was too much to do before Court. A few days ago, Attia asked Raelyn to host an important meeting with Whisper, one of Derregain's more established El'orin. Thinking it would be a welcome distraction, Raelyn agreed, but now she was regretting it. As much as she wanted to help Attia, Raelyn needed to spend every available minute preparing for Court.

Then again, there were advantages to hosting the meeting. Achillion said Whisper oversaw the criminal elements of Derregain. Between thieves, beggars, and assassins, he likely controlled a sizable network of spies. If Raelyn could make friends with Whisper, his information might help her govern the city.

Exiting her summoning room, Raelyn walked two doors down to her bedroom suite. Now that Achillion was spending most nights with her, in the House of Healing, they decided to invest in a proper bedroom. With the city starving and on the verge of civil war, it wasn't difficult for Achillion to find funding for improvements to the hospital. Raelyn suspected Derregain's nobles were prepared to give Achillion anything he asked for. After all, he was the only one standing between them and the hungry knives of the Downtrodden.

Keeping the city together was definitely taking its toll on Achillion. Even with him dressing as a woman during every private moment, it took weeks for his El'orin to recover her Aura. Raelyn grew so used to interacting with the feminine side of Achillion, she started assuming a more masculine role in their relationship. It didn't bother her. In many ways, she kind of liked it. She just wasn't sure how far she should take it.

Even if she wanted to explore their shifting gender roles more intimately, neither of them had the time. Raelyn couldn't remember the last time the two of them slept a full shift together. The best they could do was enjoy a few hours of each other's company every couple of days.

Raelyn needed more. There was no denying it, but she didn't know what to do about it. She was as much to blame for their lack of intimacy as he was. They were burning their candles at both ends, desperately racing to keep their respective aspects of Derregain from crumbling. There were only so many hours in the day.

Entering the bedroom, Raelyn approached her closet and considered what to wear. She planned to wear the same simple, practical dress to both meetings, but now she wasn't so certain. With her Demonic Court being broadcast across the Netherworld, she needed to make a statement. Wearing plain, practical clothing would send the wrong message.

She glanced at her leather dress with the risque straps and frowned. She commissioned the dress to surprise Achillion, but she hadn't found time to wear it for him yet. In her mind, the dress perfectly balanced femininity and strength. It was ideal for the Demonic Court, but would it be appropriate for a meeting with Whisper and Attia? There wasn't time to change in between.

She could always hide behind illusions, but she thought that would be seen as disrespectful. Even if Whisper found the dress appropriate, Raelyn worried how Attia might react. The girl was quite open about what she found attractive, and Raelyn knew this dress would fit the bill.

She should never have kissed Attia. Raelyn enjoyed the girl's company, and she absolutely adored flirting with her. What she wasn't prepared for was how hard Attia flirted back. By being open and honest about her preferences, Attia effectively turned the tables. When Raelyn wore modest clothing, Attia responded by either playfully pouting or by all but ignoring Raelyn. When the succubus wore more revealing clothing, Attia teased her, pointing out how Raelyn was dressing to please her.

Raelyn desperately longed to bind Attia with a second kiss. Raelyn found the way the girl toyed with her irresistible, but she vowed never to kiss Attia again. At least, not unless asked to. Breaking that vow was out of the question. That left Raelyn with little choice but to obsess over ways to convince Attia to ask for another kiss.

Did Attia know she was having such an effect on her? Raelyn didn't know if it mattered. The thought of being seduced and brought to heel by a simple girl, either accidentally or deliberately, made her weak in the knees. So far, it was nothing more than a fantasy Raelyn occasionally visited to escape the drudgery of her long days, but she feared it might eventually grow into something stronger.

Pushing the intrusive thoughts from her head, Raelyn reached for her leather dress. If she planned to wear the revealing garment, she needed to give herself enough time to cover some of her worst scars. She could always use illusions, but doing so would cost her precious power. Raelyn worked hard to save enough power to defend herself during the Demonic Court, should it become necessary. Wasting power to cover up her scars wasn't acceptable, not when skillfully applied makeup could do the job.

There never seemed to be enough time anymore. Raelyn needed another session to finish healing Attia, but with her first Court tonight, she anticipated discovering a host of new problems and responsibilities to care for. Fortunately, Conner was managing affairs for the House of Healing. Without him, she wouldn't have kept up as long as she did. Raelyn didn't like the idea, but maybe it was time to summon an assistant from the Netherworld. She knew Cinderhorn was willing to help her, but the Guardian demon was as overworked as she was.

Sighing, Raelyn arranged her powders and creams in front of the mirror, stripped out of the practical clothing she wore for the Netten and Naga show, and considered the daunting task ahead of her.

She was proud of her scars. She hated covering them up. In her mind, they were badges of honor. She received a few in battle, but most of them were inflicted as punishment for disobedience.

She cherished those most. Raelyn wasn't willing to live her life according to the whims and dictates of others. Her scars existed as testimony. They showed the world the price she was willing to pay to live on her own terms.

But Raelyn's overwhelming exhaustion was far crueler than any whip. It sapped her strength and the stole joy from her life without leaving so much as a blemish to remind her of the battle. So far, protecting the people she cared about was enough to keep Raelyn going, but she knew she was faltering.

Kissing Attia was her first warning. Feeling underappreciated, Raelyn took matters into her own hands. Attia wasn't showing her enough respect, so Raelyn seized it. Now Attia would spend the rest of her days admiring Raelyn.

Raelyn was navigating a slippery slope, and she was terrified of who she might become should she fall. For now, she could cling to her vows like precious lifelines. Because of her promises, she wouldn't kiss Attia again without permission. Conner was safe from her. So was Achillion.

But what about everybody else? In her heart of hearts, she knew she wasn't all that different from Chariden. Raelyn was strong, but her endurance wasn't endless. Cruelty and dominance rested at the core of every succubus. Overruling her natural instincts took tremendous effort, and Raelyn feared that one day, she'd grow too exhausted to fight her true nature.

2

Saro

Saro stared at Sorriah, sitting smugly behind her desk. He needed her, but he hated her all the same. She despised him as well. Saro was certain of it, but the enemy of his enemy was his friend, or so the saying went. Earlier, when the war was just beginning, he planned to betray Sorriah. Now, he didn't think it was possible.

"Ghost discussed your idea with me last night," said Sorriah, in her fake sing-songy voice. "I really like it, but I must have missed something. What's in it for the Nightcrawlers?"

Saro clenched his fists to keep from shouting. The Nightcrawlers were supposed to be his allies. Sorriah shouldn't need to ask stupid questions like that! "Releasing an army of ghouls into the ring tunnels will choke off the food supply. The Bumbles will have no choice but to respond. That means there'll be less of them patrolling the streets when we hit them."

The civil war was locked in a stalemate. The Bumbles occupied several buildings surrounding the Corners. From there, they stopped people and supplies from entering or leaving. Saro could still move through the sewers, but only in smaller groups. The Bumbles built bulwarks and barriers in the larger tunnels throughout the region, forcing Saro to rely on narrower passages. Something needed to change. Saro thought slaughtering some Bumbles was exactly what they needed to do.

"Sorry, but we tried that before, and it didn't work out," said Sorriah. Her emaciated face was mottled with oozing red sores. Saro hated looking at her.

"A lot has changed since then," said Ghost.

Sorriah smiled. A tiny trickle of blood dribbled down her lip. "Changed for the better?" she asked.

Saro absolutely hated asking the Nightcrawlers for help, but he was running out of options. "We're at war, and we're looking for a little help. Is that too much to ask from an ally?"

Sorriah smiled impishly, but her eyes looked cold and calculating. "Actually, I have something that might help. If I recall, I promised to procure a Fireball spell for one of yours." Sorriah casually smeared the trickle of blood against her lips, deepening their color. "Dimitri, if I'm not mistaken."

"You have my spell?" croaked Dimitri excitedly. "Give it to me." He rose from his chair. "Give it to me, now!"

"Calm down, brother," hissed Eirini.

Saro considered saying something, but decided against it. When he captured Dimitri, the kid was a pathetic, sniveling little bitch. In the weeks that followed, Dimitri's El'orin turned him into an absolute monster, and Saro loved it. He wished the rest of his Coterie were as eager to kill as Dimitri was.

"I think some gratitude would be appropriate," said Sorriah. There was a bit of an edge to her tone.

"She didn't have to do this for you, Brother," said Eirini in hushed tones. "Sorriah is a friend. You need to be nice to her."

Saro turned and studied Dimitri's face. The kid was sneering, and his creepy shekking eyes were darting back and forth, like they often did. If Saro were to guess, Dimitri probably lost twenty pounds since joining the Coterie.

"Very well, sister," said Dimitri after an uncomfortably long pause. "Thank you for this gift, Sorriah. May I please have it?"

"Not so fast," said Sorriah, her voice once again sweet and syrupy. "I planned to work on a few things with Eirini after this meeting. I'll send the spell home with her."

Dimitri's face contorted into a mixture of agony and rage. "Why?"

"Because I'm not comfortable with you having it inside the Warrens."

"Why?" shouted Dimitri.

"Thank you, Sorriah. That will be perfect," said Eirini, her tone forceful. "I'll take it with me after we conclude our business for today."

"So, tell me about this Fireball spell, Dimitri. Why is it so important to you?" Saro guessed the spell was a bigger version of the spells Dimitri normally cast, but with how the kid was reacting, maybe there was more to it. If nothing else, getting Dimitri to talk about it might make him stop screaming at Sorriah.

Dimitri's eyes never stopped moving as he spoke. "Anything touched by my fire explodes. The Fireball will send my beautiful flames far and wide. The conflagration will be glorious!"

Saro didn't know what to make of the response. The way Dimitri celebrated fire was downright disturbing, but if the spell performed like he said it would, maybe there was cause to celebrate. "Eirini," he said, facing the girl, "whatever business you have with Sorriah, finish it fast. I think we're going to have a little fun tonight."

"What kind of fun?" asked Eirini.

"I'm not sure I should say..." Saro glanced at Sorriah. The Nightcrawlers were still members of Achillion's treaty. They weren't allowed to hunt other El'orin. Sharing his plans in front of Sorriah might be risky. Then again, Sorriah recently sent her ghouls against the Governor. "Shek it, we're allies," he said with a shrug. "It's high time we go after the Longshadows. We're doing it tonight."

"How exciting," chirped Sorriah with a little clap.

"I'd invite you along, but you're a member of the treaty," said Saro. "Wouldn't want to get you into trouble with big bad Achillion."

Sorriah momentarily stared at him before shaking her head. "I can't be directly involved, but perhaps my children can help."

"You mean your ghouls, right?"

"Yes," said Sorriah. "My children."

Saro resisted saying what he wanted to. Sorriah was shekking crazy, but if she was offering to help, Saro wasn't in a position to refuse. "If you could hit them with your ghouls at the same time, or maybe right before us, that would help."

"I assume you're planning to attack them in their neighborhood. They still live in that large clump of row houses, just across Terrace Street, correct?"

Saro was surprised she knew. "That's right. Some homes and businesses probably aren't involved with the gang, but that don't bother me none."

"What good is a war without collateral damage?" said Sorriah sweetly.

"Yes!" cheered Dimitri.

Once again, Saro found Dimitri's enthusiasm disturbing. "We'll plan on hitting them shortly after the third bell stops ringing. Businesses will be closing up. I figure most people will be off the streets by then."

"I will send my children when the third bell rings," said Sorriah.

"We plan on approaching from the sewers. Are you using the sewers also?" Saro didn't think there was another way for Sorriah to get a pack of walking corpses into the vicinity.

Sorriah nodded. "We'll use the ancillary tunnels, just north of the ring tunnel."

"Okay," said Saro. "We'll swing around and approach from the south. You need us to avoid your, um... your children, right?"

"Unless you wish to become one of them," said Sorriah with a wink.

Saro shuddered. "We'll keep our distance."

"Suit yourself," said Sorriah with a dismissive wave of her hand. "Ghost and Eirini can walk amongst my children without fear, but the rest of your forces need to be careful.

"How many of your children are you planning to send?" asked Saro.

"Last time, we sent eight," said Sorriah. "This time, I'm thinking double that number."

Saro smiled. Finally, they were going to do some real damage to this shekking city! "That's what I wanted to hear."

"Are you sure about this?" asked Eirini, quickly glancing at her brother.

"*She's weak!*" spat Saro's El'orin. "*We need to get rid of her. She'll hold her brother back.*"

Saro thought his El'orin was overreacting. "We're not getting anywhere fighting Achillion's Bumbles. It's time we shake things up."

"I don't disagree, but shouldn't we take some time and plan this out?"

"You're not seeing the full picture. We sent our gang against the Longshadows for months. Softening them. Keeping them scared and weak." Saro set his thumbs dancing rapidly between the tips of his fingers. For whatever reason, it calmed him. "This was all before you joined us. Back then, Vallon protected them. Now that he's dead and gone, they're fattened cows, begging for slaughter."

"I just don't see why it has to happen tonight," said Eirini. "What harm is there in planning for a day or two?"

Saro shook his head. "If we have any hope of winning this war, we need to get stronger. You and your brother need to feast on other El'orin."

"Yes!" said Dimitri.

Sorriah cleared her throat. It was a sickening, raspy sound. "So, is this happening?"

Saro nodded. "Tonight, at the third bell."

"Excellent." Sorriah reached into her desk and produced a tightly bound scroll. "Given our evening plans, Eirini, we'll have to postpone our little study session. That won't be a problem, will it?"

"No," said Eirini. "Not at all."

Sorriah placed the bound parchment on her desk. "Take this scroll with you. Your brother can read it as soon as you leave the Warrens, but not before. Understood?"

"Understood," said Eirini. Dimitri lurched forward, but Eirini quickly stepped in front of him. "Behave yourself, Dimitri. You can have it after we leave."

Saro shook his head as he watched them argue over the scroll. He didn't think Eirini was soft, but even if she was, he needed her. She was the only one who seemed able to control her brother.

Maybe Mend was right. Maybe they needed to weaken Dimitri's El'orin. Whatever it was doing to the kid, it was getting worse. Saro barely considered Dimitri human anymore. He was like a wounded animal. If the rumors were true, Dimitri survived on beetles, worms, and spiders. He wouldn't eat anything else.

"I very much look forward to our date tonight, Saro," said Sorriah. Her smile was almost childlike, which made the entire scene even creepier. A childlike smile resting on an emaciated face covered with oozing sores.

"Until tonight," said Saro. "It'll be fun."

3

Attia

Attia wove her way between the deep snowbanks lining the sides of the narrow alleyway. The first few weeks of winter were exciting and new, but she was growing sick of the snow. She couldn't wait for it to melt, although it didn't seem like that would happen soon. It snowed nearly every day.

For now, the alleys between Rellistan Street and the House of Healing were still navigable. If the snow got much deeper, she might need to change her travel route, but she'd cross that bridge when she got there. Attia wanted to avoid traveling the busier streets. The fewer people who saw her, the better.

Alahn lived in an apartment, just north of Rellistan Street. It was small, but they needed little space. Attia liked it because it was private. None of her friends bothered her when she was there. Both Conner and Liam knew the address, and Eliana could always reach her with a Windword in an emergency, but so far, everyone was respecting her privacy.

Attia split her time between the greenhouse, Alahn's modest apartment, and the House of Healing. When she found herself with spare time, she tried to spend it in the greenhouse. Her friends were important to her. She didn't want them to feel abandoned. At the same time, Attia relished her newfound freedom.

Her days and nights with Alahn were surprisingly refreshing. At first, Attia worried about the awkwardness of physical intimacy, but nothing between the two was forced. They were both wounded, disfigured, and lonely. The two of them appreciated the companionship without needing it to be more. They occasionally explored each other's bodies, but it was rare. It wasn't why they enjoyed spending time together.

Since retiring from the militia, Alahn spent much of his time resting. He was still healing from his painful burns. Attia doubted he'd ever fully recover, but she was grateful all the same. Raelyn admitted she thought Alahn's injuries were fatal. The only reason she agreed to pull him from that sewer was because Professor Keldon insisted.

But that wasn't the complete story. In truth, Raelyn saved Alahn because Attia wanted her to. It came up often in Attia's frequent flirting sessions with the succubus. Raelyn made it crystal clear that she viewed saving Alahn as a way to advance her relationship with Attia. Ordinarily, Raelyn wouldn't have bothered saving the man. The power investment was too great.

Attia knew her emotions were being manipulated. She knew Raelyn's kiss ensnared her and made her feel things she wouldn't otherwise feel, but she couldn't help herself. Everything seemed so real. The succubus truly liked her, and Attia admired Raelyn long before the kiss. Attia grew up surrounded by powerful women. The Pathfinders taught her to respect strength on a deep level, and Raelyn was as strong as they came.

The fact that they were both strong is what made their relationship work. Attia noticed Raelyn shiver whenever she obeyed the succubus. At the same time, Attia quivered whenever Raelyn went out of her way to please her. Initially, all of Attia's fantasies revolved around submitting to Raelyn, but that was changing. Lately, she was dreaming about turning the tables. She enjoyed picturing Raelyn on her knees, smiling, as Attia told her she was a good girl.

Attia pushed the tantalizing thoughts from her mind. Sure, it was the middle of the day, and she was navigating a safe part of town, but she couldn't afford distractions, no matter how pleasant. Attia had many enemies, and with how often she journeyed between Alahn's and the House of Healing, someone hunting her in these alleys wasn't out of the realm of possibility.

She traveled quickly and quietly for the next ten minutes. Attia needed to step out onto the main roads a few times, but she kept to the alleys as much as possible. The streets were relatively empty, but that wasn't strange. Ever since the Downtrodden went to war against the militia, folks avoided the streets as much as possible. No one wanted to get caught in the crossfire.

Attia waved to the guards as she entered the House of Healing's walled complex. The Governor hired a large group of retired Bumbles to guard the hospital. They all knew Attia well enough not to challenge her when coming or going.

Truth be told, few people challenged Attia these days. Perhaps the tales of what she did during the War Beyond the Wall grew into legends. Maybe it was the mask she wore over half her face, or maybe it was her fake eye. Whatever the cause, she was happy not to be bothered. The underlying reasons didn't concern her.

Entering the House of Healing, Attia waved to Conner before heading toward the central stairs. Conner was always there, working. If Attia were to guess, Conner worked nearly twelve hours a day, every day. She didn't think it was healthy, but she wasn't sure how to bring it up. Conner was fiercely independent. He'd brush off her concerns, and Attia wasn't comfortable challenging Raelyn about such things. Raelyn worked so hard for all of them. The succubus was always sacrificing to make their lives better. It was only right for Conner to work extra hours. Maybe if Attia got on her knees and begged, Raelyn would reconsider...

Attia shook her head. Raelyn's influence was dominating her thoughts. She needed to be stronger than that. No matter how uncomfortable the possibility of an argument made her, Attia needed to raise the issue with Raelyn. Hopefully, there'd be time to do it after the meeting with Whisper.

Quickly climbing the steps, Attia entered the second floor of the structure. The meeting room was just down the hall. The sounds of quiet conversation drifted out from the door as Attia approached. It sounded like Raelyn and Whisper were negotiating. Attia considered waiting and listening, but decided against it.

"Sorry for being late," said Attia as she opened the door.

"You're not late," said Raelyn. "Whisper came early. Please join us." The succubus gestured toward the far side of the large room.

Whisper wore an enormous ochre robe. He was a rather fat man, but Attia suspected his frame supported a massive amount of muscle. With the way his robe hung loosely, he could have easily hidden several weapons beneath it. He bowed his head as she passed.

Raelyn was dressed in a way that made Attia's heart race and palms sweat. Her dress was composed of a series of leather straps, each carefully positioned to show just the right amount of skin, while still concealing the parts that needed to be covered. Was she wearing it for Attia's benefit? It was no secret that Attia preferred Raelyn in more revealing clothing. What surprised Attia most was that Raelyn wasn't wearing any illusions. Her wings were folded behind her, and her horns proudly poked up from her forehead. Attia didn't expect her to be so open about her demonic nature with Whisper.

"Now that we're all here, we might as well get started," said Raelyn. "There is much to discuss. Please speak first, Whisper."

Whisper cleared his throat. "It's been brought to my attention that you've come into possession of a few tools of the trade, if you catch my meaning."

"You're talking about the daggers Karilae made for me," said Attia.

"I am." Whisper ran a meaty hand across his chin. "We both know those blades are only meant for one thing." He pursed his lips. "There are rules about that sort of thing in this city, and I'm not talking about the laws the Bumbles try to enforce. If a city like this is going to hold together, all us killers got to have a code."

"These daggers are for self-defense."

"Come on now, Attia. I know about your invisible sword. You can defend yourself just fine without poisoned daggers."

Attia wasn't surprised Whisper knew about the sword. His guards forced her to temporarily surrender it at Conclave, back when she joined the treaty. Whisper's people probably studied it. She expected they examined and cataloged everyone's weapons.

"I'll tell you the same thing I told Karilae," said Attia, an edge of anger slipping into her tone. "I'm not a killer for hire. If I use one of these daggers on someone, it's for personal reasons."

Whisper held his hands out in front of him and shook his head. "This conversation isn't going how I hoped. Let me start over." He smiled and there was genuine warmth to it. "I don't give a shek about the daggers. In fact, if you need any other tools of the trade, just ask. I'll get you anything you need."

"If there isn't an issue, why are we meeting?"

"I expect you might use one or more of those daggers on members of the Downtrodden, and I have no issue with that. They are outside of the treaty. That makes them fair game." Whisper glanced at Raelyn. "But given Raelyn's new role within the city, I thought we might explore some of the other situations you might find yourself in."

Attia didn't know what situations Whisper was talking about. "I don't understand."

"Let me explain," said Raelyn. "Tonight, I officially begin overseeing all demonic activities in Derregain. As you might expect, I've already started looking into the various demons living inside the city, and I don't like what I've found."

"What does this have to do with me?"

"Earlier, we discussed the possibility of you doing some work for me. If you recall, I was particularly interested in your ability to deal with situations in, let's say... a direct and physical way."

"Yes, I remember the conversation, Raelyn, but what does Whisper have to do with any of this?"

"I would help in what you might call an advisory role," said Whisper. He smoothed the fabric of his robe. "I have spies throughout the Lowlands. I've got a fair measure in Middletown as well. I'll be able to find your target and tell you what you're dealing with."

Attia scratched her head. How long did Whisper and Raelyn talk before she arrived? It was like she walked in on the tail end of a conversation. "Someone explain this to me in clearer terms."

"As we speak, many demons are working against me," said Raelyn. "I need you to make examples of some of them. I need the demons of Derregain to see what happens to those who defy my rule."

"Look, I don't know what you thought I agreed to, but it wasn't this," said Attia.

"I know, but do me a favor and keep an open mind," sighed Raelyn. "Please believe me when I say this." Raelyn met Attia's gaze. "I won't needlessly throw you in harm's way."

Attia closed her good eye. She willed her crafted eye to stop working a fraction of a second later. She didn't want to look at Raelyn while she thought about this. Not when the succubus was wearing a dress like that.

"Is everything alright?" asked Raelyn.

Attia nodded. "Just give me a minute. I need to think."

Raelyn said she wouldn't needlessly put Attia in danger, but that meant if there was a need, she would. It didn't surprise Attia. Raelyn was clear that her safety came first, with Achillion's a close second. The question was, how far down the pecking order was Attia? She was pretty sure Raelyn cared about her. If nothing else, the succubus longed for more control over her. She did a terrible job of hiding that fact.

Attia gradually opened her eyes. Both Whisper and Raelyn were staring at her. "Let me see if I'm understanding this correctly. There are, or will be, demons that you want killed. Is that correct, Raelyn?"

"Yes."

"And Whisper's role is to find them, spy on them, and provide us with intelligence. Things like how many people or demons there are. When they come, and when they go. That sort of thing, correct?"

Whisper nodded. "Yeah, it should work something like that."

"So, my role will be to go in and wipe them out. Is that what you're thinking?"

Raelyn nodded.

"*I've worked as an assassin for a succubus before,*" whispered Attia's Ally. "*I just want to point out, it didn't end well for me. This demon already has you on a leash. You can't trust her.*"

Attia didn't think her Ally was necessarily wrong, but their situations were different. Her Ally hunted El'orin for the Demon Queen. Attia was planning on hunting disobedient demons for Raelyn. It wasn't the same. "And you think I'll be able to do this all on my own?"

"I don't know," said Raelyn, shaking her head. "That's one of the things I'm struggling with. There will undoubtedly be some weak demons we can use as examples, but probably not many. At some point, we're going to need to build a team for you."

"Wait, you're not expecting me to get my friends to help, are you?"

"No," said Raelyn. "Not unless it is something that threatens the entire city."

Attia thought that was a fair and honest answer. There was really little reason to doubt Raelyn. Maybe letting the succubus make decisions for her wouldn't be so bad. One or two more kisses would be all it took, and Attia would never doubt Raelyn again. Life would be so much simpler that way.

"*Snap out of it!*" hissed Attia's Ally.

Attia pushed the intrusive thoughts from her mind. "So, this plan is a work in progress. Neither of you really knows how this is going to play out, do you?" asked Attia.

"Like I said, I know there are demons working against me right now, as we speak. What I don't know is how they'll respond to tonight's Demonic Court. I expect many, if not most, will continue trying to undermine me, behind the scenes. Whisper plans to start gathering information on them as soon as this meeting ends."

"What happens once Whisper learns everything he can learn about a target? Do we meet again?" Attia wanted to know more about Whisper. If his spies could track demons for Raelyn, what else were they capable of?

"We could meet here, but there's really no need to," said Whisper. "I'll give whatever information I find to Alahn. He can deliver it to you."

"Wait, what?" Attia knew Alahn dealt with some of the criminal elements within the city. Alahn offered to talk with her about it, but she decided she didn't want to know. Perhaps it was time to revisit that decision.

"Alahn and I have had business in the past. Nothing major. We traded information, for the most part," said Whisper, his voice soothing. "He's one of the few Bumbles who's liked down in Undercity. A man like that is valuable to me."

Attia didn't want to ask the next question. She didn't want to hear the answer. "Has he been working for you these past few weeks? Has he been spying on me?"

"It's not like that. He reached out to me when he retired from the Bumbles. He wanted to end our arrangement. At that point, I already knew you two were spending time together. I asked him to monitor you for me, but he didn't want any part of it."

Attia shook her head. "But?"

"Alright, alright," said Whisper with a sigh. "I have a lot of spies around Rellistan Street. I would have seen you coming and going anyway, and Alahn knew that. So, in exchange for keeping tabs on you, I agreed to extend his protection. You two are completely safe when you're at his place. No thief, beggar, or assassin will ever lift a finger against you. In fact, if someone or something comes after you, my people will sound the alarm." Whisper clasped his hands in front of him, as if begging. "Don't be mad at him, Attia. He made a good deal. Not just for him, for both of you."

Attia decided she didn't like people making decisions for her. Not Whisper, not Alahn, and not even Raelyn. "For now, count me in. I'll make a final call when we have more information, but understand, I don't work cheap."

"Whatever you two have worked out for payment, that ain't none of my concern," said Whisper.

"Don't worry about it. I'm sure Raelyn will make it worth my while." Attia glanced at Raelyn and raised an eyebrow. She noticed the slightest touch of red dance across Raelyn's cheeks.

4
Malcolm

Malcolm closed his eyes and pinched the bridge of his nose, hoping to keep his headache and exhaustion at bay. He spent the morning and most of the afternoon studying. Towards the end, Professor Keldon surprised him with a copy of the Astral Whispers spell. The professor spent weeks trying to obtain a copy from the Academy. Apparently, the Academy was rethinking its generosity toward Malcolm and his friends.

The spell didn't seem taxing, but Malcolm wanted to relax for a few moments before casting it. He suspected that once he started speaking with Fahrilae, there'd be much to discuss. He only summoned her a single time since they killed Lamenica, and then only long enough for her to demonstrate the Energy Tendrils spell to Professor Keldon.

Malcolm struggled to describe how all his relationships shifted after the battle with Lamenica. Things were different, despite very little changing. Everyone still lived in the greenhouse, but most spent their time elsewhere. These days, it was rare for everyone to be together in the same room.

Conner spent most nights at the House of Healing, where he was essentially in charge of day-to-day operations. Apparently, Raelyn didn't have time anymore. After a while, no one questioned him when he started living at the hospital. It seemed like the logical answer.

Liam slept in the greenhouse, but was otherwise rarely there. The Downtrodden inflicted heavy losses on the Militia, and Liam took it personally. He started leading multiple teams each day. First, it was just morning and evening patrols, but he quickly added a third. Some days, he took part in as many as four patrols. With each lasting four hours, he rarely found time to socialize.

Attia visited the greenhouse fairly often, but unless it was to sleep, she never stayed long. Malcolm was fairly sure her main reason for stopping by was to pet Lord Rumblesnort Bunny-Fur, because that was always the first thing she did upon arrival. Malcolm knew Raelyn was working on Attia's injuries, and that her healing required many appointments. He also heard Attia was spending time with Alahn, in an apartment somewhere near Rellistan Street. Malcolm was happy for her. The War Beyond the Wall changed Attia in so many ways. Only part of her survived the fight. Many aspects of Attia died on that battlefield.

Despite rarely leaving the greenhouse, Russ and Eliana seemed to go out of their way to avoid each other. Maybe it was all coincidence, but Eliana generally worked on the far side of the greenhouse anytime Russell was out in the common areas. On the rare occasions she needed to work near Russell, he retreated into the library to study.

Malcolm couldn't blame them. He knew they broke up shortly before the battle with Lamenica. The fact that they remained together for so long amazed Malcolm. Eliana seemed unpleasant to be around, but with the way her El'orin tortured her, who could blame her? Even if Russell was strong enough to endure Eliana's mood swings, their relationship couldn't survive the revelation that Russell loved Raelyn. That it was because of an incurable charm spell, completely outside of Russell's control, made the whole thing more tragic.

"*Stop procrastinating,*" said the Other. "*Fahrilae is waiting to speak with you.*"

Malcolm considered resisting his El'orin, but his headache was already bad enough. He didn't want to risk the Other making it worse. Taking a deep breath, he opened his eyes and shifted his vision to the Astral Plane.

Fahrilae was there, gazing at him. A procession of wraiths and apparitions floated behind her. Malcolm thought he saw another spirit, a powerful one, but it was standing at the edge of his vision. He needed to get a better look to determine what it was.

Quickly chanting the words to his spell, Malcolm coaxed a trickle of power from his well. It wasn't long before the spell began working.

"Why did you wait so long to contact me?" snapped Fahrilae.

Malcolm sighed. "I just learned the Astral Whispers spell a few minutes ago. What did you expect?"

The ghost shook her head. "We don't have time to argue. There is too much to discuss."

"What's so important?"

"The neverlings sent word, two days ago," said Fahrilae. "Ul-Nong-Far has found your Ghostly Shell spell. You must summon him immediately. Spells like that are quite rare. The quicker you read it, the better off we'll all be."

Malcolm's palms began to sweat, and a knot formed in his stomach. He was trying not to think about his deal with the neverlings. Part of him hoped they never found him that spell. Accepting it would bind him to his end of the bargain.

"*You were bound to that bargain the moment you mentioned delivering them a harvest. Stop running from your destiny,*" hissed the Other.

"How soon can you summon Ul-Nong-Far?" asked Fahrilae.

"You know I can't do it near the city," said Malcolm. "I'll need to find people to escort me out into the wilds. With Alahn's retirement, and Brick's death, it might be difficult."

A dark smile crept to Fahrilae's shadowy lips. "Speaking of Brick, his spirit resisted the ravages of the Astral. He has become a ghost. A rather weak one, mind you, but a ghost nonetheless."

"Is he the spirit standing off in the distance?"

Fahrilae nodded. "I've chatted with him a few times. He's adjusting as best as can be expected. It's hard for all of us, at least at first."

Malcolm read a tremendous amount about ghosts, and how they came into being. By all accounts, a ghost's first few years were torturous. "Is it safe to summon him?"

"Probably," said Fahrilae with a shrug. "Honestly, I don't see why you'd want to, not with me around."

"With any luck, we'll have you safely placed inside a body soon. That is what you want, right?" Malcolm never thought to ask if Fahrilae wanted to be made into a revenant. Would she be particular about what kind of body she wanted?

"Of course it's what I want, but don't you dare give me some fat, old hag's remains to live in. I expect a beautiful, pristine corpse for my new home."

"*Well, that answers that question,*" said the Other with a chuckle.

Hopefully, Conner would agree to help him find a body. As much as Malcolm dreaded involving his friends with his revenants, his options were limited. For that matter, he probably needed to convince some of them to accompany him to receive the spell. He didn't know who else to ask. "Alright, I'll try to summon Ul-Nong-Far in the next day or two. What else did you need to speak with me about? You said there was much to discuss."

"Remember when I warned you that spirits were searching for you?"

Malcolm nodded.

"It's still happening, and I think it's getting worse," said Fahrilae. "The spirits only check on you every couple of days, but I've noticed they're rarely alone. I think there are neverlings with them."

"So, that confirms it. It's the Hidden Tower. They are preparing another attack."

"Probably," said Fahrilae. "For what it's worth, I think you're safe in the greenhouse."

As much as Malcolm didn't like the idea of being trapped inside the greenhouse, he was relieved to hear he was safe there. "Why is this place safe? Is there a reason they won't attack me here?"

"I'm uncertain, but I suspect they fear Eliana's ancient Fae magic. Remember, our armies were united back when we attacked Chariden. With the armies of nature and the dead walking side by side, nothing could stand in our way. But then, in our hour of triumph, the neverlings betrayed us."

"I remember," said Malcolm. Ever since Arronhelm's Painting showed him what happened, he couldn't get it out of his mind. He remembered his army of the dead, and the procession of walking trees and stone that followed. He remembered the glorious Unicorn, with eyes of molten gold, standing by his side. Most of all, he remembered the swirling portals of darkness, and the night terrors the neverlings unleashed upon him.

"Rest assured, nature also remembers," said Fahrilae. "The power of Eliana's Goldthorn Berries has filled every inch of this place. It has started spilling outside, stretching beneath the city streets, exploring the sewers below. At first, I feared it. This power, you see, it reaches into the Astral. It is not confined to your world."

Malcolm listened intently. If Eliana's Goldthorn Berries stretched into the Astral, why couldn't he see them with his

Spectral Sight? He certainly tried. Did he need to be inside the Astral to see them?

"Fortunately, this place tolerates me and the other spirits. Maybe it hasn't noticed us, or perhaps it remembers our alliance of old. I doubt I'll ever know the answer. What I do know is this," said Fahrilae. "Whatever is out there searching for you, it's afraid to enter this place. The tracker spirits approach, but the other things with them, they stay outside."

"You said the trackers show up every couple of days," said Malcolm. "How many days has it been?" If Eliana's greenhouse was guarding him, he needed to be extra careful about leaving it.

"Yesterday, young lord."

"That doesn't give me a lot of time," said Malcolm. "Not unless I wait until after the next spirit checks on me."

Fahrilae nodded.

Malcolm wanted to know more, but time was of the essence. There would be time to talk to Fahrilae later, especially if he made her a revenant. "I better get to work," he said before letting his Astral Whispers spell fade.

Exiting his suite of rooms, Malcolm walked out into the greenhouse. Despite the cold and snow outside, the greenhouse was hot and steamy. The competing temperatures left the windows fogged with moisture. Some evenings, the greenhouse was so humid it drizzled inside. It was almost like Malcolm was back in the sweltering rainforests surrounding the Citadel.

Eliana was working with a small group of arborists on the far side of the building. Malcolm didn't know what they were working on. Surveying the rest of the structure, Malcolm noticed a few groups of Bumbles chatting at picnic tables. He didn't see Russell, but the doors leading into Professor Keldon's library were open. They normally kept them closed whenever they were studying. Perhaps they were taking a break.

Grabbing his staff, Malcolm carefully crossed the greenhouse. Even with the plantings being arranged in orderly rows, the greenhouse was difficult for Malcolm to navigate without stumbling. Roots and branches crisscrossed every path, and there was no sign of the verdant growth slowing. If anything, it was accelerating.

A few of the Bumbles nodded and waved to Malcolm as he passed, but Eliana never so much as glanced in his direction. Perhaps he needed to reach out to her and force the issue. He didn't think it was healthy to let the social distance between them continue to grow. With everyone else often away, and Eliana's relationship problems with Russell, Malcolm needed to be a better friend. It wasn't a position he was used to being in.

Malcolm heard several voices as he approached the library. From the sound of it, Attia was inside, talking with Russell and the professor. Not wanting to intrude, he waited outside until the professor noticed him through the open door.

"Good to see you, Malcolm," called Professor Keldon. "Please, join us."

"I hope I'm not interrupting anything," said Malcolm as he entered the library. Russell sat on the far side of the main table, buried behind a wall of books. Attia was standing next to the table, looking at a pair of parchments.

"Not at all. We were just discussing Attia's new balance spells." The professor smiled warmly, but there was sadness in his eyes. "Sorry, but I need to get back to the Academy."

Russell closed his book and pushed it to the side. "You've been spending a lot of time there lately."

The professor nodded. "A lot changed when Lamenica died. I think we all knew she charmed a few of the Academy's instructors, but no one believed it to be as bad as it was."

Malcolm remembered Mara Young talking about it when the group fled to the Academy, right after defeating Lamenica. "If you don't mind me asking, how many?"

Professor Keldon sighed. "Three advanced instructors are still in a coma. We encouraged another four to retire. Their minds will never fully recover from what she did to them. Beyond that, another eight members of the faculty and staff are healing from relatively minor mental maladies."

"Stars above," breathed Malcolm. "She charmed fifteen people within the Academy?"

The professor nodded. "It turns out, given enough time, a single succubus can take over a sizable portion of this city. The Academy wasn't the only institution crippled by Lamenica. I'm hearing her influence across the city government was even greater."

"At least Lamenica is dead," said Russell.

"Right, but she's not the only succubus in the city," said the professor, glancing at Russell. "I know you don't like me bringing her up, but Raelyn may be our next problem. She runs the hospital, and it's common knowledge that she's sleeping with the governor."

"She's different," said Russell, his voice taking on a softer tone. "She'd never hurt us."

"Yeah, she's different," said Attia.

Professor Keldon chuckled. "Well, I really must be going." He quietly hummed as he gathered a few books and headed out the door.

Malcolm understood the professor's reaction. Russell struggled to say a harsh word against Raelyn. He was incapable of seeing her as a threat. Attia's reaction was a touch surprising, but then again, Raelyn saved her life. Attia was probably grateful. Malcolm would be too, if he were in her shoes.

"I should get going also," said Attia. "Do I need to keep these pages, Russell?"

"Not really," said Russell, shaking his head. "They're just descriptions and recommendations on how to use your new spells, but it's pretty simple."

"Let me guess. Cast them whenever I'm worried someone might try to read or manipulate my mind, right?"

"You got it."

"Can you stay for a few moments?" asked Malcolm. "I have something I want to talk to you about. Both of you, actually. It won't take long, I promise."

Attia studied him for a moment. "Sure. What is it?"

Malcolm gently pulled the entry door closed. He didn't think any of the Bumbles were close enough to overhear them, but he didn't want to take any chances. "I need your help."

"What do you need? I'm always happy to lend a hand," said Attia.

"You might not want to do this," said Malcolm, shaking his head. "I need to summon my neverlings. I can't do it inside the city, and I don't think it's safe for me to travel alone."

Russell whistled through his teeth.

Attia looked away. "After what happened at the farm, I don't think I can do that again."

"It won't be like that, not this time. There won't be sacrifices." At least not yet, thought Malcolm. What he was doing would lead to hundreds of sacrifices. If Attia was disturbed by sacrificing a few farmers, how would she feel about condemning an entire village?

"Stop feeling sorry for yourself," whispered the Other. *"You're doing what must be done. Besides, you're telling the truth about this mission. There will be no sacrifices involved with this summoning."*

"I shekking hate neverlings," said Russell. "Do you absolutely have to do this? I mean, why do you need to summon them?"

"They have a spell for me. An important spell."

"Can we get a copy from the Academy?"

Malcolm shook his head.

"What does this spell do?" asked Russell.

"It will let me build revenants," said Malcolm. "It will let me give Fahrilae a body."

"Stars above," gasped Attia.

"Is that a good thing?" asked Russell. "I mean, I know she's powerful, but the whole walking corpse thing..." Russell took a deep breath and rapped his fingertips against the table. "Are you sure we're ready for that?"

Malcolm closed his eyes and shook his head. "I don't know. Probably not, but I don't think we have a choice. We rely on Fahrilae in nearly every battle. It's dangerous for me to keep summoning her."

"And if you make her a revenant, will it be safer for you?" asked Russell.

"Much safer."

"Alright, count me in," said Russell. "What about you, Attia? I'll feel a lot safer if you come with us."

Attia looked down at her hands and sighed. "Okay, I'll help."

Russell grinned. "When do we leave?"

Malcolm breathed a sigh of relief. "Tonight," he said. "We should leave tonight, just after sundown."

5

Cinderhorn

Cinderhorn gazed past the courtyard at the ashen husk of the manor. Roughly half of Lamenica's home burned to the ground the night she was vanquished to the Netherworld. The courtyard wore countless scars. If the damage was any sign, the battle was fiercely fought.

Clearing all the debris would have been a simple enough task, but Cinderhorn decided to leave it as he found it. It's not that he enjoyed living in the surviving areas of an otherwise ruined mansion. In Nerreka, his chambers were comfortable, if not opulent, but he didn't miss them. For some reason, the ruins of Lamenica's estate seemed an appropriate home for him. He didn't want to change a thing.

If nothing else, the ruins served as a stark reminder of what happens to those who betray the Demon Queen. Lamenica schemed behind Chariden's back, and her punishment was death, but Cinderhorn doubted many demons would see it that way. Chariden didn't kill Lamenica. She made Raelyn do it. Even worse, she forced Raelyn to do it through catspaws.

It reeked of weakness.

And Chariden's weakness would tarnish Raelyn. Dissent and distrust already ran rampant through Derregain's demonic communities, and Raelyn's ascension was only making it worse. She was bound to be challenged. Cinderhorn was sure of it. The only question was by which demons and when.

The open, formal challenges didn't worry Cinderhorn. He planned to fight on Raelyn's behalf. Except for the Serpentus, and maybe Novus, he was more than a match for anything in Derregain. That wouldn't stop ambitious demons from trying, of course. For some, the prospect of vanquishing Cinderhorn and dethroning Raelyn in the process would prove irresistible.

But even greater dangers lurked in the shadows, hidden away from the formality of the Demonic Court. It wasn't uncommon for demons to plot against their rulers, even the popular ones. Many viewed such scheming as an important check and balance. Unchallenged, rulers grew dull and weak. Constant conflict honed leaders, keeping them sharp and powerful.

Daemenos already uncovered a few fledgling plots against Raelyn. A bone demon, evidently Bonewalker's apprentice, was plotting revenge. A few of Plaguebringer's agents were still lurking in the sewers, working to make the city sick. The smaller stuff didn't bother Cinderhorn. He was more concerned about Derregain's truly powerful demons.

So far, Ssalyssna, the Serpentus, seemed content playing in human politics. She was working closely with Raelyn's lover, Achillion. Cinderhorn doubted that would last, but who knew? Perhaps the Serpentus intended to remain loyal to Chariden. Time would tell.

Novus, on the other hand, was definitely up to something. Daemenos was struggling to uncover reliable information about it, but he was still searching. Cinderhorn was tempted to come right out and ask Novus about his intentions. He never met Novus, but the sixth order demon was well-regarded. By all accounts, Novus went out of his way to aid Raelyn on at least one occasion.

Questioning Novus at the Demonic Court would be inappropriate. If Cinderhorn wanted to do it, he probably needed to work through imps. A powerful imp named Horex represented Novus. Since Daemenos and Horex had a strong working relationship, sending messages through the imps would be simple.

It was a problem for another day, mused Cinderhorn as he walked across the wintery courtyard. Off to his left, a patch of ground began to bubble and shake. Clods of frozen earth tumbled to the side as an enormous creature of jagged stone emerged from the ground. It gazed at Cinderhorn, its eyes dripping magma, as it slowly raised an obsidian fist.

"Evening, Bob," said Cinderhorn. Bob was merely the first of seven syllables in the demon's name. The shortened form was much easier to pronounce.

"Greetings, Cinderhorn," said the earth demon, its basso voice echoing like boulders tumbling down a mountain.

"Were there any trespassers today?" Cinderhorn summoned the earth demon shortly after arriving in Derregain. He used him to patrol the courtyard surrounding his burned-out mansion.

"Just one," said the earth demon. "A young boy."

Cinderhorn ran a claw through his mane. "Did you toss him in the larder?"

Bob shook his head. "I planned to, but the larder was full. I could have forced him in there, but why bother? We have enough humans trapped in those stasis runes to feed us both for months."

The fully functional Runes of Stasis Cinderhorn found in the basement were among the nicest aspects of his new home. Lamenica built them to freeze humans in time, effectively giving herself a means to store food indefinitely. For all her faults,

Lamenica seemed to excel with runes. "What did you do with him?"

"I made the earth swallow him," said Bob. "His corpse is buried somewhere out by the wall."

Cinderhorn nodded. "With the larder full, try to scare off anyone foolish enough to stumble onto the property. I'd prefer to avoid slaughtering more people than necessary."

Bob's eyes smoldered, sending tiny wisps of smoke dancing across the wintery sky. It was the earth demon's equivalent to rolling his eyes. "This entire courtyard is walled, Cinderhorn. No one randomly stumbles inside." The earth demon took two enormous steps, drawing closer. "Oh, I'm sorry. I just happened to stumble into this big fucking wall." Bob was trying to make his voice sound human, but he wasn't very good at it. "I don't remember climbing over it, but I must have, because somehow, I'm inside this courtyard. Total accident. Could have happened to anyone."

"You've made your point."

"Have I?" said Bob, his voice low and rumbling once again. "Because it's bad enough that I'm working as a glorified guard dog. Don't make it worse by asking me to spare people. I'm not just some fledgling earth demon, you know. I'm fifth order."

"I asked you if you wanted a safe assignment, and you leapt at the opportunity," said Cinderhorn. "I don't see the problem."

The earth demon chuckled, causing the ground to tremble and shake. "Just like old times."

Cinderhorn grinned. "Hopefully, this assignment ends far better than the last one." Shortly after Chariden shattered the Gaea spirit, Cinderhorn summoned Bob to assist in an important battle against the Fae. Unfortunately, the earth demon didn't survive the fight.

"You did right by me. You found my prison, bought off my tormentors, and provided me an endless supply of books to read," said Bob. "Honestly, I think I needed that century of uninterrupted study to climb into the fifth order."

"I'm glad it worked out for you."

"Are you ready for tonight?" asked the earth demon.

"It's been centuries since I've taken part in a Demonic Court, let alone one that is being broadcast across the Netherworld." Cinderhorn shrugged his wings. "But if you're talking about challenges, I think I'm ready. I doubt I'll face a demon I can't handle."

"I'm here if you need me," said Bob. "You know, I could stand as Raelyn's champion in your stead."

Cinderhorn shook his head. "I prefer to keep you a secret. No one knows you're here. Not even Raelyn."

"As you wish," said Bob as he started descending back beneath the frozen earth. "I'll stay underground, but I'll keep close. If you need help, I'll be there for you."

"Thanks, Bob," said Cinderhorn.

For the first time in a long time, the Guardian demon felt like he needed protection. Daemenos was the first to find Lamenica's prison cell, deep beneath the Netherworld. They struck a bargain with her, granting her comfort during her century of imprisonment. In exchange, she agreed to answer their questions.

Working through Daemenos, Cinderhorn started questioning her earlier this week. Lamenica wasn't the first demon Cinderhorn interrogated through Daemenos. The pair had experience working together. It only took a day to discover what Cinderhorn suspected all along.

Plaguebringer wasn't working alone. Lamenica did more than just fail to report Derregain's growing sickness to Chariden. She actively helped Plaguebringer spread his disease, but the plot didn't end with just the two of them. Mael Kahn, one of the three Glabsezrii, was also involved. Cinderhorn didn't know the extent of his involvement yet, but it wouldn't take them long to get that information from Lamenica.

It was only a matter of time before Plaguebringer, Mael Kahn, or other powerful demons came after Cinderhorn. The information Daemenos was getting from Lamenica was already damning, but it was only the tip of the spear. Once they started investigating leads, and asking follow-up questions, Cinderhorn expected to learn much more.

Who knew who was all involved? The issues Raelyn recently raised on the Netten and Naga show were all valid. The Netherworld's rules were written by the demons in charge. They carefully engineered their rules to keep the weak demons weak, and the powerful demons powerful. Cinderhorn wouldn't be surprised to learn that other demon lords worked with Plaguebringer to overthrow Chariden. After all, she upset the natural order of things. In their minds, she needed to be stopped.

Maybe Cinderhorn needed to approach tonight's Court with more caution. His arrival in Derregain was no secret. Most demons probably assumed he would stand as Raelyn's champion. No one expected the succubus to take the battlefield herself, after all. Cinderhorn was fairly certain he knew about all the fifth and sixth order demons in Derregain, but with Raelyn's reign about to begin, new demons were being summoned every day.

Cinderhorn needed to be careful. He needed to take every precaution. Spinning on his heels, he walked toward the door leading to the functional portions of the mansion. In addition to living quarters, they contained an expansive summoning chamber, rivaling what Cinderhorn enjoyed back in Nerreka.

He wanted to speak with several imps. Daemenos was one of the best, but all imps had their blind spots. Cinderhorn needed to invite fresh voices into the conversation. Daemenos might not like Cinderhorn spreading his wings and searching for outside advice, but he'd understand. There was too much at stake.

Cinderhorn planned to base his next moves on what he discovered. He was nearly out of favors to spend, but that didn't mean he was without means. As much as he loathed the prospect of indebting himself to other demons, Cinderhorn was willing to consider it. He spent centuries building an impeccable reputation. Demons were begging for the opportunity to do business with him.

Fires below, it was high time he started taking advantage of it.

6

Russell

Russell carefully navigated the forest trail. It was after sunset. Even with the sparse foliage of winter, the trees blocked much of the moonlight, leaving the trail dark enough to be dangerous. Malcolm was plodding along behind him, using his staff for balance.

Attia led the way. With her runecrafted eye, she could see perfectly in the darkness. Russell told her to slow down several times before she finally found a pace the group could safely manage. For her, this was probably a casual romp through the woods. For Russell and Malcolm, every step was a treacherous exploration of roots and rocks they couldn't see.

Fortunately, the journey out to the woods went smoothly. They followed gravel roads until it was dark enough to travel through the sprawling foliage growing alongside the roads without being seen. Attia's ability to see in the dark made it easy. There was no risk of losing sight of landmarks or becoming lost in the darkness.

"We're not too far from the clearing," said Malcolm. The sudden sound surprised Russell. They traveled in silence ever since entering the forest. "I think we should talk about this beforehand."

Attia turned to face them. "What's there to talk about?"

"I don't know. I just don't want there to be any surprises. This meeting might go quickly, but I doubt it. They're giving me the spell in exchange for future payment. We'll need to negotiate." Malcolm winced and massaged his temples.

"I'm guessing the Other doesn't want you talking about it," said Russell. All things considered, he was pleased with his El'orin. The Dreamer didn't seem to punish him with headaches. Sometimes, Russell experienced cryptic or unsettling dreams, but rarely.

"The Other didn't want me to bring it up, but I suspect Ul-Nong-Far will want to discuss things with me. I don't want the two of you thinking I'm hiding anything from you."

Russell glanced at Attia. Her expression was easy to read. She didn't want to hear more, but Russell needed to know. "This spell they're giving you, is there another way to get a copy?"

Malcolm shook his head. "I don't think so. Ghostly Shell is incredibly rare. I mean, it's possible someone in the Academy knows it and would cast it into Eliana's last Elestone for me, but I don't think that's worth pursuing."

"Right. Eliana isn't likely to help with anything like this," said Russell.

"It's not that," said Malcolm. "I think the only necromancers in the Academy who know this spell are connected with the Nightcrawlers, the Hidden Tower, or both."

"Something tells me that wouldn't work out too well," said Russell.

"Considering they sent a pack of night terrors after me, I didn't think so either."

"We know the Hidden Tower sent the night terrors, but are you certain the Nightcrawlers were involved?" asked Attia.

"No, but I know the Nightcrawlers work closely with the Hidden Tower. They distribute Nevercalling spells to all the Academy's necromancy students."

"Is that the spell you found in Semilae?" asked Attia. "The one you used to call the neverlings."

Malcolm nodded.

Russell didn't want to discuss what happened in Semilae. He felt horrible enough about it already. "I think you're right about the Nightcrawlers and the Hidden Tower," said Russell. "Most of the necromancy students I spoke with in the Academy considered both groups part of one larger organization."

"Which is why I dragged you out here tonight," said Malcolm. "I need the Ghostly Shell spell, and the neverlings seem to be the only ones who can get it for me."

"It's okay," said Attia. "I understand why you're summoning them. I just don't like it."

Russell wanted to know how Malcolm was paying for the spell, but he was afraid he wouldn't like the answer, so he asked a different question. "How does the spell work?"

"You've both seen me force spirits into bodies before. This spell is like that, but it will let me send Fahrilae into a body."

"Back in the Citadel, when you animated that dead woman, her skin turned white, and her fingernails turned brown and nasty. Will it be like that?"

Russell didn't see what Malcolm did in the Citadel. At the time, Russell was exhausted from his studies, but he remembered what happened to the bodies of the sonkuon Malcolm animated. Nasty was an appropriate term for it. As hard as he tried not to, he also remembered the dead girl in the Ganna field, with her oily black skin. He never forgot how she ripped poor Tessa to shreds.

"I don't think it will be like that," said Malcolm, shaking his head. "Everything I've read suggests a body pretty much stays the same after a revenant inhabits it."

"Will it, like... slowly rot?" asked Russell. In his mind, that would be worse than it quickly turning all white and disgusting.

"No. I'm pretty sure the body stops decaying the moment it becomes a revenant."

"Oh, well, that doesn't sound so bad," said Attia, sounding relieved.

Russell shared her feelings of relief. "I mean, she'll still be a walking, talking corpse, but as long as she isn't rotting or anything, I suppose I'll get used to having her around."

Malcolm chuckled. "Somehow, I doubt the others will be so accepting."

"There's no way Liam is going to want that thing around," said Attia. "Can you see him trying to explain it to the Bumbles?"

Russell tried to imagine Liam standing in front of his troops and introducing Fahrilae, the walking corpse. He couldn't picture it. "Yeah, I can't see that happening."

"I'm not sure about Eliana," said Attia. "I mean, my first guess is she would get angry, but that's just because anger seems to be her defining emotion these days."

Russell looked away. Attia wasn't wrong, but he thought she was trivializing everything Eliana was going through. "I'm not sure either," he said after a long pause. "I don't really understand her decisions anymore."

"Sorry, Russ," said Attia softly. "I shouldn't have said it that way."

"Honestly, I think she might accept Fahrilae," said Malcolm. "Remember, Fahrilae was the one who saved her back when the demons attacked the greenhouse. Also, I remember her mentioning a dream where the Other and an army of revenants saved her El'orin from a horrible demon."

"The Eater of Worlds," said Russell. Eliana used to talk about her dreams while they cuddled in bed. "She spoke about that dream often."

"What about Conner?" asked Malcolm. "Liam won't like having a revenant around, but if all the rest of us are in favor of it, maybe he'll change his mind. I'm just worried that Conner will side with his brother out of habit."

"If anything, I'd expect him to push back against his brother," said Russell. "Ever since he started studying with Raelyn, Conner has been standing up to his brother more often." Russell's heart panged as images of the night he spent with Raelyn flooded his mind. She was so deliciously rough with him, while at the same time tender and gentle. "I hate to admit it, but I'm jealous of all the time he gets to spend with her."

"Who, Raelyn?" said Malcolm. "I wonder if she's charmed him. He defends her anytime she comes up in conversation."

Attia shook her head. "She hasn't kissed him, and she has no intention to. They made an agreement, and she's honoring it," said Attia.

Russell struggled to untangle his mixed thoughts and emotions. He felt both happy and sad for Conner. If Raelyn made a commitment, she'd certainly honor it. Then again, how could he be so sure of that? He was in love with her. He struggled to think a negative thought about her. Any time he thought about Raelyn, he remembered how magical it felt being with her, and all the wonderful things she did to him.

"How do you know that?" asked Malcolm. "I believe you, by the way. I just want to know how you found out. Did Conner tell you? Did Raelyn tell you, or did you have a conversation with both of them?"

Attia fidgeted with her hands and looked away. Russell didn't think she wanted to discuss it, but he thought she needed to. "What is it, Attia?" he asked.

"Look, I don't want to talk about it right now. We should keep moving. The sooner Malcolm summons his neverlings, the sooner we can get back to the safety of the greenhouse."

"I brought you two with me because I trust you," said Malcolm. "I considered not telling anyone about this, but I thought you deserved to know. I mean, things will be different once I start building revenants. Not only for me, but for all of us. It's not something I should hide from my friends." Malcolm paused for a moment. "What is it, Attia? You can trust us. What aren't you telling us?"

Attia hugged her shoulders and leaned back into the darkness. "Raelyn kissed me."

Russell batted at the tiny flame of jealousy smoldering within his heart.

"What?" asked Malcolm. "How did that happen? Did she attack you?"

"It wasn't like that," said Attia, shaking her head. "It was after one of the times she healed me. I thanked her for everything and offered to repay her. That's when she kissed me."

"What was it like?" asked Russell. His memories of his first kiss with Raelyn were jumbled. At the time, Raelyn wore an illusion almost identical to the one she wore as the hospital administrator. Russell generally avoided the House of Healing, for fear of seeing Raelyn, but sometimes he couldn't help himself. He remembered spotting her on one of those visits. It kind of surprised him. He expected her to build a different illusion. Did she secretly want him to find her?

"I kind of liked it," said Attia with a sigh. "I mean, I was mad when she did it to me. I slapped her, and we argued about it. She said it was a mistake and that she just couldn't help herself."

Malcolm shook his head. "Am I the only one who finds this problematic? After permanently charming you, she says sorry, and everything is forgiven?"

"Back off, Malcolm," snapped Russell. "It's not Attia's fault."

Attia placed her hand on Russell's shoulder and gently squeezed. "It's okay, Russ," she said. "And no, Malcolm, everything isn't forgiven. Raelyn understands she broke my trust. She needs to earn my forgiveness."

"You're missing my point," said Malcom. "Of course, you're going to forgive her. She charmed you. She can probably make you forgive her."

"It's not like that," said Attia.

Russell understood what Malcolm was saying. By all rights, he should hate Raelyn for what she did to him, but he couldn't stay mad at her for more than an hour or two. Whenever he tried, his resolve quickly crumbled, and his thoughts drifted back to his time with her.

He desperately wanted to spend another evening with Raelyn, but he didn't want to hurt Eliana. It didn't matter that they were no longer together. He still cared deeply about Ellie. "Spending time with her... What's it like, Attia?" he asked. He knew he shouldn't pry. Hearing about Raelyn was probably the worst thing for him, but he couldn't help himself. It was an irresistible itch he needed to scratch.

"It's wonderful," said Attia with a smile. Even in the darkness, Russell noticed the slight flush of red across her unmasked cheek. "We flirt a lot, back and forth. She watches out for me, heals me, and protects me. In turn, I watch out for her."

"How many times has she kissed you?" asked Malcolm.

"Once," said Attia. "She promised never to do it again. Not unless I ask her to."

"And you believe her?"

Russell's nostrils flared. "Of course, Attia believes her. The real question is why the shek don't you?"

Malcolm regarded Russell for a moment, his gaze cool and steady. "Because I understand monsters."

"She isn't a monster!" spat Russell, his lip trembling.

"Do you remember our conversation earlier today, when I asked you to come out here with me tonight?"

Russell nodded.

"I told you it was dangerous to keep summoning Fahrilae," said Malcolm. "Do you know why it's dangerous?"

"Not really. I assume the spell is difficult to cast, and you're worried about losing control of the magic."

"That's only part of it. The real danger is Fahrilae. She's a monster, you see."

"What do you mean? She's saved our lives many times," said Attia.

"You're absolutely right. She has, but there's something you don't know." Malcolm leaned in, making his face easier to see in the darkness. "Fahrilae fights to resist my control. She does it every time I summon her. It isn't something she wants to do. It's something she has to do. So far, I've won every battle, but only barely."

"What happens if you lose?" asked Russell. He was pretty sure he knew the answer.

"I die. She's been very clear about that. If I so much as falter when summoning her, she'll kill me."

"Can't she help herself?" asked Attia.

Malcolm shook his head. "Even after centuries, Fahrilae is still a ghost. It's much worse for younger ghosts, like Constance, and now Brick."

"Wait," said Attia, holding up her hands. "Brick is a ghost?"

"Yes. He started following me a week ago. Fahrilae spoke with him a few times. I don't think he's enjoying the transition."

"Is this something he chose?" asked Russell.

"I don't know, but we're getting away from the point of the conversation," said Malcolm. "Fahrilae is an ally, but she's still a ghost. She's driven by her need to devour life."

"Like Constance," breathed Attia. "I remember that night, leaving the Darkwood. I wanted to be there when you brought

Constance across, but you wouldn't have it. You wouldn't let Felerin be there either."

Malcolm nodded. "Constance barely resisted draining my life away. Had there been two or three of us, she would have succumbed to her hunger."

"I know," said Attia softly. "I saw her reach out toward you. I saw her struggle."

"You grew up with Constance. She was a mentor and a friend, yet she almost turned on us," said Malcolm. "Please understand, Raelyn is no different. She's a tremendous ally. Raelyn has saved our lives many times, but she's still a succubus. She's designed to enthrall and dominate those around her. It's in her nature."

"And she's really shekking good at it," mumbled Russell. He bumped into her on his way home from sharing his first kiss with Eliana, and she stole his heart. After that, she turned him into her loyal puppet, only to wash away the memories after she was done with him.

"I guess she is," said Attia with a sigh. "I was furious with her after she kissed me, yet here I am a few weeks later, furiously flirting with her. The thing is, I don't know if it's wrong. I liked her before she kissed me. The things she's asking me to do, as far as I can tell, they are good for the city."

"What is she asking you to do?" asked Russell. What if he started doing favors for Raelyn? Would she feel the need to reward him? He just wanted to spend time with her. That would be reward enough.

"Tonight, she's replacing Lamenica as the demon in charge of Derregain."

"Right," said Malcolm with a nod. "We killed Lamenica so Raelyn could assume her position."

"Some demons will resist Raelyn's rule," said Attia. "She's going to have me make examples of some of them."

"Let me help," blurted Russell before he could stop himself.

"You don't have to. I told her I'd only take assignments I felt I could handle. At least to start," said Attia. "She mentioned there might be more difficult jobs down the road. I might need help for those."

"I want to help," said Russell. Was Attia trying to keep Raelyn all to herself? Why else would she refuse his help? "If Raelyn needs demons killed, that sounds like something we should help her with. She's trying to protect the city."

Malcolm sighed, shaking his head. "You two are pathetic. Listen to yourselves."

"Raelyn is paying me. I'm not working for free," said Attia. "Besides, as strange as it sounds, I think it's something my Ally needs."

"I thought you and your Ally weren't speaking anymore," said Russell.

"We have a new arrangement."

"And does that new arrangement involve you becoming Raelyn's pet assassin?" asked Malcolm.

"Kind of," said Attia sheepishly. "Remember what Eliana said about all of our El'orin? She said they were all people of importance, and many of them were connected. Conner's Demon healed the Other, who was protecting Eliana's El'orin while they journeyed to see Liam's Guest, or something like that."

Russell nodded. "That's not a bad summary. Your El'orin wasn't involved, Attia. Then again, neither was mine."

Attia took a deep breath. "My El'orin worked as an assassin for the Demon Queen."

"Your El'orin worked for Chariden?" asked Malcolm. He glanced at Russell. He looked nervous.

"My Ally spent her life hunting other El'orin," said Attia. "I think Chariden was afraid of them."

"So, that's why you're so much better than the rest of us at tracking El'orin," said Russell. It explained why she could sense El'orin at greater distances than the rest of them. It also explained why Attia seemed so driven to hunt. Russell loved the white mists. He was certain they all did, but with Attia, it seemed like an addiction.

"So, because of that, you think you need to work as Raelyn's personal assassin?" asked Malcolm.

"Look, I don't know," said Attia. "The Other led an army of revenants, and here we are, helping you get a spell so you can make revenants."

"It's not the same."

Attia shook her head. "I'm not so sure. Conner's El'orin was some kind of demon, and Conner studies demonology. Before the city fell, Russell's El'orin ruled Semilae. Russell was the one who led us to the ruins of Semilae."

"She has a point," said Russell. "We're not reliving our El'orins' lives, but our paths seem pretty shekking similar. Maybe Attia is destined to work as an assassin for a succubus. If she is, I think hunting demons for Raelyn is an improvement over hunting El'orin for Chariden."

It wasn't lost on Russell that Raelyn was working for Chariden, but somehow, he thought this would be different. Raelyn cared about people. She went out of her way to protect Derregain and its residents. Russell knew he was biased. He knew Raelyn's charms were making him trust her, but that didn't make her untrustworthy. He wanted to believe he'd trust and adore her even without being charmed.

Russell needed to believe it.

7

Malcolm

Malcolm ran his fingers along his jawline. He was growing a touch of stubble, and he didn't like how it itched. "Maybe working for Raelyn will be an improvement, I don't know. My concern is that neither of you can think clearly when you're around her."

"Are you saying we're both supposed to avoid her for the rest of our lives?" asked Attia. "I don't really have that option. She isn't done healing me yet."

Malcolm doubted the healing would ever end. It was a convenient excuse for Raelyn to draw Attia deeper into her web. That being said, maybe there was value in what Attia was doing for Raelyn. Keeping the demonic population under control was necessary. Derregain wouldn't survive another encounter with a monster like Plaguebringer.

"We're not children anymore, Malcolm. If we want to help Raelyn, you can't stop us," said Russell.

"No one said anything about stopping you." Malcolm didn't want to get into an argument with Russell. It never ended well. "I just think someone needs to be there to look out for you two."

Attia raised an eyebrow. "Are you volunteering?"

"Let's not jump to conclusions."

"Our Mistress will happily welcome you into her service," said Attia flatly.

Malcolm backed away, instinctively reaching into his belt pouch. Was this some kind of trap? Did they accompany him out here to capture him? He doubted he could summon something quickly enough to make a difference, but if they moved against him, he'd try.

Attia's lips curled into a wicked smile. A moment later, she burst out laughed "I was joking!"

"That's not funny!" shouted Malcolm. He took a deep breath to calm his racing heart.

"Wrong," said Russell with a hearty laugh. "That was really shekking funny. You should have seen your face. You even reached into your pouch like you were going to summon a spirit!"

Malcolm waited until the two of them were done laughing before continuing. "Look, I don't mind being there to make sure Raelyn isn't taking advantage of you, but I'm not sure it's safe for me to be outside the greenhouse."

Attia looked puzzled. "You're outside the greenhouse right now. Are you in danger?"

"The Hidden Tower keeps sending spirits to find me. Fahrilae has been killing most of them, but they know I live in the greenhouse. She sees a new spirit every two or three days. They sent one yesterday. We should be fine out here tonight."

"So, the greenhouse protects you?" asked Russell.

"Fahrilae thinks so. She said whatever accompanies the spirits refuses to enter the greenhouse, even in the Astral Plane."

"Well, it's not like you'll need to be in the House of Healing often," said Attia. "A brief visit, every now and then, should be all you need. The important thing is you escort Russell whenever he visits. He's the one you need to worry about. Raelyn holds much greater sway over him than me."

"I'm not a child. I can take care of myself," said Russell.

"All the same, I think that sounds like a good plan," said Malcolm, moving the conversation forward. He didn't want to risk it turning into an argument. "Russell and I will help on your missions, but all three of us will be present to discuss each assignment with Raelyn. Agreed?"

"Agreed," said Attia.

Russell remained silent for a long moment before finally muttering, "Agreed."

"Alright, the clearing is just ahead. Let's get this over with." Malcolm gestured for Attia to lead the way. She paused for a moment before turning and continuing down the trail. While Malcolm found the previous conversation enlightening, he needed to focus on the matter at hand.

Tonight, he was crossing the point of no return. Summoning spirits was one thing, but the person he was about to become was something entirely different. Hopefully, Ul-Nong-Far wouldn't openly discuss the terms of their agreement, but Malcolm needed to prepare for the worst.

Even if the worst didn't come out tonight, it was only a matter of time. Malcolm needed to research surrounding villages before selecting his target. He needed to make several revenants to help him with his task. After that, he'd need to spend considerable time away from the city performing the deed. His actions wouldn't go unnoticed.

Today, Malcolm's friends and associates thought of him as a person. Soon, everyone would consider him a monster. It didn't matter that his magic helped to save Derregain from Plaguebringer. It didn't matter if the terrible things he planned to do were for the greater good.

Malcolm planned to sacrifice a village of innocent farmers to his neverlings. He knew the horrible fate he was condemning those people to, yet he wasn't dissuaded. In many ways, he was choosing the wellbeing of his neverling allies over the lives of innocent farmers. He was turning his back on humanity.

He was becoming a monster.

"It may seem that way, but that's not it," whispered the Other. *"Yes, you are sacrificing many lives, but think of all the lives you'll save. Always keep that in the forefront of your mind. Most people aren't strong enough to do what you are doing. Yes, you will be hated and feared for the things you do, but these things must be done nevertheless."*

"I think we're here," called Attia from ahead. She was standing next to a stump near the center of a break in the woods. The moon and stars peppered the sky above.

Malcolm was so preoccupied with his thoughts, he didn't even notice they reached the clearing. "You two don't need to stay for this. Why don't you retreat down the trail twenty or thirty yards? I'll join you when I'm done."

Russell shook his head. "I don't think so."

"I thought that's what you'd say," said Malcolm with a sigh. Why did everyone insist on watching him summon neverlings? "If you're staying, move to the edges of the clearing, and don't say a word."

"This is one of the many reasons revenants make much better companions than people. Then again, we had this exact conversation the last time you visited this clearing," said the Other.

Malcolm ignored his El'orin. Once his friends were in position, he engaged his Spectral Sight and started his Nevercalling spell. The words flowed easily, one to the next, and the phrase only took ten seconds to complete. Each repetition of the phrase sent a shiver down his spine.

Eventually, a tunnel of inky darkness appeared on the Astral horizon. It twisted and swirled as it approached, opening like the mouth of a yawning giant. Freezing wind blasted through the clearing, covering the frozen ground with a new layer of frost. A moment later, a portal of darkness appeared in the center of the clearing. Nine small beings, each clad in black robes, shuffled from the portal. Their robes were tied to their bodies with dozens of brown straps. Cowls shrouded their heads.

"Greetings, Dark Lord," said one of the creatures. Malcolm assumed it was Ul-Nong-Far. Each neverling looked nearly identical to his neighbor, making them difficult to identify. "We are pleased to answer your call."

"Greetings, Ul-Nong-Far. I've been told you have something for me," said Malcom. He didn't want to be impolite, but he thought the direct approach was the best way to get the conversation started.

The neverling reached into the folds of his robe and produced a tightly bound scroll. "We have done as we promised. We wish to know if you will do as you promised."

Malcolm sighed. He feared they'd ask him to recommit, and that's what was happening. He glanced at Russell and Attia. Malcolm didn't want to discuss his side of the bargain in front of his friends, but he didn't think there was a way to avoid it. "I will do as I promised."

"How many sacrifices will you deliver?" asked the neverling, his voice a raspy whisper.

"I don't know," said Malcolm. He still needed to do the research. "Let it be said, if the flesh I deliver is insufficient for your needs, I will deliver more."

Ul-Nong-Far remained silent, but several neverlings behind him began chittering, chirping, and clicking. Malcolm suspected they were discussing his offer. "We face common enemies," he added, hoped to sway the conversation in his favor. "It does me no good to deliver you less flesh than you require. Your tower must be strong to face the challenges to come."

The neverlings behind Ul-Nong-Far gradually stopped conversing in whatever strange language they were speaking. Malcolm suspected his argument swayed them. Why else would they have stopped their discussion?

"*Good!*" praised the Other.

"I hate this," whispered Attia. Malcolm assumed she was talking to Russell, but he heard her all the same.

"When will you make your first delivery?" asked Ul-Nong-Far.

"I can't be certain," said Malcolm. "I need time to make revenants. After that, I need to find a suitable village. Even when I'm ready, there is the Hidden Tower to consider. They are searching for me. They can't attack me in my home, but abandoning its safety for several days will be dangerous."

Chittering chirps and staccato clicks filled the clearing as the neverlings resumed their conversation. This time, Ul-Nong-Far joined them. The discussion went on for what seemed like an eternity before abruptly ending. "We can help with the Hidden Tower," said Ul-Nong-Far, cocking his head to the right and nodding slightly.

"How?" asked Malcolm.

"The Central Authority hosts many gatherings, for many purposes. Attendance is optional for many of their gatherings, but for some, it is required," rasped Ul-Nong-Far. "Our tower will request a gathering that will require the Hidden Tower to attend. This will grant you the time you need to complete your task."

Malcolm carefully considered the neverling's words. It didn't sound like this was something Ul-Nong-Far could do often. He needed to take full advantage of the opportunity they were providing. "How long will the gathering last?"

"Four, perhaps five of your days," said the neverling.

"And am I correct in assuming you can't do this often?"

"You are correct."

Malcolm nodded. He needed to come up with an easy way to communicate with Ul-Nong-Far, but if the neverlings could send spirits to speak with Fahrilae, he didn't think it was a problem. "Two weeks from now, send a messenger. If I am prepared, I will reply. If I do not reply, wait another week before sending the next messenger. Call your gathering one week after receiving my reply. Do you understand?"

"Yes, Dark Lord," said Ul-Nong-Far.

Malcolm extended an open hand and waited. Ul-Nong-Far stood there for some time, motionless. Perhaps he didn't understand the gesture. Eventually, he placed the tightly bound scroll in Malcolm's hand.

"Are they talking about what I think they're talking about?" whispered Russell.

"Yes," breathed Attia.

Malcolm took the scroll and carefully slipped it into his belt pouch. "Thank you, Ul-Nong-Far. I will begin my preparations. Our business is concluded."

"Very well, Dark Lord," said Ul-Nong-Far.

Malcolm breathed a sigh of relief. He wished he could have managed the conversation without agreeing to a firm timeline, but he didn't see any other way to coordinate it. Thankfully, the Hidden Tower would be occupied while he performed his dark deed.

One by one, the neverlings shuffled into their portal of inky blackness, leaving only Ul-Nong-Far behind. He bowed his head. "Be very careful, Dark Lord. Many eyes watch you. It is not just the Hidden Tower. Do not fail in this task." After he finished speaking, he stepped back, disappearing into the darkness.

A gust of freezing wind blasted through the clearing as the portal faded from view, leaving Attia, Russell, and Malcolm alone.

"What the shek just happened?" asked Russell.

"They delivered my Ghostly Shell spell," said Malcolm as he untied the binding and unfurled the delicate parchment.

"Good for you," snapped Russell. "Let's talk about the village you plan to feed those butchers."

Malcolm looked away from the glowing sigils etched across the parchment. As much as he wanted to read his scroll, he needed to focus on the conversation. "If we must."

"Let's be clear. There is no shekking way we're helping you do that," said Russell.

"I won't ask you to help," said Malcolm. "That's why I needed this spell. My revenants will assist me."

"But haven't we already helped you?" asked Attia.

Malcolm shook his head. "Not really. Sure, you helped me learn the Ghostly Shell spell, but you aren't responsible for what I do with it."

"It doesn't work that way," said Attia.

"Is a swordsmith responsible for every drop of blood his creations spill?" asked Malcolm.

"That's different," said Attia.

"Not really." Malcolm spoke slowly and softly. He needed to keep emotions out of the conversation. "Did you use your Breath of Battle spell when you killed the Bumbles who were trying to rape you, Attia?"

"Yes."

"Are you saying that we're all partially responsible for their deaths? Every one of us helped you get that spell, after all."

"Those Bumbles had it coming!" spat Attia, her eyes smoldering.

"Yes, they did," said Malcolm. "And if your point is that the farmers I'm planning to kill are innocent, that's a different discussion." Malcolm gazed up at the moon and stars and sighed. "The Other prepared me for this from the very beginning. He knew there were roads I would need to walk alone. What I'm about to do... This is one of those roads."

"Don't do this, Malcolm. You're not a murderer," said Russell, but he sounded uncertain.

"That's where you're wrong, Russ," said Malcolm. "This won't be the first sacrifice I've made to the neverlings. There was Ellie's mom, of course." Malcolm met Russell's gaze. He knew Russ blamed himself for the death of Eliana's mother. It was time Russell placed the blame where it belonged. "Just so we're clear, I knew they would collect a payment when I summoned them."

"Shek you!"

"Then there was that family of farmers Attia helped me sacrifice."

"Never again," said Attia.

"Exactly, Attia. Never again," said Malcolm. "This terrible thing that I need to do, I will do it alone. Neither of you is responsible. I made the deal on my own, and I intend to fulfill it on my own. The blood I spill, whether it be a few drops, a flowing stream, or an endless ocean, none of it will be on your hands. It's my burden to bear."

The three of them stood speechless for nearly a minute before Attia finally broke the silence. "How do you plan to find bodies?" she asked. "You know, for your revenants."

"I thought I'd ask Conner to help. I suspect there's no shortage of fresh corpses in the House of Healing."

"Don't ask him," said Attia. "Conner has his own dark roads to walk. I don't want him involved in this. I'll take care of it for you."

"How?" Malcolm thought he knew the answer, but Attia asked him about the bodies for a reason. She wanted to shift the conversation in this direction. He thought it best to play along.

"It's one of the perks of working with Raelyn," she said with a wry smile. "If I tell her I want this, she'll do it for me. Can I tell her about the Ghostly Shell spell?"

There was no point in keeping it a secret from Raelyn, not if they'd be working together soon. She'd find out, eventually. "Yes. Tell her."

"Alright, I will," said Attia. "Knowing Raelyn, she'll prepare a private room with a selection for you to choose from."

Malcolm didn't know what to make of Attia's willingness to help. Perhaps she felt lonely on her own dark road, working as an assassin for Raelyn. Maybe that loneliness was enough to make her want to help Malcolm with his own solitary journey. It wasn't all that strange when he stopped to think about it.

Russell and Malcolm agreed to help Attia with her work for Raelyn. Attia was now offering to help Malcolm find suitable corpses for his revenants, but she was using Raelyn to do it. She was solidifying an alliance between the four of them.

Malcolm didn't know where it left the rest of his friends. Conner was already working with Raelyn, so perhaps there was a connection there, but his brother Liam would never work with the succubus. It was even worse with Eliana. She outright hated Raelyn.

It was definitely a problem, but not one Malcolm could afford to dwell on right now. He returned his gaze to the parchment in his hands. He let his vision follow the glowing sigils etched across it. As he did, new magic raced into his mind.

8

Raelyn

Raelyn stared out at the host of demons assembled before her. She stood on a landing, four steps above the ground floor, yet several demons towered over her. Initially, she wasn't sold on Cinderhorn's idea of hosting her Demonic Court in the heavily damaged banquet hall of Lamenica's old manor, but she rather liked the effect.

Tattered and burned tapestries hung from the walls, partially concealing the blackened and scarred wood beneath. A few scattered remnants of the once luxurious carpeting remained. Fortunately, the fires that burned in this room never got hot enough to damage the stone floor.

Raelyn furnished the space with a mixture of new pieces, mostly benches and sofas, complementing the handful of surviving chairs. A few demons took advantage of the furniture, but most of them preferred to stand.

Except for a pair of imps sent by the Netten and Naga show, every demon in attendance was of the fourth order, or greater. Raelyn counted 23, which meant many boycotted her mandatory gathering. She needed to carefully consider how to handle them. Lenience would portray her as weak, but excessive punishment would paint her as a reactionary with an unsteady grip on her rule. Her discipline required careful calibration.

Raelyn wondered who summoned the imps. She didn't summon them, and neither did Cinderhorn, but their presence didn't surprise her. The Netten and Naga show wielded tremendous influence across the Netherworld. Several demons in attendance were likely connected with the show, to one extent or another. Raelyn was curious to know which ones.

"It might take a few days, but I should be able to provide you a fairly accurate list of those not in attendance," said Cinderhorn, loudly enough where many demons undoubtably heard him. He was standing to the right of Raelyn. He was one of the demons who towered over her, despite the landing. "I know many of the names already. In time, my imps will find the rest. They're certain to brag about how they defied you."

"I'm surprised so many avoided attending," said Raelyn, shaking her head. "It puts me in a difficult position." Preferring privacy, she whispered.

Cinderhorn shrugged, rustling his wings. "You were in this position the moment you accepted Chariden's offer. The way I see it, they did you a favor. You don't need to punish all of them, only some of them. With so many demons absent, you have the luxury of picking your targets."

Raelyn wasn't sure how to handle it. Ultimately, Cinderhorn was right, but the ability to choose presented a host of problems of its own. Her decisions about whom to punish and who to spare would be heavily scrutinized. "Do you think we should wait for others to arrive or just get started?"

Cinderhorn turned to face her. "I can't make that decision for you. The Queen put you in charge of this city, not me," he said in a hushed tone.

"I wasn't asking you to decide for me," said Raelyn. "I was just looking for your advice."

"I advise you proceed with confidence, bordering on arrogance," said the Guardian demon, a slight smile curling on the edges of his lips. "There are no right or wrong answers in this. Even if you do everything perfectly, they'll scrutinize you for it."

Raelyn shrugged. Maybe Cinderhorn was right. She felt like she waited long enough. "If everyone would quiet down, I would like to start the meeting." She said it loud enough to be heard, but only half the room seemed to pay attention. Swishing her tail wildly, she shouted, "Quiet down! This Demonic Court is beginning!"

All but two of the demons ended their conversations and faced her. She thought she recognized the two of them. Were they sitting with Bonewalker when Raelyn first met Lamenica? Clyve was there with Bonewalker, but there were two others as well. She couldn't be certain, but perhaps these were them.

"Keep talking," mumbled Cinderhorn beneath his breath. "You have their attention. Don't lose it."

"First, I would like to thank you all for your attendance and polite attention. Tonight, we're embarking on a new journey. Chariden, the Demon Queen of this world, has entrusted me with the responsibility of watching over this fine city." Raelyn surveyed the crowd. Some seemed amused. Others wore angry expressions, but most of the demons looked bored. "From this point on, I am the steward of Derregain. My decisions and policies, as they apply to Derregain, are extensions of the Queen's will."

"I thought the Queen wanted you dead," came a breathy voice echoing from within the crowd.

Raelyn couldn't identify the speaker. Netten and Naga's imps insisted on flooding the stage with bright light. They said it would make for a better broadcast, but the lights made it difficult to see portions of the room. "At one time, she did," said Raelyn forcefully. "We have a much better relationship now."

"Word down below is that you're the one who vanquished Lamenica," said a shadow demon reclining on a couch near the front of the room. In many ways, he looked like any wraith or apparition a necromancer might summon, but there were differences. Thin lines of crisp, crimson light decorated his shadowy body in places, drawing on facial expressions, fingernails, and what seemed to be a pair of pants. "Why should we respect your rule?"

"Because the Queen put me in charge," said Raelyn. "It's as simple as that."

"Nothing is ever that simple." The strings of crimson light marking the shadow demon's mouth twisted and turned until he looked like he was grinning. "If you killed her, you violated her right of Dominion, and none of us need respect your authority."

"Are you issuing a challenge, Darkthane?" growled Cinderhorn.

"Relax, Guardian. I'm only asking questions."

"It's okay, Cinderhorn," said Raelyn. She needed to strike a balance with the Guardian demon. She wanted everyone to understand that he backed her, but at the same time, she needed to appear independent. It was a delicate dance. "To answer your question, I didn't kill her. A group of humans did."

"But you work with those humans, don't you?" asked the shadow demon. "My imps tell me you're teaching one of them demonology, and that many of them serve your pet, the Governor."

Raelyn's forced her eyes to smolder as she ran a finger across her scarred cheek. She didn't expect to intimidate any of the assembled demons, but she wanted to strike a strong pose, nonetheless. "And is that a bad thing? Whether we like it or not, our survival in this city requires that we work with humanity."

"But that's not how it is in the other settlements," said Darkthane. "In most villages, humans are kept as slaves, or even livestock."

Cinderhorn cleared his throat. "The Queen tried something different with Derregain. She wanted to see what happened if she let a human city live and thrive freely."

Darkthane rose to his feet. It was eerie to watch. His shadowy limbs quivered and bent as if they were made of watery ink, yet they still maintained their shape. "And look where it got us. The humans killed Lamenica! Even if the Queen had a hand in it, are we really going to let their arrogance go unpunished?"

Raelyn swept her gaze across the banquet hall. Some demons looked to be barely containing their anger. She didn't want to inflame their rage, but she wasn't about to back down. "What about Plaguebringer? Should we punish the humans for fighting him?"

The strings of crimson light marking the shadow demon's mouth bent into a gentle frown. "Last I checked, the humans didn't vanquish Plaguebringer. He's still in this world."

"Many of his most powerful servants aren't, though," countered Raelyn. "Clyve, for instance, was killed."

"Actually, the humans didn't kill Clyve. I did that," said Novus. He was standing along the back wall. Maybe she was imagining it, but even through the poor lighting, Raelyn thought he looked amused.

"My point still stands!" said Raelyn, flapping her wings in agitation. "If not for the humans, Plaguebringer would have destroyed this city. Without Derregain, there isn't enough blood to support our continued existence in this world. We don't have to like it, but we can't deny it. Our survival, at least in this world, depends on theirs."

"I've heard enough of this blasphemy!" hissed a demon with an echoing voice. Raelyn guessed he was some type of wind demon. Three sets of long, angular wings flowed behind him, each ending in gleaming razor-edges. Similarly razored spurs lined the demon's arms and legs, making his wicked claws among the least threatening of his features. "Raelyn is in bed with the humans!" the demon shouted. "She serves them, not us!"

"Order!" shouted Cinderhorn, but it was too late. Other demons were cheering and shouting, and the wind demon seemed thrilled by the attention.

"Raelyn is not fit to rule!" screamed the wind demon. "I challenge her!"

A smothering silence spread across the assembly. Demons who were shouting encouragement, egging the wind demon into action, immediately stopped shouting.

"Are you certain?" asked Raelyn. "Notice how all your friends have grown silent. They're fine with you risking your life, but we both know they lack the courage to mount their own challenges."

The wind demon quickly glanced around the assembly. If he was hoping for renewed support, he didn't get it. None of the demons said a word. "I stand by my challenge, bitch. You are not fit to rule."

"As you wish," said Raelyn with a sigh. "Cinderhorn, will you stand as my champion?"

"Of course," said the Guardian demon, his words a dissonant choir of voices.

"Coward!" spat the wind demon. He spun to face the assembly. "Look how she cowers and hides behind the Guardian demon."

Raelyn feigned an exaggerated yawn. "The Queen knew there would be challenges. She sent Cinderhorn to support me. I would be a fool to turn my back on her aid. After all, a good leader should avoid taking unnecessary risks."

Cinderhorn unfurled his wings as he stepped forward. All across the banquet hall, other demons backed away, leaving as much space as possible for the combatants. "As the appointed champion of the challenged, I set the terms," said Cinderhorn. "We fight here, within this hall. Magic will be allowed."

The wind demon snorted. "There's barely room to fly in here. Your terms are hardly fair!"

Cinderhorn shrugged. "Then, withdraw your challenge. I have no desire to vanquish you."

The wind demon raised his arms and chanted. Thin tendrils of electricity began dancing across his razor-sharp wings and claws. "I don't need to fly to slaughter you, Cinderhorn. They say you're the weakest of the Guardians," growled the wind demon. "They say you're a coward who hides behind his imps."

Cinderhorn laughed, but with his voice a discordant choir, the sound was utterly terrifying. Several demons shuddered, and even the wind demon backed up a step. "The only imps in the room are over there," said the Guardian demon, pointing at the pair broadcasting the event for the Netten and Naga show. "Rest assured, I won't hide behind them."

"Your time has come, Guardian. I can't wait to rip you to shreds and send you screaming back to the Netherworld!" shouted the wind demon. "You think you're powerful, but your arrogance will be your undoing. Today, the Netherworld will learn my name. Today, the Netherworld will celebrate Bladestorm!"

"My arrogance?" taunted Cinderhorn with a sneer.

Screeching like a bird of prey, the wind demon flapped his many wings and leapt at Cinderhorn. He moved so fast, he was a blur. A stream of electricity followed the charging demon, and thunder reverberated throughout the hall. Raelyn couldn't help but retreat a step. She knew wind demons were fast, but she wasn't prepared for anything like this.

But Cinderhorn was.

The Guardian demon held up a single paw and Bladestorm slammed to a halt. It was as if he flew into a granite wall. Raelyn was surprised the wind demon didn't cry out, but maybe he wasn't able to. Cinderhorn must have used some kind of Telekinesis spell to capture Bladestorm. The magic was well beyond anything she thought herself capable of.

Several demons gasped, and many exchanged nervous glances. Novus looked on intently, and the Serpentus crept a few steps closer to the action. Raelyn guessed everyone was just as surprised as she was by the Guardian demon's display of raw power.

"Look at all those blades," said Cinderhorn, his sickening choir of a voice teasing and taunting. "They look so deadly. I wonder what might have happened had you slammed into me with all those knives. How sharp are they?" The Guardian demon wiggled his claws and the wind demon's wings twisted, curling inward. "Let's find out, shall we?"

Cinderhorn clenched his fist and Bladestorm's wings bent in on themselves, lancing into his helpless body. Gouts of steaming pink blood splattered across the walls and floor. Raelyn resisted the urge to shield herself with her wings, letting the blood splash across her body instead. She thought it would make for a stronger image.

The wind demon coughed and sputtered, but failed to scream. Raelyn was certain Cinderhorn's Telekinesis spell was preventing it. Slowly, Bladestorm's wings began to dig and tear, cutting his muscles and viscera into bloody ribbons.

"My, my, those blades are sharp. You really should be more careful with them," said Cinderhorn with a macabre laugh. He flicked his wrist, and the wind demon collapsed. The sickening plop of wet, torn flesh and shattered bones slamming against the floor echoed across the hall. "I believe this challenge is over. Is there another challenger?" Cinderhorn slowly swept his gaze across the crowd. "Anyone? Anyone at all?"

Based on the astonished expressions throughout the hall, Raelyn knew no one was going to take Cinderhorn up on his offer. She assumed most expected the Guardian demon to win the fight, but not like that. Bladestorm never had a chance.

Raelyn waited until the gasps and hushed whispers quieted down before speaking. "Moving on," she said, keeping her tone as calm as possible. She wanted the room to think she wasn't surprised like the rest of them. She wanted them to believe she was fully aware of Cinderhorn's power the entire time. "I would like to discuss the Traditions. Most notably, Hospitality, and the rare conditions under which I plan to grant it. It's time we establish some rules about summoning demons in Derregain."

9

Dimitri

Dimitri carefully climbed up onto the street. As embarrassing as it was having two kids helping him navigate the sewers and the snowy streets, he appreciated the help. Even before his possession, Dimitri was anything but agile. Now, with only limited control over his motor functions, Dimitri was clumsy to a fault.

The plan was to attack after the third bell stopped ringing, but the ringing never ceased. Scattered screams and clanging bells continuously echoed across the snowy streets. Dimitri assumed it was because of Sorriah's ghouls. He knew little about necromancy, but his sister assured him Sorriah's ghouls were absolutely terrifying.

"Just wait, my little meatsuit," whispered the voice in Dimitri's head. *"Our Fireball will be glorious! I can't wait to watch this city burn. Do well tonight, and perhaps I'll reward you with a few pieces of bread to go with your spiders and worms."*

Dimitri hated how his stomach growled, and his mouth watered at the mere mention of spiders and worms. The spirit inside him was in complete control. It could make him savor and crave things that should disgust him. There was no doubt in Dimitri's mind that the voice in his head could reduce him to some kind of disgusting animal. In many ways, it already did.

"Good job, meatsuit, you're finally learning," teased the voice. *"You exist to serve me. The more you fight me, the more tortured your miserable existence will become. Except for your sister, the people around you have already stopped thinking of you as a person. Rest assured, I can make it much worse."*

Dimitri wondered how long it would be before Eirini stopped seeing him as her brother. These days, she seemed to avoid him as much as possible. When they spent time together, he noticed the horror and revulsion in her eyes. Who could blame her?

"Stop feeling sorry for yourself, meatsuit, or I'll give you more reasons to loathe your life," whispered the voice in your head. *"Focus on the task at hand. Saro is almost ready."*

All around him, dirty, emaciated gang members assembled in the street. Saro was out front, issuing orders. Both Eirini and Mend were close to Dimitri, off to the side. He didn't know where Ghost was. Dimitri assumed the necromancer was scouting in his insubstantial form. With Sorriah's enhanced ghouls roaming the streets, scouting seemed critical.

"When we move, we move as a group!" shouted Saro. He was hard to hear over the clanging bells. "Our target is that building," he yelled, pointing at a large structure towering over the squat row houses lining either side of the street. "Here we go!"

Dimitri lurched and shuffled down the street, his escorts flanking him the whole way. He wondered if those kids resented being made his babysitters. Truth be told, it was probably the safest job available. In Dimitri's estimation, Saro treated most young gang members like fodder. He didn't expect many of the kids to survive the night.

Up ahead, three people raced around the bend. "Help us!" they shouted as they ran towards Saro and the rest of the group. Dimitri doubted they recognized the threat Saro, and the others, presented until it was too late. The three of them screamed and wailed as daggers, shards of glass, and stones tore through their bodies until each of them collapsed against the slushy street.

"Stay back!" called Mend, her shrill voice cutting through the screaming and clanging. "Okay, we're clear. The ghouls have found new targets."

Dimitri knew Mend could read the thoughts of other members of the Coterie. He was certain she read his mind enough to understand what he was going through. Dimitri saw the fear and sympathy in her eyes. In this case, Mend was probably reading Ghost's mind and relaying the details to Saro.

"Charge!" shouted Saro as he raced down the street. Mend and most of the gang members ran after him, but a small group remained behind to escort Dimitri and Eirini. There was no way for him to keep up. With the spirit inside of him controlling his legs, the best he could do was clumsily shamble along.

By the time Dimitri finally reached the intersection, the battle was already underway. Saro and his gang were facing opposition from both sides of the street. The attacks were coming from the windows and doorways of several row houses. Thrown weapons seemed the most common, but Dimitri thought he saw arrows raining down from some of the second-story windows.

"Can you help them, Brother?" asked Eirini.

"*Oh, you most certainly can,*" whispered the voice inside his head.

Dimitri watched his hands slowly rise in front of his face. He could make casting spells more difficult by resisting the spirit, but he didn't think it would get him anywhere. Besides, a part of him wanted to see what his Fireball spell did. In this situation, it was best to be helpful. There was no sense in earning more punishment.

Between Dimitri's hands, a tiny spark of brilliant fire coalesced. It grew, quickly becoming a sweltering ball of roiling flames. The air shimmered from the heat, and thin trails of smoke rose from Dimitri's healthy arm. His withered one seemed barely involved. He was surprised the spirit bothered to raise it.

Pointing with his good arm, Dimitri sent the ball of fire roaring out into the night. It sputtered and spun as it flew through an open second-story window. Once inside, it exploded, sending a swirling cloud of superheated flame into the night sky.

A pair of screaming, burning bodies leapt from the window. Showers of brilliant, smoldering sparks followed. A slender awning covering a modest deck was the first to catch fire, followed by the entry door and the closest sections of wall.

It only took a few moments for the entire townhouse to erupt into roiling flames. Several other burning people raced out into the snowy streets, hoping to extinguish themselves somehow, but Dimitri knew it was futile. His flames were beautiful, terrible, and unforgiving. Few survived their kiss.

"*Yes!*" cheered the voice in his head. "*Again! We must do it again!*"

"Shek," breathed Eirini from off to his right. Dimitri wasn't sure if she was happy, sad, or terrified. He couldn't tell from her voice, and with the spirit turning his head towards another row house, he wasn't able to see Eirini's expression.

Once again, a tiny orange spark formed between his hands. This time, the spark grew slowly, gradually taking on an almost crimson hue. Smoke billowed from Dimitri's good arm. A moment later, searing pain followed. Dimitri knew his arm was on fire, but there was nothing he could do about it. The spirit wasn't about to stop casting.

The Fireball that leapt from Dimitri's fingers differed from the last. This one looked more like a condensed meteor of magma than a roiling ball of fire. It sizzled as it raced across the night sky, leaving a swirling trail of smoke in its wake.

"Don't just stand there! Smother that fire!" shouted Eirini at Dimitri's escorts.

Both kids grabbed at his burning arm, but Dimitri ignored them. He wanted to watch his magic explode. He needed to see its flames feast on his enemies. Dimitri knew these weren't his thoughts. He knew his spirit was forcing them inside his head, but he didn't care. On a certain level, he was proud of himself. Sure, his magic was violent and cruel, but at the same time, it was also beautiful and powerful.

The brilliant ball of magma struck the row house just above the main entryway. It shattered on impact, sending countless globs of superheated flame in every direction. Each individual glob exploded as it contacted whatever happened to get in its way. The door was the first to burst into flames. The roof and a pair of second-story windows immediately followed. Even nearby cobblestones erupted when struck by one of the glowing globs.

The overall effect was breathtakingly destructive. Roaring flames enveloped the row house in short order. A half-dozen people fled the building for the streets. Three of them were unfortunate enough to make contact with patches of the superheated magma. They immediately burst into flames. With Saro and the gang outside waiting, the others fared little better.

"That spell is amazing, Brother," said Eirini, but once again, Dimitri thought there was more fear in her voice than anything else. "The others are advancing. We need to follow them."

Dimitri's legs started moving on their own. The light from the burning buildings lit the street like a sunny day, making navigating the slushy cobblestones far easier. Fortunately, Saro and the gang weren't moving quickly. Two of the row houses were in flames, and the fire was threatening to spread to others, but a few enemies were still fighting.

A sparkling barrier of green energy snapped into existence around Dimitri just in time to deflect an arrow. The enemy must have realized who was responsible for the Fireballs. They were trying to fight back the only way they knew how.

"We'll use a smaller explosion this time. The last one burned you. I prefer my meatsuits rare. Medium rare, at most," whispered the voice, Dimitri's Master.

The recognition of their true relationship sent shivers down Dimitri's spine. He couldn't deny it. The spirit within him controlled virtually all aspects of his life. Dimitri was being trained into utter obedience, and there was nothing he could do to stop it.

"Yes, I think I like that. From now on, think of me as your Master."

Dimitri's wizardry Shield spell flashed as it deflected a second arrow, reminded him of the imminent danger. He pointed at the window the arrows were coming from and a tiny ball of bright orange flame sprung into existence. There was heat, but not nearly so much as with the last Fireball. This one seemed cool in comparison.

The tiny ball of flame leapt into the air. It swelled as it traveled across the winter sky, racing toward the window in the distance. Dimitri smiled as a woman jumped from that second-story window, desperate to escape her fate. He knew there were others up there. He knew his fires would feast on them.

The seething ball of flame reached the window and exploded into a smoking cloud of superheated fire. The roof, and much of the second floor of the row house, burst into flames. This time, the flames didn't spread to the lower level, or the streets below. Watching two burning bodies leap from the window, Dimitri decided this smaller Fireball was nearly perfect.

10

Liam

Liam staggered back a step, nearly slipping in the slush and snow covering the cobblestone street. He fought ghouls before. Stars above, back in the Citadel, he spent an entire afternoon training with the one Malcolm created and bound within a circle of runes. The pair of ghouls he was currently facing were faster, tougher, and far stronger.

These monsters lacked the bleached skin of ordinary ghouls. In fact, they wore no skin at all, exposing their glistening muscles and slender tendons to the open air. Neither appeared to have an ounce of fat on them. Curiously, they wore pristinely polished ribcages around their bodies like armor.

"These are just like the ones we fought in the sewers," said Sinnow. He was standing directly behind Liam, staying close enough to provide healing support.

"Stand your ground!" shouted Liam to the rest of the team. The pair of ghouls lunged at him, sweeping their claws wildly. Liam allowed his shield to dance into position, intercepting one attacker. He extended his glowing blue sword to keep the other at bay, but it swept the weapon aside, landing a staggering blow against his shoulder.

Freezing cold mingled with the blinding pain in the back of Liam's skull. Remnants of his burns, a constant itching sensation crawling across his seared skin, weren't helping matters, either. The headaches were nearly constant now, and despite his brother's urging, Liam refused to let Raelyn use her recently learned Regrowth spell to treat his horrible burns.

He spent most days somewhere between misery and agony. Fortunately, his troops seemed to understand what he was going through. If they hated him for his quick temper and surly attitude, they hid it well. Given his ability to sense lies and half-truths, Liam didn't think them capable of hiding it from him, even if they wanted to.

Retreating a step, Liam brought his shield to bear. As expected, the ghouls followed. Liam didn't think they had a choice. Undead craved life, and he was the nearest living thing. As the ghouls charged, spears raced forward to meet them.

Liam took an active role in customizing the teams he worked with. He required a healer in each and filled the rest of the positions with spearmen and archers. He saw little value in relying on additional swordsmen. With Liam standing alone at the point of attack, others, wielding spears, or crossbows, could attack around him. Additional swordsmen would just get in the way.

Two spears impaled one ghoul, while a single spear impaled the other. If the spears hurt the undead monsters, they didn't show it. Fortunately, the ghoul attacking Liam's sword side was the one struck twice. It struggled to advance against the two spears in its belly. The weapons were angled such where the ghoul couldn't just walk its way down the shafts.

The monster attacking Liam's shield side was only dealing with a single spear. The weapon barely slowed it down as it delivered another series of heavy blows against Liam's shield.

Each impact caused his headache to flare and patches of his burned skin to ache, but the power of the monster's strikes wasn't what terrified Liam. It was the accumulation of all the deadly wounds he previously survived. They threatened to bring him to his knees.

"Yelnor... Collins, keep that ghoul pinned," shouted Sinnow.

Cooling waves of healing suddenly raced through Liam's blood, chasing away the darkness pushing against the edges of his vision. Reinvigorated, Liam pivoted, turning his back on the ghoul impaled by the two spearmen. Advancing behind his shield, he plunged his glowing sword into the other ghoul's belly.

Blue and white flames surged at the moment of impact, causing the glistening flesh around the wound to bubble and blister, but the ghoul didn't seem capable of feeling pain. It kept pressing forward, frantically trying to slip its claws past Liam's shield.

With his blade all the way through his enemy, Liam worked the edge until he cut a path out the side of the monster. Wasting no time, he reversed his motion, following the path of the wound and hacking into the creature's spine. It took him three hacks to finally sever the spine, completing his cut.

The ghoul lunged forward, but with its torso no longer connected to its legs, it toppled to the ground in pieces. The top half kept reaching for Liam, but with no legs to propel it, it was easy to avoid. The rest of the team would deal with it.

Liam turned to face the remaining ghoul, and not a moment too soon. Yelnor and Collins managed to hold it so far, but they were losing control. The force of the thrashing ghoul already knocked Collins to his knees. With only Yelnor standing to anchor the impaling spears, the ghoul was breaking free. Why weren't the archers finishing it? They would not get a clearer shot.

Turning to check on the rest of his team, Liam's blood ran cold. A third ghoul was charging from the edge of the alley.

Several crossbow bolts ripped into its thighs, but it wasn't slowing down. "Sinnow, help the spearmen!" shouted Liam as he raced into position, bracing himself to intercept the approaching ghoul.

The smoky sky above was tinged with oranges and reds. Buildings were burning, and the fires were spreading. The smoldering light cast flickering shadows against the wall that made Liam's head hurt worse. The constantly clanging bells only magnified his misery. Fighting back waves of nausea, Liam resisted the urge to wretch.

The bone-rattling impact of the charging ghoul forced Liam to stagger back several steps. Most of the archers fell back with him, but one, a woman with a crossbow, didn't move fast enough. With Liam knocked away from the ghoul, she suddenly became the closest living thing. It spun on her in an instant. Without a shield or armor to protect her, the ghoul's claws quickly tore into her soft flesh.

The woman screamed as the ghoul tore wriggling viscera and clumps of wet meat free from her body. She backed away, punching at it with the butt of her crossbow, but to no avail. Mercifully, she didn't survive long. Liam knew the instant she died, because the ghoul snapped its head to the side, locking its attention on him.

"Finish the other two before helping me!" shouted Liam as he set his stance. His head was swimming from all the clanging bells and flashing lights, but he couldn't afford to be sick just yet. The ghoul was advancing, and he was the only one capable of holding it off.

Liam thrust, but the ghoul twisted, knocking his blade to the side with both claws. Before Liam could recover, the ghoul swept both claws back at him. With his sword out of position, Liam tried to pivot, but he wasn't fast enough. Fortunately, his Guest forced his shield to intercede, or the damage would have been much worse.

Unrelenting fingers of frost crept through Liam's muscles and bones, sapping him of his strength and quickness. With his shield already in place, he protected himself from the worst, but the ghoul snuck a claw past the protective metal shield. Liam's armor stopped it from tearing him open, but his muscles were slowing faster than he'd like. Paralysis would soon follow. He wouldn't last long after that.

"Liam!" screamed Sinnow as he raced in, slamming his shoulder into the ghoul.

"Sinnow... no," said Liam, but his voice was too weak to compete with the clanging bells. He didn't want his friend putting himself in harm's way. He didn't want him risking his life.

The ghoul spun on its new opponent in an instant, sweeping both claws in a wide arc, but Sinnow was ready. Carefully angling his staff, Sinnow pivoted into the attack, lowering his body as he did. When the ghoul's claws slammed into his staff, they deflected up, harmlessly passing over the healer's head.

The power of the ghoul's strikes forced Sinnow's staff to spin. In many ways, it became a lever, with Sinnow's steady hands acting as the fulcrum. As the bottom half of the staff swept up, Sinnow pivoted and sank into a stance. He quickly reversed his grip and used his body to complete the motion, delivering a powerful, arcing blow to the undead monster.

The ghoul staggered into the wall of the alley, but it was undaunted. It spun, faced Sinnow, and lunged all in one smooth motion. Liam tried to intercept it, but his muscles were sluggish and weak. Try as he might, he was powerless to help.

And those shekking bells kept clanging! The excruciating pain in the back of Liam's head seemed to take on a life of its own, surging and swelling with each earsplitting clang. Liam's vision faded with every breath, growing dimmer with each crash of the bells.

Sinnow dropped his hands to the bottom of his staff as he snapped it into position, using it much like a spearman setting his spear against a charging horse. The ghoul swatted at the staff, trying to knock it aside, but it was like swatting water. Sinnow relaxed, letting his staff dip to avoid the ghoul's wide swings, only to snap it back rigid at the last moment.

The ghoul slammed into the tip of Sinnow's staff with incredible force. Had it been a spear, the monster would have easily impaled itself. Instead, the weight and force of its charge caused Sinnow to stagger back several steps. At first, it looked like he might maintain his grip on his staff, but the force must have been too great, because the weapon went flying.

Frigid, sluggish muscles screaming in protest, Liam staggered into the ghoul. Unarmed, and only lightly armored, Sinnow was as good as dead against the undead monster. Liam's shield and armor would protect him, at least for a little while.

The horrible clanging bells grew louder as Liam's sword clanged against the cobblestones. He must not have noticed it tumble from his hand. His shield was actively protecting him, but Liam's Guest did that. There wasn't enough strength left in Liam's muscles for him to protect himself.

Whistling arrows slammed into the ghoul's side, causing it to lurch, but only for a moment. Liam barely took a breath before the monster resumed its relentless attack. His shield protected one side of his body, but his other side was completely defenseless. Liam couldn't even raise his arm to defend himself. He was just standing there, his armor slowly denting as it absorbed blow after blow.

More arrows ripped into the ghoul. At one point, Liam felt the refreshing sensation of healing magic race through his body, but he was having trouble focusing. Every time he tried to concentrate on his surroundings, those shekking bells rang!

Each clang drove needles and knives through the base of his skull. Everything was moving so fast, or perhaps he was moving too slow. The shadows on the walls were spinning, though he guessed his eyes were playing tricks on him.

"Liam!" shouted Sinnow.

Staggering, Liam fell, slamming his back against the wall of the alley. He expected the ghoul to lunge in to finish the job, but it was lying against the far wall, motionless. When did that happen? He must not have been looking. He probably had his eyes closed. His head hurt less when he kept his eyes closed.

CLANG!

Liam closed his eyes, wincing. He retched, tasting the burning bitterness of bile in his throat.

CLANG!

Liam slammed the back of his head against the alley wall. It hurt so shekking bad! He needed to make it stop.

"Liam!" screamed Sinnow. "Someone help!"

CLANG!

Liam frantically whipped his head back against the cool, unrelenting stone. Anything to make it stop! The pressure was too much. It felt like his head might explode.

CLANG!

11

Eirini

Eirini yanked her brother behind an overturned cart. A steady stream of arrows peppered the street a moment later. Both of Dimitri's escorts died in the last barrage of arrows. At first, Eirini assumed there were multiple archers, but now she was certain it was just one. Whoever it was, he or she was definitely trying to kill Dimitri. Eirini wasn't about to let it happen.

Sections of the enormous building at the end of the street were burning. Dimitri's Fireball spells made sure of that. Eirini guessed the building served as some kind of communal living quarters for the Longshadows gang. It probably wasn't too different from the Corners, although it seemed much nicer. Then again, this was Middletown. Everything in Middletown was nicer than the Corners.

Saro and the rest of the gang were engaged in a pitched battle near the building's main entrance. The fires were enough to cause the inhabitants to flee. Saro's team slaughtered the first groups exiting the building, but they quickly encountered resistance. The Longshadows knew how to fight. Even outnumbered, they were giving Saro all he could handle.

"Let me go, Sister," hissed Dimitri as he tried to pull away. "I must make them burn!"

Eirini shook her head. "Not with that archer out there."

Dimitri sighed, but stopped struggling.

The battle in front of the Longshadows' home wasn't the only thing to worry about. The fires Dimitri set earlier were spreading, causing the residents to panic. Some were trying to collect buckets of slush to fight the fires, while others were running for their lives. Packs of Sorriah's ghouls were out there too, roaming the streets, slaughtering anyone unfortunate enough to stumble across them.

Eirini assumed several teams of Bumbles were already in the area, with others on the way. If the constant ringing bells weren't a sign of trouble, the roaring fires couldn't be ignored. Part of her wanted to hunt and kill the Bumbles. She still blamed them for what happened to her father. Unfortunately, Saro looked like he needed help. She would have to wait to hunt Bumbles another day.

As much as Eirini wanted to help Saro, she struggled to find a safe way to get close enough. Dimitri moved slowly, and Eirini wasn't about to abandon him. She stayed with her brother throughout the battle. As a result, Saro and his team were already fighting when Eirini and Dimitri arrived.

It might not have been a problem, but Dimitri started casting Fireballs before they reached the safety of the rest of the team. The archer found them shortly after that. Eirini was sure the archer was using the rooftops. With how close the buildings were in this region, the archer could be just about anywhere, not that it mattered. Eirini didn't think she could do anything, even if she located the archer. Her spells were only effective at shorter ranges.

If the archer could target them from any rooftop, they wouldn't be safe behind the overturned cart, at least not for long. Moving might be dangerous, but so was sitting tight. "We need to get out of here, Dimitri," she said, squeezing her brother's hand. "Do you see that awning?"

Dimitri nodded.

"We're going to run to it. Once there, we'll make a break for Saro and the others. Do you understand?"

Dimitri nodded again.

Eirini knew her brother moved slowly. Hopefully, they'd catch the archer off guard. She didn't know how many more arrows her brother's Shield spell could deflect. She thought about standing in front of him, but it wouldn't do any good. Her necromancy Shield protected her by making her body momentarily insubstantial. The arrows would pass through her and still end up striking her brother.

"Here we go," she said as she helped her brother to his feet and started leading him toward the awning in the distance. They didn't make it four steps before the first arrow whizzed past. Eirini tugged on her brother's hand, encouraging him to run, but the best he could manage was a clumsy shuffle.

"Sister, please," he said as he pulled away from her.

Eirini faced her brother in time to see his wizardry Shield snap into existence, deflecting a perfectly placed arrow. A tiny ball of fire coalesced between his hands. Squinting, she spotted the archer on the roof of one of the row houses on the far side of the street. She didn't think there was any way her brother's Fireball would catch the archer, but now that he started casting his spell, there was no stopping him.

Emerald sparks exploded from Dimitri's Shield as it deflected another deadly arrow, but his spell was nearly complete. Waving his good arm, he sent his globe of searing flame racing out across the night sky. It left a swirling trail of smoke in its wake.

The archer must have been expecting Dimitri's counterattack. Based on the silhouette, Eirini thought the archer was male. He sprung to his feet and sprinted to his right, easily leaping to the next rooftop. Dimitri's Fireball gently turned in flight, attempting to track its target, but the archer was too fast.

When the Fireball reached the roof, it exploded, sending streaming meteors raining down on the streets below. Clouds of smoke radiated out from the point of impact, momentarily obscuring Eirini's view of the rooftops. If she couldn't see the archer, she doubted he could see them. "Now's our chance, Brother!"

Pulling Dimitri along behind her, Eirini ran to the awning. It stretched out from the side of a building with shut doors and closed windows. Hopefully, the inhabitants were too scared to join the fight. The last thing Eirini wanted to deal with was an ambush, especially with that archer hunting them.

Keeping the row houses to her right, Eirini advanced down the street. To her left, several carts, many of them toppled on their sides, provided cover. It wasn't much, but Eirini was grateful for it nonetheless. The thud of an arrow slamming one of the wooden carts hammered home the point.

"We're almost there, Brother," said Eirini. Saro led sixty kids on this attack. Even with some of them dying along the way, there had to be nearly forty still fighting. Once Eirini and her brother were safely within the crowd, the archer would be less of an issue. They only needed to cross a few more steps to reach safety.

Dimitri yelped. Eirini spared a quick glance behind her and saw an arrow lodged in the shoulder of his good arm. He must have nearly drained his well casting Fireballs. Now, he lacked the magical energy to protect himself with his Shield spell.

"Help us!" shouted Eirini to the kids in the back ranks. Most of them ignored her, but two of them, both young women, turned to face her. She gestured at her brother, and they seemed to understand. Both raced over to him. They wasted no time ushering him into the safety of the ranks.

"Now that he's safe, shall we have some fun?" asked the voice in her head.

A smile crept to Eirini's lips. She found her spirit's voice comforting. The fact that the spirit waited until Dimitri was safe was not lost on her. Yes, she thought. Let's have some fun.

"Excellent," purred the spirit. *"Now, focus on the battle. I see some opportunities for us, but what do you think?"*

The Downtrodden were arranged in a loose circle around the burning building's main entrance. Poorly armed children formed the front ranks. Many were lying on the ground, dead or bleeding out. Still, what they lacked in skill and weaponry, they made up for with sheer numbers. Saro was approaching this fight the same way he approached his fight with the Governor and those Bumbles, down in the sewers.

The Longshadows were rallying behind a single warrior, a woman with a long, double-edged spear. She wielded it with tremendous speed and precision. The extreme length of the weapon allowed her to keep Saro's forces at a distance. Any time one of them crept forward, attempting to get into range, the spear cut them. Most of those cuts appeared lethal.

Saro and others were throwing daggers, rocks, and other small projectiles at the woman whenever the opportunity presented itself, but a shimmering green barrier protected her. It meant she was more than just a skilled warrior. She studied wizardry as well.

Behind her, other members of the Longshadows tested the edges of Saro's ring of people. They seemed careful not to encroach on the woman and her wildly whipping spear, but they were free to attack to either side. By doing so, they were forcing Saro's troops to shift to the far sides of the formation, softening the center.

"Excellent observations," praised the voice in her head. *"If we do nothing, the woman with the spear will gradually break through the formation, dividing it. Once that happens, expect her gang to charge one side. They will still be outnumbered, but not by much. They are much better fighters than the children Saro brought with him. I expect it to be a short and bloody fight for our side."*

With all the bodies littering the battlefield, Eirini thought her opportunity was fairly obvious. All she needed to do was summon wraiths. Each would quickly find a body to inhabit, creating a small army of ghouls. Sure, hers were weak compared to Sorriah's, but they were still deadly.

"Yes, of course, but we need to be careful," advised her spirit. *"You won't be controlling any of them, so you need to create them well away from our own troops. Also, avoid the woman with the spear. I don't expect any of our ghouls to last long around her."*

Eirini pressed her way through the crowd until she got a better look. A few random screams from behind her told her that the archer was still out there, doing what damage he could do, but there was nothing she could do about him. She needed to focus on the areas of the battle she could influence. Dwelling on matters outside her control would get her nowhere.

"Have I told you how much I appreciate your thoughts? Focus, such as yours, is rare."

Bolstered by her spirit's compliments, Eirini scanned the battlefield. She noticed several corpses in the back ranks, close to the building itself. They must have been some of the first to flee the burning building before Saro faced any opposition. Animating some of those bodies seemed the best course of action.

"I agree."

Eirini retrieved a Soulstone from her pouch and activated her Spectral Sight. The spirit inside immediately responded to her.

Shifting her vision to the Astral, she noticed dozens of spirits floating around. Buildings were burning, and people were dying in the streets. There was no shortage of spirits to call.

Gently coaxing the soul from the Soulstone, Eirini beckoned one of the wraiths to cross over from the Astral. Making the exchange was easier than ever before. She attributed it to her El'orin. Once the wraith was fully within this world, she repeated the process, summoning a second wraith.

Eirini shivered against the strain of controlling two wraiths, but she knew she didn't need to control them for long. Pointing, she sent her wraiths drifting towards the corpses closest to the building. A few kids yelped and cried out as the wraiths drifted next to them, perhaps even making contact, but Eirini didn't care. The kids Saro brought along on this raid were fodder. If her wraiths inadvertently froze one to death, so be it.

A few members of the Longshadows pointed and shouted an alarm as the wraiths drifted in their direction, but no one attacked the deadly spirits. Once the wraiths were among the fallen corpses, they broke apart into wispy fragments, each flowing into a dead body. A moment later, a pair of ghouls rose from among the dead.

"*Excellent,*" praised Eirini's spirit. "*Do it again. Summon another pair of wraiths.*"

Eirini turned, quickly scanning the surrounding crowd. While the battle was important, her brother's safety was more important to her. It took a moment, but she finally spotted Dimitri. To her relief, Mend was with him, her hands glowing white with healing magic.

Satisfied that Dimitri was going to be alright, Eirini reached for another pair of Soulstones and started summoning more wraiths.

12

Saro

Saro missed Claw. Shek, he even missed Stone. In theory, he didn't think the Downtrodden needed skilled warriors among its El'orin. With countless young gang members to throw at their problems, it made more sense to bolster their El'orin ranks with casters, like Eirini and Dimitri, but it wasn't playing out quite like Saro hoped.

Sure, Dimitri's fire spells were powerful, and Eirini's undead were valuable, but neither were helping him deal with this crazy woman and her shekking spear. Claw would have been fast enough to trade blows with the warrior, and Stone would have been tough enough to stand against her deadly spear. All Saro's gang members were accomplishing was littering the street with their bodies.

If the goal was to burn buildings and inflict massive casualties, the mission was a smashing success. Ghost was monitoring Sorriah's ghouls, and according to Mend's last report, half of them were still wandering the streets, slaughtering people. Saro didn't need Mend or Ghost to tell him about the fires. He could see those for himself.

Dimitri did an excellent job lighting buildings on fire. The creepy kid was almost too good at it. As much as Saro wanted to see Derregain burn, he still lived there. With how fast Dimitri's fires were spreading, there was a real possibility of half of Middletown burning to the ground, or worse.

It meant they needed to be more careful using Dimitri's fire magic in the future. Buildings in Middletown were close together, but the Lowlands were much more densely populated. A few carefully placed Fireballs in the slums might burn the whole place down. Then again, maybe that's what this war needed. Either way, Saro wanted to take time to think it through.

A sudden commotion behind the crazy shekking spear lady caught Saro's attention. Something was causing all the Longshadow cowards to react. It took Saro a moment to realize what happened. Ghouls. There were ghouls ripping through the back ranks. Eirini must have finally made it to the fight. Better late than never.

The lady with the spear didn't seem to notice, but Saro didn't think that would last. Eventually, the ghouls would cause serious damage, forcing her to deal with them. Saro didn't believe the cowards in the back could handle them, and his people, sure as shek, weren't going to let any of them make a run for it.

"Keep it up, Eirini," shouted Saro. He didn't know where the girl was, but she had to be close if she was animating ghouls in the back ranks.

"As you wish."

Exactly what he wanted to hear. Sinking into a crouch, Saro studied the spear lady's patterns. By extending and retracting the shaft, she seemed to have excellent control over her ranges. Whenever she needed to bring the blade around behind her, she raised it over her head so as to not injure the people cowering behind her.

Saro wasn't sure the woman had a weakness, but if there was one, it was tied to the length of her weapon. If he could somehow get into close quarters with her, he thought he might have an advantage. Her double-edged spear was perfect for carving up people at a distance of anywhere from four to ten feet, but what if he got right in her face?

His daggers wouldn't do a lot of damage, but his cuts would add up. Eventually, her wizardry Shield would fail. More importantly, once he was on her, some of the kids he brought might muster the balls to charge in and help. Right now, they were all hanging back, probably pissing themselves at the mere thought of approaching the woman and her deadly spear.

"Where are you, Saro?" screamed the woman with the spear. "Show yourself, coward!"

Normally, Saro never responded to taunting, but this time, he wondered if it might not be the right decision. The woman wasn't reacting to the ghouls yet, but it was only a matter of time. The longer Saro kept her from dealing with the threat behind her, the worse it would be once she recognized the danger.

Saro gracefully rose from his crouch. "I'm right here," he said with a wave. "Put down that fancy spear of yours, and I'll let the people behind you go free."

"Like I'd believe you!" spat the woman as she thrust her spear at him with blinding speed and deadly precision.

Saro leaned back and away as fast as his superhuman reflexes would move him, and he still barely avoided the tip of her weapon. Shek, she was good! "And here I thought you just wanted to talk."

"You're a murderer!" she shouted. "Even if it takes my final breaths, I will put an end to you."

Saro drifted back several steps and waited. He didn't want to risk engaging the deadly woman too soon. Behind her, the ghouls were creating havoc. Saro didn't know how many Eirini animated, but he guessed at least four. They were murdering defenseless people with ease. It wouldn't be long before one of them focused on the woman with the spear.

The first charging ghoul took the woman by complete surprise. She must have assumed all the shouting behind her was because of the burning building, because she never turned around to look. Her wizardry Shield flashed vibrant green as it protected her from the ghoul's slashing claws, but she was left no choice but to turn and face her attacker. That brief moment of vulnerability was all Saro needed.

Leaping into a somersault, Saro dove into the fray. The woman's back was to him, but with how often she spun, he figured she'd notice a shadow or a flicker of motion if he remained upright. By tumbling toward her, he hoped to keep beneath her field of vision, and it seemed to work. He made it within striking range of her legs without being noticed.

Saro lashed out, driving daggers into the tendons beneath her calves. Her wizardry Shield flashed and sparked, absorbing the damage. Saro climbed to his feet as she spun to face him. Her eyes smoldered with anger, but Saro saw hints of fear as well. She never expected him to get this close to her.

With him in close quarters, Saro expected her to retract her spear and wield the bladed section, much like a sword. That would leave the butt end of it projecting behind her. Anticipating her movements, Saro circled around her, forcing her to turn. He was careful not to circle too far around. He didn't want to get close to the ghouls, or the surviving members of the Longshadows.

"I'll gut you like a fish," spat the woman. As expected, she withdrew the shaft of her spear, bringing the blade into their fight. Saro's daggers were much quicker, but her blade looked far deadlier. He couldn't afford to let her hit him.

Fortunately, it didn't take too long for Saro's gang to respond. By forcing the woman to turn, Saro made her expose her back to some of his forces. One of them, Saro didn't see who, mustered enough courage to grab the shaft of her spear. All it took was one and others quickly followed suit.

The woman struggled with her spear, and failing that, she twisted, delivering several powerful kicks behind her. A few kids cried out, but now that they were swarming her, there were plenty to replace those she knocked aside.

As much as Saro wanted to taunt the woman, he knew he couldn't risk it. She was far too dangerous. He started delivering deadly stabs, one after the other. Saro knew her Shield spell was protecting her, so he didn't wait to assess the effect of his attacks. He simply kept attacking. Eventually, he'd cut through her defenses and start doing real damage.

Dropping her spear, the woman clenched her fists. Both began glowing as if she were grasping molten rocks, and wisps of smoke escaped between her fingers. She struck with surprising speed and precision, striking Saro in the chest, and landing a glancing blow across his shoulder. Pain exploded throughout his body, but it didn't matter. The gang was on her. Dozens of grasping hands grabbed hold of her arms. Others wrapped around her waist, while a few circled around her legs.

Saro waited until she was completely immobilized before driving his blades into her neck. Her Shield spell flashed again to protect her, but he knew her power was fading. Fortunately, she didn't seem to know the Blink spell, or she might have gotten away. With how shekking good she was at everything else, it surprised him she wasn't great at that as well.

"My brother will avenge me," she hissed.

Saro shrugged and kept stabbing her, repeatedly. He didn't stop when the green lights no longer flashed, and he didn't stop when her screams turned to wet, gurgling sounds. He waited until the white mist exploded from her body. Only then did he stop.

Swirling streams of white mist leapt through Saro. Out of the corner of his eye, he saw other streams of mist blasting through the crowd. He knew Eirini, Dimitri, and Mend were close. Hopefully Ghost was close enough to benefit, but Saro wouldn't lose sleep over it if he wasn't. Ghost was a whiney little bitch. If he missed out, it served him right.

Saro threw his head back and laughed as the white mist surged through his body, making every nerve cry out in ecstasy. He waited far too long to savor this feeling again. He never should have agreed to the Governor's treaty. Nothing in life felt so good. He needed to feel this again and again! It was what he was made for.

Gradually, the ecstasy slowly faded, and the reality of the battle returned. The building in front of Saro was rapidly becoming a bonfire. Terrified people frantically ran in every direction, desperately trying to avoid the ghouls in their midst. He was fortunate none of the ghouls found him while the white mists incapacitated him.

Saro quickly retrieved the deadly spear from the ground and drifted back into the crowd. With the dangerous woman dead, Saro's gang members were back to slaughtering people. Between them, the ghouls, and the burning building, few were likely to escape.

Carefully weaving through the crowd, Saro searched for Eirini, Mend, and Dimitri. As far as he was concerned, their work was done here. The gang members he brought along could continue the fight. The smart ones would figure it out and run. The dumb ones would die in the streets. Saro didn't care either way.

They did what they came to do. They set Middletown on fire. They slaughtered countless people in the streets. Most importantly, they feasted on the essence of another El'orin.

Saro couldn't be happier.

13
Eliana

Eliana watched the flickering flames lick the sky and wondered where her friends were. She knew where Conner was. He was working in the House of Healing, and she had a rough idea of where Liam was. He was somewhere out there in the streets, probably fighting for his life. Russell, Malcolm, and Attia were nowhere to be found.

She sent Windword spells to each of them. Hopefully, they were already on their way, rushing to come help her, but she knew her hopes were misplaced. Russell and Malcolm rarely left the greenhouse. Perhaps Attia was on her way to help, but if Russ and Malcolm were gone, Eliana didn't think they were nearby.

Where could they have gone?

Lord Rumblesnort Bunny-Fur meowed, forcing Eliana to focus on the matter at hand. She was in the middle of the street. All around her, panicked people screamed and shouted. The cacophony of constantly clanging bells adding to the chaos, and ahead of her, Middletown burned.

Eliana wondered what could have started such aggressive fires. With so many buildings burning, and in so many places, it had to be a concerted effort. Why would anyone do it? Were demons still loyal to Plaguebringer trying to cripple the city? That didn't seem likely, but no other explanation seemed plausible. Maybe Saro and his gang did it as an act of civil war, but if so, why were they hitting Middletown? She would have expected them to go after High City. That's where the wealthy people lived.

Farther down the street, someone screamed. Eliana tracked the sound to an older woman backing away from an alley. Something strange and horrible was charging her. It was slender, muscular, and its bloody red flesh was entirely exposed. It was skinned, from head to toe. Whatever it was, everyone was terrified of it. Instead of rallying to assist the horrified woman, people were desperately fleeing.

The creature pounced on the woman with the quickness of a jungle cat. A moment later, her blood sprayed across the snowy streets. In the next breath, the creature climbed to its feet and started chasing the closest person. Eliana didn't think he even knew he was being chased.

Based on its behavior and appearance, the creature was some kind of undead. Eliana remembered Sinnow and Professor Keldon describing how powerful the strange, skinned ghouls they encountered in the sewers were. This must be one of those.

As much as Eliana wanted to send electricity racing through the ghoul until it burst into flames, she needed to be efficient. There was no telling how many of those things were roaming the streets, and she knew fire was the most effective way to handle them. Taking the time to build an elemental was the smart choice, but it wouldn't be fast enough to save the ghoul's next victim. "Sorry," she mumbled, even though no one was close enough to hear her.

Chanting quietly, Eliana focused on the closest burning building, drawing patches of flame together until they formed a single raging fire. She sent her magic into that fire, stoking it, and giving it a sentience of its own. Her El'orin immediately took control of the living flames, lifting that responsibility from Eliana's shoulders. With her Savior directing the elemental, Eliana was free to focus on her surroundings.

The ghoul caught the man it was chasing. Blood splattered across the snow as it tore his innards out through his back. The scene was absolutely grisly. Everyone else on the street was running away from the monster. It rose and darted after its next victim, a young girl, but Eliana was close enough to help this time. "Run to me!" she shouted. "Don't look back. Run as fast as you can!"

Her eyes wide with terror, tears streaking down her cheeks, the girl ran toward Eliana. The ghoul was much faster, but the girl had a healthy head start. As she approached, Eliana's elemental swirled into motion. Singularly focused on its prey, the ghoul didn't even notice the deadly entity of concentrated fire. As the ghoul prepared to leap at the girl, seething gouts of flame enveloped it. It sizzled and smoked as the fires quickly incinerated it, reducing it to a collection of smoldering bones and ash.

The girl ran a few more steps before she collapsed, sobbing. Others in the area shouted and cheered. Looking around, Eliana guessed there were a dozen people nearby, all looking at her. She wasn't used to crowds. She wasn't used to seeing the people she protected. This was different, and she didn't understand how it made her feel. There was definitely pride, but there was something else there, beneath the surface. She couldn't quite put her finger on it.

"There are more of those things roaming the streets," shouted a man. Between the clanging bells and roaring flames, he was difficult to hear. "Can we stay with you?"

Eliana nodded as she slowly advanced down the street. She heard snippets of conversations as people gathered around her. Some questioned why she had a cat on her shoulder. Others wondered if she was the girl from the greenhouse. She did her best to ignore most of the comments. With all the noise, it wasn't difficult.

Up ahead, another ghoul rounded the bend. Like the last one, it was skinned, though for some reason it was wearing a ribcage on top of its muscles. It locked its eyes on Eliana and charged, propelling itself with both hands and feet across the slippery, snowy street.

Eliana kept walking, though she slowed her pace. She wanted to make sure her elemental was out in front of her. Rumblesnort issued a low growl and dug his claws into her shoulder. Even though it hurt, Eliana found it comforting. It meant her cat was alert and prepared to hinder the monster should the elemental fail to destroy it.

The ghoul never made it to her. The elemental started bathing it in flames as soon as it approached within thirty feet. As it got closer, the flames got hotter, until eventually all the ghoul's flesh burned away, leaving nothing more than smoking bones skidding across the ice.

The crowd cheered!

With the ghouls no longer a concern, Eliana focused on the burning buildings. Not so long ago, she gathered ice and snow, forming a weapon to destroy Lamenica, but she didn't do it alone. The wind spirit, Debhara, helped her. She didn't know what she was capable of without the spirit, or if Debhara was still watching over her, but she planned to find out.

Pointing her hands to the sky, Eliana attempted to gather the ice and snow. The wind swirled in response, but she needed far more than wind if she hoped to deal with the burning buildings. If anything, whipping winds would make the problem worse.

"What's happening?" called a voice from behind her.

"I don't know," came an answer.

"Is she summoning a storm?" asked another.

A storm was definitely what she needed, and not just any storm. She needed heavy snow and drenching rain. The blowing winds and gentle snows that seemed nearly constant in Derregain these days wouldn't help her.

"Why do you call upon me, child?" whispered the spirit. Eliana didn't see her, but she felt her presence like a chill wind blowing across her neck.

"You know why I call upon you," answered Eliana.

"Who's she talking to?" asked one of the people gathered around her.

"These fires are born from human hands," whispered the spirit. "They are of no concern to us. Let the humans suffer the consequences of their actions. Let their shelters burn so that they can finally feel the true depths of winter's bitter embrace."

Eliana didn't think it was that easy. Derregain was already enduring as much as it could withstand. People were starving. Letting large parts of Middletown burn to the ground would make it much worse. "I don't care about the buildings that are already burning," she said out loud. She thought there needed to be witnesses. "Help me stop the fires from spreading. That is all I ask."

"All you ask?" spat Debhara incredulously. "You speak of it like it is a small thing. Listen to me child and heed my words." The wind began to whistle and howl, echoing the words Debhara whispered in Eliana's ears. "Humanity is a plague upon Gaea's world. The sooner they are purged, the sooner the demons will flee. Only then will we be reborn."

Eliana processed what the spirit told her, but she didn't want to believe it. What if there was another way? There had to be another way. She understood that the demons somehow needed humans to remain in this world, but surely that didn't justify the eradication of the human race. "I don't believe it. There must be another way."

"What if there isn't?"

Eliana shook her head. "I'm asking for your help. Will you help me? Will you lend me your power?"

"Come on, help her!" shouted someone from the crowd.

"Yeah, help her out."

Eliana didn't think their words were convincing the spirit to aid her, but she didn't think she could make them stop. With Debhara's voice echoing in the wind, they probably heard most, if not all, of the conversation. She couldn't blame them for trying. Most of them probably lived in the area. Of course, they didn't want their homes to burn to the ground.

"Be careful what you ask for, child," whispered Debhara. "If I bolster this storm for you, even for an hour, it will remember, and it will grow stronger. Perhaps the winds will blow harder, or the snow will climb deeper. Maybe the air will grow colder, it's hard to say. Every storm is a living thing. They all behave differently."

The crowd murmured behind Eliana, but it wasn't long before they began voicing approval. The entire conversation struck Eliana as strange. Was the spirit negotiating with them or her? "I understand the risks, Debhara. Please help me."

"As you wish, child."

The winds surged and swirled, both inside and outside of Eliana, as she felt the spirit's energy rush through her body. The sky flashed, and a thunder crack split the night, momentarily drowning out the bells. Almost immediately, a gentle rain started falling.

"The storm is responding to you, child. Gaea's tears fall for you," whispered the spirit, her words continued to echo in the winds. "Walk, and the storm will follow."

Eliana's feet tingled as she trudged through the thick slush toward the next burning building. Her elemental hissed and popped next to her. The pouring rain and blowing snow constantly diminished it, but there was no shortage of fires to draw upon to refresh it.

She definitely needed the elemental. She encountered two more ghouls during her journey through the streets. The elemental easily incinerated both of them, though one of them got disturbingly close to her before succumbing to the flames.

Over time, the crowd behind Eliana grew. She didn't ask anyone to stay with her. With how heavily the rain was coming down around her, it was probably miserable. The rains weren't falling anywhere else. They only fell in a roughly hundred foot radius of her.

Eliana suspected the people stayed with her out of gratitude. They didn't understand the strange magic causing the rain clouds to follow her, but they knew those rains were quenching the fires burning throughout their neighborhood. The people wanted to help, but they didn't know how, so they stayed with her, if for no other reason than to provide company.

They encountered many dead littering the streets. Many of the bodies were torn to shreds, likely victims of the ghouls, but others were killed by the fires. Weapons killed some, and others were trampled to death. Eliana quickly lost count of the dead.

At one point, they stumbled across a group of Bumbles who took it upon themselves to become Eliana's escort. She didn't need them. If they encountered another ghoul, the Bumbles would only get in the way, but like the people following behind her, she didn't have the heart to send them away. They were trying to do their duty in whatever way they knew how.

Everywhere Eliana walked, the fires slowly died out. Sometimes she needed to stand near a burning building for several minutes. Other times, the fires extinguished in mere moments. There didn't seem to be any rhyme or reason to it, and Eliana decided it wasn't worth questioning. Gaea was shedding her precious tears because Eliana asked her to. That knowledge was all that mattered.

Eventually, Eliana and her growing crowd of supporters came across Sinnow and his tattered group of Bumbles. Her heart sank when she saw they were carrying Liam between them. Even from a distance, she knew he was alive. Liam was a member of her Coterie. On a certain level, she could sense him.

"What happened?" she called when she thought Sinnow was close enough to hear. At some point, the bells stopped ringing. She didn't remember when.

"Some of those super ghouls attacked us. They were like the ones we faced in the sewers," said Sinnow. "Liam held them off, but something happened to him. I think..." Sinnow paused, looking at the enormous crowd gathered behind Eliana. "I think it was the old wound. It's been getting worse, day after day. I tried healing him, but he won't wake up."

Eliana saw the fear and concern etched across Sinnow's face. As much as she hated the thought of sending Liam near that shekking succubus and her foul home, that's where Conner was, and as much as Eliana hated to admit it, Raelyn was probably the only one who could help Liam.

"What should we do?" asked Sinnow.

"Take him to the House of Healing," said Eliana. "Take the rest of the Bumbles as an escort."

"We prefer to stay here, with you, ma'am."

Rage raced through Eliana's veins. Lightning danced across the sky above, and another crack of thunder crashed through the night. "I don't give a shek what you want!" she shouted. "Liam is my friend. Make sure he reaches the House of Healing safely. That's an order!"

A smile crept to Eliana's lips as she watched the Bumbles rush to obey.

14
Conner

Conner rubbed his stinging eyes and shook his head. He knew what his brother wanted, but he didn't care. Liam was a stubborn ass. There was no way he would let Raelyn lay a finger on him, but he was unconscious. Conner didn't know if his brother would ever wake up again. As far as Conner was concerned, it was his decision to make. "Heal him," he breathed through dry, cracked lips. "Try your Regrowth spell."

Raelyn sighed. "I can try, but I don't think it will help."

"Try, dammit!" snapped Conner. He knew Raelyn held her first Demonic Court earlier in the night. He asked for her the moment she returned to the House of Healing, and she came right away. She didn't even ask for time to change into real clothes. She was still dressed in what amounted to a set of leather straps that barely covered her.

"Okay," she said, holding up a hand. "Just give me a minute. It's an expensive spell. I need to unravel some of my defensive magic before I attempt it. I might not have enough power to complete it otherwise."

Conner wanted to tell her to hurry, but he knew he was being unreasonable. Raelyn was doing everything she could, given the circumstances. "Thanks," he said after a long pause. "I know I'm asking a lot."

Raelyn shook her head. "You're not asking a lot, Conner. As far as I'm concerned, I owe you this, and so much more." Her hands glowed with brilliant white light as she gently worked them behind Liam's head.

Conner stripped his brother out of his armor before Raelyn arrived. He wasn't prepared for the sight of Liam's burned skin. Some areas of it didn't look bad, but other sections looked absolutely ghastly. Liam accepted basic treatment in the House of Healing for his burns, but he refused to let Raelyn touch him. Alahn's burns, which Raelyn treated with her Regrowth spell, looked far better by comparison.

"The spell is trying to recreate the tissue as it was before Liam received the wound, but I don't think it knows how," said Raelyn.

"Liam suffered that wound when a giant stone statue killed him," said Conner. He hated remembering it. "It slammed his head into the ground."

"I know. We've spoken about it before," said Raelyn softly.

"It's not going to work, is it?"

Raelyn closed her eyes. "I don't think so, but the spell isn't done trying yet. Let's give it a minute."

Conner didn't want to wait. He felt so shekking helpless. Here he was, a powerful healer, and none of his spells could help save his brother. It wasn't fair. He healed that wound at the base of Liam's skull countless times, but it kept coming back. Wounds weren't supposed to work that way!

Liam gasped and his eyes snapped open. He looked around, appearing disoriented and terrified for a few moments, until he saw Conner. The two brothers met each other's gaze for a long moment before Liam finally spoke. "Maybe it's finally time to let me go, Conner."

"Don't say that, Liam. The city still needs you," said Conner. "I still need you."

"But it takes so much to heal me for even a few hours now," said Liam. He closed his eyes and winced. "The pressure... the pain... it's just too much."

Raelyn caught Conner's eye. Her expression was serious, yet considerate and compassionate. She was standing at the head of the bed, outside of Liam's field of vision. Her hands were still pressed against the back of Liam's head, so he likely knew she was there, but he wasn't reacting to her.

"We're still looking for a cure. We just need more time, Liam," said Conner, but he didn't think he sounded convincing. Conner was hoping Raelyn's Regrowth spell was the solution, but if it wasn't, he didn't know what to do.

"Please don't lie, Brother. I don't have a lot of time."

Liam's words made Conner's heart hurt. "Sorry," he said softly. "I hoped the spell Raelyn used to heal Attia's back would be strong enough."

Liam gently slipped his hand alongside his head until he found Raelyn's wrist. Conner expected him to swat her away, but he gently rested his fingers against her wrist. "Thanks for trying."

"You're welcome," said Raelyn.

"My vision is darkening, Brother. I can already feel the pressure building. Stars above, this hurts."

"Isn't there something you can do for him?" asked Conner.

Raelyn shook her head.

"There's nothing to be done, Conner," said Liam with a wry smile and moisture in his eyes. "I died. It's as simple as that. I've been living on borrowed time ever since."

"Don't say that, Brother."

"No, it's okay, Conner. It really is," said Liam. "I'm proud of how I've spent the time my Guest gave me. Just think about all the things we've done. The people we've touched. The lives we've saved..." Liam closed his eyes and pushed his head back against the pillow. He looked like he was in agony.

"But think of all the things we've yet to do. Think of all the lives we'll save in the days to come."

"I love you, Brother," whispered Liam. "I'm so proud of you... I'm proud of the man you've become." Liam let his head roll to the side and his breathing grew shallow.

"Brother?" said Conner, his heart pounding. "Liam? Are you still with me?"

Raelyn gently traced a glowing white finger around Liam's head until it rested on his forehead. "He's alive, but I'm not sure he'll wake up again. The wound at the back of his head..." Raelyn paused, shaking her head. "I think the Regrowth spell may have made it worse."

"How is that possible?"

"The magic tried to rebuild Liam the way he was, before the injury, but that wound was fatal," said Raelyn. "I don't know, but maybe it changed things for the worse."

"So, what happens now?" asked Conner. He was nearly shouting. He couldn't help it.

Raelyn began massaging Liam's skull, one glowing hand on his forehead, and the other still at the base of his skull. "I can feel the wound swelling, even as we speak. If it gets much worse, I don't think he's going to make it."

"Can you stop the swelling?"

Raelyn frowned. "I'm trying to right now. The moment I stop healing him, the swelling continues. I could try a Rejuvenation spell, but I used most of my remaining power casting Regrowth."

"That isn't good enough! He's my brother!" shouted Conner, his cheeks burning. He knew everything she was telling him was true. Conner never learned the Rejuvenation spell, but he knew how difficult it was to cast. Still, Raelyn was the strongest, most resourceful healer he ever met. He couldn't let her give up. He couldn't let Liam die. "What would you do if it was Achillion dying in this bed?"

Raelyn's eyes smoldered with red light, and her nostrils flared. She stared at him for what felt like an eternity, and her gaze was terrifying. Conner wanted to look away, but he refused to. After a pause that stretched on for ages, Raelyn sighed and said, "Go to my chambers. You'll find Powerence there. It's in the mahogany cabinet. Bring me all of it."

Conner started to leave, but stopped. "Then what?" he asked. Convincing Raelyn to burn through her emergency reserves was a moral victory, but he was having second thoughts. What if she used all her Powerence and only kept Liam alive for a day?

"I don't know, Conner," said Raelyn. "If the Rejuvenation spell keeps him alive, we'll have to find a way to keep it running on him. I just wish I knew more healers with that spell. Lehnai was the only other one in the House of Healing who knew it, and... well..."

Conner looked away as memories of Lehnai's death flooded his mind. The man's agonizing screams were horrifying, but it was the smell, an overpowering mixture of copper, rotten eggs, and rust, that Conner couldn't push from his mind. "I'm sorry he's gone. He was a good man."

Raelyn smiled sadly and nodded. "There is a spell in demonology that would help. It's called Gather. Cinderhorn used it to temporarily steal my power the night he summoned me into the Citadel. That's how he summoned so many demons."

"You have any other horrifying memories you want to bring up?" snapped Conner.

"Sorry."

Conner pushed past his momentary outburst. "Can Cinderhorn teach you that Gather spell?"

"I doubt it," said Raelyn, shaking her head. "It never hurts to ask, but as I understand it, Gather is one of the harder demonology spells to come by."

"So, that's not going to happen, is it?"

Raelyn sighed. "No."

"Do you think there are healers in the Academy who can help?"

"Probably, but it might be difficult to get their help," said Raelyn. "The Academy has been donating fewer resources to us lately. They're undertaking what they call a necessary reevaluation and reallocation of Academy resources. That's what they told me when I inquired about the reductions."

A lump grew in Conner's throat. "If it's just you, how long do you think you can keep up?"

Raelyn closed her eyes for a moment. "Using all the Powerence I've managed to save, and leaning on Achillion to purchase more with emergency funds, a week, maybe two."

Conner looked down at his brother through blurry, tear-soaked eyes. He wasn't ready to let Liam go, but he didn't see another way. He could demand Raelyn burn through all her resources, but what was the point? All it would accomplish was keeping Liam alive for another week or two.

"It might be worth it," said Conner's Demon. *"A lot can happen in two weeks. Liam's Guest might do something useful for a change. We can always speak with a few imps and try to bargain for a solution. You've fought too long and hard to give up now."*

"I'm sorry to ask this of you, but I want you to do everything in your power to keep my brother alive," said Conner. "We just need time."

Raelyn looked away for a moment. Conner expected her to be angry, but when she turned to face him again, she was grinning. "I think I have an idea, but you might not like it."

"Will it save my brother?"

Raelyn nodded. "It will keep him alive until we're ready to treat his injuries, even if it takes us months to research a cure."

Conner couldn't believe what he was hearing. "How is that possible? Just a minute ago, we were discussing how long you could keep him alive with Rejuvenation spells. What did you figure out?"

"We'll discuss it later," said Raelyn. "Right now, I need you to fetch that Powerence. We need to keep Liam alive long enough to get him to Cinderhorn."

"Get him to Cinderhorn?" gasped Conner. "What are you talking about?"

"You're going to have to trust me, Conner."

Memories of Silver's dying screams trickled into Conner's mind, joining the memories of Lehnai's last moments, and the horrifying host of demons assaulting the Great Hall. Somehow, Cinderhorn was scarier than the rest of Conner's memories. He was the demon behind the scenes, pulling all the strings.

Cinderhorn was the one who tore Silver's veins from her arms, manipulating them like a puppeteer would a marionette. Conner hated relying on him to save Liam's life, but he was prepared to do whatever it took.

15
Achillion

Achillion clenched his fists as he silently counted the bodies scattered across the blood-soaked snow. He knew the Downtrodden were dangerous, but he never expected them to be so mindlessly violent. They could have harvested El'orin from the Longshadows without nearly burning down the neighborhood. The Downtrodden didn't need to slaughter so many innocent people in the streets. They didn't need to do any of it. They did it because they wanted to. Need never factored into the equation.

"Sadly, it seems this civil war is escalating," said Counselor Jurgenson.

Achillion knew the counselor was just a skin the Serpentus was wearing. With the militia out in force, Achillion thought appearing as Counselor Jurgenson was a good choice. He was in charge of the militia, after all. "They've been quiet ever since we defeated them in the sewers, back when we fought for control over the mushroom fields. I was hoping it would stay that way."

"I so enjoyed watching Raelyn slaughter them with her Telekinesis spells," said Counselor Jurgenson. "The Netten and

Naga show replays that episode constantly. It's simply spectacular."

Achillion vaguely understood what the demon meant. Raelyn tried to explain how her pane of obsidian glass functioned, and the roles similar sheets of obsidian served within the Netherworld, but Achillion never saw one in action. He wasn't able to see anything in Raelyn's obsidian. Evidently, it only worked for demons.

"I've watched it many times," said the counselor. "I must say, the stacks of corpses surrounding you, Governor, impressed me. Your skill with sword and shield must be superb."

"Not that it did much good," said Achillion as he studied the buildings lining either side of the street. Several of them were badly burned. According to the reports, Eliana summoned storms to douse the flames. If not for her, the fires would have spread, possibly spiraling out of control.

"Don't sell yourself short," said the Serpentus masquerading as Counselor Jurgenson. "I've spoken with some of the survivors. They witnessed your actions down in those sewers, and every one of them is terrified of you. They saw your sword slice their brothers and sisters to ribbons. They saw you slam your shield against Quick's skull until it was a sloppy mess. Most of all, they felt your overwhelming aura. They tested its strength, and they succumbed to it."

Achillion kicked a clump of wet snow into a smoldering pile of rubble. "We can't turn our back on what they did here tonight," said the Governor, shaking his head. "They've gone too far. There must be retribution."

The Serpentus nodded. "Are you asking if my offer still stands?"

"Yes." As much as Achillion didn't want to rely on the soul-stealing demon, he didn't see a better option. Sending the militia into the Corners was too risky. Even if they succeeded, the collateral damage would likely lead to countless deaths. Sending the Serpentus to infiltrate the Downtrodden and assassinate Saro was the best option.

Counselor Jurgenson pursed his lips. "I must admit, given what you told me about El'ominae spirits, I've reconsidered the risks. I will need a promise of recompense before I accept this task."

"I would think protecting Derregain would be reward enough," said Achillion without conviction. "After all, this city is as much your home as it is mine."

"Not exactly," said the counselor, shaking his head. "While I would love to call this city my sanctuary, sadly, I'm a creature of the Netherworld. Carelessly rushing into risky missions is a recipe for my imprisonment. I'm sure Raelyn discussed that with you."

Achillion nodded. "Yes. She's explained what happens."

"Good," said the Serpentus. "Then I suspect you can appreciate my concerns. I'm risking a century of suffering, after all. Asking for recompense is only reasonable."

"Very well," said Achillion with a sigh. "What do you want?"

The counselor smiled. "Demon and human politics within this city should stand separate from one another, but sadly, they've grown intertwined." The counselor paused, waving to a trio of Bumbles as they passed. "You're asking me to insert myself into human affairs. It seems only reasonable for me to ask the opposite of you."

"I don't understand what you're asking."

"How do I say this delicately," mused the Serpentus. "You're sleeping with Raelyn, the appointed viceroy of this city."

"It's more than that."

"Perhaps. Perhaps not. It matters little to me," said the Serpentus with a dismissive wave. "What matters is that she listens to you."

"Raelyn listens to me, but she's incredibly independent."

"Of course," said Counselor Jurgenson. "If I were to guess which of the two of you were pulling the strings, it wouldn't be you, Governor." The counselor smiled. "No offense."

"None taken."

"All I'm asking is that you whisper a few good words about me," said the Serpentus. "Discuss our alliance, and my service to this city."

Achillion traced a finger across the scar he suffered when Saro sent that army of children against him. He didn't see an issue with the demon's request. If anything, he wondered why it was so modest. "I can do that, but to what end?"

The counselor stared at him for a moment. "At this second, we serve the same Mistress, Raelyn and I, but the future is a sea of shifting sands. Someday, should my relationship with the Queen sour, I would prefer Raelyn to be on my side. It's as simple as that."

Raelyn warned Achillion about how dangerous the Serpentus was. She questioned Chariden's decision to summon it in the first place. Was the demon planning on breaking away from the Demon Queen? Achillion didn't know how that worked, but he didn't think he needed to. "How long do you think it will take you?"

"To slay Saro?"

Achillion nodded.

"It's hard to say," said the counselor. "At this stage, I'm uncertain killing Saro accomplishes the mission."

"I'm not worried about Mend and Ghost," said Achillion. "Neither of them scares me. Saro is the true killer. He's the one behind all this."

"Some suggest the new ones, the brother and sister, are the most dangerous." Counselor Jurgenson gestured at the burned buildings. "Based on all I've heard, I suspect the brother was responsible for these fires. Some question if he is even human.

What would happen if he stepped into Saro's role? I doubt we'd enjoy it."

"Then kill them all," said Achillion.

"I was under the impression those with El'orin spirits protected one another," said the counselor. "Isn't there a treaty?"

The Serpentus' knowledge of El'orin surprised Achillion, but perhaps it shouldn't have. The demon was deeply involved in the city's politics. Who knew who all was feeding the Serpentus information? "They are no longer members of the treaty. That makes them fair game."

"I see," said the Serpentus. "And what of the El'ominae spirit? Won't it just summon new El'orin spirits to possess new hosts? That is how it works, isn't it?"

"Yes, I suppose so," said Achillion with a nod. "Either way, it won't happen immediately. There will be a window of time where the Downtrodden will be without leadership. That's when we'll hit them."

"Perhaps that won't be necessary," said the counselor. "No promises, but if I get a chance to destroy the El'ominae spirit, I won't hesitate."

Achillion doubted it would happen the way the demon wanted. He suspected the El'ominae would find a way to escape. Then again, maybe the Serpentus had a way of tracking the powerful spirit. "You'll let me know before you make the attempt, right?"

Counselor Jurgenson nodded. "I'll send a message before I start, but it may be several days. I have things to research, and preparations I must care for..." The counselor's voice trailed off. He stood there, for a moment, staring at the burned buildings and scattered corpses. "Is there anything else you wish to speak with me about?"

"No."

"Then I shall take my leave," said the counselor as he turned and made his way down the street.

Achillion watched the demon go. Something about the way the counselor ended the conversation disturbed him. The prospect of putting an end to Saro and his gang was appealing, but Achillion worried there would be hidden costs. He planned to discuss the matter with Raelyn. If anything, he wanted to explore any possible ramifications of this decision with her.

Privately, Raelyn was exploring new relationship roles with Achillion, and he wasn't sure how he felt about them. He understood his El'orin's need to feel feminine in order to recharge, and he appreciated Raelyn adopting a masculine role to help that happen. But lately, he wondered if Raelyn was assuming a masculine role more for her own benefit.

It's not that he minded. It's more that he didn't feel like he was making decisions anymore. She was the one guiding their relationship. Achillion trusted Raelyn's decisions, but he still enjoyed having some say in the matter.

At least, with the Serpentus, it felt like he just made a decision. He asked the demon to act against Saro and the Downtrodden. In truth, nothing was stopping the Serpentus from taking action without his permission, but the fact that he asked for action gave him a sense of control, even if it was just an illusion.

Deep down, Achillion knew he didn't control the Serpentus. If the soul-stealing demon was discussing the possibility of falling out of favor with Chariden, Achillion wondered if anyone controlled the Serpentus.

16
Attia

Attia waved for the others to join her as she considered the plumes of smoke off in the distance. The slow progression of a large caravan forced them to avoid the roads during much of their journey back to Derregain. It was already the dead of night by the time they returned to the city.

Having done it many times before, Attia was comfortable using the sprawling network of alleyways to navigate Middletown. She didn't see any reason to risk traveling the city streets. The Governor provided them all permits for their weapons, but Attia preferred to avoid the Bumbles altogether. It was easier that way. She remembered how her last interrogation ended. She didn't want it to happen again.

"Looks like there was a fire," said Malcolm as he crossed the street and joined Attia in the next alley. "I wonder if this is what Eliana sent us Windwords about."

The message was simple. Eliana asked for help north of the greenhouse. She seemed to send the same message to each of them. "It must have been."

"That isn't our old neighborhood, is it?"

Attia shook her head. "Our old neighborhood is there," she said, pointing. "If I were to guess, I'd say those fires are coming from the Longshadows' territory. They control roughly nine square blocks of Middletown."

"I'd ask how you know that, but I'm not sure I want to hear the answer," said Russell as he slipped into the alley.

"I spent weeks casing the Longshadows' neighborhood, back when I was hunting Bioja. That's how I know," said Attia with a shrug.

"That was the answer I didn't really want to hear," said Russell, although he didn't sound annoyed.

"Why?" asked Attia. "After all the secrets we shared tonight, this shouldn't surprise you."

"I knew about your hunting. After Vallon and Stone argued about it at Conclave, we all knew. It's just strange talking about it," said Russell.

"I think it's good that we're discussing it," said Malcolm. "You mentioned you have a new arrangement with your El'orin. Is she no longer driving you to hunt El'orin?"

Attia faced Malcolm and Russell. "I wouldn't say that. I still crave the white mists, but we all do."

"I remember how you were, back after Achillion rescued us from the Academy. He was doubled over, throwing up. Your Ally was trying to force you to behead him," said Malcolm, leaning heavily against his staff. "I saw your Ally inside of you. I felt her strength... The sheer intensity of her will."

"Shek," mumbled Russell.

Attia shook her head. "Nothing like that will ever happen again. My Ally and I have started a new life together. I can't really explain it, but it's like we trust one another now. I understand her need to evolve and grow. At the same time, she understands my needs as a protector. I grew up as a Pathfinder. It's who I am. I won't turn my back on it, and she understands that."

"That was well said. Thank you," whispered Attia's Ally.

"Do you think we should investigate?" asked Russell, gesturing at the plumes of smoke.

In the past, Attia would have jumped at the opportunity. If the Longshadows' neighborhood was burning, the Downtrodden were likely involved, and she wanted nothing more than to hunt the Downtrodden. "We shouldn't. Let's get back to the greenhouse. Once we make sure everyone is safe, maybe we can investigate."

Malcolm peered at her, his gaze uncomfortably intense. He regarded her for a long moment before nodding. "Agreed."

Attia resumed her journey through the alleys, picking up the pace. Some streets were filled with people, probably curious about the smoke and fires, but in other neighborhoods, the streets were barren. Many of the residents of Middletown woke hours before dawn to begin their workdays. Attia expected they slept through the strange events of the evening, and would only learn about them in the morning.

Weaving through a final series of narrow alleys, Attia stepped out onto the street in front of the greenhouse. The building looked like it always did this time of night. Its many opaque glass panes glowed softly as the light within struggled to pierce the veil of fog on the inside and frost on the outside. Attia noticed a few silhouettes moving around inside, but that wasn't out of the ordinary. Between the arborists and Bumbles living in the greenhouse, someone was always up and working.

Attia beckoned her friends to follow as she crossed the street and opened the door at the far end of the greenhouse. Her quarters weren't far from it. Most nights, she could enter the greenhouse and slip into her room unnoticed, but tonight wasn't one of those nights.

The piercing blue eyes of Lord Rumblesnort Bunny-Fur greeted Attia as she entered the greenhouse. Russell and

Malcolm filed in behind her a moment later. Rumblesnort meowed dismissively before spinning and sprinting out of sight.

"Anyone else find it strange that Ellie's cat was waiting for us at the door?" asked Russell.

Rumblesnort often waited for Attia at night, but he generally waited on her bed. This behavior was new. "Whatever's happening, I suspect we'll find out soon."

Malcolm pointed. "The cat went and got Eliana. She's on her way over to us."

"She looks pissed," mumbled Russell.

Attia wasn't surprised. Eliana was often angry these days. Attia liked to think it was all because of Eliana's El'orin, but it was impossible to know. Perhaps Ellie felt ignored by her friends. She spent so much of her time working in the greenhouse alone. Before, Russell was often there to give her company, but that stopped when they broke up. Maybe Attia needed to make a point of spending more time with her friend.

"Where were you?" shouted Eliana.

"We needed to take care of something outside the city," said Malcolm after a long pause.

"Why didn't you tell me?" asked Eliana. She was closer now. She spoke loudly, but she was no longer shouting. "Why didn't you ask me to come?"

"You wouldn't have wanted to."

"How do you know?"

"I needed to contact my neverlings."

"How dare you!" Eliana's face twisted into a sneer. "And you went along with him, Russ? How could you?"

Russell sighed. "He asked for my help. What did you expect me to do? I wasn't going to let him journey outside the city alone, not with the Hidden Tower after him."

"You should have turned him down!" shouted Eliana. A forest of vines and branches twisted around to face Attia and the others, their tips rigid, like deadly spears.

Attia activated her Shield spell and stepped in front of Russell. She didn't think Eliana would attack them, but she wasn't sure Ellie was in complete control of her actions. Off to the side, Rumblesnort watched intently. Attia thought the cat looked concerned.

"No," said Russell sternly. "I don't turn my back on my friends."

"Well, while you were out there chatting with the monsters that murdered my mother, Liam almost died!" shouted Eliana.

The vines and branches undulated like angry snakes, coiled and ready to strike, but Attia was no longer concerned about them. Making sure Liam was safe was the only thing that mattered to her. "What happened to Liam? Is he alright?"

"There were ghouls in the streets," said Eliana. "He and his Bumbles fought them, but something happened. He was unconscious when I came across him. I made the Bumbles take him to the House of Healing."

Attia watched the vines and branches gradually calm as the anger in Eliana's voice receded. "Have you heard from Conner?" asked Attia.

Eliana nodded. "He sent a messenger. They have him stabilized. He said not to worry, but I don't believe him."

"What happened out there?" asked Malcom. "We saw plumes of smoke, and you said there were ghouls in the streets."

Eliana stared off into the distance, her eyes unfocused. "The neighborhood was on fire by the time I arrived. I'm not sure how many ghouls were out there. The Bumbles dealt with some of them. I only encountered a few."

The mention of fire got Attia thinking. Alahn often spoke about the Downtrodden's creepy kid and his deadly fire. Alahn's memories of the encounter seemed so visceral and terrifying that Attia considered asking Raelyn to soften them. "Was the boy there? Was he the one who set all the buildings on fire?"

Eliana nodded. "Some of the Bumbles saw him. They described him tossing balls of fire into several of the buildings, but the descriptions don't line up with how fast those fires spread. With all the snow and rain, the fires should have spread slowly, if at all." Eliana shook her head. "It must be something his El'orin is doing."

Attia suddenly regretted accompanying Malcolm on his mission. She vowed to kill the kid who burned Alahn so badly. He was out there tonight, and she missed her opportunity. Who knew when she would get another chance? Ever since Saro and his Coterie attacked the Governor in the sewers, they rarely poked their heads out of their hiding places.

"I can't believe you all abandoned me!" snapped Eliana, her anger violently returned. "You left me all alone here. Friends don't do that!"

"It's very rare that I leave the greenhouse, but this is something I needed to do," said Malcolm.

"You didn't have to take Russell and Attia with you."

"Leaving the greenhouse is dangerous for me. For whatever reason, the Hidden Tower avoids this place," said Malcolm. "It wouldn't have been safe for me to go by myself."

"That doesn't make it alright to leave me alone."

"Even when we're here, it's like you're alone, Ellie," said Russell, choking on the words. He looked like he was on the verge of crying.

"That's not fair!"

"Isn't it? You spend all your time working with your plants. You don't talk with us, spend time with us, or anything. It's like we're not even here," said Russell.

"My work is important," said Eliana. The anger was gone from her voice. She sounded exhausted and sad. "Without me, the city would have fallen to Plaguebringer. Now, with Derregain starving, I'm trying to grow my Ganna crop. It never ends. It's like I'm constantly running, but I never gain any ground."

"I know, honey," said Russell. "I'm so proud of you, and everything you've done. We all are." Russell looked down at his hands, and his shoulders shook like he was on the verge of sobbing.

Attia let the silence stretch on for several breaths, hoping Russ and Ellie would continue, but they didn't. It seemed like they said as much as they were going to say tonight. "I'm sorry, Ellie. We should have told you we were going out for a few hours. It won't happen again."

Eliana flashed her an angry, almost pained glance before nodding.

Malcolm cleared his throat. "Since we're talking, there's something else we need to discuss. I'm not sure how to say this, Eliana, but the time has come for me give Fahrilae a body. Is that going to be a problem for you?"

Eliana stared at him for a moment, her breathed rapid. Off to the side, Lord Rumblesnort Bunny-Fur hissed. "Give her a body? Are you talking about animating a corpse?"

Malcolm nodded. "As I understand it, she'll be nothing like a ghoul. From a distance, she might not even seem undead."

"But you're still talking about animating a corpse," said Eliana, shaking her head. "And you plan to do what? Keep her in your quarters?"

"That sounds about right."

Eliana looked away. Vines and branches twisted around her, protectively. Attia wasn't sure what the behavior meant. After what seemed like an eternity, she returned her gaze to Malcolm. "I haven't forgotten how Fahrilae saved my life, so she can stay. If anyone asks questions, I'm sending them to you. As far as I'm concerned, it's none of my business."

"Thanks, Ellie," said Malcolm. He glanced at Attia. "At sunrise, would you be willing to escort me to the House of Healing? I want to take care of this quickly."

Attia wanted to talk with Raelyn about it in advance. Truth be told, she was fantasizing about the conversation. Part of her wanted to order the succubus to do it for her, just to see how Raelyn reacted. Another part of her wanted to beg for it. What would Raelyn make her do to earn the favor? "I need to talk about it with Raelyn first."

"There is no time," said Malcolm, shaking his head. "If I don't take care of this quickly, I'll be forced to wait until after the Hidden Tower searches for me again. That could take days, or even longer."

Attia wanted to refuse him, but she knew he was right. She didn't think Raelyn would have any problem with helping Malcolm find a suitable body. Attia simply wanted to flirt with the succubus. but she couldn't allow her infatuation to take priority over Malcolm's safety.

She remembered Malcolm's accusations from earlier in the night. He questioned Attia's and Russell's ability to think for themselves when dealing with Raelyn. She thought he was being foolish at the time, but maybe he was right. Her fantasies about the succubus were becoming intrusive.

Playful flirting was one thing, but this was bordering on obsession. Attia was familiar with addiction, and how it twisted her personality. Going forward, she needed to be more careful with Raelyn.

17
Cinderhorn

Cinderhorn sighed as he swept the banquet hall. Given the overall condition of the room, he questioned the value of doing it at all, but he didn't want to let the messes grow out of control. Demons were filthy creatures, and Raelyn was planning on holding Court often enough where uncleaned messes were likely to accumulate.

If only he summoned something other than Bob to protect him. A water demon could have easily washed the banquet hall after the gathering. A wind demon could have simply blown the debris outside. Instead, Cinderhorn was left with Bob. A recalcitrant earth demon, unwilling to perform even mundane tasks. He claimed it was beneath his station.

Cinderhorn could have forced the ancient earth demon to assist him, of course, but he didn't think it was worth the potential repercussions. Bob recently became a member of the Union, and he wasn't shy about parroting his rights and protections. Cinderhorn thought it was just a phase. The Union catered to imps and other weaker demons. There was little for a fifth order demon, like Bob, to gain from membership. Then again, maybe Bob joined simply to antagonize Cinderhorn. That sounded like something he might do.

"You missed a spot," called the earth demon from the entryway.

Cinderhorn growled. "Unless you plan to help, keep your comments to yourself."

"But I am helping," said Bob with a grin. "I'm pointing out areas you missed.

Cinderhorn sighed and continued sweeping. He was nearly done. With any luck he'd finish before Bob drove him into a blinding rage.

"In fairness, you only have yourself to blame for most of the mess," said the earth demon as he leaned into the room. He was standing on a patch of earth, exposed by cracked and rotted flooring. "From what I heard, you kind of made a mess of that air demon. What was his name again? Knifeknave?"

"Bladestorm."

"Ah, yes," said Bob. "That was it, though I have to say, I like my name better."

Cinderhorn set his broom against the wall. He was done cleaning for the day. "I really didn't have much choice. That Telekinesis spell was all or nothing. Once I caught him, there was no way I was letting him go."

Bob reached down and tore away a few planks of flooring, extending the patch of exposed earth far enough to allow him to enter the room.

"Please don't destroy the place."

"Why? It's already in shambles," said the earth demon, gesturing around the ruined banquet hall. "Besides, exposing more ground will make it easier for me to respond should you need help. I mean, what would have happened if your spell failed?"

"It wasn't going to fail," said Cinderhorn. "I spent all day crafting it. The faster the opponent, the stronger the responding force. With his incredible speed, Bladestorm was dead the moment he charged."

Bob cocked his head to the side. "So, you knew Knifeknave was going to mount a challenge, didn't you?"

"I was tipped off by one of my new imps," said Cinderhorn with a nod. "Using a situational spell like that was risky, but it paid off."

"If all the chatter in the Netherworld is any indication, it definitely paid off," said the earth demon. "Most of the Netherworld is absolutely terrified of you. I doubt anyone is going to challenge Raelyn anytime soon."

"At least not any of the demons currently in Derregain," said Cinderhorn. "And with Raelyn's moratorium on summoning, there shouldn't be many new threats entering the city."

Bob crouched and touched one of his huge obsidian fists to the ground beneath him. "Someone has entered the grounds. Based on the hooves, I suspect it's Raelyn, but she's not alone. Someone is walking beside her."

Cinderhorn frowned. Why was Raelyn coming back so soon after adjourning her Demonic Court? He would have thought she was busy speaking with imps, plotting her next moves. Did she need his advice on something? "Please leave me, Bob. If it's Raelyn, I should meet with her in private."

"Are you sure?" asked the earth demon. "There's someone with her. Do you want me to wait around until we know who it is?"

Cinderhorn shook his head. "I trust her. I'll be alright." He questioned the honesty of his words after uttering them. He wasn't sure he trusted anyone.

"Suit yourself," said Bob as he quickly descended beneath the ground.

Cinderhorn lacked any real way of knowing if Bob honored his wishes and left the area, or if he was hiding nearby, just beneath the surface. Perhaps he was far more trusting than he gave himself credit for. After all, he rarely second guessed the information he received from his imps, and here he was trusting Bob to honor his wishes for privacy, despite having no means of verifying it.

The Guardian demon waited for several minutes before Raelyn finally entered the banquet hall. A man's unconscious body was draped over her shoulder, and a boy walked alongside her. Cinderhorn didn't immediately recognize the boy, but it didn't take him long to put the pieces together. Conner, one of the El'orin from the Citadel, was with her. It shouldn't have surprised him. Conner was her student, after all. Cinderhorn found his presence unsettling, nevertheless.

"I'm glad you're still awake," said Raelyn as she approached.

"I was just cleaning up," said Cinderhorn, gesturing to the broom in the corner. "To what do I owe this visit?" he asked, casting a quick glance at Conner.

Raelyn sighed. "I'm sorry for bringing humans into your home without your prior consent, but the matter is pressing." She crouched and gently lowered the man she was carrying to the ground.

Cinderhorn immediately noticed the man's resemblance to Conner. "Is this the other brother?"

"His name is Liam," said Conner. There was defiance in his voice, but Cinderhorn smelled his fear.

Raelyn rose, gently placing her hand on Conner's forearm. "As you can see, Liam poses no threat. His life is hanging by a slender thread."

Cinderhorn grabbed a nearby chair and sat down. He was much taller than Raelyn, and he absolutely towered over Conner. If Raelyn brought a pair of El'orin into his home, there had to be a good reason. Cinderhorn thought removing his tremendous height advantage might benefit the conversation. "Why did you bring him here? You're the healer, not me. If you can't help him, what do you expect me to do about it?"

Raelyn glanced at Conner. "Liam suffers from a wound we can't seem to cure," she said. "No matter how many times we heal it, it keeps coming back."

"Then it's time to say your goodbyes, and move on." Cinderhorn didn't want to be cruel, but the answer seemed obvious enough to him.

"No," said Conner sternly.

"Did I misunderstand something?" asked Cinderhorn, suppressing a chuckle. "The wound keeps coming back, even after it's healed."

"Sure, with our current spells," snapped Conner. "I'll find new spells if I must."

Cinderhorn ran his claws through his mane. Raelyn recently used the Netten and Naga show to bargain for a spell. "I take it Raelyn's new spell didn't work?"

Raelyn shook her head.

"So, are you here to ask for my help in seeking new healing magic?" Cinderhorn was out of favors. Given her connections with Nettan and Naga, Raelyn controlled more bargaining power than he did.

"Actually, no," said Raelyn. "We may seek your advice, but Conner will bargain for the spell himself."

A smile crept to Cinderhorn's lips. He knew Conner successfully bargained with Daemenos, but this was far more dangerous. The kid was willing to take risks. Cinderhorn had to give him that. "Then what do you need from me?"

"We need time," said Raelyn.

"I'm sorry. I'm not sure I understand."

"Runes of Stasis," said Conner. "We encountered some when we battled Lamenica. Raelyn said you have another set of them in the basement. I want you to freeze my brother in time."

Cinderhorn flashed Raelyn an angry glance. "What else have you told this boy?"

"I'm sorry, Cinderhorn, but I owe him," said Raelyn, with a slight bow of her head. "He's loyal to me, and as you know, that means I'm loyal to him."

Cinderhorn rose from his chair, towering over the two of them. He spread his wings for good measure. "Since when are your debts mine? You may trust this boy, but that doesn't mean I do!" Cinderhorn shook his head violently. "Liam was there when my brother fell. He was involved in the battle. I'd like nothing more than to watch him die."

"Your brother didn't die," said Conner. The stench of his fear was overwhelming, but he wasn't backing down.

"No," growled Cinderhorn. "What happened to him is far worse! He's rotting in a prison beneath the Netherworld."

"Spare me the horror stories. Raelyn told me all about it," said Conner, shaking his head. "She also told me how hard you worked to find him and how you bargained for his safety. He may be stuck there for a century, but he isn't suffering."

"Of course, I did that for him. I'd do anything to protect him. He's my brother," said Cinderhorn dismissively. Erranaekis and Nesharon would have done the same for him had he been the one to fall. At least he hoped so.

"And Liam is my brother!" shouted Conner, advancing. "How is it any different?"

Cinderhorn retreated a step. It's not that he feared Conner. He simply didn't know how to respond. By all rights, the boy was correct. His brother was dying, and he was doing everything in his power to save him. Their situations weren't all that different.

"If it helps, please understand that it's within my power to keep Liam alive," said Raelyn. "Doing so would drain most of my power every single day, but I'll do it if I must."

Cinderhorn glowered at the succubus. She wasn't fighting fair. Chariden sent him to Derregain to help Raelyn rule.

Spending most of her power keeping Liam alive would leave Raelyn tremendously vulnerable. He couldn't allow that to happen. "Fine," said Cinderhorn with a sigh. "I'll do as you ask. I'll place Liam within the Runes of Stasis."

Conner shook his head. "Not good enough. I want to be there. I want to see it with my own eyes."

"Out of the question," snapped Cinderhorn. The Runes of Stasis weren't the only important things in the basement. Lamenica's old Runes of Transport were still down there, fully intact. It turned out the Runes of Transport Cinderhorn built in both Nerreka and Derregain were unnecessary, but it was more than that.

The Inscription Chariden used to Portal to Derregain was in that basement. The Demon Queen hadn't visited in decades, but Cinderhorn expected that to change. He couldn't let Conner see that Inscription. Even with the Banishment spell, Cinderhorn didn't think Conner was all that threatening, but the entire group of Citadel El'orin, working together, was terribly dangerous. He couldn't, in good conscience, let them know the whereabouts of Chariden's Inscription.

"I need to know that he's alright," said Conner, his tone much softer.

"Please, Cinderhorn," said Raelyn. "Do it as a favor for me."

The Guardian demon closed his eyes and sighed. He wasn't prepared to trust Conner, or any human, for that matter. Trusting Raelyn, on the other hand, was a necessary evil. How else could he hope to support her in Derregain? "Very well."

18

Conner

Conner took a deep breath, trying to calm his racing heart. Seeing Cinderhorn up close wasn't something he was prepared for. He knew the Guardian demon was enormous, but being close to him gave Conner an entirely new appreciation for what that meant.

Cinderhorn's massive head displayed some human aspects, but was dominated by feline features, including fangs, an extended snout, whiskers, and a thick mane. A pair of thick black horns twisted out from his temples, and large leathery wings sprouted from his back. Dense, rippling muscle covered his athletic frame, and heat radiated from his body.

It took every ounce of Conner's self-control to keep from running away. He remembered watching this monster hurl bolts of force at Devin and magically rip Silver's veins from her body. That's what terrified Conner the most. Despite Cinderhorn's physical size and power, it was his magic that made him truly dangerous.

"Lead the way," said Raelyn.

"I'd prefer if you lead," said Cinderhorn. "After all, you know the path as well as I do. The corridors are narrow and difficult for me to travel. If it's all the same to you, I would prefer not to have two healers with the Banishment spell following behind me where I can't see them."

"Fine," said Raelyn as she approached the far wall of the dark room.

Conner guessed the room might have been a banquet hall. They never entered this room when they attacked Lamenica, but based on the soot and burned tapestries, the fires from their battle must have spread to here. Something about the room smelled foul, like rotten eggs. At first, he thought the smell belonged to Cinderhorn, but it definitely came from the room.

Reaching the wall, Raelyn ran her palm along the surface until she found a particular spot. She pressed, and a small rectangular section of the wall sank inward a couple of inches. A moment later, a door slid open, revealing a dimly lit corridor with a set of descending stairs.

With the door open, Raelyn quickly retrieved Liam, gently draping him over her shoulder. Once he was safely situated, she returned to the door and slipped inside. She turned and gestured for the others to follow.

Conner was grateful Raelyn was carrying his brother. As much as he wanted to, he wasn't strong enough to lift Liam. He might have managed it with Telekinesis, but probably not safely. Conner didn't enjoy thinking about his frailty, but moments like this made it hard not to.

"After you," said Cinderhorn, gesturing to the corridor.

Conner stood there, dumbfounded. Did the enormous demon really expect Conner to walk in front of him? "I'd prefer to stay in the back," said Conner, struggling not to stammer.

"I'd prefer you to leave, and never return," said Cinderhorn. "It seems neither of us gets what we want today."

"Would you two stop arguing and come along? I haven't got all night," called Raelyn from the stairs.

Conner took a deep breath before rushing to join Raelyn. The rotten eggs smell made him want to retch, but neither of the demons seemed bothered by it. He knew Cinderhorn was following him, but he found it necessary to glance back to confirm the fact. The enormous Guardian demon barely made a sound when he moved. Conner would have expected a creature that size to shake the ground with each step, but nothing could be farther from the truth.

"No reason to worry, little one," said Cinderhorn, his voice an unsettling choir of voices, each just slightly out of tune from one another. "I'm not going to hurt you."

Conner carefully followed Raelyn down the steps as he considered his next words. "I believe you, but at the same time, it's hard for me to believe. Does that make any sense?"

"It makes perfect sense," said Cinderhorn. "The last time you saw me, I was destroying your civilization. I did unspeakable things to people who were probably your friends. Earlier that day, your father sacrificed himself to save you from the Black Tide. I know you're terrified of me. I can smell it, but I certainly don't blame you for it. You should fear me."

Talking about the day forced Conner to remember parts of it. The sickening crunch of Devin's chest shattering, and the sound of Silver's tortured screams. Most of all, he remembered the image of his father turning into a miniature exploding sun. "Why? Why did it have to happen?"

Cinderhorn sighed, filling the narrow stairs with the faint scent of cinnamon. "I wish I knew, Conner. The barrier protecting your civilization vexed the Queen. Over time, her desire to conquer the Citadel grew into an irresistible obsession. She sent army after army across the rainforest, and when they all failed to defeat you, she gave me the task." Cinderhorn stopped speaking as they worked their way through a narrow place on the stairs. "Summoning that army took me nearly a decade of work. So many favors traded to gather each and every name. In the end, what good did it do?"

"What good did it do?" spat Conner incredulously. "You shekking won! You destroyed the Citadel."

"I wanted to conquer the Citadel, but I never wanted to destroy it, Conner. That was the Queen's folly. My plan, all along, was to give it to Raelyn to rule."

Up ahead, Raelyn turned to face Conner. "It's true. He argued with Chariden, begging her to leave the Citadel under my dominion, but she wouldn't hear a word of it."

"When was that?" asked Conner.

"After I used the Bloodgate to pull Chariden into the Citadel," said Raelyn. "At the time, you and your friends were away, on your mission to the Darkwood."

"So, you lied about their whereabouts when you told the Queen to search the southern swamps," said Cinderhorn. "I always assumed as much, but I wasn't certain."

Raelyn nodded. "Chariden was being such a bitch. I wanted to hurt her, and that was the only way I knew how."

Conner discussed some of this with Raelyn in the past, but the conservation was much different with Cinderhorn involved. In many ways, Conner was as much an observer as a participant in the discussion. "What happened to the Citadel? There was an army of orcs marching down the Black Scar. We fled before they reached us. A group of us went through the Theleram. The rest planned to flee through the swamps, but I never found out what happened to them."

"They loaded up their boats and fled south," said Cinderhorn. His voice was much calmer. Each word still produced a dissonant chord, but when he spoke softly, the effect was much more tolerable. "My demons pursued them for several weeks, but Gunther was with them. Eventually, they killed so many demons that I stopped following them."

"So, they're still alive?"

"As far as I know," said Cinderhorn.

Conner didn't want to get his hopes up. He knew many dangerous creatures lived in the swamps. Still, if Gunther was with them, and the demons stopped chasing them, maybe they survived. Their plan was to sail along the coast until they reached Derregain. No ships from the Citadel ever arrived, so that didn't happen, but maybe they found a safe place to build a new home.

"We're almost there," said Raelyn as she turned and continued down the winding stairs. "There are many things in this basement that don't concern you, Conner. I brought you along so you could see your brother safely frozen in time. Focus on that, and try to ignore the rest."

"Hey, Raelyn," called Cinderhorn. "Don't think about a fire breathing goose banging on a drum."

"What are you talking about?" hissed the succubus.

"You thought about the goose, didn't you?"

"Of course, I did!"

"Just like Conner is going to look for all the things that don't concern him the moment he sets foot in that basement."

Conner suppressed a snicker. He hated to admit it, but he liked Cinderhorn's sense of humor. "I'll try not to look, but I have to say... Raelyn's warning made me curious."

"Whatever," mumbled Raelyn, as she trotted around the bend.

Conner followed and soon found himself in an expansive chamber. Dozens of globes of Liquidlight hung from the ceiling, bathing the room in ample light. Several circles of neatly scripted runes lined the perimeter of the room. Tall stacks of crates and boxes rested against the walls in various places, and if Conner wasn't mistaken, he noticed an Inscription carved into the floor in the far corner of the chamber.

But the Runes of Stasis commanded the most attention. The runes themselves were little more than lines of script carved into the floor, but their contents took Conner's breath away. There were so many bodies! Conner expected to see a few people suspended within the runes, but he wasn't prepared to see scores of people frozen in time.

They were stacked, folded, and wrapped around each other. To Conner, seeing so many people compressed into a motionless brick of flesh reminded him of the disgusting monsters the neverlings sent after Malcolm. He struggled to think of them as human. Was he really planning to add his brother to the pile?

"Here we are," said Raelyn as she gently lowered Liam to the ground.

"Why are there so many of them?" gasped Conner.

"Careful what you ask. Are you sure you want to know the answer?" asked Cinderhorn.

Conner nodded. He suspected he already knew the answer. Raelyn told him about needing to consume blood to remain in this world.

"Food," said Cinderhorn. "We're using these runes as a larder."

It made sense, but it chilled Conner's blood, nonetheless. The people imprisoned within those ruins would never age. They didn't experience the passage of time. They were little more than bags of blood for the demons to feed on.

"If there are no objections, I would like to place Liam here, along this edge," said Raelyn, pointing.

Conner fought back waves of nausea. "I guess so."

"I know this is difficult, Conner, but your brother will be safe down here," said Cinderhorn. His tone was surprisingly tender. "You have my word."

Raelyn met Conner's gaze. "Cinderhorn's word is no small gift, Conner."

Conner nodded to the Guardian demon before approaching Liam's unconscious body. He didn't want to do this, but he didn't see another option. He needed to keep Liam alive until he found a spell to cure him. The Runes of Stasis were the best way to accomplish that. "Will I be able to visit?"

"I'm not sure," said Raelyn, pursing her lips. "I don't think so."

"I'll permit it, but only if you come alone," said Cinderhorn. "I know when anyone sets foot on these grounds. If you bring any of your friends with you, let's just say you won't like the outcome."

Conner faced the Guardian demon and nodded. "I understand."

"As long as you come alone, and as long as Raelyn approves, you can come anytime you like." Cinderhorn ran his claws through his mane. "The similarities are not lost on me, Conner. You're bargaining with the Netherworld to protect your brother, much like I bargained to protect mine. I respect that."

Conner met Cinderhorn's intense gaze for a moment before turning back to face his brother. He knew Liam wouldn't approve of this. He hadn't even started searching for the right spell yet, and he was already making dark deals with demons.

Then again, he started walking this road long ago. The knowledge and magic he gained along the way already saved his friends' lives on several occasions. He saw no point stopping his journey now, especially with his brother's life hanging in the balance.

19

Gunther

Gunther peered across the swollen river. He didn't think the term river even applied at this point. It was closer to a lake than anything else. Countless days of torrential rains caused the river to escape its banks, and there didn't seem to be any end in sight. Not that it mattered anymore. The waters were already deep enough for the Lurker.

And the Lurker was coming. Gunther knew it. He felt it in his bones.

The talons made little effort to disguise their movements over the past few days. They seized the few sodden pieces of land within sight of New Citadel, using felled trees and floating debris to expand each into a tiny island. Then, using the islands as muster points, they gathered for the upcoming battle.

Their numbers were staggering. There had to be thousands, and those were just the ones Gunther could see. Who knew how many of them were hiding beneath the surface? He doubted they were all skilled warriors. Gunther suspected some were too young or old to fight, but he didn't think it mattered. There were more than enough warriors to get the job done.

It wasn't that New Citadel couldn't defend itself. The city was built into the side of a hill, with combinations of magical and natural walls providing endless obstacles for any invading force to contend with. Between archers and mages, Gunther expected his forces to inflict tremendous damage to the invading talons.

But the Lurker would change everything. How were they supposed to repel something like that? Gunther remembered how its tentacles towered like mighty trees over Deliverance, the Citadel's largest ship. The sheer size and power of the Lurker would overwhelm New Citadel. Sure, Gunther's people engineered defenses and countermeasures to battle the gigantic squid, but he didn't think any of them would matter.

They built a battery of six ballistae into the side of the mountain. The weapons were hidden in the lower levels of the city, each aimed up and out. While normal arrows were unlikely to pierce the Lurker's thick skin, the ballistae might manage it. Gunther gave Falstaff credit for trying. Many leaders would have surrendered to despair, but Falstaff refused to. Still, if Falstaff was counting on one of the ballista bolts striking a lethal blow, he was relying on wishful thinking.

If the ballistae didn't work, the plan was to resort to magic, flaming pitch, and boiling oil. Gunther had even less faith in those measures than the ballistae. The Lurker was a sea monster. The most fire was likely to accomplish was to force it to retreat beneath the waters for a short time. It wouldn't be enough.

Gunther feared he was New Citadel's last best hope for fighting the Lurker. The people worshipped Gunther like a God. It didn't matter that he was just a man, being asked to fight a monster 1000 times his size. Somehow, the people expected him to win.

To their credit, New Citadel's alchemists and herbalists did their best to prepare him. They gave him potions to accelerate his movements, regenerate his wounds, and grant him flight. They gave him pouches of edible herbs designed to heighten his awareness, enhance his strength, and thicken his blood. Between all the potions and herbs, Gunther wasn't sure he'd manage to choke it all down.

"You might as well come in out of the rain," grumbled Kostanus from behind him.

"What's the difference?" said Gunther. "As soon as the attack starts, we're all getting wet."

"But the attack might not happen for days."

"We don't have days," said Gunther, shaking his head. "I suspect they'll attack before sundown. Tomorrow at the latest."

Kostanus jammed the butt of his staff into the muddy ground. "Why do you say that?" he asked as he deftly untied several leather straps, revealing the Runes of Flame covering the top third of his staff.

"They've finished organizing their forces," said Gunther, pointing out across the water. "They have four primary muster points. Two near, one on either side of us, and two farther back, closer to the middle."

Kostanus' staff sputtered and popped as the Runes of Flame ignited beneath the heavy downpour. He rubbed his hands together above the smoldering runes and nodded. "You're probably right. Still, you never know. They might hold off for a few days yet."

Gunther knew what they were waiting for. "They're waiting for the Lurker. They'll attack shortly after it arrives."

"You sure it ain't already here?" asked Kostanus. "The water is plenty deep. For all we know, that monster is swimming around beneath the surface as we speak."

Gunther glanced at Kostanus. "We'd know it if it were here."

"If you say so."

"You weren't there the night it attacked us, but you saw the ships we built," said Gunther. "The Lurker towered over our largest ship. I've seen nothing so large. Its tentacles climbed higher than the tallest trees." Gunther closed his eyes and pinched the bridge of his nose. The chilly rain was causing his forehead to ache. "If it were here, we'd know it."

A deep, powerful croaking rang out across the surface of the water, momentarily drowning out the sound of the rain. Gunther thought it sounded a little like a frog, but the sound was much deeper, and orders of magnitude louder.

"Well, piss on me," grumbled Kostanus. "Looks like your monster is arriving, right on time."

Gunther spotted the advancing wall of water first. It was like an enormous dam burst, and all the water held behind it was suddenly surging down the river, but it wasn't long before the Lurker's muddy brown tentacles came into focus. Sharp barbs jutted out from them at odd angles. The tentacles seemed to propel the massive creature. Some of them likely pushed against the river bottom, while others pulled against submerged patches of land on either side of the river.

Even laying flat in the water, the monster's enormous body rose high above the surface of the river. Sickly green light emanated from countless creases and cracks along the Lurker's carapace. Gunther remembered the monster's glowing green eye the night it capsized their ships, but he didn't notice the light shining through its carapace. Then again, everything from that night was a blur.

"I hate to admit it, but I guess you're right," grumbled Kostanus. "Even with the water level as high as it is, there's no way that thing is hiding."

Gunther wiped the rain from his eyes. He struggled to believe what he was seeing. "That damn thing is even bigger than I remembered."

"Its body looks longer than the tallest trees in the rainforest. If it's built like a normal squid, its tentacles will be quite a bit longer. Double the length, or even more."

"We're dead. There's no hope," said Gunther with a sigh. He knew the upcoming battle would be his last, and he was at peace with that. Gunther longed to end this life and begin his new life with his friend, Arronhelm. He dreamed about it nearly every night.

"What are you talking about?" said Kostanus. "Last I heard, you were going to fly through the air and cut that thing to ribbons. That's still the plan, ain't it?"

"I think so," said Gunther. "That's how I know we're as good as dead. I might as well leave my sword behind and just piss on the Lurker. I probably have a better chance of hurting it that way."

"Well, or at least pissing it off," said Kostanus with a nervous chuckle.

The wall of water flowed into the lake in front of Gunther, causing the ocean of talons to violently bob across the surface. A few of them began to cheer, and it wasn't long before others lent their voices to the effort. Within moments, the talons' cheers grew deafening. The scattered clanging of metal weapons made the sound more horrifying, but it was the bellowing croak of the Lurker that caused Gunther's blood to run cold.

A series of bells rang out behind Gunther. New Citadel's watchmen saw the Lurker and were sounding the alarm. Throughout the city, soldiers were probably saying goodbye to their loved ones before manning their posts. From here on out, no one would rest until this grisly conflict was over, one way or another.

The Lurker was surprisingly graceful as it pulled itself into the lake surrounding New Citadel. Its tentacles moved with such fluidity that they barely caused ripples across the surface of the water. It didn't seem possible for something that large to move so effortlessly through the water, but then again, the Lurker was an Ancient. Who knew what kind of primal magic it commanded?

A few cries of fear rang out behind Gunther. He suspected the clanging alarm bells drowned out most of the cries. Gunther couldn't blame anyone for their fear. He couldn't think of a more rational reaction to the monstrous horror floating in front of them. Anyone who thought New Citadel was going to win this battle couldn't possibly believe it anymore. Not after seeing the Lurker.

Slowly, the Lurker rotated in the water until its enormous glowing eye was facing them. Gunther felt his heart skip a beat. It wasn't something he was used to feeling. He remembered feeling similar sensations back when he hunted El'orin with his friends. The anxious feeling wasn't exactly the same, but it was similar.

What if the Lurker was something like an El'orin? Maybe it didn't care about Gunther's people. Maybe the foul beast was after him the entire time. In his heart of hearts, he knew that wasn't true. Gunther would gladly sacrifice himself if it would save the rest of them, but he knew that was folly. The Lurker was there to destroy their civilization.

The likeliest outcome of the upcoming battle was that Gunther would sacrifice himself, but it wouldn't make a difference. He might be one of the first to die, but he certainly wouldn't be the last. By the end of the day, everyone in New Citadel was destined to join him in death.

20
Malcolm

Malcolm shivered as he tried to shake off the cold. The wind and snow picked up overnight, making for a chilly walk to the House of Healing. On the brighter side, the stormy weather forced many people to stay indoors. The streets were nearly barren as Attia and Malcolm worked their way through the Lowlands. They passed a few groups of Bumbles, but little more than that.

Then again, most residents of the Lowlands understood they were embroiled in a civil war. The Downtrodden attacked Middletown, nearly burning down an entire neighborhood. Everyone expected the Bumbles to strike back. If not today, soon. Families who didn't need to venture out into the streets were likely hiding in their homes, waiting for the conflict to calm down.

"Busy night?" asked Attia, as she approached the group of armed guards patrolling the entry hall.

One of the guards nodded. "A lot of folks came in here after getting caught up in the fighting over in Middletown. Some of them looked pretty rough."

"Saw a bunch of Bumbles come in too," added another guard.

Malcolm wanted to ask about Liam, but he didn't know any of the guards. Attia seemed to know them. Maybe she would ask. Either way, if a lot of seriously injured people came in throughout the night, there were likely fresh corpses to choose from. He hated himself for thinking that way, but he couldn't help it.

"*Don't chastise yourself for being focused on the task at hand,*" whispered the Other. "*What you're doing is incredibly important, but terribly dangerous. You can't afford distractions. Not today.*"

"Did you see Liam?" asked Attia.

"No," said a guard. "I heard his team brought him in before our shift. Sometime around midnight."

"Okay, thanks. I'll go find his brother," said Attia as she grabbed Malcolm's hand and led him past the guards.

Malcolm waited until they were out of earshot before speaking. "Do you know all the guards who work here?"

"Pretty much all of them," said Attia. "I'm here fairly often, and with my mask and false eye, I'm pretty memorable."

Malcolm was about to ask her how often she visited when they spilled out into the House of Healing's admissions center. The sheer volume of wounded people scattered about the expansive chamber caught Malcolm off guard, breaking his train of thought. While this wasn't the first time Malcolm visited the hospital, he wasn't exactly a frequent visitor.

"Conner looks awful," said Attia beneath her breath.

He was standing behind a large desk topped with several open books. Based on his position, Malcolm guessed he was leaning back against a chair or stool. His eyes were bloodshot, distant, and unfocused. Attia waved, but Conner didn't seem to notice.

"Conner," called Attia. "Is everything alright? How's Liam?"

Conner startled when he heard his name, but it only took him a moment to recover. He quickly waved them over. Once they were in comfortable speaking range, he said, "I'm not sure." He looked down at one of his open books, but he clearly wasn't reading. "He's alive. I just don't know how to fix him."

"Can we see him?" asked Attia.

Conner shook his head. "That won't be possible."

"I don't understand," said Malcolm. "Are his wounds so bad he can't have visitors?" Raelyn didn't let the group visit Attia very often while she was recovering from the War Beyond the Wall. Maybe Liam's situation was similar.

"Look..." Conner sighed and rubbed his eyes. "If I tell you this, promise not to talk about it with anyone."

"You mean we're not supposed to tell Russ and Ellie?" asked Malcolm. He tried to keep his voice calm and soothing. Conner appeared exhausted, and if his brother was as wounded as it seemed, he might not be thinking clearly. The last thing Malcolm wanted to do was come off as combative.

"Yes," said Conner, but he shook his head. "I mean, they're going to find out. How can they not? I just want to be the one to tell them."

"Tell them what, Conner?" asked Attia with surprising tenderness.

"Do you remember the Runes of Stasis?"

"You mean the ones I disabled during the fight with Lamenica?" Malcolm remembered the Other showing him the weakness in the runic script. Once he knew where the runes were vulnerable, they were fairly easy to dismantle, which was definitely a good thing. Runes like that could hold a person imprisoned in time forever. "Wait," gasped Malcolm as the realization hit him. "Did someone figure out how to repair those runes? Is Liam frozen in time?"

"Kind of," said Conner. "There is another set of those runes in the basement of Lamenica's manor. When Raelyn couldn't keep Liam alive, she took him there. We'll keep him frozen in time until we find a spell to fix him."

"Lamenica's old manor?" breathed Attia. "Raelyn warned me never to go there."

Conner nodded. "That's where she held her Demonic Court, and she's right about avoiding that place. I can visit, but no one else should."

Malcolm didn't like the sound of that. "What's living in those ruins, Conner?"

"Look, I'm not going to talk about it. At least, not right now." Conner flipped one of his books open and pretended to read the page. "Is there anything else you need?"

"Don't be like that, Conner. We're just concerned about Liam," said Attia.

"*Let him keep his secret, for now,*" said the Other. "*We have other business to attend to. The longer you remain outside the greenhouse, the greater the risk.*"

"No problem, Conner, we understand. We'll talk about it when you're ready," said Malcolm. "You wouldn't happen to know where Raelyn is? We need to speak with her."

Conner looked up from his book, glancing at Attia. "Can it wait? She needs to rest."

Attia shook her head. "It can't wait."

"Fine," said Conner with a sigh. "If you want to head up to the critical treatment room, I'll let her know you're here."

"Thanks, Conner," said Attia. "Let's go, Malcolm." She wasted no time grabbing him by the hand and leading him through the Hospital's congested admissions center, carefully avoiding the areas with the most heavily wounded patients. A few guards and medical staff nodded to Attia as she passed, but no one challenged them.

After entering the large stairwell in the center of the Hospital, Attia faced Malcolm and spoke. "I don't know what lives in the ruins of Lamenica's manor. I just know it's powerful."

"How do you know?"

"Raelyn and I talk fairly often. I guess you'd call it flirting, but whatever." Attia smiled and shook her head. "After I heard she planned to hold her Demonic Court in the ruins of Lamenica's manor, I started asking questions here and there. She was deadly serious when she warned me never to go there."

Malcolm considered the implications. Raelyn kept the Governor as her lover. She worked hand-in-hand with Conner, and she was seemingly romantically involved with Attia. He suspected many demons would find fault with her behavior. Then again, it wasn't like the citizens of Derregain were going out of their way to support people who worked with Raelyn. Distrust seemed common among both demons and humans.

Still, what if the demon living in the ruins wasn't fully aware of everyone Raelyn was involved with? Conner said it was safe for him to visit the ruins, but that it wasn't safe for anyone else, but could Conner be trusted? Maybe he was charmed. Attia claimed Raelyn would never break her word and charm Conner, but what if she did? How would Attia find out about it? Even if she did somehow find out, couldn't Raelyn just rewrite Attia's memories? There were no shortages of opportunities for her to do so.

"Anyway, we should get going," said Attia. "The room isn't too far. It's just one floor up. Are you going to make it up the stairs?"

"I'll be fine," snapped Malcolm, more harshly than he intended.

"I wasn't trying to be hurtful," said Attia. "I just thought your legs might be tired after all the walking you did last night."

Malcolm sighed. "Look, I'm sorry." He massaged his forehead in anticipation of a sudden headache. "The Other has this thing about me asking for help."

"Yeah, I've noticed."

"It's annoying at times, but his reasoning is sound," said Malcolm. He paused, waiting for the headache. When it didn't come, he continued. "The farther I go with my necromancy, the more isolated I'm likely to become."

"It doesn't have to be that way, Malcolm," said Attia. "After all, I'm helping you find a fresh corpse to animate. That should count for something, shouldn't it?"

"It does," said Malcolm with a nod. "And I'm grateful, but you know what I mean. There are certain roads I need to walk alone. If I'm going to succeed on those journeys, I can't afford to depend on other people."

Attia stared at him for a moment, her face unreadable. "I understand." Without saying another word, she turned and climbed the steps.

Malcolm followed as quickly as he could manage. Attia wasn't wrong about the fatigue and soreness in his legs. If he hadn't relied on his balance magic for much of last night's journey, he doubted he'd be able to walk today, let alone climb stairs. But he didn't dare drain his well on balance magic this morning, not with the prospect of casting Ghostly Shell ahead of him. He needed to conserve as much magical energy as possible for that moment.

After ascending the stairs, it wasn't far to the treatment room. Attia walked in silence, but there was an almost childlike skip to her step. Malcolm didn't know what to think. He suspected she was eager to flirt with Raelyn, but maybe he was making too big a deal of the situation. He knew there were degrees of charms, and if Attia was to be believed, she was only lightly charmed by the succubus.

"I don't know what to think either," said the Other. *"She seems so much happier, but that in itself should be cause for concern. Attia has never been a cheerful person. As much as I enjoy seeing her happy, we need to be careful. If her personality has changed, there might be other changes."*

The two of them took seats in the treatment room and waited for Raelyn to arrive. Fortunately, they didn't need to wait long.

Malcolm didn't even think a minute passed before the succubus entered the room, which made little sense to him. He wondered if Conner could somehow contact Raelyn magically. How else could he have gotten word to her so quickly?

Raelyn was wearing the illusion of the hospital administrator, Reya, as she generally did when moving about the House of Healing. Even covered by her illusion, Malcolm knew she was exhausted. He understood exhaustion better than most. It showed in the way she held her head, and how she seemed to hang onto the door handle for a moment as she closed it.

"Thanks for seeing us on short notice," said Attia. "I wouldn't wake you if it wasn't important."

"It's okay, Attia. Now, what can I do for you?" said the illusion of the hospital administrator, her weary voice not even remotely matching her smiling, energetic face.

"Attia is here on my behalf," said Malcolm. "I need a favor."

The hospital administrator turned to face Malcolm. "I'm intrigued. Go on…"

"Do you mind dropping your illusion? It's unsettling."

The image of the hospital administrator briefly shimmered before melting away, leaving a haggard-looking succubus in its place. Raelyn was wearing a loosely tied black nightgown. Her hair was tussled as if she just woke up. Both her wings and tail drooped against the floor. "As you wish," she said, suppressing a yawn.

"It's complicated," said Malcolm, immediately regretting it. He clearly interrupted Raelyn's sleep. The least he could do was be direct with his request. "Are you familiar with the Ghostly Shell spell?"

"Necromancy isn't my strongest suit."

"You know what a revenant is, right?"

Raelyn nodded.

"Ghostly Shell is the spell you use to make one."

Raelyn closed her eyes for a moment. When she opened them again, she seemed more alert. "And you know this spell?"

Malcolm nodded. "I often work with a powerful ghost, and I want to make her a revenant."

"And what do you need from me?"

"I need to find a suitable corpse for her body," said Malcolm. "Fresh, cleanly killed, and preferably young."

Raelyn cast a quick glance at Attia. "I'm sure I can help, but I must say, it's an odd request."

"I'll make it worth your while, ma'am," said Attia softly.

"There's no need to be formal," said Raelyn, her tone stern.

"It's okay," said Malcolm. "I know about your relationship with her. Attia told me about it last night. Russell knows too, for what it's worth."

Raelyn raised an eyebrow, and a slight smile crept to her lip. "In that case, yes, you definitely will make it worth my while, Attia. Do you understand, girl?"

"Yes, ma'am."

Malcolm shifted nervously. He knew little about flirting and sexuality, but it didn't take an expert to understand what was playing out in front of him. "How do we proceed?" he asked, hoping to interrupt whatever was happening between Attia and the succubus.

"Not so fast," said Raelyn, licking her lips. "You look deliciously uncomfortable, Malcolm. You're normally so calm, focused, and in control. Perhaps I should get to know this side of you a little better. You'd like that, wouldn't you?"

"*Focus!*" hissed the Other.

"That won't be possible," said Malcolm, shaking his head. "What I'm about to do is very dangerous. I can't afford any distractions."

Raelyn playfully pouted. "Why did you have to ruin my fun like that?" Her eyes flashed burning crimson. "Okay... talk to me about the dangers. Is there anything I can do to make this safer for you?"

Malcolm tried to mask his relief, but he suspected the succubus was reading his reactions like a book. "Summoning Fahrilae is quite dangerous. If I lose control of her, even for just a moment, she'll kill me."

"Fahrilae is her name?"

Malcolm nodded. "She's ancient. Centuries ago, she was one of the Dark Lord's revenants."

Raelyn took a step back, her eyes wide. "Is there much risk of losing control? You've summoned her before, haven't you?"

"Yes, but usually with the aid of Eliana's cat."

"Conner explained the cat to me," said Raelyn. She pursed her lips and ran a finger along the length of one of her horns. "I'm not unfamiliar with the struggles of summoning powerful beings. Strong demons often fight against their summoners. Is it fair to say Fahrilae will fight even harder against the Ghostly Shell spell? That spell binds her to you, does it not?"

"Yes. I expect her to fight my control. I don't think she has a choice in the matter. She has to fight me."

Raelyn stared at him for a long moment. "I don't think we can do this today. If we're going to do this right, I need to build a safe place for this."

"It can't wait. I have to do this today."

"Why?"

"Reasons."

"You're the one asking for help," said Raelyn, a hint of anger creeping into her tone. "If you want my help, I expect you to answer my questions. It's common courtesy."

Malcolm shook his head. "I don't have the time or the patience to explain the intricacies of necromancy to you. If we're going to work together, you're going to have to trust me."

"Trust is a two-way street, boy."

"I'm already trusting you."

"What are you talking about?"

"You charmed and raped Russell. Conner spends all his time here, to the point where you could do anything you wanted to him, and you've got Attia eating out of your hand like a pet."

"That's not fair!" hissed Attia.

"You've given me endless reasons not to trust you, Raelyn, yet here I am, willing to work with you. Willing to trust you," said Malcolm. "As far as I'm concerned, it's your turn to trust me."

Raelyn looked away. "Very well. If you say it must happen now, then I'll have to trust you on that." She returned her gaze to Malcolm, her eyes smoldering. "We'll use my summoning chamber. I'll show you the way."

Malcolm knew he touched a nerve. He saw the tension in Raelyn's shoulders and heard the anger swelling beneath her words. The glowing red eyes weren't subtle either. If he were to guess, it was his comment about Russell. Rape was a harsh term, but it wasn't unfair. Maybe it was consensual with Attia. With Russell, it wasn't debatable. She stripped him of his freedom, pure and simple.

Malcolm wasn't about to let her forget it.

21
Raelyn

Raelyn did her best to hide her agitation as she led Malcolm and Attia up to her summoning chamber. Malcolm had no right to judge her! He didn't know the long, twisting roads she walked. He couldn't comprehend how much she suffered and how hard she worked to reach her station in life.

Still, he wasn't wrong. What she did to Russell could be fairly described as rape, and she knew kissing Attia was an abuse of trust. Malcolm was well within his rights to think of her as a monster. Fires below, she helped destroy their civilization. How could he not see her as a monster?

Raelyn didn't understand why she cared what Malcolm thought. She destroyed countless lives over the centuries. Twisting hearts and minds was part of being a succubus. It was her birthright, and no one could judge her for it. She was no more guilty than a jungle cat feasting on its prey. She was acting within her nature, pure and simple. Russell and Attia were prey, no more, no less.

But they were more than that to her.

Chariden, and a host of other heartless demons, would see them as prey, but Raelyn wanted to be better than that. She was better precisely because she cared, and sometimes caring meant she needed to sit there and take a verbal beating when some arrogant necromancer kid insulted her.

Especially when he was right.

"Here we are," said Raelyn as she stepped across the hidden runes, triggering the sealed door to open. "Understand that neither of you can enter this room on your own. I need to let you in." She decided not to mention that the runes also opened for Conner. They didn't need to know that.

"This is the room where you and Conner fought the flesh demon, isn't it?" said Malcolm.

"Yes, that's right." Evidently, Conner already told his friends about this room. Hopefully, he didn't tell them he could open the door, but what if he did? Raelyn never swore him to secrecy. In retrospect, she probably should have.

"Do we need to be concerned about any of those runes?" said Malcolm, pointing to several concentric circles of runes carved into the floor.

"Do you think I would have brought you here if the runes were dangerous?" Raelyn was getting tired of justifying herself to Malcolm. All it would take was a few kisses, and he would treat her with the respect she deserved. Oh, how she would enjoy watching him grovel for her attention! Raelyn closed her eyes and pushed the intrusive thoughts away. She needed to be better than that. She wasn't Chariden.

"You're right," said Malcolm softly. "It all comes back to trust, doesn't it?" he said as he stepped across the runes and entered the chamber.

Raelyn smiled and gently nodded. At least Malcolm understood he was being difficult. It made her feel less guilty for fantasizing about charming him. "Don't get too comfortable. We need to select a body."

"Do you want me to bring some up from the morgue?" asked Attia.

Raelyn noticed she didn't call her ma'am or bow her head as she sometimes did when they were flirting. It was probably for the best. There would be time for fun later. "That won't be necessary, Attia. Malcolm can choose from one of the comatose bodies I keep on hand." She pointed to a door halfway down the hall. "Go ahead, Malcolm. Take your pick."

The boy shot Raelyn a nervous glance as he left the summoning chamber and approached the closed door. To his credit, he didn't hesitate after reaching the door. He peered inside for a moment before speaking. "They're still alive. What did you do to them?"

"I did nothing to them," said Raelyn. "They suffer from various maladies that prevent them from waking. Left untouched, most would die in a day or two. I'm keeping them alive for their blood. Many of my rituals require it."

"Ghostly Shell requires a corpse."

"Find a body you like, and make it a corpse," said Raelyn. Malcolm was doing a good job hiding it, but she knew he was uncomfortable. Certainly, he had to have killed before. He was a necromancer, after all.

"Why don't I just grab one from the morgue? It will be easier," said Attia.

"No, it's okay, Attia," said Malcolm. "Fahrilae deserves a fresh body, killed without visible wounds. Raelyn's right. This is for the best."

"You're not really going to kill one of them, are you?" asked Attia.

Raelyn enjoyed watching the little drama between Attia and Malcolm unfold. Both were capable killers in battle, there was no doubt of that, but murdering a defenseless person was much harder.

"Of course I am," said Malcolm. There was an edge of icy finality in his tone. "Think about what I offered the neverlings in exchange for the Ghostly Shell spell, Attia. If I can't do this, stars above, how will I ever be able to do that?"

Attia nodded, but said nothing. She wasn't okay with any of this. Had Raelyn known how Attia was going to react, she would have handled the situation differently. The last thing she wanted to do was make Attia uncomfortable. She adored the girl. She hated seeing her like this.

Malcolm disappeared into the room for several minutes. The entire time, Attia just stood there, gazing at the wall. Raelyn needed to make it up to her. Later in the day, she planned to invite Attia back for a little fun. Achillion was going to be away for several days, dealing with the recent attacks on Middletown. No one would disturb them.

"It's done," said Malcolm as he stepped back into the hallway. "I hate to ask, but can someone help me carry the—"

"I'll do it," blurted Raelyn. She didn't even give Malcolm a chance to finish his sentence. The last thing she wanted to do was make Attia carry the body.

"Thanks. I chose the young woman on the left. The one with the dark hair."

The pillow Malcolm used to suffocate the girl was still resting on her stomach. Raelyn gave Malcolm credit for performing the deed himself. She half expected him to summon a spirit to take care of the grisly task. By all accounts, Malcolm did a good job. Other than a few specs of red in her eyes, there wasn't a mark on the girl's body.

Carefully cradling the dead girl in her arms, Raelyn carried her into the next room. Both Malcolm and Attia quietly followed along. The moment of silence was nice. In many ways, it was the calm before the storm. Raelyn took advantage of it by letting her thoughts drift to more pleasant topics. Perhaps she'd share a bath with Attia this afternoon. Would that be too forward?

Raelyn set the corpse on the ground, just outside the concentric circles of runes. "If you're standing inside the runes, will you be able to make Fahrilae appear outside of them?"

Malcolm shook his head. "I don't think so. These are Runes of Protection versus Undead, I take it."

"Yes," said Raelyn. "One of the circles, at least."

"I don't have great control over where she appears, but it shouldn't matter," said Malcolm. "As long as I don't lose control when I bring her across, she'll remain friendly until I start casting Ghostly Shell. At least, that's what the Other says should happen."

"The Other is the Dark Lord, right?" asked Raelyn. Conner refused to talk openly about his friends' El'orin, but scattered details emerged throughout their conversations. Those details, combined with the extensive notes Russell prepared for her back at the Citadel, made things relatively easy to piece together. Burning those notes was unfortunate, but letting Chariden get her hands on them wasn't an option.

Malcolm stared at her for a long moment before nodding. "In life, he was the Dark Lord. He died roughly three centuries ago."

If what Raelyn knew of the history was true, the Dark Lord fell while assaulting Chariden, in Nerreka. Had the neverlings not betrayed him, he might have defeated her. Netherworld scholars held differing opinions about what might have happened had the Dark Lord vanquished the Demon Queen. Some thought demons would have been cast out of this world. Others speculated that what Chariden accomplished could not be undone, and that demons would remain.

"Are we ready?" asked Malcolm.

"Are you sure I can't convince you to wait until tomorrow?" asked Raelyn.

Malcolm shook his head.

Raelyn's power was diminished from saving Liam. Another day of rest would largely replenish her. If Malcolm lost control,

Raelyn wasn't sure how much help she'd be. "If we must do this today, let's get it over with."

Malcolm reached into a pouch and produced three Soulstones. He carefully arranged them in his left hand before placing his right palm on top of them. He rested his staff in the crook of his right arm. Taking a deep breath, he slid his hands back and forth slowly. His eyes were milky white, his pupils barely visible.

Gradually, three distinct shadowy figures manifested in front of Malcolm. Raelyn thought she saw thin lines of shadow flowing out from Malcolm's hands, but she couldn't be sure. An instant later, a slender disc of darkness materialized above them. In the blink of an eye, the three shadows were sucked up into the disc of darkness. At the same time, a single, much more vibrant creature of shadow appeared.

Icy wind raced through the chamber with enough force to blast Raelyn's wings back. Attia took a step back, shivering. Fingers of frost stretched across Malcolm's forehead, and patches of ice appeared in his hair. He shivered violently, but the intensity of his gaze never wavered.

"Greetings, young lord." The ghost's voice was like frozen wind howling through the city at night. "I must admit, I'm pleased with the vessel you've chosen for me. She's young, pretty, and undamaged." The ghost faced Raelyn. "You have my thanks, demon."

Raelyn bowed her head slightly. She was used to facing ancient, powerful beings. Fires below, she just held her first Demonic Court, yet something about Fahrilae disturbed her. "I was happy to help."

"This next part will be difficult, young lord. I hope you're prepared," said the ghost, returning her attention to Malcolm.

"So do I," said Malcolm.

Fahrilae's face was featureless shadow, but Raelyn somehow perceived a wicked smile cross the ghost's lips. "The runic circle will help you, but only so much, young lord. Remember, I am an ancient wizard. A simple Blink spell is all it will take for me to enter your protective circle."

Raelyn cursed under her breath. "That's a problem."

Malcolm gripped his staff in one hand. He used his other to trace a sigil of golden light in front of him. It quickly condensed to a brilliant star before racing off toward Fahrilae, where it vanished from view.

"One Dispel won't save you, young lord," said the ghost.

"I'll cast another, but that's about all I can afford. Ghostly Shell is costly to cast," said Malcolm as he quickly crafted another sigil of golden light.

"Allow me to help," said Raelyn as she quickly built a series of four Dispels. She sent each at Fahrilae, where they would remain to counter any spell the ghost tried to cast. Combined with Malcolm's magic, Fahrilae needed to fight through six bursts of Countermagic before she could cast a spell. Raelyn hoped it would be enough. She wanted to conserve what little power she had left.

"I will kill Malcolm quickly, should he fail to bind me," said Fahrilae. "If Malcolm perishes, I highly recommend that no one else moves against me. I don't wish to harm either of you, but if you pose a threat to me, I won't hesitate."

Raelyn didn't like Fahrilae's tone. Sure, the ghost was ancient, but Raelyn was nine centuries old. She didn't think she would fall easily to Fahrilae, but she wasn't willing to risk it. If Raelyn was at full power, things might go much differently. Right now, she thought Fahrilae was providing good counsel.

"I can't heal you, Malcolm," said Attia. "Not until I harvest another El'orin. I'm not sure how much help I can offer."

"This isn't your fight, Attia. You don't need to be here."

Attia shook her head. "I want to be here. I care about both of you. If either of you are in danger, my place is here, at your side."

Raelyn quickly parsed Attia's words. The girl was definitely loyal to her friends. Attia's comments about harvesting an El'orin to restore her ability to heal Malcolm intrigued her. Back when Raelyn fought for her life against the flesh demon, Conner used his El'orin to restore her power. Could Attia's El'orin heal her, potentially saving her from a mortal wound?

"Please stand next to the body, Fahrilae. I'd like to get started," said Malcolm.

The ghost drifted over to the body of the dead girl. The moment she got there, before she even turned around, Malcolm raised his arms and began chanting. Once again, icy wind blew through the chamber, causing a stack of Raelyn's parchments to swirl chaotically around the room.

Malcolm shouted as Fahrilae spun around. She lunged at him, impossibly fast, but a barrier of emerald light snapped into existence, forcing the ghost to retreat. The Runes of Protection versus Undead worked.

Fahrilae wasted no time. Sapphire light danced at her fingertips, but quickly faded behind a pair of miniature golden explosions. It took both of Malcolm's Dispels to stop a single Blink spell from Fahrilae.

The ghost resumed casting, and the first of Raelyn's Dispels flared to life. Fires below, Fahrilae was strong! Her magic easily ripped through the first Dispel before fading against the second. Undaunted, Fahrilae started preparing another spell.

Raelyn quickly crafted another Dispel, completing it just as Fahrilae's magic tore through Raelyn's remaining two. No wonder the ghost was so confident. Her magical skills surpassed Raelyn's. To make matters worse, Blink spells were quick and relatively cheap to cast. Trying to hold Fahrilae at bay with Dispels was a losing battle.

Malcolm screamed, and several slender tendrils of mist began flowing away from Fahrilae's ghostly body. If Fahrilae noticed it was happening, she didn't care. She continued weaving her spells, triggering the new Dispel Raelyn just put in place. With all competing magic spent, Fahrilae disappeared in a flash of blue, reappearing next to Malcolm, within the runic circle.

Fahrilae passed her hands through Malcolm's body twice, causing thick patches of ice to form. To his credit, Malcolm never lost focus. He kept chanting, his hands held high. Gradually, the slender tendrils of shadowy mist thickened into swirling vortices. Fahrilae's body dimmed. She reached out for Malcolm, but it was as if she was being sucked into the corpse on the other side of the room.

She screamed and howled, but the suction grew stronger, until Fahrilae's ghostly body broke apart, only to be quickly absorbed by the corpse on the ground. A moment later, the body of the dead girl climbed to her feet. She was smiling. "Well done, young lord. You've made your first revenant."

Raelyn should have been overjoyed, or at least relieved, but an irresistible anger washed over her. Malcolm should have waited. He should have listened to her! Fahrilae nearly killed him, and who knew what would have happened afterwards.

Malcolm sank to his knees, coughing and panting. One of his arms hung limply at his side, and he was violently shivering. Fahrilae's touch nearly froze him to death. "That... That was harder than I expected," he stammered.

"Let's talk about trust," hissed Raelyn. She didn't understand where her anger was coming from, but it was powerful, passionate, and righteous. This child dared to question her honesty. He called her a rapist and a monster! "I just saved your life."

Malcolm closed his eyes. "Yes, you-you da-da-did." His teeth were chattering so badly he barely managed to get the words out.

"Good," said Raelyn. "From now on, I expect your respect. I've more than earned your trust. Now say it. Tell me you trust me!"

"I... I tru-tru-trust you."

Raelyn felt a wave of joy wash over her. Seeing this arrogant boy kneeling before her, pledging his trust, made her dark heart sing, but she needed more. "That's not good enough. I want to hear the Dark Lord say it!"

"Stop it, Raelyn. You're scaring me," said Attia as she stepped in front of Malcolm.

"He tr-trusts." Malcolm took a series of deep breaths until his teeth stopped chattering. "He trusts you, Raelyn. We both do."

The burning anger faded, disappearing as quickly as it arrived. "I'm sorry, I don't know what came over me," said Raelyn. She wasn't sorry for challenging Malcolm. She felt she more than earned his trust today, but she wasn't accustomed to losing control like that.

"Well, that was exhilarating," said Fahrilae. Her voice was breathy, with a pleasant, almost musical tone.

"Once you've safely escorted them home, please return to me, Attia," said Raelyn. "Achillion will be gone all day, and I'd like some company."

Attia looked at Malcolm nervously. She seemed scared. "I don't know, Raelyn."

"Please," said Raelyn, her voice almost a whisper. She didn't want to beg, but if Attia resisted, she feared she might. What was happening to her? One moment she was seething with righteous anger, and the next, she was desperate, almost simpering.

"Okay," said Attia.

"Thank you," said Raelyn, relief washing over her.

"You're welcome."

Raelyn rolled her neck and stretched her wings. "It has been quite an interesting morning, I suspect for all of us. Thank you for trusting me enough to let me help you, Malcolm. If you don't mind, I'll take the liberty of preparing you a special room here. It will come in handy if you need to make more revenants."

"I appreciate it," said Malcolm.

"Don't mention it. I'm happy to help." Raelyn couldn't read Malcolm's reaction. For all she knew, he thought she was crazy. Then again, maybe she was.

Something was happening to Raelyn, and she needed to find out what.

22
Eliana

Eliana peered through the window at the frozen streets outside the greenhouse. The snow was coming down much harder than last night, and the temperature seemed to be dropping. She couldn't help but remember Debhara's warnings. She said the winds might blow harder, or the snows might grow deeper, or the air might grow colder. As far as Eliana could tell, all of that was happening.

But the bitter weather wasn't preventing Eliana's followers from gathering. She started noticing them a few weeks ago. At first, it was just a handful of people. A few carried colorful flags or banners proclaiming her as some sort of Harvest Goddess. All in all, Eliana thought they were harmless. Liam offered to station a team of Bumbles outside to prevent them from gathering, but she turned him down.

Eliana wondered if she needed to revisit that decision. Over the weeks, their numbers swelled, but not dramatically so. She wasn't worried about twenty or thirty people gathering each morning. On a certain level, she didn't blame them. The city was starving. They were desperate for food, and despite the horrible winter, Eliana's crops were flourishing. It was only a matter of time before some came to view her as a Goddess.

But Eliana wasn't a Goddess, she knew that. Then again, her connection with the natural world was supernaturally deep. The Goldthorn Berries responded to her, and her alone. Vines and branches leapt to life in her presence, eager to defend her at the slightest signs of danger. Plants flourished beneath her touch, and the winds and weather answered her call.

Perhaps people were right to worship her.

Dozens of new followers gathered in the streets this morning. Despite her difficulty seeing through the blowing snow, Eliana recognized some of them from last night. They were out there, in the streets of Middletown, following her as she summoned snow and rain to extinguish the roaring flames. For all she knew, some of them heard her call out to Debhara. To them, she was the person who bargained with the storm itself to save the city from fire and ash.

To them, she was a Goddess, and they were here to worship her.

The sound of a door closing shook Eliana free from her thoughts. Malcolm and Attia were back. A small figure, wrapped in dark robes, was with them. Eliana didn't know who the newcomer was, but she suspected it was Malcolm's ghost, Fahrilae, in her new body. That was why Attia took him to the House of Healing, after all.

Lord Rumblesnort Bunny-Fur hissed and growled at the robed figure. Attia crouched and beckoned the cat over, but Rumblesnort backed away, preferring to hide within a nearby forest of Ganna trees.

"Well, the cat definitely hates you," said Malcolm.

The robed figure pulled back her cowl, revealing pale skin and long black hair. Something about her eyes troubled Eliana, but she couldn't quite put her finger on it. Otherwise, she thought the young woman was rather pretty. If Eliana were to guess, she thought the girl was a few years older than she was.

"I'm pleased to finally meet you in the flesh, Eliana," said the woman. "If you haven't figured it out yet, I'm Fahrilae."

A couple of arborists and a passing group of Bumbles noted the newcomer and the conversation, but no one seemed alarmed. It didn't surprise Eliana. She knew Fahrilae was a corpse, yet she struggled to notice anything odd about her. Perhaps her skin was a shade too white, and there was something creepy about her eyes, but otherwise, she looked perfectly normal. "You're not what I expected. I thought you'd look more..." Realizing that she was about to say something cruel, Eliana let her words trail off.

"Dead?" asked Fahrilae.

"I guess so," said Eliana.

Malcolm glanced at a group of arborists tending some nearby Ganna trees. "Shall we resume this conversation in my chambers?"

"If you don't mind, I should probably head back to the House of Healing," said Attia. Eliana wasn't certain, but she thought Attia looked nervous.

"By all means," said Malcolm as he made his way to the entrance of his suite of rooms. "After you, ladies," he said, beckoning Eliana and Fahrilae to join him.

Eliana waited for the revenant to enter before following. She didn't know what she hoped to gain by the delay. She probably felt uncomfortable walking in front of a living corpse, but she knew she wasn't being rational. Fahrilae wasn't her enemy.

Once inside, Malcolm gestured to a table and chairs. His main room was surprisingly pleasant. The doors leading to his sleeping chambers, library, and workroom were closed. Rich green and white tapestries hung from the walls, and a thick brown rug covered much of the floor. A small hearth was inset into the far wall, but it wasn't lit. Despite the winter weather outside, the greenhouse remained surprisingly warm.

Fahrilae took a seat on the far side of the table, leaving Eliana the closest chairs to choose from. Malcolm yawned as he took his seat at the head of the table. He looked more exhausted than usual. Eliana didn't feel like sitting, but she didn't want to seem rude, so she took a seat next to Malcolm, as far away from Fahrilae as she could without being obvious about it.

"Thank you for offering me a home within your greenhouse," said Fahrilae.

Eliana didn't remember making any such offer, but then she remembered her conversation with Malcolm. As a ghost, Fahrilae was always near Malcolm, hidden with the Astral Plane. She, of course, heard the conversation. "You saved my life. This place wouldn't be here without you. Actually, without both of you."

Fahrilae glanced at Malcolm. "Still, it is rare for a revenant to experience kindness from one of the living. I'm not used to it." She paused and fixed her creepy, piercing gaze on Eliana. "It means more to me than you might know."

Eliana resisted the urge to push her chair away from the table. Although Fahrilae's words were kind, she was still a corpse. "You're very welcome."

"I will do my best to remain within Malcolm's chambers as much as possible," said Fahrilae. "Even within a body, my ghostly touch devours life. I suspect your lovely plants will suffer around me."

A wave of anger surged through Eliana. "Do not harm my plants," she hissed.

"I will take great care around them," said Fahrilae with a disarming smile. "Fortunately, Malcolm's chambers rest on the far side of the greenhouse. It should be easy for me to slip in and out without damaging the foliage."

Malcolm gently tapped the table with his fingers. "Slip in and out? Are you planning to explore the city?"

"I think patrol would be a better term for it. With Attia often away, and with Liam indisposed, this greenhouse is vulnerable."

"Vulnerable to what?" asked Eliana. She worked so hard to put the demon with the red suit out of her mind, she stopped considering how vulnerable her greenhouse was.

"For starters, the sewers beneath this place connect with the ring tunnels, making them accessible to anyone or anything living beneath the city."

Malcolm frowned. "You raise a good point. I suspect some of Plaguebringer's forces are still living down there."

"The Hidden Tower is down there also," said Fahrilae.

Malcolm leaned forward. "I thought the neverlings were afraid of the greenhouse. You said they tend to avoid it."

"In the Astral Plane, yes," said Fahrilae. "It's because of Eliana's Goldthorn Berries, but I suspect the berries are far less frightening to the neverlings in the real world."

"My Goldthorn Berries are visible in the Astral Plane?" asked Eliana.

Fahrilae nodded. "They're quite breathtaking. They permeate this entire place. Recently, their golden tendrils have crawled beneath the streets, and dug deep into the sewers."

Eliana grinned. It was nice to hear about her Goldthorn Berries, though she worried their visibility might attract the wrong kind of attention. "So, can spirits see them from great distances?"

"It's difficult to explain," said Fahrilae. "The simplest answer is no. Most spirits won't notice them unless they happen to pass by this place, but spirits that know how to look for them can spot them from miles away."

"Is that something I need to worry about?"

Fahrilae shrugged. "Powerful spirits that know what to look for will have an easy time finding you. Whether that is good or bad is hard to say."

Eliana couldn't decide if it was good or bad. Spirits seemed to find them, one way or another. So far, her interactions with spirits were positive. Perhaps that would change in the future, but she didn't think it was worth dwelling on. "I understand."

"Speaking of spirits, be careful around the Fury," said Fahrilae. "She's far more powerful than you know."

"Are you talking about the spirit that touched Eliana the night we fought Lamenica?" asked Malcolm.

"Yes," said Fahrilae. "There are four of them, one for each element. I don't know if they've always been here, or only appeared after Chariden shattered the Gaea spirit, but they embody aspects of each element."

Eliana thought back to the warning she received last night. "The wind spirit is named Debhara. Last night, she helped me quench the fires. Otherwise, they might have spread throughout the city."

"Did she say there would be a cost?" asked Fahrilae.

Eliana nodded. "Yes, how did you know?"

"With primal spirits like that, there is always a cost," said Fahrilae. "What did she say?"

"She said if she strengthened the storm for me, the storm would remember. She warned me it might lead to a harsher winter."

"Then I expect that's what will happen."

"Starvation is already becoming an issue," said Malcolm. "The mushrooms they harvested from the mycon fields helped, but they won't last forever."

Eliana wondered if she made a terrible mistake, but how could she have known? Sure, the spirit warned her, but

Debhara's warnings were vague. The fires were a very real and immediate threat. Eliana didn't think there was much choice. Besides, she was doing everything she could to expand the Gana crops. Her crops would never be enough to feed everyone, but every little bit helped.

"Hopefully it won't be too bad," said Malcolm, but he lacked conviction.

"Perhaps, but I'd prepare for the worst," said Fahrilae. "Debhara has been observing Eliana for quite some time. I've studied her from afar, and I must admit, she scares me. Nothing good will come from working with her."

"How can you say that?" snapped Eliana. "She helped me kill Lamenica. She extinguished the fires last night."

"My apologies," said Fahrilae, bowing her head. "May I try to explain?"

Eliana wasn't sure she wanted to hear it, but she nodded.

"The Astral Plane is not kind to spirits who resist its oblivion. It erodes their minds, slowly stripping away memories and aspects of their personalities, leaving terrible voids. For ghosts, those voids are often filled with an insatiable hunger to feast on the living. With Debhara, I suspect the Astral filled her voids with seething anger."

"But you can resist it, right?" asked Eliana. "After all, you're sitting here talking with us. You don't seem like you're on the verge of feasting on our life energy."

"Malcolm's magic is protecting me," said Fahrilae. "Every time he summons me, we fight. Fortunately, he's won every battle, though I think it's more accurate to say your cat, Rumblesnort, won most of the battles for him."

"I don't understand. What is his magic protecting you from?"

"For starters, the Astral Plane," said Fahrilae. "But more importantly, Malcolm's magic protects me from my hunger."

"So, without it, your hunger would drive you to attack us?"

Fahrilae nodded.

"Do you remember when I summoned Constance outside the Darkwood?" asked Malcolm.

"Yes, but my memory of that night isn't great," said Eliana, looking down at her hands. "I had a lot on my mind."

"I didn't attempt to bind Constance. I simply brought her across into our world," said Malcolm. "You might not have seen, but she nearly attacked me. After less than a day in the Astral, her hunger was nearly strong enough to turn her against us."

"And it gets worse and worse as the days pass," said Fahrilae. "The Astral never stops. It constantly erodes those spirits that dare resist it."

"But you seem to know who you are," said Malcolm. "You've been a ghost for centuries, yet you remembered enough of your past to find the Dark Lord within me."

"I've forgotten far more than I remember."

"Do you remember fighting the Eater of Worlds?" Eliana wasn't sure if she should bring it up. If nothing else, she wanted to move the conversation away from Debhara. "It was centuries ago. You were one of the Dark Lord's revenants."

"That name, the Eater of Worlds, sounds familiar to me, but I can't picture it." Fahrilae closed her eyes and shook her head. "Sadly, so much of my memory lies in jagged shards and disparate fragments."

"I'm sorry for bringing it up."

"No, not at all," said Fahrilae. "If you wouldn't mind, please tell me the story. Maybe it will help me remember."

Eliana nodded. "I can only tell you what my El'orin shared with me, but who knows, maybe you'll remember something I wasn't shown." She looked at Malcolm and smiled. "Or perhaps the Other will remember something."

She thought about waking Russell, but she decided it was best to let him sleep. The two of them spent most of the night talking. Their conversations were superficial, but pleasant all the same. Neither of them was willing to delve into areas that might hurt the other. Instead, they just retold old jokes and kept each other company. It was nice.

Eliana didn't realize how much she missed it, but she couldn't dwell on it now. She needed to focus on the story she was about to tell.

23
Felerin

Felerin patiently lined up her shot before releasing her arrow. It flew true, sinking deep into the shoulder of a talon, two stories beneath her. She hadn't missed a single shot this morning, but it was becoming increasingly difficult to find undefended targets.

Enormous, armored crabs monsters were interspersed throughout the talon forces. Their gigantic, chitinous claws were strong enough to deflect arrows. They used them to create mobile shields for their allies to move beneath. If Felerin waited long enough, she always found a clear shot, but many of her fellow archers weren't so patient.

Not that she was worried about wasting arrows. Once they determined war was inevitable, the fletchers went to work crafting hundreds of arrows. Even without the crabs defending the talons, Felerin didn't think she'd run out of arrows. With the annoying crabs in the way, she didn't expect to use half her arrows before the day was done.

So far, the battle was going better than she expected. The Lurker started the assault by tearing apart the earthen walls protecting the lowest levels of the city. It didn't take the horrifying beast long to accomplish its task. Dozens of excellent soldiers died in the process, but there was no time to mourn them.

Not now. That would come later.

The first waves of talons attacked immediately after the walls came down, flooding into the breach the Lurker created for them. With so many defenders fleeing the Lurker's initial assault, the talons quickly occupied the lowest level of the city, but advancing beyond that position proved difficult.

In the weeks leading up to the assault, earth mages carved out tunnels and conjured walls, forcing the enemy to navigate a maze of narrow passages to climb beyond the lowest levels of the city. The bottlenecks provided massive advantages to the defenders, especially those with strong armor.

And then there was Gunther.

Standing alone, Gunther guarded one of the wider paths into the higher regions of the city. Despite how hard the talons tried, nothing managed to slip past him. Gunther moved with horrifying speed and precision, spinning his enormous blade around him in wide arcs, leaving little to no space on either side of him.

Felerin didn't understand why the talons continued to fight Gunther. Surely, they saw how easily he was cutting them down. The other pathways up into the city were narrow and heavily guarded, but navigating them had to be safer than facing off against Gunther. She wondered if their willingness to fight him was tied to their honor. It was hard to be certain from such a distance, but she thought she saw talons saluting Gunther before engaging him.

Taking a deep breath to center herself, Felerin lined up her next shot. One of the crab monsters pulled a spearman out of the ranks in one of the side pathways. With the defensive formation weakened, the defenders were being forced to give up ground. They needed help.

Felerin let her arrow fly and was satisfied to see it rip through a talon's back. She quickly let a second and then a third arrow fly. With the talons densely packed, and their crab monster grappling with a spearman, it was difficult to miss. There wasn't a better opportunity to fire. Strangely, Felerin seemed to be the only one shooting. Why weren't the other archers taking advantage of the opportunity?

Taking a moment to survey her surroundings, Felerin's heart sank. Off to the side, a pair of archers were fighting for their lives against a trio of talons. She didn't think they stood a chance in hand-to-hand combat. The talons were faster, stronger, and far more experienced. How did they make it up to the archers' balcony?

Felerin nocked an arrow and patiently waited for a clear shot. Somewhere behind her, she heard a strange sound. It was like a pot or vase shattering. Slowly exhaling, she let her arrow fly. It passed between both archers and slammed into a talon's chest.

One down, two to go.

Behind Felerin, someone screamed her name. She spun around in time to see a talon charging her. Where did he come from? She backpedaled and quickly launched an arrow at his belly. The talon tried to sweep the arrow aside, but was only partially successful. The arrow struck his gut, but didn't strike deep enough to stop him.

The talon lurched forward, a wicked sneer on his face, but he only made it a step before an arrowhead burst through the meat of his shoulder. Felerin flashed a quick grin at the man who fired the arrow, but she caught a flicker of motion out of the corner of her eye. Tracking it, she noticed a pot shattering against the floor of their archery platform. Why? How?

Felerin suddenly understood what was happening!

The talons were using magic to turn their bodies into water. It was something she saw them do in the past. They were filling clay pots with their liquid bodies, hurling the pots deeper into the city, and canceling their spells after the pots shattered. It was ingenious, but terrifying.

Felerin drew back her bowstring and watched as the small puddle of water gradually expanded and grew, taking on a humanoid shape. She didn't think it was facing her, so she wasn't worried about it deflecting her arrow. She waited until the talon's watery body took on the color of skin before letting her arrow fly. It ripped into her target's body, showering the area with blood.

An arrow whizzed past Felerin's shoulder, reminding her there was a fight taking place behind her. "Take care of the other talons. The ones behind me," she shouted to the archer in front of her.

Moving to the railing, Felerin carefully scanned the battlefield beneath her. She wasn't entirely sure what she was looking for, but it didn't take long to spot the problem. A small group of talons were operating what was either an enormous slingshot, or a tiny ballista. Felerin couldn't decide which description was more accurate. She watched as they fired, and sure enough, she noticed a clay pot racing towards her.

Felerin carefully took aim, waiting until the pot was closer before letting her arrow fly. The pot shattered when her arrow struck it, spraying water everywhere. She wondered what scattering a liquified talon would do, but she didn't have time to dwell on it. Focusing on the team of talons below, she rained a volley of arrows down on them.

Many of her shots missed, but Felerin wasn't bothered by it. Her goal was to get their attention and stop them from launching more pots in her direction. As far as she could tell, her plan worked. It only took a few arrows thudding into the ground to convince the talons to retreat beneath cover. Felerin didn't believe her solution was likely to last throughout the morning, but if it lasted even five minutes, she'd count it as a victory.

A deafening, guttural roar echoed across the rainy landscape. Looking beyond the battle raging across the lower levels of the city, Felerin saw the Lurker. Its tentacles coiling and writhing above the surface of the water. Slowly, it snaked its tentacles onto shore, twisting them around trees and solid walls. The tentacles grew taut as the impossibly enormous squid pulled itself closer to New Citadel. She didn't know what it planned to do, but it was definitely getting ready to do something.

"Felerin, watch out!" shouted an archer.

She spun just as the crouching talon leapt at her. She didn't know where it came from, but it didn't matter. Felerin swept the length of her bow across her body, pushing one of her enemy's blades to the side, but the other one bit into her side. Blinding needles of pain raced through her body. The icy burn of poison flowing through her veins immediately followed.

Felerin frantically backpedaled, hoping to escape, but the talon was too fast. She retrieved an arrow and tried to stab him with it, but he stabbed her first, this time driving his blades into her belly. The pain paralyzed her, but only for a moment.

This was not how she was going to die!

Memories of Constance's melting body raced through her mind. She remembered the glowing tornado of insects, the excruciating pain that ripped through her body that night, and how she fought through it all to deliver a raft to her friends. Felerin was a protector, a warrior, and a Pathfinder. Too many people were counting on her!

Screaming at the top of her lungs, she sent her battlemagic racing through her veins. She registered the talon's blade, plunging into her belly again, but she no longer felt pain. Dropping her bow, she drove her arrow into the meatiest part of the talon's shoulder. Once she was satisfied it was buried in his flesh, she retrieved another from her quiver.

The talon thrust into her again. A chill washed over her as blood poured from her eviscerated belly, but she couldn't afford to slow down. Ignoring his deadly weapons and her lethal wounds, Felerin drove her next arrow through the hollow of the talon's throat. The arrow slowed as she bit into his windpipe, but the resistance only lasted a moment. Pressing with all her might, screaming at the top of her lungs, she forced the arrow clean through her enemy's throat.

He stared at her for a moment, confused, before crumpling to the ground. Felerin tried to walk, but with the immediate danger gone, her legs were no longer responding. She stumbled and fell, landing next to the dying talon.

Felerin shivered as the blood raced from her body. She heard people shouting all around her, but she couldn't make out the words. Her fingers trembling, she slipped her hand around her necklace, feeling for the tiny vial it held.

24
Gunther

Gunther fought the urge to throw up. The combination of oily potions and bitter herbs wasn't sitting well with him, but he couldn't complain about the effects. He never felt faster or stronger. His wounds were healing on their own. Hell, he could even fly.

But he knew it wouldn't make a difference. Right now, he was fighting through hordes of talons. Gunther felt like he could do that all day, but all his successes would come crashing to a halt once the Lurker joined the fight. When it roared, he thought it was calling out to him. As it gradually pulled some of its massive bulk onto shore, he knew it was coming for him.

Another wave of talons bowed their heads before spreading out before him. Gunther nodded to the group, accepting their challenge. He couldn't help but respect them. There were many paths leading farther into the city. None of the talons needed to fight him, but they were lining up for the opportunity. Gunther believed it was a matter of honor for the talons. He didn't understand the first thing about their culture, but he didn't need to. They were warriors, just like him.

Some things transcended culture.

The first two talons approached from the left, one with long blades mounted to her wrists, and the other carrying a wicked-looking spear. Another talon, carrying two slender blades, carefully approached from the right. All three moved cautiously. They undoubtably witnessed what happened to all the talons who haphazardly charged, thinking they might overwhelm Gunther. It didn't end well for them.

Taking a step forward and to the right, Gunther thrust his blade, forcing the talon with the twin swords to retreat. In the same motion, he pivoted, swinging his sword to the left in a waist-high arc. The passage Gunther chose to defend was the perfect width for him. Standing in the center, reaching with one hand, he could barely touch his blade to the walls on either side. It was easy for him to cover the entire width of the passageway, making it next to impossible for anyone to slip behind him.

Throughout the morning, many tried and a few even succeeded at gaining his back, but in each case, Gunther's armor protected him. He suffered several wounds, but nothing serious. The Potion of Rejuvenation he drank was healing many of his injuries before he even noticed them.

The talon with the blades on her wrists dove, somersaulting beneath Gunther's cut, while the one with the spear waited for Gunther's sword to pass by before lunging. Pain exploded from Gunther's shoulder, but he didn't think the wound was dangerous. The spear pierced his armor, but it didn't strike deep.

Sliding back to the center, Gunther delivered a push kick to the talon who somersaulted toward him. While she seemed prepared for the attack, Gunther's surprising speed caught her off guard. She tried to roll with the kick, but with the wall there, she didn't have room to complete her roll. Gunther cut her down before she regained her footing.

Blades clanged against Gunther's legs as the one with the swords slid in behind him. The talon was smart to direct his attacks low. The armor was weaker there, but it was easily strong enough to deflect cutting blades. Using his outstretched blade to challenge the spear, Gunther turned and backhanded the talon with the twin swords. His opponent was quick enough to roll his shoulder, protecting his jaw, but the impact forced him to stagger back.

Pressing his advantage, Gunther finished his turn, swinging his sword in the process. The talon pivoted, crossing both his swords in front of him to defend, but his blades were far too slender to deflect the magic and weight of Gunther's blade. The talon didn't even flinch as the enormous sword carved into his chest. He merely bowed his head for a moment before collapsing.

Gunther turned, but the remaining talon was too fast. His spear slid perfectly through the seams of Gunther's plate armor. Normally, the chain resting beneath the plate would slow the spear, but the talon wielded his weapon with incredible skill and strength. Gunther winced as the spear slid through muscle and slipped between his ribs, puncturing his lung. He would have laughed if the wind wasn't suddenly knocked out of him.

Gunther grabbed the spear a few inches from where it entered his body. The shaft was made of some form of petrified wood, reinforced with strips of metal, but Gunther snapped it easily. Even without potions and herbs to bolster his strength, he was strong enough to shatter spears and staves.

The talon retreated, surprised, but he quickly regrouped, brandishing the broken shaft as if there were still a spearhead attached. Gunther bowed his head, for just a moment, before swinging his sword at the nearly defenseless talon. At the last moment, he swiveled his wrist, striking with the flat of his blade. The impact was great enough to send his opponent flying into the wall. He likely broke several ribs, but the blow wasn't lethal.

Another group of talons, waiting for their turn to fight, looked at their fallen comrade, unsure of what to do. Gunther pointed at the body and flicked his fingers. He wanted them to pull the warrior to safety, but he didn't think the talons understood. Gunther pointed to the spear sticking in his side, then to the talon on the ground, then finally away from the battle.

It took a moment, but eventually a pair of talons crept forward and grabbed their fallen companion, pulling him to safety. One of them never took his eyes off Gunther the whole time, but the other was brave enough to turn his back. That one understood. He knew Gunther was showing respect to the only opponent who seriously wounded him. He understood that Gunther wouldn't harm him for his efforts.

A shadow stretched across the battlefield as the Lurker sent several of its tentacles high into the sky, blocking out what little light the overcast sky provided. Gunther kept his gaze on the next group of talons, but when they turned and faced the sky, he knew he was safe to shift his focus. Compared to the Lurker, they were all insects. Even if the enormous squid was fighting on behalf of the talons, Gunther knew it wouldn't think twice about crushing them. It probably wouldn't even notice.

Grabbing the tiny vial around his neck, he popped the cork and downed the precious few drops of the Water of Life he brought with him. Many, if not most, of the soldiers fighting today carried similar vials, leaving New Citadel with very little to spare.

A deafening, guttural roar echoed across the rainy landscape as the Lurker's tentacles came racing down. The talons cried out and ran, doing their best to scatter from the deepening shadows appearing around them. As much as Gunther didn't want to abandon his post, he thought the talons had the right idea. At least one of those tentacles was likely to land nearby, and Gunther wasn't about to risk getting crushed.

Leaping into the air, he willed his Potion of Flight into effect. This was only his third time using such a potion, but he thought he was getting the hang of it. He controlled the magic with his thoughts, but he felt all the exertion within his muscles. If he twisted in the air, his sides ached. If he forced himself to fly faster, his legs burned, almost as if he were sprinting.

Gunther flew high into the air as the tentacles came slamming down to earth. He counted four of the monstrous appendages. The crash of them smashing into earthen walls and pavement was nearly loud enough to drown out the screams of the poor creatures the enormous tentacles crushed.

And the Lurker wasn't done. Two of its tentacles twisted and coiled around some of the pillars supporting the base of New Citadel, while the two longest tentacles reached out for supporting structures higher within the city. All at once, the Lurker's tentacles tightened, causing the entire hill to rumble and groan. Gunther couldn't believe his eyes. It was climbing! As far as he was concerned, the Lurker belonged in the water. Nothing that massive should be able to climb!

The Lurker's green, glowing eye flashed, blazing with new intensity. The light from the eye was so bright, it beamed, like how a lantern might paint a path across a predawn fog. The beam danced around the battlefield, glimpsing its surroundings, until it came to rest on Gunther.

Why did it care about him? Maybe the talons warned the Lurker about him, or maybe it sensed the El'orin inside of him. Gunther didn't think it mattered. If that enormous squid was coming for him, he didn't plan to make it easy. Taking a deep breath, Gunther flew straight up, climbing high above New Citadel and the Lurker.

Several streams of electricity flowed down from the upper reaches of the city, striking the Lurker all across its body. The monster howled and smoked, but otherwise ignored the blasts. Gunther guessed it would take the Lightning of a hundred or more wizards to destroy the Lurker. By his count, they were about ninety short.

Slowly, the Lurker climbed. It was horrifyingly beautiful to watch how it rhythmically flexed and released its tentacles, tightening its coils, inch by inch. At the same time, it pressed several tentacles against the ground beneath it, both pushing and stabilizing its incredible mass.

More bolts of electricity rained down from above, but if the Lurker noticed, it wasn't showing it. Gunther considered diving and hacking at the thing, but what good would it do? If the strongest mages in New Citadel weren't even getting its attention, what did Gunther hope to accomplish? Maybe he could stab it in the eye, or slice into one of the tentacles supporting the Lurker's weight, but he doubted any of that would hurt the enormous squid.

"Don't sell yourself short, old friend," whispered a familiar voice.

Gunther wondered if the potions and herbs were playing tricks on his mind. Arronhelm was gone. He said his last goodbyes to the ancient wizard long ago. Was that really his voice?

"You set me free, but I never left you," said Arronhelm. *"Gallisandra and I have been watching over you. Remember, she sees the future. She knew this day would come."*

The Lurker shook and howled as a pair of massive arrowheads tore through its body, sending a stream of bright blue blood showering the streets below. Falstaff must have triggered some of the ballistae. Despite what appeared to be direct hits, the Lurker didn't release its grip. If anything, it was climbing faster now.

"I know how hard it's been for you...how lonely you've become," said Arronhelm. *"If you're ready, we'd love for you to join us."*

Gunther was exhausted to his core. The mere thought of joining his good friend in the next world made his eyes sting with tears. He lived far longer than he was meant to. His world died when the Citadel fell. Ever since, Gunther lived as a shadow, drifting through a world he didn't belong in.

"Again, don't sell yourself short, old friend. Yes, the Citadel fell, but its people live on, in no small part, because of you."

What was the point of rebuilding if it was all destined to come crumbling down? The Lurker was going to destroy them all. They were powerless against it. All the suffering and hard work that went into building their new home was wasted effort. In the end, they would have been better off dying to defend the Citadel. They never should have fled into the swamps.

"Nonsense," said Arronhelm, his voice gentle. *"Do you really think I would do that to you? Like I said, Gallisandra sees the future. She knew this attack would happen, but she couldn't see how it would end. In my mind, that means there's still a chance we might win."*

Gunther drifted to the side, narrowly avoiding a swiping tentacle. Despite the ballistae and all the lightning raining down from above, the Lurker's glowing green eye seemed fixated on him. Could it see Arronhelm and Gallisandra? The Lurker was an incredibly powerful creature. It wouldn't surprise Gunther if it could see spirits and other things outside of ordinary sight.

"I would like to help you, if you'll let me," said Arronhelm.

Of course, Gunther wanted Arronhelm's help! Why was his friend even asking?

"It will be different this time," said Arronhelm. *"Before, I was a part of you, but things changed when you released me.*

Accepting me back inside you again will be excruciating. It won't take long for my presence to kill you." Arronhelm paused. *"I know you said you're ready to join us in the next world, but are you absolutely certain? Once I possess you, there's no going back."*

"What are you waiting for?" shouted Gunther. "You know I want this!"

Incomprehensible pain washed over Gunther's body as the spirit of Arronhelm entered him. It was like nothing he ever experienced before. The sensations were too intense for him to process. He couldn't decide if he was burning or freezing. He didn't know if he was screaming in agony or crying in ecstasy. It was simultaneously both. The best and worst things he ever felt.

And Gunther welcomed it!

25
Conner

Conner winced as he pressed the long cut running across his palm, forcing the flow of blood to resume. As much as he hated using his own blood when Communing with the Netherworld, he couldn't afford not to. It made the imps happier, and happy imps were more likely to help him.

Conner needed all the help he could get.

Fortunately, Raelyn designed her summoning circles with narrow channels. According to her, they required far less blood to fill than standard summoning circles. Conner had little reason to doubt Raelyn. She was always honest with him. Sometimes to a fault.

Turning his hand sideways, Conner watched his blood flow into the summoning circle's channels. He hoped Daemenos answered his call today. The last time he attempted to reach out to an imp, Barrister Valargus answered his call. Conner found the experience incredibly unpleasant. The obnoxious tap-dancing imp refused to do anything for Conner unless he agreed to appear on the Netten and Naga show, but that wouldn't happen. Conner wasn't dumb enough to agree to anything like that.

Conner quietly chanted as streams of his blood crawled through the channels. Deciding there was enough, he forced a tiny burst of healing into his hand, barely sealing the wound. All the while, his blood oozed around the channels, finally coming together to form an uninterrupted circle. The moment the circle closed, there was a sighing hiss, and the room grew much hotter. The stone floor inside the circular river of blood became black and reflective, like obsidian. A transparent, slightly wavering face became visible against the darkness.

"Who dares summon Justinivious the Magnificent, almost the greatest among imps?"

A streak of white ran the length of Justinivious' nose. Conner thought it was some kind of face paint. Countless earrings hung from each ear. Most of the pieces were almost comically fake, but a few of the earrings looked valuable. A pair of glowing, colorful rings hung from each nostril. Raelyn made those for him. He also wore a surprisingly tasteful necklace. For whatever reason, the mixture of quality pieces and laughable fakes somehow worked for the strange little imp.

"Speak, mortal!" commanded Justinivious in a high-pitched, almost squeaky voice. "I was nearly Imp of the Year. My time is way more important."

Conner suppressed a snicker. Raelyn talked about Justinivious before. She genuinely seemed to like him, and now Conner understood why. At first blush, he seemed obnoxiously arrogant, but it was all a show. "Oh, great imp," said Conner, playing along. "I hope you find my blood a welcome offering."

Justinivious regarded him for a moment, his eyes narrowing to slits. "Yes, indeed. Very tasty."

"Good, I am pleased." Conner closed his eyes and considered how to phrase the next part. Daemenos was who he needed to talk to, but he didn't want to offend Justinivious. "While you could easily answer my questions, I feel it is beneath you, oh mighty imp. Perhaps another in your office would be more appropriate for my simple request. Is Daemenos available?"

Justinivious peered off to the left. "I suppose that might be better. I is super busy, after all."

"Is that Raelyn?" came a muffled voice from off to the side. Conner thought it sounded like Daemenos.

"No," whispered Justinivious. "It's her hooman."

"Perfect. I've been meaning to talk to him." The voice sounded clearer and closer now. Conner was certain it was Daemenos.

Justinivious faced Conner. He leaned forward and squinted one eye, almost like he was winking. "I've decided I'm too busy for you. One of my servants will take over now."

"Thank you, oh wise and powerful imp."

"Yes, of course," said Justinivious with a dismissive wave of his hand before slowly backing away.

As Justinivious disappeared, another imp slid into view. Conner immediately recognized him as Daemenos. "Good to see ya, kid," said Daemenos. "Cinderhorn warned me... Eh, I mean told me you might reach out." The transparent image of Daemenos smiled, showing off his diamond studded teeth.

Conner didn't appreciate Daemenos' humor, but it was part of the cost of doing business. "I take it he told you about my brother?"

"Yeah, he did," said Daemenos, looking down. "Tough break, kid, but I think you and Raelyn found a good solution with them Runes of Stasis."

Conner wasn't sure how he felt about Cinderhorn discussing his problem with Daemenos. On one hand, it was a violation of trust, but Cinderhorn may have been legitimately trying to help. As much as Conner wanted to believe he could solve this problem on his own, he knew it was folly. He needed Cinderhorn's and Raelyn's help. "So, you know what I'm looking for, don't you?"

"Of course, I do," said the imp with a nod. "Before we begin, how about you pour some more blood into that circle. It's drying out. A crackly connection makes it hard for me to concentrate."

The summoning circle wasn't drying out. Daemenos was just trying to coax him into spending more of his blood. Conner considered refusing the request, but decided against it. Daemenos seemed to crave the upper hand in their discussions. Things would go better if he let the imp have his way.

Pressing against the cut on his palm, Conner reopened his wound. He let a few healthy globs of blood splash into the channels, but nothing more. He wanted to comply with Daemenos' request without offering too much. Once again, he sealed the wound with a tiny burst of healing magic.

"Oh yeah, that's the stuff!" Daemenos leaned back, closed his eyes, and inhaled deeply. "Come on now, don't be stingy. Keep it coming."

"We haven't even started negotiating yet," said Conner. "Let's not get ahead of ourselves."

"Well done. Never bargain against yourself with an experienced imp. Force him to set the terms," advised Conner's Demon.

"Alright," said Daemenos, waving his hands. "What exactly are you looking for from me?"

"I thought you already knew."

"I know what Cinderhorn told me, but I want to hear it from you," said the imp. "I'm a professional. You know... thorough."

"Careful," warned Conner's Demon.

Conner took a deep breath. "I need to heal my brother, but none of my spells can help him. Raelyn's spells can't do it either."

"So, you're looking for magic from another world. Specifically, you're looking for a powerful demon, who happens to be a powerful healer, who happens to know magic from another world, and who might be willing to share it with you, for a price." Daemenos pursed his lips and shook his head. "Did I get that right?"

Conner nodded.

"That's a tall order, kid."

"I know."

"Did you ask Raelyn about this? She recently learned healing magic from another world. I get it didn't work out for you, but she seems like a much better candidate for this kind of thing."

"Raelyn worked with the Netten and Naga show to get the last spell," said Conner. "If I involve her, she'll probably be forced to work with them again, and I don't think that's a good idea. I want to protect her from that."

Daemenos leaned in, his eyes bright. "You're not wrong about that. You like her, don't you?"

"Who, Raelyn?"

"Who'd you think I meant, Naga?" Daemenos chuckled. "Of course, I meant Raelyn."

Conner didn't know what Naga looked like. The obsidian panes of glass only worked for demons, but Raelyn described both Netten and Naga to him. He didn't think he'd get along with either of them. "I guess so, but probably not in the way you're thinking." Conner looked down at his hands. "I respect Raelyn. She has been a great mentor to me. I only want success for her."

"Okay," said Daemenos with a nod. "Good to know."

"Each and every piece of information you divulge is valuable to this imp. Stop over sharing!" hissed Conner's Demon.

"Before we go any further, is this something you're capable of?" asked Conner.

"Sure, kid," said Daemenos with a nod. "Healing magic is pretty rare among demons. It won't be hard for me to narrow down a list of potential candidates, but what do we do if none of them have the right spell?"

Conner's mouth dropped. He never even considered the possibility that the spell he wanted didn't exist. "I don't know."

"That's the trouble with this kind of thing. There are no guarantees." Daemenos flashed him a reassured grin. "That doesn't mean we shouldn't try. I mean, even if we can't find the spell you need, we might be able to send a demon to another world to find it. For the right price, mind you."

Conner thought he had useful knowledge to trade, but he was beginning to doubt it would be enough. "Is this a good time to talk about the price?"

"No, not yet," said Daemenos, shaking his head. "First things first, we need to discuss the cost of retaining my services. As much as I like you, I can't do all this legwork for free. Besides, with this kind of thing, you really want to have me on retainer. Trust me about that."

"*He's right,*" said Conner's Demon. "*You need to share your information with him before he can negotiate on your behalf. By paying him, you protect your information. He won't be able to take your information and sell it on his own. Does that make sense?*"

Conner nodded. "I want you to act as my agent in this matter, and I want you to negotiate on my behalf."

"Slow down, kid," said Daemenos. "Just so we're on the same page, you're asking me to do a lot more than legwork here. If you want me to negotiate for you, you need to tell me what you have to offer." Daemenos paused to peer at Conner. "Here's what I need you to understand. If I don't think there's enough there, I'm not going to move forward with this, but you have to pay me all the same. Is that part absolutely clear?"

"So, I need to pay you before having the conversation. Once I've agreed to your terms, I'll share what I have to offer. If you think it's enough to make a deal, you'll try to broker one on my behalf."

"Exactly," said Daemenos. "You pay me before we discuss this any further. If I can work with what you have to offer, I'll give it a shot."

"I understand," said Conner with a nod. "Name your price."

"*You're such a useless twit,*" teased Conner's Demon. "*Name your price? Is that the best you could come up with? I bet his price just went up.*"

"Gotta love the moxie," chuckled Daemenos. "Okay, kid, here we go. I want you to promise never to cast your Banishment spell on Cinderhorn. And just so we're clear, we're talking for like the rest of time here. If you piss him off and he tries to kill you, you'll have to find another way to defend yourself. The Banishment spell is off limits."

"But just against Cinderhorn, right?"

"Correct," said Daemenos with a nod. "Feel free to cast it on other demons, though I'd prefer you didn't."

Agreeing to the terms would forever destroy Conner's ability to oppose Cinderhorn. Banishment was his only chance against a demon like that. Then again, his odds of landing that spell against Cinderhorn were next to nothing to begin with. Was he really giving up all that much? Was the deal even binding?

"*If you agree to his terms, consider the deal binding,*" said Conner's Demon. "*It will be entered into the official ledgers in the Netherworld. Breaking the deal will make you an Oathbreaker. They will hunt you down, but it won't end there. So much suffering. So much agony. Torture is considered a sacred art in the Netherworld.*"

"I agree to your terms," said Conner, before he could reconsider his decision.

"Really? That was easier than I thought," said Daemenos. "Well, now that that's settled, let's get down to business. What are we working with here? Tell me what you have to offer."

"Normally, Plaguebringer's ooze monsters are impossible to kill. No matter what you do, they keep coming back."

"Not exactly," said Daemenos. "I've heard Disintegration spells work, but I catch your meaning."

"We found a spell to stop them from regenerating," said Conner. He didn't know everything about the magic, but hopefully, he knew enough. "It's a necromancy spell. Basically, it creates a vortex in the Astral Plane. Plaguebringer's ooze monsters were being reanimated by spirits in the Astral. The vortex gets rid of those spirits."

"Sounds promising, kid. Everyone hates Plaguebringer. Please tell me you know how to make this spell."

"There are some difficult reagents involved, but I can get you the recipe."

Daemenos rubbed his hands together and grinned. "We're in business, Conner. I can work with this."

Conner closed his eyes and smiled. Liam might not like him making deals with demons, but it was the only way. He wasn't there yet. For all he knew, it could take months to track down a suitable spell, but the first part was done. Conner set things in motion, but now came the hard part.

The waiting.

26

Gunther

Gunther's world dissolved into an endless pool of deep blue light, but only for a moment. When it faded, he was once again floating thirty feet from the Lurker, his sword extended in front of him. He waited for the coiling tentacles to shift. Once he saw a clear path to the Lurker's torso, he charged, flying as fast as he could.

His sword burrowed through the Lurker's carapace. Gunther pressed all his weight and momentum behind the blade until he was up to his elbows inside the monster. The creature snapped and coiled its closest tentacles, trying to crush Gunther. Once again, the world dissolved into blue. After a moment of vertigo, Gunther found himself floating in the air, lined up for another attack.

Not all of his attacks were successful. Gunther had a few cracked ribs, and a fractured femur to remind him of the times the Lurker swatted him. It hurt, but the broken bones were nothing compared to the seething burn of Arronhelm's icy touch. Pain rarely slowed him down, but this was different. Without his battlemagic, Gunther would be curled up in a ball, begging for the pain to end.

"This is working, but it's taking too long. The Lurker is still climbing. We're not doing enough damage," whispered Arronhelm.

Sickly green light shone through each of the places Gunther punctured the Lurker's carapace. He guessed there were a dozen or more punctures. The pair of wounds inflicted by the ballistae were much larger. If those didn't slow the Lurker down, his smaller attacks were pointless. Relatively speaking, his stabs were the equivalent of poking someone with a needle. Sure, getting poked by needles hurt, but it wasn't exactly lethal trauma.

If Gunther was little more than a needle to the Lurker, he needed to attack more sensitive targets. A needle in the arm was barely noticeable. A needle in the eye, on the other hand, would get its attention.

"It's not going to be easy to get to the eye, but I'll see what I can do," said Arronhelm.

Leaping to the side to avoid a lashing tentacle, Gunther dove toward the Lurker. It was using several of its tentacles to climb, leaving it only a handful for defense. While it was easy for the Lurker to protect its body with only a few tentacles, they weren't lethal without momentum. Coiling, undulating tentacles could easily knock Gunther out of the way, but they did little to damage him.

Once close to the Lurker's body, Gunther started working toward the eye. He immediately found his way blocked by a tentacle, but after a brief flash of blue light, he was beyond it. Continuing, he encountered a second, and even third tentacle, but each time, Arronhelm managed to build a Portal to carry him out of harm's way.

Flying along the ridge of the Lurker's carapace, Gunther spotted its enormous eye. He turned and sprinted toward it, but it wasn't long before he was swept into one of Arronhelm's

Portals. When the overwhelming blue light faded, Gunther faced a wall of sickly green, crisscrossed with a spiderweb of yellow and orange veins.

He was at the eye.

Thick patches of glistening black tendrils surrounded the eye, each perhaps ten feet long. There were scores of them. Gunther guessed they functioned much like eyelashes, but with him so close to the eye, they sprung into motion. Before he could react, a dozen tendrils wrapped around his arms and legs. They were coated in serrated barbs, but Gunther didn't think the barbs were strong enough to pierce his armor.

He twisted and turned, trying to break free, but the tendrils were too strong. More tendrils whipped towards him. Instead of twisting around him, these tried to rip and tear at him with their barbs. As Gunther expected, they lacked the strength to pierce his armor. Given time, they'd shred his exposed flesh and find the seams between his stronger plates, but Gunther didn't think Arronhelm would let that happen.

Attacking the eye while the lashes defended it seemed a fool's errand. They were too quick to avoid and strong enough to hold him. Then again, they weren't all that long. The Lurker's eye was massive. If Gunther were floating next to the eye, he didn't think the tendrils on the far side could reach him. He really only needed to deal with half the tendrils, perhaps even less.

Gunther's world dissolved into an endless pool of deep blue light. When his vision returned, he was floating to the left of the Lurker's eye. All around him, writhing tendrils lashed out, seeking to recapture him, but Gunther's sword was already in motion.

His blade barely met a whisper of resistance as it sliced through a large patch of the Lurker's eyelashes. Several lashes twisted around his arms and legs, but in limited numbers, they weren't strong enough to stop him. Gunther could still maneuver his sword, and that's all he needed to free himself. It didn't take him long to clear the rest of the tendrils within reach of him.

Seizing the opportunity, Gunther plunged his sword into the Lurker's eye. He didn't wait to see if his strike was effective. He quickly retracted his blade and plunged it back into the eye, over and over again. The Lurker howled and shook.

Thick, twisting tentacles whipped and writhed all around him. Gunther couldn't get a good look, but he thought the Lurker must have halted its climb. Maybe it found a place to rest its tremendous weight, because there were definitely more tentacles than before. Hopefully, the monster didn't have a way to grow them magically, or something similarly horrifying.

Gunther's world momentarily flashed blue, but he didn't seem to move more than a few inches, if at all. He quickly glanced around him and suddenly understood. Arronhelm pulled him through a Portal to avoid a sweeping tentacle, but Gunther doubted even Arronhelm could protect him for much longer. The Lurker's tentacles were everywhere.

He was hurting it!

Screaming at the top of his lungs, Gunther plunged his sword deep into the Lurker's eye. He twisted it before pulling it out and striking again. A massive impact struck him in the shoulder, making his teeth painfully crash together, but Gunther didn't stop stabbing.

Once again, blue light flashed around Gunther. He assumed Arronhelm protected him from another potentially lethal blow, but whatever his old friend was doing, it wasn't enough to stop the next tentacle from slamming into his lower back.

Gunther suddenly lost sensation in his legs. Hopefully, the Potion of Flight would still allow him to move, but he suspected he was paralyzed from the waist down.

"I can't defend you much longer, old friend. There are too many tentacles."

The Lurker howled and lurched back several feet. Sparing an instant to look around, Gunther noticed a pair of thick shafts sticking out of the monster's belly, not too far from where he was floating. He didn't know if the ballistae bolts truly hurt the Lurker, or just pissed it off, but he welcomed them all the same. He'd take any help he could get.

"Archers... Mages," shouted Falstaff, his voice magically amplified to the point where it all but drowned out the battle. "It's wounded. Give it everything you've got!"

Taking several deep breaths, Gunther plunged his sword into the Lurker's eye. After striking it so many times, the ordinarily thick surface of the eye was little more than jelly in some places. As much as he hated the thought of it, Gunther plunged his arms, head, shoulders, and torso through the jelly. He knew he wouldn't survive much longer attacking the Lurker from the outside.

It was time to move inside.

"I must say, ever since the night you freed me, it has been a pleasure watching over you," whispered the spirit of Arronhelm. *"You've been a part of my life for longer than I can remember. Stars above, you're even part of my afterlife."*

Gunther struggled to push through the thick, gloppy jelly inside the Lurker's eye. The smell was so disgusting as to be intriguing. It was kind of a mix of spoiled fruit, rotting fish, and rancid piss, but somehow much worse. The pressure against the parts of Gunther's body he could still feel was intense. He couldn't feel his legs anymore.

"I can say, with absolute honesty, that I've never seen you happier than you've been these last couple of months. Kostanus, Norinae, Urgo, Felerin, and that fat fisher, Ajax, have truly become your family. I know the bitterness and anger were never your fault. Your El'orin pushed those emotions upon you, but seeing you finally able to experience joy and share deep friendships has made me truly happy."

Using his Potion of Flight to propel him, Gunther squished through the viscous jelly. He did his best to bring his sword's edge to bear against any cords or tubes he came across. He never dissected a squid before, but he cut open his fair share of people, monsters, and bugs throughout his life. Anything that looked like a string might be a nerve. Anything that looked like a tube might be a vein. Hopefully, it was the same inside the Lurker.

"And think about everything you've done!" praised Arronhelm. *"The people of the Citadel escaped the orcs because of you. Sure, I was there to help, but in the end, you're the one who did the work."*

Gunther's lungs burned. He was good at holding his breath, and his battlemagic was helping, but he couldn't keep going forever. Wherever he was inside the Lurker, and he didn't think he was in its eye anymore, there was no air. The jelly was everywhere, and the pressure was growing more intense by the second.

"And when the ships fled south, through the swamps, and the demons kept attacking, remember how you finally stopped them?" Arronhelm's voice gradually grew louder as he spoke. Gunther found it comforting. *"You, flying through the clouds, with a handful of air mages behind you. I'm sure that was the last thing those demons expected to run into."*

Gunther struggled to push through a wall of muscle. He was definitely outside the eye now. There were cords and tubes all around him, and thicker sheets of flesh. He did his best to cut through them, but he was growing weaker. If only he could find a pocket of air somewhere inside the Lurker. He just needed one more breath.

"And here you are, saving our people once again," said Arronhelm, his voice warm and resonate. *"I suspect you're in the space between the eye and the brain right now. With all the things you're cutting, I imagine you're killing it, or at least crippling it. Without the Lurker, I hope the talons flee."*

Gunther's vision was fading, but Arronhelm's words helped guide him. Pushing deeper through jelly and muscle, he worked his sword between a tight cluster of nerves, severing them one by one. Ahead, in the distance, he saw what he imaged was a thick artery. He swam towards it.

"The goal, all along, was to bring the next generation of Citadel El'orin safely into this world, and afterward, help guide our civilization to safety," sang Arronhelm. There was another voice singing in unison with Arronhelm's words. Gunther guessed it was Gallisandra. *"Together, even against impossible odds, we did that."*

Pressing forward with the last of his might, Gunther plunged his sword into the large artery in front of him. Sheets of muscle contracted around him, squeezing and crushing him. He felt his armor begin to buckle beneath the tremendous pressure. Whatever ribs weren't already broken, suddenly cracked.

"And now, good friend and tireless soldier, you may rest. We've waited patiently for you to join us. There is so much we want to show you. It's time to cross over, Gunther. You've struggled longer and harder than any man should. Your journey is finally at its end. Be at peace and know that you've made a tremendous difference in this world."

Gunther tried to push forward, but the crushing weight of the Lurker was too strong to fight. He felt his jaw give way, and his teeth shatter. His vision faded and his thoughts slowed. Finally, after one last agonizing moment, there was no more.

27

Nathanial

Nathanial Norwitch did his best to ignore Archmage Torgolo's rambling retelling of recent events. Mara Young gave him a highly detailed report on everything that had transpired over the past eighteen months. The only new information the archmage might offer pertained to the library in Semilae, but so far, he hadn't mentioned anything Nathanial didn't already know from his discussions with Deninger.

As usual, Todd Torgolo brought little of value to the conversation. It wasn't that Archmage Torgolo completely lacked purpose. His blind ambition and unquenchable greed made him reliably predictable. Nathanial could always count on Todd to put his personal interests ahead of everything else, which made it easy to cast him as the villain. Todd was a useful distraction, and Nathanial used him accordingly.

"I'm just relieved you're back, Archmage Norwitch," said Todd. "The Academy hasn't been the same without you. We lack discipline..."

Nathanial held up a hand and waited for Archmage Torgolo to stop babbling. If it was an option, Nathanial would never have returned to the Academy, but it seemed necessary. He needed to learn Russell's version of the Portal spell. Returning to the Academy gave him the best chance of success. "Tell me about your efforts to learn Russell's Portal spell."

"I tried to detain him, along with the rest of his friends, but that incompetent traitor, Keldon, got in the way," growled Todd, his face turning a violent shade of red. "Why is Mehlo Keldon allowed to remain in the Academy after what he did?"

Nathanial heard about the altercation in the Inscription room. As much as he shared Todd's opinions of Professor Keldon, he didn't think discipline was a useful tool in this circumstance. "I will evaluate Professor Keldon shortly. I've thoroughly reviewed his behavior, along with the parameters of the special assignment Mara granted him, and I must admit, I have concerns."

"Finally, someone who understands what I've been saying all along. Mehlo Keldon is an infection. He must be purged from this institution!" howled Archmage Torgolo. "Things would have been so much better had we detained Russell and his friends. They've caused nothing but problems, and Professor Keldon has been there all along, hiding in the shadows, advising them at every juncture. It's a travesty! Keldon's disloyalty and careless disregard for the interests of the Academy should not be tolerated!"

"Your feelings on the matter are duly noted. Now, please leave me," said Nathanial with a dismissive wave of his hand.

"But I have more to say on the matter."

"I'm sure you do, but you'll have to save it for another day. I have other business to attend to," said Nathanial, doing his best to contain his rising disgust for the man.

Archmage Torgolo stared at him with a shocked expression plastered across his meaty face. He looked like he wanted to say something, but he must have reconsidered, because he turned and left without uttering another word. He slammed the door on his way out.

Nathanial Norwitch closed his eyes and tried to ignore his blinding headache. It took Kora more than a week of intensive work to untangle the twisted knots in his mind. The Mindars did more damage than Nathanial originally realized. They devoured dozens of spells and all but shattered his personality. If not for Kora's tremendous expertise, Nathanial would never have fully recovered.

Now that his memories were restored, Nathanial was growing impatient. He needed to resume his work, but he couldn't risk it until he recovered more of his lost spells. Many of the spells the Mindars took were common. He already replaced those, using spells from the Academy's supply, but a few of his lost spells were incredibly rare. It might be years before someone stumbled across the necessary reagents to make those spells, and Nathanial couldn't afford to wait.

But Russell's new version of the Portal spell would fix everything. With it, Nathanial could bring Deninger, Kora, and the rest of the Halls of Research with him. Alone, he was vulnerable to attack, but with others present, he doubted the Mindars would dare attack him.

He was close to untangling the secret of the magical barrier surrounding Vorrenkempe. He knew it was similar to the barrier that once protected the Citadel, although he didn't know how it was powered. The spirit of a Greater Unicorn powered the Citadel's barrier. Arronhelm showed Nathanial the Painting. Whatever was powering Vorrenkempe's barrier, the Mindars assumed control over it. They twisted it, using its power to broadcast their crippling, mind-warping abilities throughout the city of Vorrenkempe, affecting all who lived there.

With their thoughts twisted and distorted, the entire city lived under a false version of reality. The Mindars dictated right and wrong, friend and foe, love and hate, and everything else that mattered. With their perception of reality redefined, the people of Vorrenkempe were little more than slaves, destined to live out their lives serving the Mindars.

Unless Nathanial set them free.

A gentle knock on the door snapped Nathanial back into focus. Professor Keldon wasn't due for another couple of minutes, but perhaps he was early. "Enter," he called, hoped it wasn't Archmage Torgolo returning to share more of his childishly banal insights.

"You wanted to see me," said Professor Keldon as he quietly slipped into the office, carefully closing the door behind him.

"Yes. Please have a seat," said Nathanial, gesturing to the chair opposite his desk.

Professor Keldon approached and slowly lowered himself into the chair. Nathanial couldn't quite read his expression. "I assume you want to discuss the group from the Citadel," said the professor flatly.

"There are several things I wish to speak to you about, but I won't lie. The children of the Citadel are my highest priority. Specifically, Russell."

Professor Keldon sighed. "You know he can't produce copies of his enhanced Portal spell, right? I've spoken with him at length about it. If the recipe for that spell was somewhere in that library, I imagine Todd or Deniger would have found it by now."

Nathanial tended to agree. Deninger made several trips to the library in Semilae, cataloguing every book within it. The recipe might very well be buried in some innocuous tome, but Nathanial doubted it. Still, there were other ways to learn new magic. "I'm told Russell has access to an Elestone. Is this not true?"

Professor Keldon leaned back in his chair. Nathanial caught him off guard. He was certain of it. "I believe Eliana has an

Elestone, but convincing her to part with it might prove difficult."

The professor's honesty surprised Nathanial. He expected the professor to evade or distort the question. "Well, that's where you come in."

"I doubt she'll surrender it," said the professor, shaking his head.

"She has to."

"It doesn't work that way, not with this group," said the professor. "You can't force them to do something, especially not now."

"You'll find I can be incredibly persuasive," said Nathanial.

Professor Keldon shook his head. "Stop it! These kids don't respond to threats. It didn't work for Archmage Torgolo, and it won't work for you."

"I'm far more powerful than Todd Torgolo." With both Vallon and Arronhelm dead, Nathanial was the most powerful wizard in the world. He was certain of it.

"And you think that makes it okay to threaten and abuse these kids?"

"You don't understand how much I want that spell," said Nathanial. He shouldn't need to justify himself to anyone, but something about the professor's tone challenged him. "But I'm not taking this simply because I want it. Thousands of lives are at stake."

"Then maybe you should approach them and explain your need instead of immediately resorting to threats."

Nathanial leaned back in his chair, stunned. He didn't have the time or patience to explain the situation to a group of children, but maybe the professor was right. "I'm afraid there isn't time for that."

"Russell and his friends are backed by the Governor. Raelyn supports them as well. No matter how powerful you are, you won't be able to force them to do anything." The professor leaned forward. "You understand that, don't you?"

"Achillion is my friend. He'll see my side of this."

"Honestly, I doubt it," said the professor. "While you were away, and while the Academy watched from the sidelines, those kids helped save Derregain from Plaguebringer."

"It's not my fault. If I could have been here, I would have been," said Nathanial, but he wasn't sure it was true.

"It doesn't matter," said Professor Keldon. "What's done is done. You weren't here, and in your absence, the children of the Citadel saved this city. They have the gratitude of the Governor, the demons, the militia, even the common citizens."

Nathanial ground his teeth from side to side. He was beginning to understand why Archmage Torgolo hated the professor. "You seem to know these children better than anyone else. What do you suggest?"

Professor Keldon looked away for a moment. "If convincing them of the need is out of the question, have you considered bargaining with them? Russell bargained with the Academy before. He very well may do so again. I think he enjoys it."

"Do you have any idea what a spell like that is worth?" said Nathanial, shaking his head. "I doubt the Academy can afford it."

"Maybe, maybe not, but I don't see a lot of other options," said Professor Keldon. "By the way, you're not just bargaining for Russell's Portal spell. You'll need to pay for the Elestone as well. It's not like Eliana is just going to give it to you."

"That's preposterous!" spat Nathanial.

The professor shrugged. "If you want that spell, you need to be prepared to pay for it, and I promise you it won't be cheap."

Nathanial steepled his fingers in front of his face as he considered the professor's suggestion. The Academy held a wealth of spells in reserve for its aspiring members. Even after being away for so long, Nathanial was still the most influential member of the Academy. As long as Russell and his friends didn't ask for many rare spells, he could probably get away with paying them a considerable amount. "Hypothetically, let's say I entertain this negotiation. How would we proceed?"

"The Academy has already gone through the trouble of forging a working relationship with the children of the Citadel. I teach them out of a small library the Governor built in Eliana's greenhouse."

Nathanial smiled. That was the professor's angle. He wanted to leverage the situation to ensure that his cushy job continued. "You're speaking of the special arrangement you worked out with Mara Young, correct?"

The professor nodded. "I see no reason we wouldn't use my library to conduct your transaction. We've done it before."

"Do you have a sense of what Russell might want in exchange for the spell?" asked Nathanial.

"It's hard to say. In this case, he may try to bargain for several smaller items to share amongst his friends. As far as the Elestone is considered, I suspect Eliana can be bought with elemental spells. She already knows how to conjure a fire elemental, but she lacks the other elements."

"Interesting," mused Nathanial. "I know the Academy has a spare copy of Summon Water Elemental on hand. I'm not sure about the others. Is there a reason she prizes those spells more highly than the rest?"

Professor Keldon met Nathanial's gaze. "Each of the kids possesses certain gifts. An affinity for elementals is one of Eliana's gifts."

Nathanial plastered a smile on his face. It was the easiest way for him to hide his surprise. Did the professor know about El'orin, or just that the children of the Citadel were somehow more powerful than ordinary people? "Do you know the nature of all their gifts, or just this aspect of Eliana's?"

"I don't pretend to understand much of it," said the professor. "While I've seen how effective Eliana's fire elemental can be, truth be told, she asked me to look for copies of the other elemental summoning spells for her. That's how I know what she wants."

"And the others?"

"I suspect Russell will be interested in some of the more advanced spells in wizardry. As for the rest of them, I'm not sure."

Nathanial pinched the bridge of his nose. His headache was becoming difficult to ignore. He needed to end this conversation before the pain got much worse. "Negotiate this deal for me. You know what spells the Academy has readily available. As best you can, try to steer them toward those spells. Do this for me, and I'll find a way to make your special arrangement a permanent position."

The professor regarded him for a long moment before nodding.

"Thank you, Professor Keldon," said Nathanial as he gestured toward the door. "If you would be so kind, please gently close the door on your way out."

"Yes, of course."

Nathanial watched the professor leave. He wasn't sure he trusted the man, but he didn't think it mattered. If he didn't like the deal Professor Keldon negotiated, he'd try to strike a better deal on his own. If necessary, he thought there might be a way to steal the spell from Russell's mind.

After all, Mindars could rip spells from people's minds. If they could do it, Nathanial was confident he'd find a way.

28

Saro

Saro paced back and forth. He knew he was making the others uncomfortable, but he couldn't contain himself. After playing nice for far too long, they finally harvested a rival El'orin. It felt better than sex, but that was only part of it. His entire Coterie benefited from the successful hunt. They were all stronger, each in their own way.

"How long do you think it will be before the Governor strikes back?" asked Mend.

"What makes you think he will?" asked Saro. "If the militia had the balls to come after us, they would have done so long ago."

"But this was different," said Mend, shaking her head. "If not for that freak storm, the fires might have spread all across Middletown. Even if the Governor wants to avoid a fight, I'm not sure he can. The city leaders will demand action."

Saro glanced at the others. Ghost appeared interested in what Mend was saying, but Saro doubted the annoying necromancer was concerned. What the shek did it matter to him? He'd turn into a spirit and drift away at the first sign of danger. Eirini looked calm, but Saro felt her seething anger, just beneath the surface. That girl loathed the Bumbles. She wanted nothing more than to destroy every last one of them. Then there was Eirini's brother, Dimitri. Saro didn't want to know what that kid was thinking. Some things were best left alone.

"We have rebuilt our small army of ghouls. We'll unleash them on the Bumbles if they attack," said Ghost.

Saro held up a hand to silence the conversation. "At the end of the day, it doesn't shekking matter. If and when the Bumbles come, we'll fight them. Until then, let's focus on what matters." Saro spread his arms and grinned. "We just downed one of Longshadows' El'orin. I know I got stronger. What about the rest of you?"

At first, no one said anything. Saro wasn't sure they understood the question. Eventually, Ghost cleared his throat and said, "My spirit form improved."

"How so?" asked Saro.

"Before, the only things I could do in my spirit form were float through walls and talk to people." Ghost looked around the room, a smile gradually spreading across his lips. "Now I can cast some spells while spiritual. At least, that's what my El'orin tells me. I'm not sure which spells, or how it works, but I can't wait to try it out."

Saro didn't know what to think about Ghost's newfound abilities. They sounded incredibly useful, but, ultimately, he didn't know if he could trust Ghost. If the creepy necromancer kid remained loyal, this was great news. If he turned on the Coterie, his new powers might prove problematic.

"I don't know if my El'orin got stronger," sighed Mend. "She hasn't said anything."

"You were there for the white mists," said Saro. "They touched you, right?"

Mend nodded.

"So, something had to happen to you," said Saro. He didn't trust Mend. She was hiding something.

"Look, I'm sure I got stronger, I just don't know how yet," said Mend. "I'm guessing it has something to do with my mindreading. Would you like me to test it out on you?"

"Don't you shekking dare!" snapped Saro. He didn't want Mend anywhere near his mind.

"Alright," said Mend softly. "Then, it might be some time before I explore my new abilities."

"You can explore my mind," said Dimitri, his eyes darting back and forth, his voice verging on a deranged cackle.

The color drained from Mend's face. "No, that's quite alright," she said, shaking her head.

An uncomfortable silence spread across the room. Earlier, Mend expressed concerns about how Dimitri's El'orin was torturing the boy, but Saro didn't think it was nearly as bad as she was making it out to be. Based on how Mend reacted when invited into Dimitri's thoughts, Saro wondered if he was wrong about the situation. Maybe Dimitri's El'orin was truly torturing the poor kid.

"I guess I can go next," said Eirini, breaking the awkward silence. "I haven't tested it yet, but I'm pretty sure my undead are more powerful now."

"How so?" asked Ghost.

"According to my El'orin, whenever one of my summoned spirits enters a body, the undead that rises will be faster and stronger."

"So, if you send a wraith into a body, you'll create a more powerful ghoul?" asked Ghost.

"I think so."

Ghost whistled through his teeth. "Better not let Sorriah know about that. She really loves her ghouls. If she finds out you can make even stronger ones, who knows what she'll do?"

Saro didn't understand Sorriah's strange attachment to her ghouls, and he didn't want to. She talked about them like they were her children. It was pretty shekking gross. Still, if Eirini's new ability appealed to Sorriah, maybe there was a way to leverage it. So far, the Downtrodden benefited from Sorriah's ghouls. Maybe Saro could work out a trade. "Are you thinking Sorriah will want Eirini's help?"

"Probably," said Ghost with a shrug. "Look at how much time Sorriah spends preparing her corpses. She skins them and trims away all the fat. If the spirits Eirini summons develop into stronger ghouls, Sorriah is going to be interested."

Saro stopped pacing. Could it really be so simple? Could he loan Eirini to Sorriah in exchange for access to the Nightcrawlers' army of ghouls? After all, if Eirini could craft stronger ghouls, wouldn't Sorriah prefer to replace her existing army with newer, stronger creations? "How soon until she needs to make more ghouls?"

"Wait," said Eirini, holding up a hand. "What are we talking about?"

Ghost cocked his head to one side. "Sorriah tries to keep 200 ghouls prepared, at all times. I don't know why she sets the number at 200. Maybe the Nightcrawlers have limited space for them, but I know she only gives us bodies when her larder is full."

"If she sent sixteen to help us last night, she'll need to build new ghouls to replace the fallen, right?" asked Saro. The timing couldn't be more perfect. Eirini would help Sorriah replace her fallen ghouls, demonstrating her new capabilities. After that, the true negotiations would begin.

"If this involves me, I'd like to be part of the conversation," said Eirini.

"I think you're right, Saro," said Ghost. "Sorriah's probably already building new ghouls as we speak."

"Then we don't have time to waste." Saro grinned. This was too perfect. "Take Eirini and go meet with Sorriah. Take Dimitri with you too, for good measure. Show Sorriah how much stronger her ghouls can be if Eirini is involved."

"I'm not going anywhere!" shouted Eirini.

"What the shek is your problem?" asked Saro. He knew why she was mad. After all, he was having fun deliberately pissing her off.

"If you need me to do something, you ask me," said Eirini, her tone icy. "I don't respond to demands."

"That's not really how things work around here," said Saro, his tone easily as icy as Eirini's. "It's pretty simple. I'm in charge. The rest of you do what I say." He stared at Eirini for a long moment before asking, "Is that clear?"

"Right now, you're the one who needs me, not the other way around," said Eirini. "I don't mind working with Sorriah, but if you're going to treat me like a child, you can go shek yourself." Eirini met Saro's gaze. "Is that clear?"

Ghost giggled.

A tiny ball of flame popped into existence above Dimitri's palm. He bounced it back and forth between his hands, a maniacal grin stretching across his twisted face.

Saro wasn't sure how to respond. He didn't like being challenged, especially by the newcomers, but he couldn't help but admire their courage. "Oh, we're definitely clear," said Saro, casually brushing aside the conflict as if it never happened. "So, you're going to show Sorriah your new powers. With any luck, that crazy bitch will want you to help rebuild her army."

"Okay. What happens after that?" asked Eirini.

"Hopefully, Sorriah won't be able to get enough of you," said Saro. He spoke slowly to give him time to think. He was making the plan up on the spot. "That's when I'll step in and negotiate a stronger alliance with the Nightcrawlers."

"Are you sure they'll make a deal?" asked Mend.

Saro wasn't sure, but it seemed like the right time to press the issue. "They've been trying to have it both ways this whole time.

On one hand, they're trying to play peaceful with the Governor, honor the treaty, and all that kind of shit, but on the other hand, they're working against him whenever they can. Sorriah just sent ghouls to help us harvest the Longshadows. She's ready to join us in burning it all down. All she needs is a little push."

"For what it's worth, I think you're right," said Eirini.

"Why?"

"Back when Sorriah first showed me her ghouls, I asked her why she had so many," said Eirini. She looked around the room. "Sorriah said she needed them to purge the living."

"Well, that's comforting," mumbled Mend.

Saro wasn't surprised. He didn't expect Sorriah's goals to match his own. He just needed her to be useful in his war against the Governor and the city. "Don't worry about it. We'll deal with Sorriah when the time comes. Until then, she'll make a great ally."

The room grew quiet as everyone seemed to consider his words. Eventually, Ghost broke the silence. "So, what about you, Saro? What new powers did you gain from the white mist?"

"You'll see," said Saro. It wasn't that he didn't trust them, he just wasn't ready to share. His El'orin hadn't spoken since receiving the white mists last night, but Saro was receiving visions, nonetheless. The Bull was communicating with him. He knew it in his bones.

"Oh, come on. We told you about our new powers," said Ghost.

Saro grinned and shook his head. As the leader of the Downtrodden, he knew the Bull worked through him. He could feel the anger in everyone around him. If he concentrated, he could stoke the embers of hatred and rage that burned deep within people's hearts.

The Governor might be the Peacemaker, but Saro would soon become the Ragebringer. Where the Governor silenced voices, quelled riots, and prevented violence, Saro would do the opposite. He would fan the flames of rebellion, finally forcing the poor oppressed people of Derregain to break their shackles and cast off their chains.

The next time Achillion hid like a coward behind that unbreakable aura of his, Saro would be there to stop it. He'd match the Governor's power with his own. Finally, the people would be free to make their own choices. Saro knew, if given half a chance, they'd turn on the Governor and everything he stood for.

Saro grinned. "Don't worry. When the time comes, you'll all see what I can do, and I promise you, you're going to love it!"

29
Eliana

Eliana shook her head. She understood what Professor Keldon was saying. The Academy wasn't shy about its desire to learn Russell's version of the Portal spell. They were going to get their hands on it, one way or another. She knew the professor was right, but she didn't care. She didn't want to give up her final Elestone.

But she knew she didn't really have a choice. Archmage Torgolo nearly threw them all in prison during his attempt to learn Russell's magic, and he was nothing compared to Nathanial Norwitch. According to the professor, Nathanial was the most powerful, most ambitious wizard in the Academy. It wasn't lost on her that Arronhelm knew and trusted Nathanial. Maybe there was a way to strike a reasonable bargain with him.

"What if we refuse?" asked Russell. "It's not like he can force us to give him the spell."

"I wouldn't be so sure of that," said Professor Keldon. "I know you don't like anyone trying to push you around, Russ, but please trust me on this one. Nathanial Norwitch is a very dangerous man. I wouldn't cross him, not if I were you."

Russell bit his lip, like he often did when he was trying to control his emotions. If it were anyone other than the professor, Eliana expected Russell would have started shouting. "What's he going to do, attack us?"

Professor Keldon shook his head. "I don't think he'd do anything direct. Nathanial is more likely to work through the Academy. He'll start by closing down this library." The professor gestured around the room.

"What will happen to you if he does that?" asked Eliana. As much as she disliked the Academy, she cared for the professor. He was always kind to her.

Professor Keldon shrugged. "Don't worry about me. Worry about yourselves. Once Nathanial shuts down the library, he's likely to cut you off from all Academy spells, services, and resources. From there, I wouldn't be surprised if he withheld Academy support to the House of Healing and other important institutions within the city until he gets his way."

"What a shekking donkey cock," mumbled Russell.

"That seems like an accurate assessment," said the professor.

"Let's say we decide to do it," said Eliana. "What does that look like? How would we proceed?"

"Ellie, no. It's your last stone," said Russell.

Eliana smiled at Russell. Even though it was his Portal spell everyone was interested in, he understood she was being asked to give up something of tremendous value. Still, it was her decision to make. She needed to weigh the pros and cons. "Let's just hear what the professor has to say."

"If you decide you want to make a deal, you'll work through me," said the professor. "I already told Nathanial how much I thought the spell and the Elestone were worth, and he didn't like what I had to say."

"What do you get out of it?" asked Eliana. She hated having to ask, but she wanted everything out in the open.

"Nathanial said he would make my appointment here, with all of you, more permanent, but please, none of this should be about me," said Professor Keldon. "Whether I'm punished or rewarded shouldn't play into your decision. Do what works best for all of you. I'll be fine."

"I understand," said Eliana. "I just needed to know where you fit into all of this." Lord Rumblesnort Bunny-Fur was sitting in her lap, purring, and rhythmically pressing his paws into her thigh. It stung when his claws occasionally pierced her skin, but she didn't mind.

Russell cleared his throat. "You said you told Nathanial how much the spell and stone are worth. Mind sharing that information with us?"

"It's hard to say," said the professor. "The combination of the spell and the stone is basically priceless, but that isn't particularly useful to us. Since Nathanial will stop at nothing to get what he wants, we need to arrive at some kind of price."

Eliana nodded. What the professor said made sense. "I've been searching for the other elemental spells. If I get those, I guess I'm happy."

"Out of the question," said Professor Keldon, shaking his head. "You're asking for far too little. There is no way I'm letting Nathanial get off that easy."

Russell grinned. "Now we're getting somewhere. What do you recommend?"

"First, I intend to get you one or two of your missing elementals, Eliana," said the professor. "Water and earth, I suspect. The Academy only has one of them in reserve at the moment, but I know a mage in the Academy who should be able to pen the other for you."

Eliana was glad the professor was looking out for her interests. She knew her friends cared about her, but at times, she felt taken for granted. Eliana knew her El'orin was magnifying her feelings of discontent, but she didn't think her concerns were completely unfounded. For instance, everyone knew how much she hated Raelyn, yet they didn't think twice about asking her to work with that foul creature.

"Are we limited to spells the Academy has readily available?" asked Russell.

"Yes and no," said the professor. "I suspect we could force Nathanial to come up with rare magic, but we can only push him so far. The better option is to ask for several valuable but relatively easy to obtain items. I could be wrong, but I'm pretty sure Nathanial doesn't care about the overall cost to the Academy. He only cares about his own time and effort."

"Other than Eliana's elementals, I'm not sure what other simple spells the Academy can offer us," said Russell, scratching his chin. "Malcolm seems to get his spells from other sources. Conner is learning spells from Raelyn, and the Academy isn't likely to part with any of the spells I'm interested in. They seem to have a thing about giving out widely destructive magic."

Professor Keldon nodded. "They certainly do, but Nathanial has the power to suspend that rule for you. I already planned on making that part of the arrangement."

"What about Attia and Liam?" said Eliana. Her friends often ignored her, but she wasn't about to ignore them. If there was a way for all to benefit from this bargain, she wanted to pursue it.

"I thought about that as well, and I think I might have a solution," said the professor. He flipped through a small book, making soft grunting noises until he found the page he was looking for. He spread the book out on the table in front of him, pointing at two pages, each featuring pictures of rings surrounded by dense blocks of intricate writing.

"Help us out, professor," said Russell. "What are we looking at here?"

"Rings of Power, and Rings of Protection," said the professor.

"Like Malcolm's ring?" Eliana thought Malcolm's ring was incredibly valuable. Surely, they weren't in a position to ask for several rings like that.

"Not exactly," said Professor Keldon. "Malcolm's ring is among the most powerful rings in the world. Yes, it is a Ring of Power, but it is much more than that. The rings I am suggesting are much weaker than Malcolm's."

"If they're weak, what's the point?"

"I didn't say they were weak," said the professor, shaking his head. "I said they were weaker."

Eliana held up a hand to stop Russell from quipping back at the professor. She could see the mischievous look in his eye. "Okay, what will these rings do for us?"

"In the most basic sense, they'll deepen your well," said the Professor. "They'll allow you to cast more spells, and do so more often. They are highly sought after by aspiring students within the Academy." Professor Keldon leaned in. "I couldn't help but notice that neither of you possess one. If I'm not mistaken, Conner is missing one, as well."

Studying all four elements, Eliana's well was deep. Still, it wouldn't hurt to make it deeper, even if only a little bit. She reached down and massaged Lord Rumblesnort's cheeks, causing him to deliver his purrs in a series of snorts. "What do you think, Rumblesnort? Do you like the idea of a Ring of Power?" The cat meowed softy. Eliana didn't know if he was expressing agreement or annoyance, but since he was purring, she decided he was happy with the suggestion.

"What about Rings of Protection? What do those do?" asked Russell.

"I trust you've both seen Achillion's ring in action," said the professor.

"You mean the one that creates a disc of energy on the back of his hand?" asked Eliana.

Professor Keldon nodded. "That's a Ring of Protection. Mind you, Achillion's ring is much stronger than anything we're likely to get from the Academy, but the principle is the same."

"So, you're thinking we get Rings of Protection for Attia and Liam?" asked Russell.

"Precisely," said the professor. "Getting as many as five rings will be difficult, but I don't think it's an impossible task. The rings are easy to make, it's just costly and time consuming. The Academy won't be giving up any resources it can't replace. That being said, they only create three or four rings a year, so what we're getting represents a significant amount of work."

Eliana considered her options. Nature led her to that grotto in the Theleram. The only reason they discovered those Elestones was because Nature wanted the group to have them. So far, they spent one stone teaching Attia her Breath of Battle spell, and another stone on Conner's Banishment spell.

Both spells were tremendously helpful to the group. Eliana didn't think they would be alive today if not for those spells. As much as she wanted to hold on to the third stone for another piece of rare magic, maybe trading it for several items, benefiting all of them, was the right answer.

Beyond that, part of her wondered if this decision went deeper than the material gains they were bargaining for. Arronhelm trusted Nathanial, and for whatever reason, Nathanial was desperate to learn Russell's Portal spell. What did he need it for? If Arronhelm trusted him, it was entirely possible that Nathanial needed the spell to save lives.

If only Arronhelm knew how to cast Russell's Portal spell back when everything started falling apart. He could have safely delivered the entire group to Derregain. Arronhelm wouldn't have needed to limit it to just Eliana and her friends. Given enough time, he could have safely moved everyone living within the Citadel.

Most importantly, Arronhelm would have transported Eliana's mom. Malcolm wouldn't have needed to summon those nasty neverlings, and Eliana's mom wouldn't have needed to sacrifice herself. With her mom there to hold her close, Eliana wouldn't be so lonely.

She understood her El'orin was magnifying her loneliness. Eliana understood she was the one who broke up with Russell, not the other way around, but none of that made her miss her mom any less.

30

Achillion

Achillion trudged through the snowy streets, oblivious to the bitter winds and stinging sleet of early evening. It took him most of the day to convince the council not to do anything stupid. With both Senator Ominar and Counselor Jurgenson absent from the meeting, Achillion, as Governor, assumed leadership over the militia. He was amazed by the wide variety of creatively stupid suggestions he was forced to endure regarding the militia and how best to use it. Few of Derregain's legislators had military experience, and it showed.

Still, he'd gladly endure a dozen such meetings if it meant finally putting an end to Saro and the Downtrodden. The Serpentus sent him a message earlier in the day, using a Soundsend spell. Achillion wasn't aware that the Serpentus knew that spell. It was something worth remembering, but it was a small matter when compared to the message itself.

The Serpentus was planning to attack Saro and his people tonight. Achillion was surprised how quickly it was happening, but he certainly didn't mind. The sooner the Downtrodden were crippled, the better. There was even a chance of outright destroying the El'ominae, forever ending its ability to rebuild its army. If the Serpentus managed that, the Downtrodden would never be a threat again.

Then again, there was a chance the attack would fail. Achillion considered trying to help, but he wasn't sure how best to do so. If the Serpentus wanted to involve the militia, she easily could have done so. After all, she controlled both the senator and the counselor in charge of the militia. Achillion's only real way of helping would be to convince the children of the Citadel to become involved, and that was out of the question.

They were doing too much for the city already. He needed to let them sit this one out. As Achillion approached the greenhouse, he resolved to not even mention the Serpentus, and her upcoming attack on the Downtrodden. He was there to pay his respects and to thank Eliana for her help last night. Achillion was done feeling guilty about asking Liam and his friends for help, while constantly pressuring them to do more and more. He couldn't have it both ways.

Carefully opening the door, so as to not allow the wind to grab it, Achillion entered the greenhouse. He noticed the usual teams of arborists tending the crops. Groups of soldiers sat and drank at various wooden tables, but none of them waved to him. Most wouldn't even look at him, not that he blamed them. They were probably worried about Liam. Achillion wouldn't be surprised if some thought he was responsible for what happened to their leader. On a certain level, he was responsible.

The door to Professor Keldon's library was closed, which generally meant the professor was sleeping, or teaching. With any luck, the professor was in there working with one or more of the children, but if not, Achillion didn't mind waking the man. As far as the Governor was concerned, Professor Keldon owed him for getting this library built in the first place.

The sounds of quiet conversation drifted out from the library as Achillion approached it. A few of the soldiers noticed him as he passed. One nodded, one spat on the ground, and one quickly looked away. That range of reactions was about what he expected.

Achillion gently knocked before pushing the door open. Professor Keldon, who was facing the door, immediately noticed him, but he said nothing. Eliana was sitting on one side of the table with her cat in her lap. Russell was on the opposite side of the table.

"If Eliana will part with her Elestone, I guess we're doing this," said Russell. "How long do you need to negotiate with the donkey cock?"

"I expect it will take a few days, perhaps more," said the professor. "Even if he accepts our bargain, with no renegotiation, it will take several days for the Academy to gather everything we're requesting."

"Well, what do you say, Eliana? Once we set this in motion, there's no turning back," said Russell.

Achillion was amazed none of them addressed him. They had to know he was there. If nothing else, they heard the door open and close, and even though neither Russell nor Eliana were facing him, Russell should have seen him with his peripheral vision.

"Let's just get it over with," she said. "Nathanial will never stop until he gets the spell he wants. We might as well get as much as we can for it."

Nathanial!

The name hit Achillion like a hammer. Was Nate really back in town? When did he return? Why didn't he reach out? Achillion spent years adventuring with Nathanial, back when they were younger. "Did you say Nathanial?" he stammered, even though he already knew the answer.

"Evening, Governor," said Russell.

"Yes, Nathanial Norwitch has returned to the Academy," said Professor Keldon.

"When?"

"Several days ago," said the professor. "As I understand it, he has been back in Derregain for weeks, although I'm told he wasn't himself. Evidently, his mind needed extensive healing."

The possibilities and ramifications swirled around Achillion's thoughts like annoyingly evasive gnats. Try as he might, he couldn't pin one down long enough to explore it. Was Nate back for good? What happened to him that he needed such extensive healing? Was he planning on abandoning the city again? Why didn't he reach out? Achillion and Nathanial always planned to lead Derregain together as a team. That all ended when Nathanial left the city without warning, ages ago.

"Based on the look on your face, this is the first you're hearing that Donkey Cock... I mean Nathanial, returned to the city," said Russell. "Just so you know, he's desperate to learn my special version of the Portal spell. Professor Keldon is helping us come up with a fair price."

"Hold on," said Achillion, shaking his head. "I need a minute." If Nate was trying to learn Russell's Portal spell, he wasn't planning on remaining in Derregain for long. The only reason to learn that spell would be to transport groups of people out of the city. Was he planning on taking Deninger, Kora, and others along with him?

Did he even plan on visiting Achillion? At one point, they were such good friends. With parts of the city crumbling and starvation running rampant, Nathanial Norwitch was precisely the savior Derregain needed at this moment, yet he was planning on leaving without so much as saying hello?

That couldn't be possible.

Of course, Nathanial wanted to learn that spell, but he wasn't going to abandon Derregain, not again. Surely, he'd stay around long enough to help cleanse Plaguebringer's forces from the bay, and perhaps liberate the farms to the south. Maybe he wasn't ready yet. Perhaps Nathanial still needed to recover. Surely, that was the answer. Once he was fully healthy again, he'd offer his help.

"You okay, Governor?" asked Russell, his tone a touch more teasing than Achillion cared for.

"I don't know," said Achillion with a heavy sigh. "Me and Nate, we were the best of friends. I'm surprised he hasn't reached out to me since returning."

"I'm sorry to be the one to break it to you, but I doubt Nathanial planned to contact you," said Professor Keldon.

That couldn't be true! The professor was wrong. "Why do you think that?" said Achillion softly, a pit slowly forming in his stomach.

The professor gently closed his book, placing his palms on the table in front of him. "He's been quite active since returning to the Academy. He's resumed his leadership role over all major institutions, but I suspect only temporarily. I've heard whispers about him draining resources from the Academy. Draughts of Powerence, and various potions. Things he wouldn't need to gather if he intended to remain. There have been other rumors as well—"

"Stop!" commanded Achillion, holding up a hand. "I've heard enough."

"Very well," said the professor.

"The three of you were negotiating a fair price for Russell's spell," said the Governor. He spoke slowly in an effort to stop his growing anger from bleeding into his words. "Have you arrived at a price?"

"I believe we have," said the professor, quickly glancing at both Russell and Eliana, probably searching for objections.

"Then, let's go," snapped Achillion. "Let's broker this deal."

"I planned on bringing it to him privately," said Professor Keldon. "I suspect Nathanial will argue with me. He may even threaten me, but in the end, I think I can persuade him."

The Governor shook his head. "I'm going with you. We're going now!" He abandoned all attempts to hide his anger. What was the point?

"Well, this escalated quickly," said Russell. "I'm coming along."

"I guess I should go too," said Eliana.

"No," said the professor. "I think we want you and your Elestone here, safe within the greenhouse. Don't you agree, Governor?"

Professor Keldon often appeared smug, but the man wasn't stupid. Among other things, Nathanial was an incredibly powerful enchanter. With both Russell and Eliana present, he might attempt to coerce the spell out of them. Once Nathanial learned that spell, there would be nothing to keep him in Derregain. "I agree. Eliana and her Elestone are our only leverage. She needs to stay here."

Achillion relaxed his Aura of Influence as he approached the door to Nathanial Norwitch's office. A small army of various Academy functionaries followed behind him, expressing discomfort, but stopping short of forbidding him from continuing. Without the Aura, they would have presented a problem. With it, they were merely an annoyance, easily ignored.

The door wasn't locked, which was a good thing. It probably saved the Academy the cost of replacing it. Achillion wasn't about to let a simple door slow his progress. He needed Nathanial to explain his behavior. Achillion wasn't planning on accepting excuses or apologies. He just wanted honest answers, not that he expected to receive them.

"How dare you barge in..." Nathanial Norwitch's voice trailed off as Achillion, Professor Keldon, and Russell entered the room.

"How dare me?" growled Achillion. On his way through the Academy, he envisioned remaining calm throughout this confrontation. That wasn't happening. "How dare you! Did you really think you'd pull it off?"

"I have no idea what you're talking about," said Nathanial, his voice icy and smooth. "I heard you fell prey to a succubus. Perhaps she twisted your thoughts, old friend."

"Don't give me that shit," spat Achillion. He took a deep breath before continuing. His anger was spiraling out of control. "You're bartering for Russell's Portal spell. How long did you plan to remain in Derregain after learning that spell? A few days, a few hours, or even less?"

"My business is none of your concern."

Achillion imagined a hand slapping his face, leaving his cheek stinging and red. "You better believe it's my shekking business! We had an agreement. We were supposed to lead this city together, but you turned your back on that."

Nathanial held his hands in the air, gesturing in a way much like a parent trying to quiet a screaming child. It was insulting! "Don't be so melodramatic," said Nathanial. "I didn't abandon you. I spent years building the Academy, making sure it was powerful enough to defend the city in my absence."

"The Academy," snorted Russell. "What a shekking joke."

"Control yourself, Russell," whispered Professor Keldon.

"The Academy sat on the sidelines, watching Derregain burn," said Achillion, his tone much more measured. He was grateful for Russell's brief outburst. The kid said what needed to be said.

"Hyperbole and exaggeration aren't helpful, Achillion," said Nathanial. "I understand you may be dissatisfied with the efforts of the Academy, but they certainly didn't sit by and watch Derregain burn."

"Have you bothered to tour the city since you returned?" asked Achillion, even though he already knew the answer. "Crapland is gone. Burned to the ground by Plaguebringer and his army. We needed to build a shekking wall to keep the monsters from overrunning the rest of the city."

"I heard that there was an invasion, or something of the sort," said Nathanial. He sounded less arrogant. Less sure of himself.

"Most of our farms were destroyed, their crops so tainted and poisoned that it may take years for them to recover."

"Yes, I know. I read there were food shortages."

"Shortages?" bellowed Achillion. "People are starving in the streets."

"I don't see how that's the Academy's fault," said Nathanial, shaking his head.

Professor Keldon cleared his throat. "The Academy did essentially nothing to aid the city during the war against Plaguebringer. The Governor has consistently needed to beg, threaten, and, I suspect, steal to get even minimal support out of the Academy."

Nathanial regarded them. It looked like he was fighting not to roll his eyes. "Well, if that's the case, it's an institutional failure that can be easily addressed. I built the Academy to serve the city. If it is failing in that regard, I will correct the problem before I leave."

"Before you leave?" said Achillion. He let the words hang in the air like a damning allegation.

"I have important work to attend to elsewhere," said Nathanial. "So, yes. I do intend to leave. Frankly, it's none of your business."

"Actually, that's where you're wrong," said Russell. "It is his shekking business."

"I don't catch your meaning."

"You see, what the Governor didn't tell you was how we survived Plaguebringer, and how we fought off starvation as long as we did," said Russell. He sounded like he was having fun. "We did it all as a team. My friends, the Governor, and even Raelyn, the succubus you mentioned earlier. We all worked together to save the city, despite the Academy's constant attempts to sabotage us."

"Yes, yes," said Nathanial, waving his hands dismissively. "Get to the point."

"You don't get a copy of my Portal spell until the Governor says so. It's as simple as that."

Nathanial sneered, but held his tongue. Achillion let the silence stretch for several breaths before speaking. "First, Professor Keldon has drawn up a list of items he expects in return for an Elestone containing Russell's version of the Portal spell. You will provide him with everything he's asked for."

"If I may," said the professor, raising his hand. "There is one additional item that hasn't been added to the list yet. Russell will need one of the more destructive wizardry spells given to him. We haven't determined which one yet."

"Nate and I will work that out," said Russell, a smile in his voice. "That won't be a problem, will it, Nate?"

"No problem at all."

"Good. Now to the second item," said Achillion. "There is a warship anchored out in the bay. Plaguebringer's demons captured it early in the war. As long as that ship is there, we can't fish the bay. Its weapons can strike at considerable distances, and with their wind demons, they can easily sink anything we send at them. I need you to destroy that warship."

"And if I do this for you, you'll let my deal with Russell and Professor Keldon move forward?" asked Nathanial.

As much as he wanted to force Nathanial to stay and help, he knew it was a lost cause. It was best to get as much out of him as he could and then let him go. "Yes," said the Governor with a nod.

"Fine. Meet me down by the High City docks in two hours." Nathanial sighed. "For what it's worth, I'm sorry. It's not my fault the Academy turned its back on you. That's not how I wanted things to be."

"Save it." He wasn't interested in excuses. None of them mattered. Derregain was starving, and Achillion needed to find a way to feed it. That's what mattered. "Two hours from now, at the docks, in High city," said Achillion as he turned to leave.

31
Dimitri

Dimitri miserably shuffled through the slushy sewer tunnel. Both his sister and Ghost were moving slowly, allowing him to keep up, but he was miserable all the same. His El'orin, his Master, was forcing him to slam his toes into rocks and jagged sections of the wall. Twice now, Dimitri's Master made him deliberately slip and fall, face-first, into chilly streams of human waste.

"*So pathetic, my little meatsuit,*" teased Dimitri's Master. "*After everything I've done to you, somehow you still think you have a choice. Our fires are truly glorious, and in time, you will come to love them every bit as much as I do. The smell of smoldering flesh will become more appealing than fresh flowers. The frantic screams of burning people will replace the finest music in your ear. The sight of blistered, blackened flesh will become the highest art in your eyes.*"

In his heart of hearts, Dimitri knew it was all true. He already craved the juicy pop of worms between his teeth and the crunchy texture of spiders on his tongue. His Master could easily rewrite his other senses to savor similarly horrible things. Dimitri was already a monster, and it was only going to get worse.

The creature he was becoming terrified him. Dimitri hated the horrible things his magic did to people, but he knew it was only a matter of time before he came to celebrate them. His Master already planted the seeds. There was nothing Dimitri could do to stop them from growing within the garden of his soul. His soil was carefully tilled and fertilized for just that purpose.

"There, there, little meatsuit," whispered Dimitri's Master. *"It won't be so bad. Right now, it bothers you when you burn people to a crisp. Think of how wonderful it will be when burning people becomes your favorite thing in the entire world. I may even make it sexually satisfying for you. Would you like that?"*

Dimitri wanted to die, but he knew his Master wouldn't allow it. He tried holding his breath, but his Master made him gasp. He tried letting himself drown in the rivers of effluence he kept falling in, but his Master dragged him back to his feet. It was hopeless. He was destined to live in misery, at least until such a time as he became the creature his Master wanted him to be.

"Your best opportunity to die was at the hands of that archer, but I've taken care of that for us. I used the power from our latest harvest to enhance our fire. Now, our glorious flames will protect us, reducing thrown objects and even arrows to ash before they so much as break our skin. After all, I must keep my precious meatsuit safe."

"Is there any way you can stop your brother from wallowing in streams of shit?" asked Ghost. "We're not even halfway there, and the stench is already unbearable."

"Stop it! It's not his fault," said Eirini.

Ghost spun to face her. "It's not my fault either. I shouldn't be forced to smell it."

"No one is forcing you to be here. You can go back to Saro, for all I care. It's not like we don't know where we're going."

"My orders were to accompany you to see Sorriah," said Ghost.

"Then go on ahead," said Eirini. "We'll meet you there."

Ghost shook his head. "I'll stay."

"Fine, but I don't want to hear another nasty word about my brother," said Eirini. "None of this is his fault. The Bull did this to him."

Ghost looked down at his hands. "I know. Mend visited his thoughts. She told me what it's like inside his head." Ghost looked back at Dimitri, a strange expression on his face. Maybe it was concern, or perhaps pity, it was hard to say. "Sorry Dimitri. Whatever you're going through, I know it has to be shekking hell."

"Thanks, Ghost," whispered Eirini.

"*Oh, how touching, but we don't need their sympathy,*" said Dimitri's Master. "*Sympathy is for the weak. The Bull summoned me because he needed strength. Once I've molded you into the creature I need you to be, we'll reduce this city to ashes. The weak ones, Mend, Ghost, and even your sister, they'll grow stronger, or they'll die along the way.*"

A tiny ember of resistance flared to life within Dimitri's heart. His Master could make him do many things, but Dimitri still controlled a kernel of agency. There was no way he was going to allow any harm to befall his sister. Back in that ballroom, he was able to look away, forcing his fires to go astray. It wasn't much, but it was a start.

"*How adorable!*" praised the voice in Dimitri's head. "*I must say, I truly cherish how you struggle against me. You see, if you haven't figured it out yet, I'm a sadist. Nothing thrills me more than torturing others.*" Dimitri's Master paused. When he spoke again, his voice was a keening whisper. "*I love it when you fight me. It gives me a reason to punish you. Torturing, tormenting, breaking you... These are the things that make my heart sing.*"

Eirini stepped to the side and waited for her brother to catch up before continuing her journey. She reached out and cradled Dimitri's hand. The simple sensation of his sister's hand holding his meant the world to him.

"To be honest, I feel sorry for both of you," said Ghost.

"Why?" asked Eirini.

"Saro seems to be using you for leverage with Sorriah and the Nightcrawlers."

"I noticed," said Eirini. "Is that a problem?"

"It might be," said Ghost. "Saro is neither trusting nor trustworthy. Since I spend so much time with the Nightcrawlers, he questions my loyalty. I imagine he'll develop similar issues with you."

"Let him. I don't really give a shek what he thinks," said Eirini.

Dimitri closed his eyes, focusing on his good hand. It took tremendous concentration, but he eventually forced two of his fingers to tighten. It wasn't much of a gesture, but it was the best he could do. Hopefully, his sister would find it as comforting as he found her touch.

"You should," said Ghost. "Saro is a murderer, and he isn't above killing his own."

"Can he do that? I thought we were a Coterie."

"He killed our previous leader, Stone," said Ghost. "Not directly, mind you. He arranged for all of us to abandon him on the battlefield."

"And you went along with it?"

"We didn't have much of a choice," said Ghost.

"*How touching,*" taunted Dimitri's Master. "*You worked so hard to gently squeeze your sister's hand. Allow me to help you.*"

Dimitri's hand violently contracted, forcing him to dig his nails into his Eirini's hand. It didn't seem bad at first, but it wasn't long before he felt her skin rip and blood flow. He tried to stop it, but his hand wasn't responding to him anymore. Rage burned in his heart, but it was purposeless. His Master was in complete control.

"Ouch," hissed Eirini. "Stop it, Dimitri. You're hurting me!"

Dimitri closed his eyes and attempted to lean back and to the side. With his Master focusing on his hand, Dimitri lost his balance. He welcomed the vertigo as he fell. Maybe he'd get lucky enough to hit a rock and crack his skull.

Forced to control the rest of Dimitri's body, the vile spirit let go of Eirini's hand. Dimitri twisted and threw his good arm in front of his face as he crashed hard against the sewer floor. Even with his arm there for protection, the impact was enough to rupture the skin, leaving a deep gash along his forehead. Blood flowed into his eyes, and he couldn't be happier. Dimitri's Master could force him to do many things, but he would not hurt his sister.

"Alright, meatsuit, you've made your point. Since you have just enough control over our body to be dangerous to us, I'm willing to make a deal," whispered Dimitri's Master. *"I want you to stop trying to kill us immediately. In return, I won't harm your sister. Not directly, at least. If she falls in combat, or happens to get trapped in a building we set on fire, so be it, but I won't do anything to deliberately hurt her."* Dimitri's Master paused, probably to let him think about it.

"What the shek, Dimitri," said Eirini. "Ghost, come help me get him back on his feet."

"Looks like he cut himself."

Dimitri felt several hands snake beneath him and lift gently. There was a jagged rock, just inches from where he landed. If only his head had struck that instead of the stone floor, he might have killed himself. He expected his Master would be especially careful with him going forward.

"Do we have a bargain?"

"The cut isn't too deep," said Eirini. "I'll heal him once we get him back on his feet."

With the prospect of killing himself unlikely, if not impossible, Dimitri decided to take the deal. His life was no longer his to control. He needed to strive for the minor victories within his reach. Protecting his sister was an important one in his book.

"Excellent," praised Dimitri's Master. *"See, when you work with me, instead of against me, good things happen. I know I'm being very hard on you, but it will get better, I promise. Maybe not tomorrow, next week, or even next year, but eventually you'll look back on all the things we've accomplished together with pride."*

Eirini pressed a glowing white hand to Dimitri's forehead, pouring healing energy into his cut. All the while, blood dripped down her wrist from where Dimitri's tore her skin open. It hammered home the reality of the situation. His sister still loved him. Enduring his Master's endless tortures was the best way Dimitri could love her back.

"I'm so sorry, sweet sister," said Dimitri, though he wasn't the one speaking. His Master was in complete control of his voice. "I was losing my balance, and I guess I just instinctively gripped you too hard."

"It's okay, Dimitri. It'll be easy enough to heal. I'm just happy that you're alright. You could have cracked your skull." Eirini was glancing at the ground, probably noticing the same jagged rock Dimitri noticed.

Dimitri felt his lips curl into a smile. "I don't know what came over me, but rest assured, it won't happen again."

Dimitri didn't like the way his Master forced him to emphasize the last couple of words. He was speaking to Eirini, but the actual message was meant for him. His Master was highlighting the deal they just struck.

Dimitri's Master was making it clear. There was no escape.

32

Attia

Attia couldn't help but smile as she darted through the alleyways on her way to Rellistan Street. There were definitely reasons to be concerned, but she enjoyed her afternoon with Raelyn, nonetheless. Now, she was looking forward to spending a relaxing evening with Alahn. In a brief time, her romantic life went from completely barren to nearly overflowing.

Raelyn was definitely not herself this afternoon. She was much calmer than she was earlier in the day when she and Malcolm argued. Still, something was bothering her. It was almost like she was fighting herself. Attia never felt like she was at risk. She was in control of the encounter, at all times, but there was definitely tension in the air.

Despite that, the bath was wonderful. Attia wasn't used to letting anyone see her body, but she gradually became comfortable with Raelyn's attention. With how wounded her back was, there was really no way to avoid it. After dozens of healing sessions with the succubus, Attia didn't think twice about being shirtless in her presence.

Bathing with Raelyn took things to a different level. It wasn't that it was more intimate than their healing sessions. Healing brought its own kind of intimacy. To Attia, it was a fluid power exchange. Raelyn was often exhausting herself to bring Attia comfort. On the other hand, Attia was exposed and vulnerable, and very much in need of Raelyn's care.

The bath stripped away that playful fluidity. Both of them were there to enjoy the others' presence. They saw each other for who they were, scars and all. While they lightly played at dominance and submission, neither let it muddy the waters they were enjoying together.

Attia even let Raelyn feed on her. She knew the succubus needed to consume human blood to remain in this world. All demons did. It was something Raelyn shared with her early on, when they were first getting to know one another. Attia wasn't sure why she did it, but she found herself pressing back into Raelyn's embrace, bearing her neck, and commanding the demon to drink.

The sting of Raelyn's bite was like a surge of electricity. Throughout Attia's life, pain was a trusted companion. She was a Pathfinder, after all. She trained from a young age to endure all varieties of discomfort. The extensive wounds she received across her various battles raised things to a new level, but this was different. By commanding Raelyn to bite her, Attia took control of her pain. She made the rules. She set the boundaries, and when she was ready, she invited that meaningful pain into her life.

Before departing, Attia raised her concerns about how hard Conner was working. They didn't argue about it. If anything, Raelyn seemed grateful Attia brought it up. It was something that had been troubling her, and Raelyn assured Attia she was searching for a solution.

Attia stepped back, drifting deeper into the alley, allowing a patrol of Bumbles to pass on the street up ahead. She knew most of the Bumbles who patrolled the region. None of them messed with her, but she preferred to avoid them all the same. Better safe than sorry.

Satisfied they were continuing on their way, Attia crossed the street and entered the alley on the far side. Something didn't feel right to her. Her heart skipped a beat and her breath caught in her throat. It felt like she needed to cough. Was there another El'orin nearby?

"I feel it as well. I think it may be more than one," said her Ally.

Attia crouched and carefully peeked out onto the street, looking both directions. Other than the patrol of Bumbles and a few staggering drunks, the street was uninhabited. It wasn't unheard of for people, looking to avoid attention, to travel along the roofs, but with all the ice and snow, it wasn't safe. Still, it was probably worth checking.

"It's more than one person, I'm certain of it," whispered Attia's Ally. *"I can't imagine a group of them would use the roofs. What about the sewers? If I'm not mistaken, the ring tunnels cross through this area."*

Attia thought that was right. She wasn't an expert when it came to the sewers, but Alahn knew them well. He drew her maps on a couple of occasions. He promised to show her the wonders of Undercity whenever they found the time.

Kicking away the snow, Attia quickly found a sewer grate. The alleys were full of them. The grate was held closed by a lock and chain, but testing the lock, Attia found it opened easily. She wasn't surprised. Alahn claimed that most of the sewer grates in Derregain were unlocked. The people who lived beneath the streets prided themselves on picking every lock within days of installation.

If there ever was a ladder attached to this grate, someone ran off with it. That didn't surprise Attia. If she lived beneath the streets of Derregain, she'd make a point of stealing a ladder to carry with her.

Focusing on her false eye, Attia peered down into the sewers. Gradually, her ability to see in the dark took hold, giving her a clear view of what was below. The fall was approximately twelve feet. The stone floor was covered with slush, but it appeared even. Deciding there was little time to waste, Attia pushed the grate aside and jumped down.

She landed in a crouch. The splashing slush made more noise than she would have preferred, but the sound quickly faded, eclipsed by the plops and splashes of melting slush dripping down from the streets above.

Attia took a deep, calming breath to activate her balance magic. She needed it to soften her footfalls. Moving without sound, and maximizing her El'orin's ability to conceal her within the shadows, gave her tremendous advantages. Being able to see in the dark only improved her situation.

"This is what we're built for, Attia, but even with all our advantages, we must be careful. Now that we're closer, I believe there are three of them. One of them seems far more powerful than the others. You can feel them, can't you?"

Attia nodded. They were moving away from her, but slowly. Once she felt confident her balance magic was working, she began making her way down the tunnel. She moved slowly at first, gradually picking up speed as she learned how best to navigate the sewer quietly.

It wasn't long before the narrow tunnel emptied into a much larger corridor, a ring tunnel. Most who traveled beneath the streets favored the ring tunnels. Attia assumed the people she was hunting were no different.

Keeping to the sides of the spacious tunnel, Attia could move fairly quickly. The floors of the tunnel were slightly sloped, forcing most of the liquid into channels running down the center.

It made it easy for her to avoid noisily walking through slush and slop.

Avoiding light was a touch more difficult. While the ring tunnel wasn't well lit, the walls were peppered with occasional Liquidlight globes, housed in glorified sconces. She approached each cautiously, making sure no one was in sight before darting past them. While she was nearly invisible in the shadows, any strong source of illumination countered her stealth.

"*We're getting closer,*" said her Ally. "*I think they're just beyond the next bend. Proceed with caution.*"

Heeding her Ally's warning, Attia crept forward. She could make out snippets of a conversation, or perhaps an argument. Attia didn't immediately recognize any of the voices, but that didn't surprise her. She only met Derregain's El'orin a few times, at Conclave, and none of them seemed to go out of their way to be social during those gatherings.

Carefully rounding the bend, she spotted her targets. There were indeed three of them, but only one of them mattered to her. The creepy boy with the withered arm was there. He was the one who nearly burned Alahn to death. He was the one she planned to kill first.

Attia guessed one of the other two was his sister. She believed the girl was a necromancer of some skill, though nothing compared to Malcolm. The other one was definitely Ghost. She saw him on a few occasions before. His black hair, framed against incredibly pale skin, made him easily recognizable.

"*Ghost is the one who can become like a spirit,*" said her Ally. "*If you kill the fire-maker first, Ghost will get away. I'm not challenging your decision. I'm merely offering advice.*"

Attia didn't care about Ghost. As far as she was concerned, it was probably best if he turned into a spirit. She didn't think she could successfully kill all three of them. With Ghost out of the fight, her odds of killing the other two improved.

None of the three of them seemed aware of her yet, but Attia knew that would change as she approached. The only sensible strategy was to charge them, hoping to close the distance before they could turn and cast spells against her.

Using her magic to further soften her footfalls, Attia broke into a sprint. She was much faster than most people, and it wasn't long before she closed to within a few dozen feet of her targets. The next few steps were critical. Attia knew they would sense her El'orin any moment now.

The boy with the withered arm was the first to notice. He raised his good arm and spun around. Strangely, instead of calling out an alarm, he coughed out an unintelligible series of sounds. Was it some kind of spell? Whatever he did, it did the job. His sister and Ghost immediately spun around.

Attia took a series of long strides before diving into a somersault, closing the rest of the distance. It looked like all three of them were casting spells. With any luck, she'd gut the boy with the withered arm before he completed his spell. Attia thought he was the dangerous one. Ghost and the girl were necromancers. They were likely summoning spirits. She planned to kill them before their spirits became a problem.

"I agree. The boy with the withered arm is the dangerous one. His El'orin is the strongest, by far," advised Attia's Ally.

Rolling to her feet, Attia drew her blade into a deep cut, targeting the boy's belly. She would have preferred to impale, but she ended her somersault too close to her target. She expected him to retreat a few steps, and he didn't.

Blinding orange light flashed across the corridor, and intense heat washed over her. Smoldering sheets of flame sprung up around the boy before Attia's blade could bite into his soft flesh. Had she been prepared, Attia might have completed her cut, but the fires caught her by complete surprise, forcing her to spring back before she could complete her deadly strike.

Searing pain erupted across Attia's hands, forearms, cheeks, and forehead. Whatever spell the boy cast, it was powerful. Even having avoided the flames, she suffered serious burns. Knowing she couldn't afford to waste even an instant, Attia sprung to her feet and prepared another strike.

Out of the corner of her good eye, Attia caught the faint glow of lavender. She tried to drag her gaze away from the scintillating light, but it was too late. The sight of the girl's lovely lavender eyes was breathtaking. Attia couldn't bring herself to turn away.

"I've got her. There's nothing she can do," said the girl. "Burn her to ashes, Dimitri."

"Wait!" shouted Ghost. "That one is named Attia. She's the hunter who killed Claw."

Ghost was just outside of Attia's field of vision. She could see the blocky silhouette of his shadow painted across the slushy floor, so she knew roughly where he was standing, but she couldn't see what he was doing.

"So shekking what? I'm sure she'll burn like anyone else," said the girl.

The boy with the withered arm waved his good hand, and a tiny ball of fire sputtered into existence. There was something about him that just didn't add up. His face was twisted into a tortured sneer, but his eyes were all wrong. They were darting back and forth, and if Attia wasn't mistaken, tears were dripping down his cheek.

"You're holding her with your Captivate spell," said Ghost. "Let's not rush this. Let me summon a few wraiths. Give Dimitri a few moments to craft the perfect fire spell. The last thing we want to do is let her get free, even for a moment."

I think we underestimated Ghost, whispered Attia's Ally.

Attia tried to rip her gaze away, but there was nothing she could do. Her false eye, interestingly enough, seemed completely fine. The Captivate spell did not affect it, but it didn't help her much. With her good eye held by the magic, she was helplessly paralyzed.

"I have my first wraith," said Ghost. "Give me a moment to summon a second one. How much longer can you hold her?"

"I can hold her as long as you need," said the girl.

The ball of bouncing fire in the creepy boy's hand expanded. Whatever was going on inside his head, Attia didn't think it was going well. One of his eyes was shut, but the other was wide open, with the pupil rapidly bouncing back and forth. His lips and mouth were so contorted it looked painful. Tears were pouring down his face now.

"Do it, Dimitri!" shouted the girl. "Blast that bitch!"

Dimitri tossed the ball of fire high in the air, where it hovered for a moment. Slowly, it inched towards her, gradually picking up speed. Attia's heart raced, and she tried to close her eye, but the Captivate spell was too strong. Maybe the fire wouldn't kill her. Alahn survived a blast. Maybe she would too.

Attia didn't think she would be so lucky. She might have welcomed death a few months ago, when her back was horribly shredded, and even her friends avoided looking at her. But things were so different now. Raelyn truly cared for her, and Attia loved her for it.

There it was. She finally said it. She loved Raelyn. Attia knew it was silly. Raelyn's kiss twisted her heart and mind. None of her feelings were real, but Attia didn't care. It felt authentic enough to her. She enjoyed every minute she spent with the succubus, and she knew the feeling was mutual. Raelyn was incredibly busy, yet she always found time to spend with Attia.

Not that any of it mattered. She was about to die, and there wasn't a single thing she could do about it. She was helplessly transfixed, waiting for some superheated ball of fire to burn her flesh from her bones. What a terrible way to go.

Dimitri coughed, sputtered, and gasped. He forced his eyes shut, and he turned away. The swirling ball of roiling flames responded, drifting, ever so slightly, to the side. It slipped past Attia with barely an inch to spare. An instant later, it exploded, showering the area with tiny meteors of bubbling fire.

"What the shek just happened?" shouted the girl. "Dimitri, what have you done?"

One of those tiny meteors landed on Attia's shoulder. It took a moment for it to burn through her leathers, but when it did, intense pain raced through her body, instantly shattering the magic of the Captivate spell.

"*Shut your good eye!*" barked Attia's Ally. "*Do it now!*"

The girl quietly uttered a phrase, and fresh lavender light flooded from her eyes, but it didn't matter. Attia's real eye was closed. Her magical eye seemed completely unhindered by the Captivate spell. Using only her runecrafted eye, Attia's sight was far from perfect, but it was more than enough to guide her next moves.

Stepping to the side, she delivered a high cut, hoping to cleanly cut the creepy boy's throat. She kept her distance, trying to hit with the farthest part of the blade. She knew the boy's fires would lash out against her, and she wanted to be as far away as possible.

Attia's world melted into a sea of swirling red and orange, but she didn't fall back. She understood she'd be badly burned, but the only way to put an end to the fires was to kill their creator. The smell of burning hair and smoldering skin filled her nostrils as searing agony raced up and down her arms. The pain grew so intense she thought she might pass out.

And then the pain abruptly faded, washed away by a crashing wave of white mist. Joyous ecstasy replaced Attia's agony. She knew she was horribly burned, but she didn't care anymore. Every fiber of her being drank in the white mist, exalting in its joyous power.

"*That one was much stronger than I thought. Yes! So much power!*"

"Dimitri!" cried his sister. "No!"

Attia shifted her focus to Ghost. He was standing two paces behind where Dimitri's headless body collapsed in a crumpled heap. Two tall, slender wisps of swirling shadows danced near him. As she watched, a third materialized off to the side. They were wraiths.

Taking the briefest moment to center herself, Attia activated her Breath of Battle. She was so practiced with that particular piece of magic, casting it was like second nature to her. The moment her spell took hold, she sprung forward, her blade whipping into motion.

She directed her cut toward Ghost's arms. They were the easiest available targets. As her sword closed in on her enemy's flesh, the trajectory slightly changed. Attia didn't know what was happening at first, but it quickly dawned on her that her Ally was controlling her sword. In the past, Attia's vision often narrowed, assisting and directing her toward her opponent's points of vulnerability, but this was new.

"I can guide your cuts now, much like Liam's El'orin guides his shield, though not to that extent, I suppose," whispered her Ally. *"We'll need to practice often, but this should make us far more deadly."*

Attia's blade caught Ghost in the wrist, just beneath the meat of his hand. The sword ripped through his vital veins and arteries, but it didn't stop there. It cut down the length of his forearm, making sure the wounds were too wide to be easily closed. Without healing magic, Ghost was certain to bleed to death.

Ghost screamed as streams of blood spurted from his slit wrist. Attia reversed her blade, quickly drawing it back with a second cut, but Ghost's body shimmered and faded. Her sword passed through his translucent body as if it weren't there. The speed of his shift from flesh to spirit surprised her.

"Your Captivate spell isn't working, Eirini," shouted Ghost. "You need to run."

The trio of wraiths Ghost summoned sprung into action, whipping their impossibly long shadowy arms at Attia. She managed to avoid all of their freezing shadows, but she needed to rely on her balance magic Shield spell to help pull her out of the way. Each time Attia dodged, her Breath of Battle drew her blade into a quick counter strike. None of the attacks were particularly powerful, but she expected they would add up over time.

Attia turned to face Dimitri's sister just as two more wraiths coalesced into existence. The girl heeded Ghost's advice, giving up on her Captivate spell. Like her late brother, she was crying. Based on the expression on the girl's face, Attia didn't think the tears were born from sadness or pain.

Dimitri's sister was pissed.

33
Eirini

Eirini wanted to scream! The Bumbles murdered her father. Her aunt was little more than a slave, serving the Governor and his bitch succubus. She could survive all of that as long as her brother was with her, but that was over now. Dimitri was dead, beheaded by Attia, another one of the Governor's pets! Eirini didn't know who she hated more, but right now, it didn't matter. The Governor wasn't here, but that shekking bitch, Attia, was.

She needed to die!

"*Calm down,*" advised the voice in Eirini's head. "*I'll help you kill her, but now might not be the time. Maybe, with enough wraiths, there's a chance, but Attia is dangerous. Her El'orin is incredibly powerful. She's a hunter, and right now, you're her only prey.*"

Attia leapt forward, and Eirini fell back. She wasn't nearly as fast as Attia, but Ghost's wraiths were slowing Attia down just enough. Closing her eyes momentarily, Eirini forced her wraiths to join the fight. Surely, five wraiths would be too much for anyone to deal with.

The dancing cloud of wraiths surrounded Attia, each sweeping its shadowy arms at the woman, but surprisingly, nearly all of them missed. A few patches of frost crystallized around Attia's leathers, but not nearly as many as Eirini expected. To make matters worse, Attia was somehow weaving in counterstrikes each time a wraith attempted to hit her. Her sword was moving so fast it was a blur. Eirini never saw anything like it.

"She's relying on her balance magic to protect her, I'm sure of it," said the spirit inside Eirini. *"I don't understand all the counterstrikes. It must be some kind of battlemagic or balance spell, but it's nothing I'm familiar with."*

Ghost floated next to Eirini. "Summon as many spirits as you can, but you must run. We're close to the Nightcrawlers' warrens. We'll be safe there."

"I know you don't want to hear it, but Ghost is right. We'll get our revenge, I promise, but now isn't the time."

Eirini tried to ignore the voice in her head, but she knew he was right. Even as she backed away from the battle, Attia was fighting her way closer. There were only four wraiths attacking her now. Attia brought one down with her rapid counterstrikes. At a certain point, Attia was likely to ignore the wraiths and charge. Eirini's necromancy Shield would protect her, but she didn't know for how long.

Taking a deep breath, Eirini retrieved a pair of Soulstones from her pouch. Gently coaxing a soul from each, Eirini beckoned a pair of wraiths to cross over from the Astral. Normally, she summoned one at a time. Summoning two at once was surprisingly taxing. It felt like buckets of slushy water being dumped over her head. Eirini's teeth chattered, and she shivered uncontrollably.

"You have four wraiths now. That's too many. Controlling so many wraiths will drain our well in less than a minute. We

won't have enough energy left to power our Shield should Attia come for us."

Eirini backed away as fast as she dared. The ground was covered with slush and ice. One slip or fall, and Attia would pounce. Right now, the swarm of six wraiths was the only thing keeping the deadly assassin at bay. Eirini felt like she was dead either way. If she didn't keep sending wraiths into the fray, Attia would be free to charge her. If she kept sending new wraiths, she wouldn't have any magic left to defend herself.

"Look, I know you don't want to hear this, but it's the only way," said her El'orin. *"Quick, before you get farther away, send your wraiths into your brother's body. Attia will probably pounce on us, getting in a strike or two, but hopefully, our defenses will hold."*

Eirini bit her lip and shook her head, but she knew her El'orin was right. Once her wraiths entered a body, she'd be freed from the responsibility of protecting them from the Astral Plane. Regrettably, Dimitri was the only corpse in the area. She didn't have another option.

Concentrating, Eirini sent her cloud of wraiths racing away from Attia, leaving only a pair of spirits left attacking the deadly woman. Attia immediately responded by leaping into a somersault. As expected, once most of the wraiths left her, she focused only on Eirini.

Eirini shivered as Attia's sword passed through her neck. If not for her necromancy Shield making her body momentarily insubstantial, the cut would have been lethal. As terrifying as the prospect of staying near the deadly assassin was to Eirini, she needed to focus on her collection of wraiths. They were near her brother now. Thin streams of mist were flowing from them into the fresh corpse.

"What are you doing?" said Ghost. "You need to run."

"Not until I leave this shekking murderer a little present!" hissed Eirini. "And if my brother doesn't kill you today, Attia, don't worry about it. I'll kill you later. I'll kill you. I'll kill your lovers. I'll kill your friends!" Eirini coughed up a glob of phlegm and spat it at Attia. "Shek, I'll kill anyone who's ever said a single friendly word to you!"

Attia easily sidestepped Eirini's glob of phlegm. As she did, her blade flashed, delivering a blindingly fast cut. There wasn't a lot of force behind it, so Eirini didn't spend the magical energy on her necromancy Shield, but she regretted it. Blood poured down her arm from the deep slice across her shoulder. Even quick cuts from Attia were potentially deadly.

In the distance, the headless corpse of Dimitri climbed to its feet. With four wraiths inside it, the corpse didn't shamble. It moved with eerie speed and fluidity. The fact that it lacked a head didn't seem to hinder it either. The spirits within it didn't need eyes to see. They saw things in their own special way, and the first thing they saw was Attia.

The headless corpse of Dimitri raced across the sewer tunnel. Attia must have heard its footfalls, because she turned to face it just before it reached her. Eirini cursed under her breath. She wanted to see it drive its claws through Attia's body, ripping out bones and organs, but that didn't happen. The ghoul that had been her brother leapt at Attia, but the agile woman dove to the side at the last instant.

"We need to get out of here!" shouted Ghost.

"*He's right,*" whispered the voice inside Eirini's head.

Eirini wanted to stay and watch the fight, but she knew it wasn't safe. The headless ghoul was incredibly fast, but Attia seemed a hair faster. Ghost was down to a single wraith now. Attia must have killed another with her annoying counterstrikes. As much as Eirini wanted to stay and summon another wraith, she knew she couldn't. Her well was nearly empty. All it would take was a single precision strike from Attia to end her life.

If Eirini died, there would be no one left to avenge her family. The Bumbles who murdered her father would go unpunished.

The Governor wouldn't be punished for giving the orders. Most importantly, Attia would never answer for her crimes! Eirini needed to survive if she ever hoped to avenge Dimitri's death.

The ghoul leapt at Attia, forcing the woman to retreat a few steps. They were fighting along the far wall of the ring tunnel now. Attia was circling to put the ghoul between her and Eirini. It looked like Attia was making sure her own lines of retreat remained open. Interesting. Perhaps the ghoul was too much for her.

"Ghost, drop out of spirit form and summon more wraiths," commanded Eirini.

"Are you mad?" whined Ghost. "I'm going to bleed to death shortly after my body becomes flesh again. I leave my spiritual form with the same wounds I had going in. I need to find a healer before I dare return to flesh."

"I'm a healer," said Eirini.

"A healer with little left in her well," said Ghost. "If you had enough power to heal me, you'd summon more wraiths yourself. I'm not an idiot."

Eirini sighed. Unfortunately, Ghost wasn't an idiot. Assessing the battle, Eirini didn't think it mattered. Attia killed the last of the wraiths. It was just her and Dimitri now. Well, what was left of Dimitri. His headless corpse. Even if Eirini summoned more wraiths, Attia would probably get away. Attia was retreating down the ring tunnel as she fought. It wouldn't be long before she was out of sight.

"Fine," said Eirini, shaking her head. "There's nothing we can do here. Let's go." She took one more last look at the undead creature that had been her brother before turning and jogging down the sewer tunnel. Ghost floated next to her.

Eirini barely noticed the passage of time as she traveled the tunnels. Her jogging eventually transitioned into a run, at times verging on a sprint. Her lungs ached and burned, but she loved the sensation. In the back of her mind, she wondered if she needed to be worried about the deep cut on her shoulder, but she didn't care. If she bled out before she made it to the Nightcrawlers' warren, so be it.

"You're bleeding badly, but I don't think you'll bleed out," whispered her El'orin. *"Still, let's not be stupid about this. Stop running for a second and spare yourself a small burst of healing. You have enough power left in your well to do that. Why risk bleeding out when there is no reason to?"*

Eirini stopped running, sank to her knees, and screamed. She touched her shoulder and felt her bloody flesh move. She planned to heal the wound before continuing, but she wasn't ready yet. For now, she needed the pain. It was the only thing keeping her going.

Dimitri was dead. Nothing was ever going to change that. That shekking bitch, Attia, snuck through the sewers and took him from her. She had no right! If the Downtrodden were at war with Attia and her friends, it might make sense, but they weren't. This attack came out of nowhere. How did Attia know where they were in the first place? Was she hunting Eirini and her brother? If so, for how long?

Ghost drifted to a stop next to her. It looked like he wanted to say something, but he wisely kept quiet. Eirini didn't want to hear a single shekking word from Ghost's mouth. She didn't blame him for what happened to her brother. He fought hard and even suffered a nearly lethal wound. Eirini should be grateful for Ghost's efforts, but she simply didn't like him. She hated the way he whined about everything.

Taking a deep breath, Eirini willed a gentle trickle of healing magic into her sliced shoulder. She didn't close the wound entirely. She left a portion of it open. Eirini liked the pain and how the blood felt as it dripped down her arm. Hopefully, the cut was deep enough to form an angry scar. She wanted a permanent reminder of Attia, and all the horrible things she represented.

Climbing to her feet, Eirini resumed her journey. Once again, she jogged, but this time she was careful not to accelerate to a full run. They were very close to the Nightcrawlers' warrens now. Soon, they would encounter some of the acolytes who patrolled the region.

Most of the Nightcrawlers knew who she was. If not, they'd certainly recognize Ghost. He was there so often, Sorriah had a room specially prepared for him. Still, Eirini wondered how the Nightcrawlers might react. Even after healing herself, she was wounded. Ghost's wounds were potentially fatal.

With how prevalent Life Flowers were in the area, the wounds weren't likely to be a problem. The Nightcrawlers were well-supplied with Healing Potions. Eirini was more interested in how Sorriah might react. She pretended to be an ally, but was she really one? Would she even care about Dimitri's death?

Would Sorriah casually dismiss Eirini's quest for vengeance as a childish waste of time? Somehow, Eirini didn't think so. Saro planned to trade Eirini's newfound skills for additional support from the Nightcrawlers, but Eirini had a different plan. She'd happily stay with Sorriah, animating ghoul after ghoul, as long as Sorriah helped Eirini with the one thing she wanted.

Vengeance!

34
Ssalyssna

Ssalyssna sat against a secluded wall in the commons, watching all the commotion with mild amusement. She was wearing the skin of a street tough she claimed some time ago. He lacked friends or family, making him the perfect skin to wear when exploring the Corners, the towering, rundown buildings the Downtrodden lived in.

Even though it was one of her least favorite, Ssalyssna made a point of wearing this skin every couple of days. He was unremarkable in nearly every way. His combat skills were middling at best. He studied no magic, and his basic survival skills were barely satisfactory.

Yet somehow, he was well-respected among the Downtrodden. That told Ssalyssna all she needed to know about this street gang. The fact that they respected such a simple specimen meant most of them were likely even less accomplished, although she struggled to understand how such a thing was possible.

The impoverished people of the Corners were on edge today. While some celebrated their recent assault on Middletown, many feared the Bumbles would soon sting them in retaliation. These people were safe from the Bumbles, of course. By taking care of the situation personally, Ssalyssna was removing the militia from the equation.

She wondered if it was worth it. She knew the Governor was a skilled manipulator. Was he using her? She didn't think it was likely, but it was worth considering the possibility, nonetheless. She was the one at risk, after all.

Not that she thought there was much risk.

Even with her predominantly holding souls for their social value, Ssalyssna doubted Saro, or his friends, could hurt her. Her capabilities in her serpent form would be sufficient for the task. Now, if Novus, Cinderhorn, or the children of the Citadel moved against her, she might be in trouble, but she didn't think there was any actual risk of that happening.

Behind the scenes, Ssalyssna was the one orchestrating everything. She knew which strings to strum, which strands to pull. The Governor might not trust her, but he had little choice in the matter. He needed her. That took both Raelyn and the children of the Citadel off the board, at least for now.

Novus was slippery, almost secretive. Ssalyssna knew he served a powerful Ancient, known as the Wanderer, but she knew little more than that. His motivations were masked. Even Ssalyssna's imps struggled to discern his true aims. Perhaps Novus was merely seeking sanctuary in this world, but she doubted it. Ssalyssna knew he was amassing a small army of changeling demons. To what purpose?

Cinderhorn presented a potential problem, but Ssalyssna wasn't so sure. She always knew Cinderhorn was powerful, but what she saw at Demonic Court astonished her. His mastery over Telekinesis was staggering. Still, she questioned where his loyalties rested. While he served the Queen, many in the

Netherworld whispered tales of his growing dissatisfaction. Some suggested he preferred Raelyn over the Demon Queen.

Ssalyssna needed to solve the Cinderhorn puzzle before she severed ties with Chariden. Finding someone else to summon her back to this world was a simple matter, but Cinderhorn's imps saw everything. The Guardian would know she returned to the city, but what would he do with the information? Would he inform both Chariden and Raelyn? What would happen if he did?

Ssalyssna hoped Raelyn would speak up for her. That was why she bargained for the Governor's words on her behalf. She needed to establish herself as a valuable supporter of the city, prior to severing her ties with Chariden. This mission was an important step toward achieving that.

If Ssalyssna consumed Saro and his immediate supporters, she could easily use his skin to seize control over his street gang. With control of Senator Ominar and Saro's army of impoverished wretches, Ssalyssna would wield true power in Derregain.

With such power, she doubted the Demon Queen would be in any position to oppose her. Simply put, Ssalyssna would have the power to destroy Derregain. Without Derregain's blood supply, countless demons would be forced to return to the Netherworld. Chariden's rule couldn't survive such a blow.

But she was getting ahead of herself. Ssalyssna needed to deal with Saro first. Based on conversations she recently overheard, Ghost, and the siblings, recently left the building, exiting through the sewers. No one was certain where they were going and when they might return.

Ssalyssna wasn't sure how to respond. She considered working her way up to the top floor and dealing with Saro now, while three of his associates were missing. On the other hand, there were advantages to waiting for their return. The last thing she wanted to do was leave loose ends. It would be cleaner to kill them all in a single battle.

Of all of them, Ghost was the one that interested her the most. His power to become insubstantial intrigued her. She knew Ghost's El'orin controlled it. What she didn't know was what would happen when she consumed a soul with an El'orin. Would she consume both souls? If so, would the souls combine to occupy just one of her seven slots, or would they occupy two? If consuming a soul and El'orin occupied two of her seven souls, would she be able to pick and choose which remained? Keeping all the El'orin and releasing the mortals seemed the strongest option to her.

The possibilities were endless. If she could access the abilities of El'orin, her power might grow to rival those of the Ancients. Not even the strongest of demons would dare stand against her if she had the power to make her body spectral, or summon the same Aura as Achillion did. Most of the El'orin were a mystery to her, but she couldn't wait to discover what each was capable of.

And what would happen if she consumed Saro's El'ominae? Achillion described El'ominae as being incredibly powerful. Among other things, they could summon new El'orin spirits. How would that work? Would Ssalyssna gain the ability to call new El'orin? Would she be able to select the strongest of them and consume them, claiming their powers as her own?

Chariden held dominion over this world, but her control was tenuous at best. Her most powerful servant, Cinderhorn, doubted her. Her newly installed viceroy, Raelyn, overshadowed her. One of the demon lords she summoned, Plaguebringer, waged war against her. The other, Vahruul, seemed to be marshaling armies for his own purposes. It wouldn't surprise Ssalyssna if Vahruul followed in Plaguebringer's footsteps and betrayed the Demon Queen.

Intrigued by the possibilities, Ssalyssna bode her time. She needed to attack tonight, but there was no need to rush it. She could afford to wait a couple of hours. Hopefully, Ghost and the others would return by then. If not, she could always hunt them later, if it proved necessary. She was an excellent huntress.

Ssalyssna wondered what the best strategy might be. She needed to wear this skin throughout the building, at least until someone questioned her. Once challenged, she thought the skin of Selandra Mayes might be useful. That skin granted Ssalyssna access to many spells.

She thought the best plan was to shift into Selandra's skin the moment she was challenged. Ssalyssna could use Selandra's sonic magic to create a bubble of silence, preventing others from sounding the alarm. Selandra's Lightning spell would also prove useful against weaker threats.

Ssalyssna planned to shift into her serpent form before starting her final assault. Saro, and his close allies, would be far stronger than simple street toughs. If Ghost was present, she planned to consume him first. If Ssalyssna managed to master his ability to become spectral, she planned to use it during the rest of the battle.

Saro probably needed to die second. Ssalyssna didn't entirely know what he was capable of, but she doubted his powers were trivial. After all, he was their leader. There had to be a reason for it. Ssalyssna knew Saro moved significantly faster than normal human specimens and that he wielded small blades with surprising precision. Fortunately for her, small blades struggled to penetrate her thick scales.

The real problem with Saro was his speed. Ssalyssna didn't want to let him get away. At a minimum, she needed his skin in order to assume control of his gang. She suspected his thoughts and memories might prove useful as well, but her desire to claim him ran deeper.

Ssalyssna relished the opportunity to torture Saro. She wasn't particularly fond of the Governor, but she certainly respected him. If Saro was responsible for even half the sins Achillion blamed him for, he deserved to suffer endlessly.

If there was one thing Ssalyssna excelled at, it was torture. The souls she stole spent their miserable existences screaming in agony. Even those she tried to protect suffered tremendously. There was simply no way to steal a soul without crippling it. It wasn't Ssalyssna's fault, but even if it was, she wouldn't change a thing.

Ssalyssna loved the way her enslaved souls helplessly wept. She so looked forward to hearing Saro's screams. She imagined how he might cry, shamelessly begging for even a whisper of relief. Ssalyssna planned to tease him with the promise of freedom, only to snatch it away at the last second, over and over again.

She didn't plan to keep him forever. Ssalyssna could only enslave seven souls at a time, and with the prospect of capturing El'orin a real possibility, she knew Saro was too weak to remain with her for eternity. Still, she planned to torture him as long as possible, savoring every delicious scream.

35

Conner

Conner rubbed his stinging eyes and yawned. He hadn't slept, and he didn't expect to soon. Raelyn was finally resting. Conner needed to oversee the House of Healing until she woke. Afterward, he planned to visit Liam and Cinderhorn. If everything went well, he'd catch a few hours of sleep after that.

He knew of a spell in balance magic that suspended the need for sleep. Healers in the Citadel occasionally used it when observing a patient for long periods of time. Conner suspected some of the Pathfinders relied on it as well. Until now, he never saw a purpose for it, but maybe it was time he learned it. He wondered if Attia knew it, and if so, could she teach it to him?

Conner wasn't sure what he hoped to accomplish by visiting his brother. Daemenos warned him things wouldn't happen quickly. Apparently, nothing happened quickly in the Netherworld. Without access to new healing magic, Conner didn't dare remove his brother from the Runes of Stasis. So, what was the point of visiting?

Was he really going to forego sleep just to gaze at his frozen brother and chat with Cinderhorn? In his heart, he felt like he needed to be there, but he struggled to see any real value in it. Cinderhorn was incredibly influential. There was a possibility that the demon, moved by Conner's devotion to his brother, would intercede and tip the scales in Conner's favor, but that seemed like wishful thinking. Was he visiting out of guilt?

A slight commotion out in the hallway shook Conner from his reflections. A few of the guards were following someone, but they weren't acting aggressively. As they drew closer, Conner recognized Attia. She was limping badly. Her dirty leathers were caked in blood in a few places.

"I need Raelyn," called Attia as she staggered into the admissions center.

Conner rushed out from behind the admissions desk. He wouldn't know the severity of Attia's wounds until he removed her leathers. He only planned to wake Raelyn if it was absolutely necessary. "Let's get you into a private room. I want to take a look."

"I want Raelyn to take care of me."

"She's sleeping. If we don't let her rest, her well will never refill," said Conner, shaking his head. Now that he was closer, he noticed several severe burns on Attia's forearms, with less intense burns all across her face and neck. What happened to her?

"Why are you being so difficult?" asked Attia. "Raelyn always treats me. That's how she wants it."

Conner gestured towards a closed door on the far wall. "We'll talk about it, but not here." He waited until Attia started walking before following. Her leathers were torn in a few places, mostly along her back and shoulders. With the way she was limping, he was surprised there were no rips around her knees or thighs.

Despite Attia's wounds, Conner struggled to keep up with her. He found himself, at times, needing to jog to keep pace with her, even with her limping. Conner's frailty never seemed to be a serious issue before, but he couldn't ignore it any longer. It was bad enough that he needed Raelyn to carry his brother the other night. Struggling to keep up with a hobbled Attia was borderline humiliating.

Conner waited for Attia to enter the room before following, gently closing the door behind him. He gestured toward a small bed in the corner, observing Attia's movements as she climbed on top of the bed and turned to face him. "What happened?" he asked.

Attia looked away. "I stumbled across some of the Downtrodden."

Suddenly, the wounds all made sense. "Which members?"

"Ghost, and the two new ones," said Attia softly. "The brother and sister."

"Dimitri and Eirini." Conner remembered them from the many times they visited their aunt, Stitches, not that he really interacted with them. They stopped showing up a while ago. Probably after they became members of the Downtrodden. "And you suffered these injuries fighting them?"

Attia looked at him and nodded. "The creepy one with the withered arm—"

"Dimitri," offered Conner.

"I killed him, but he burned me pretty badly in the process."

Conner wasn't surprised Attia killed one of the Downtrodden. It was no secret she was hunting them. "And what about all the other wounds?"

"Ghost and the other one summoned a swarm of wraiths," said Attia. "At one point, they animated Dimitri's corpse, making some into some kind of ghoul. It was far stronger and faster than any I've fought before. It nearly ripped me apart before I managed to put it down."

Conner was growing tired of hearing about ghouls. They seemed to be everywhere these days. Ghouls slaughtered the

Bumbles when they went to arrest the Downtrodden. Later, ghouls entered the mushroom fields and slaughtered the harvest teams working there. Last night, ghouls roamed the streets of Middletown. They played a part in what happened to Liam. And now, a ghoul nearly killed Attia. It wasn't lost on Conner that the Downtrodden seemed to be at the center of everything. "What happened to the others? Did you kill Ghost or Eirini?"

"Ghost turned into a spirit a second after I cut him," said Attia. "There was nothing I could do to him after that. Eirini got away while I was fighting her brother's corpse."

A flash of jealousy raced through Conner's heart. He would have benefited from tasting Dimitri's white mist. Attia was selfish to hunt alone. She needed to involve Conner, or even the entire group. Conner took a deep breath and pushed the intrusive thoughts away. "Well, let's take a look at those wounds."

Attia shook her head. "I want Raelyn to look at me."

"I told you, she's sleeping."

"I'll wait."

"What's going on with you two?" Conner immediately regretted asked the question. He knew Attia and Raelyn were spending a lot of time together. If he really wanted to know about it, he could have easily asked Raelyn, but he didn't think it was any of his business.

"It's..." Attia fidgeted nervously with her hands. "It's complicated."

"Raelyn went to bed just an hour ago," said Conner. Now that the conversation was in motion, he didn't think it wise to stop it. "If you're going to insist on waiting for her, we have plenty of time to talk about it."

"She kissed me," blurted Attia. "It was an accident, alright?"

"Raelyn doesn't really do things by accident," said Conner.

"I know, but it doesn't matter," said Attia with a sigh. "What's done is done."

That explained why she only wanted to let Raelyn heal her. The kiss probably happened during one of their earlier healing sessions. Attia spent a lot of time in the House of Healing. She tried to be discreet about her comings and goings, but Conner basically ran the House of Healing. He was well aware of how often Attia visited. After a long pause, he asked, "Is she good to you?" He didn't think it was a particularly good question, but he was at a loss for words.

Attia nodded. "I was so mad at her for doing it. I never thought I would forgive her, but it didn't take long for that to happen."

"You know how Raelyn's kiss works, right?" asked Conner. "You never really had a choice about forgiving her."

"Spare me," said Attia, rolling her eyes. "I just had this conversation with Malcolm the other day. Just because she charmed me doesn't mean she isn't genuinely kind to me."

"Malcolm knows?"

"Yes."

"Who else?"

"Russ knows too," said Attia. "We didn't tell Eliana, and we didn't have a chance to tell Liam." Attia closed her healthy eye. "Sorry, that didn't come out the way I wanted it to."

"It's alright," said Conner. He wasn't being entirely truthful, but he didn't want to make this conversation about his feelings. "How many times has Raelyn kissed you?"

"Just once."

That was a relief. One kiss held Achillion, and he seemed to keep a great deal of agency. Hopefully, it would be the same with Attia. "Has she given you assurances that it won't happen again?"

"Yes. She said she'll never kiss me again unless I ask her to."

Conner didn't like Attia's answer. A simple yes would have answered the question. The fact that she added that second part meant that she might be considering it. "If she made that promise to you, I think you're safe. Oaths are very important to Raelyn. They're a way of life for her."

Attia pursed her lips and nodded. She remained silent for a long time before speaking. "You didn't want to talk about it the other night, but you said Liam was being held in the ruins of Lamenica's Manor. You warned us not to go there. What's in those ruins, Conner?"

Conner still didn't want to talk about it. He felt that discussing it would violate his trust with Raelyn. Then again, Raelyn should have told him she kissed Attia. Wasn't that a violation of trust? Attia was a close friend. Raelyn should have told Conner about the kiss. "I'm not sure I should discuss it," said Conner with a sigh.

"I just shared something very private with you," said Attia. "I'm asking you to return the favor."

Conner didn't think the two discussions were related. If anything, Attia should ask Raelyn about it. The information wasn't Conner's to share. Still, the fact that Raelyn was keeping secrets from him touched a nerve. "Cinderhorn lives in those ruins," said Conner, before he could talk himself out of it.

"Cinderhorn?" gasped Attia. "There's a Guardian demon in Derregain?"

Conner nodded. "Chariden sent him to assist Raelyn. Apparently, many demons loyal to Plaguebringer and Lamenica remain in the city."

"Doesn't it make you nervous?" asked Attia. "Having your brother so close to a demon like Cinderhorn?"

"Not really," said Conner, shaking his head. "The way I see it, Liam is in the safest place he can be. I mean, nothing's going to mess with Cinderhorn."

"Can you trust him?"

"Actually, yes," said Conner. "I think Cinderhorn respects my devotion to Liam. The three Guardian demons are brothers.

Apparently, Cinderhorn traded countless favors to protect his brother, Erranaekis."

"Erranaekis was the Guardian Arronhelm killed, correct?"

"Right. When demons die in this world, they return to the Netherworld, where they suffer for a century," said Conner. He thought Attia might know some of this, but it didn't hurt to make sure. "It's possible to bargain for kind, or even gentle, treatment during that century of imprisonment."

"I know you love your brother, but what do you hope to gain by freezing him in time?" said Attia, her tone uncharacteristically gentle. "If Raelyn doesn't know a spell to help Liam, how do you expect to save him?" Attia paused, taking a deep breath. "I just don't want you holding on to false hopes."

"I struck a bargain with a powerful imp," said Conner. "He's searching for a spell that might help my brother."

"Wait, you struck a bargain with an imp? You meant to say Raelyn struck the bargain, right?"

Conner shook his head. "I struck the bargain. Liam is my brother. I felt like I was the one who needed to do it."

Attia stared at him for a long moment. "You remember, back in the Theleram, when you promised to tell me before you learned anything beyond the basics of demonology?"

"I remember, but I thought it was fairly obvious what I was doing when I started studying with Raelyn."

"Of course, it was. You didn't violate my trust," said Attia with a smile. "I'm just pointing out how far your studies have come. I'm not saying it's bad, or dangerous, or anything like that, but think about it. You're bargaining with imps, and it seems like you're on a first name basis with a Guardian demon."

"And you're dating a succubus. What's your point?" snapped Conner. He could tolerate his brother questioning his connection with demons. He didn't think Attia was in any position to judge.

"Like I said, I'm not saying it's a bad thing. I'm just asking you to stop and think about it. You're starting to play with fire. I don't want you to get burned."

"*She's right, you know,*" whispered Conner's Demon. "*I think you struck an excellent bargain with Daemenos, but the information you traded directly hurts Plaguebringer, a demon lord. Whether you like it or not, Conner, you're in the game now.*"

"Speaking of burns, let me look at your arms," said Conner, changing the subject. "I know you want to wait for Raelyn, but I can't leave you sitting in this room for most of the day with untreated wounds."

Attia frowned, but extended her badly burned wrists toward Conner. "And for the record, I'm not dating Raelyn. We're just flirting and having a little fun."

White light poured from Conner's hands as he gently touched Attia's angry burns. He didn't know the difference between dating, flirting, and having a little fun. As far as he was concerned, he didn't need to know the difference.

These days, he had enough things to worry about. Fortunately, dating wasn't on the list.

36

Russell

Russell leaned against the railing as he watched Nathanial Norwitch float down from the streets of High City, bypassing the icy stairs the rest of them used to descend to the docks. In the Lowlands, the city and the docks sat at roughly the same elevation, but the architects of Derregain built High City atop a steep slope, overlooking the ocean. The docks were built close to the water, while the rest of High City stretched out across the hills above.

The evening was frigid and wet. As far as Russell was concerned, the chilling sting of the ocean surf only made things worse. He spent his youth despising the hot wetness of the rainforest, only recently to discover cold wetness was far worse.

"At least he showed up," said the Governor beneath his breath.

"Of course, he showed up. He's desperate to learn Russell's Portal spell," said Professor Keldon. "You didn't give him another way to achieve that."

"You brought the potions with you, right?" asked Russell.

The professor nodded. "Three Potions of Flight. I added them to your spell's price tag."

"So, is that the vessel you need destroyed?" called Nathanial as he drifted closer to the group. He was pointing across the bay. There were a few small skiffs, but only one large ship out on the water.

"Yeah, it's the only warship anchored out there," said the Governor. "You can't miss it."

Russell wanted to laugh at the Governor's quip, but something seemed wrong. He couldn't quite put his finger on it. He felt restless and short of breath. A small but sharp pain flared to life between his eyes. The Dreamer never gave him headaches, so that didn't seem likely. Russell protected himself with several Dispels prior to this meeting, so he doubted magic was behind his sudden headache.

"*He has it!*" croaked the Dreamer, startling Russell. He wasn't used to the sound of his El'orin's voice. "*That man has the Orb of Planes. I can feel it calling to me!*"

Russell remembered the Orb of Planes from the first visions the Dreamer shared with him. It was the strange orb that allowed the Dreamer to project his thoughts into the Astral Plane. He used it to bargain with the Vel Sathir, back when Plaguebringer was infecting Semilae.

"Just making sure," said Nathanial. "We wouldn't want me destroying the wrong ship."

Based on the way his many pouches rested against his robes, Russell thought the Orb of Planes sat inside the pouch on Nathanial's right hip. He wasn't sure that piece of information was useful. Maybe the Dreamer wanted the orb back, but Russell doubted it.

"*The orb is dangerous,*" said the Dreamer. "*It brought the Vel Sathir into this world. Everything crumbled after that.*"

"So, Nate... Orb of Planes," said Russell with a whistle. "How's that working out for you?"

Nathanial spun to face Russell, a confused, angry expression on his face. "How do you know?"

Russell shrugged. "My El'orin owned it three centuries ago."

"Well, you can't have it," snapped Nathanial. "So, don't even try to add it to your already unreasonable list of demands."

"Don't worry," said Russell. "As far as I'm concerned, you can keep it."

Professor Keldon cleared his throat. "Speaking of unreasonable demands, I've added three Potions of Flight to the list of compensation Russell is collecting in exchange for his spell."

"Fine, whatever," said Nathanial with a dismissive wave of his hand. "Be warned, if you plan to fly out over the water with me to observe the battle, you're on your own. I'm not responsible for your safety. After all, demons can be quite unpredictable."

"I'm sure we'll manage," said the Governor, his tone icy.

"Suit yourselves," said Nathanial, as he retrieved a vial of glowing purple liquid from one of his belt pouches.

Russell didn't remember ever seeing a potion that looked like that. "What's that potion do, Nate?"

"It increases the intensity of my damaging spells."

"He calls it a Potion of Potency," said Professor Keldon. "It's one of the many secrets Nathanial failed to share with the Academy."

Russell considered added the recipe to his list of demands, but thought better of it. Although the potion sounded promising, he wasn't terribly interested in Alchemy. He didn't think it was a good idea to get too deeply entangled in the Academy's struggles with Nathanial.

"If the three of you are going to insist on foolishly following me, I suggest you drink your Potions of Flight now. I'd like to get started before it gets any colder out here," said Nathanial, before popping the cork and guzzling his purple potion.

Russell pinched his nose and quickly downed his potion. He was yet to find a potion with a pleasant taste, and he doubted this was going to be the one. The strange, oily, yet powdery texture of the liquid was almost enough to make him gag. Adding taste to that already confusing mix of sensations wasn't likely to improve the experience.

"Oh, that's awful," said the Governor, wiping his face.

"Power comes at a price," said the professor.

Slowly, the three of them rose into the air. Russell wasn't used to the sensation. Eliana described what it was like to fly to him, but her descriptions didn't do it justice. The feeling of weightlessness was exhilarating, especially for Russell. Despite losing a lot of weight recently, he still considered himself on the heavy side.

"You both know how to control the magic, right?" asked Professor Keldon. "You direct your motions with your thoughts, but you will feel the exertion in your muscles. I must warn you, it's easy to overexert yourself. Try to fly slowly."

Russell remembered Eliana waking up one morning with pulled muscles throughout her legs, so he knew about the overexertion, but he wasn't worried about it. He planned to fly as fast as he needed to. He'd gladly suffer sore, aching muscles if it meant avoiding getting ripped apart by an angry demon.

Nathanial began to chant, and a series of colorful stars flashed into orbit around his head. Most were Arcane Orbs, but Russell noticed a pair of Eldritch Orbs as well. A moment later, a protective field of green energy appeared around Nathanial, immediately followed by another field of translucent energy. The second field was blue. Russell knew the first was a Shield spell. He believed the second was Nathanial's Flight spell.

Following Nathanial's lead, Russell quickly raised his own Shield spell. While he didn't expect to see much battle, he thought it was best to be prepared. Russell started chanting the words to his Arcane Orbs spell, but he waited until his El'orin joined in before committing to the magic. He only spent enough energy to create two orbs, but with the aid of the Dreamer, he managed to build four.

"I see Russell is prepared," said Nathanial. "How about the rest of you? Are you satisfied with just a Shield spell, professor? I'd like to get started."

"I'm ready," said the professor.

The Governor floated out over the water without answering. A scintillating disc of amber projected from the back of his sword hand. Russell knew it was his Ring of Protection. He tried to picture how Attia and Liam would look with similar rings. In his imagination, they looked amazing with their magical rings. He couldn't wait to see the real thing.

"Here we go," said Nathanial, as he gracefully drifted out over the water. He floated up and to the side, distancing himself from the Governor. Russell guessed Nathanial didn't want to be near the rest of them, and that was perfectly fine with him. Nathanial was the likeliest to be attacked. The farther away he was, the better.

Concentrating, Russell willed himself into motion. He found it refreshingly simple to guide his weightless body. His muscles, particularly those in his legs, tingled as he moved, warning him of their exertion, but it didn't feel any worse than a brisk walk.

"Follow," called Nathanial, as he flew across the bay.

Russell floated behind Nathanial. Professor Keldon and the Governor drifted along next to him. The image of the ship in the distance gradually grew clearer as they approached it. Eerie red lights flickered across its decks, and pulsing green light flooded out from the many gun ports lining the side of the vessel.

"As long as we stay high above the water, their guns won't be able to touch us," said the Governor.

Russell noticed several silhouettes race across the deck. They didn't look human. Truth be told, Russell couldn't figure out what they were. Their bodies seemed to shift and change as he watched them. Some sprouted wings. Others melted, morphing from bipedal creatures into misshapen animals that walked on four or more legs. It was hard to tell at this distance. "It looks like they've noticed us."

A swarm of winged creatures leapt from the deck of the ship in the distance. Some, with large bat wings, flew high into the sky, while others, supported by several smaller insectoid wings, hovered close to the surface of the water. Behind them, a pair of enormous avian creatures raced high above everything, slipping out of sight as they passed through the sheets of grey clouds that dominated the overcast winter sky.

Nathanial raised his hands above his head and began chanting. Russell was surprised he could hear him. It was something to do with the spell Nathanial was casting, Russell was certain of it. There was no other way he could have heard. Nathanial was hundreds of feet away.

A brilliant mix of orange, gold, and crimson light appeared around Nathanial's hands. Off in the distance, a similar collage of colors formed against the hull of the enemy ship, close to the surface of the water. Compared to the ship, the vibrant ball of swirling colors wasn't large. Russell guessed it covered maybe a twentieth of the hull. What was Nathanial trying to accomplish?

The swirling colors grew brighter, tinging the night sky in oranges and reds. The water beneath Nathanial's terrible magic began to bubble and boil, and it looked as if the ship's hull was melting. A thunderclap blasted through the night as the colors faded, leaving behind a gaping hole in the ship's side. Whatever spell Nathanial cast, it completely disintegrated whatever it touched.

"Well, shek," said Russell, though he didn't think Professor Keldon, or the Governor were listening. "That got the job done."

"Here they come!" shouted the Governor.

Russell tore his gaze from the gaping hole in the ship's side. A dozen of the smaller demons flew toward them. They looked like grotesque combinations of people and flies. Long human arms and legs hung beneath them, though all their limbs ended in serrated claws. Several sets of shimmering wings sprouted from their backs. Their faces seemed human, if not for the enormous, insectoid eyes sprouting from their temples. Long, flexible stingers trailed behind them as they skimmed across the bay.

The Governor descended, floating a few feet above the water. With his armor, shield, and Ring of Protection, he seemed the only one capable of weathering the charging swarm of demons, but Russell wondered for how long. Each demon looked to be smaller than an adult man, but there were many of them.

A shimmering bolt of electricity ripped into one of the closest demons, immediately causing all of its wings to erupt in flames. A moment later, the flying demon tumbled into the water, its limbs twisting and tangling before it sank beneath the surface of the bay.

Deciding the professor had the right idea, Russell spread his hands and began chanting. He didn't think he needed a large Lightning spell to deal with these demons. With four Arcane Orbs, each of his spells was likely to pack quite a punch.

Electricity danced up and down Russell's forearms as he sent his first bolt of magical energy into the swarm of flying demons. He didn't wait to see the results. He quickly crafted a second blast and sent it into the enemy ranks. Only one demon crashed into the water, though he saw smoke rise from another.

Russell quickly retrieved his wand from his belt, using it to send a quick jolt into the demon he wounded. The extra electricity was enough to set its wings on fire and force it to crash into the water below.

Demons slammed into the Governor, knocking him back several feet, but the powerful warrior maintained his balance. Alternating between his sword and shield, Achillion slashed and bashed demon after demon.

Another of Professor Keldon's Lightning spells blasted into the host of demons, further thinning the herd. With nearly half of the demons wounded or killed, Russell thought the Governor was more than capable of dealing with what remained. Free from the battle, Russell looked around, scanning for other threats.

He was glad he did!

The water beneath Russell spun and churned. A moment later, a massive storm of tentacles and teeth burst from the water, leaping up at him. With no time to fly to safety, and little interest in deflecting the fearsome creature with his Shield spell, Russell's world quickly faded to blue.

He appeared a dozen feet away, safe from the terrifying beast's deadly tentacles. The creature was much larger than the flying demons Russell had just fought. Its many tentacles and mouths stretched twenty feet from the water. Russell couldn't see how much of the creature was hidden beneath the surface.

Willing his body into a sprint, Russell quickly ascended high into the air. Professor Keldon seemed to have the same idea. Unfortunately, the Governor was too occupied with his own battle to respond to the dangerous monster in the bay.

Russell was about to cry out a warning when the rest of the monster erupted from the bubbling waters, flapping its enormous wings to climb above the surface. Surprisingly, there wasn't much more to the monster beyond what Russell already witnessed. It was pretty much a collection of barbed tentacles, snapping jaws, glowing eyes, and flapping wings.

It screeched as it fixed its gaze on Russell. With a mighty whoosh of its wings, it raced toward him, its tentacles chaotically whipping around it. Russell considered using another Blink spell to get out of the way, but now that the thing was out of the water, he didn't think he could easily escape it. A shower of emerald sparks rained down as his Shield spell flared to life, deflecting a sea of heavy tentacles.

Deciding that he didn't have a choice, Russell faded, reappearing off to the side. He didn't wait for the beast to adjust. Quickly chanting, he cast a second Blink spell, immediately followed by a third. When he was done, he was perhaps a dozen feet behind the monster.

Continuing its motion, the beast flew off into the distance before abruptly stopping and spinning around. How could a monster that size turn so quickly? Once again, it fixed its baleful gaze on Russell before it charged.

A thick blast of Lightning crashed into the creature's side, causing it to screech in pain, but it didn't alter its course. Once again, Russell's Shield spell flared to life, protecting him. The impact was enough to send him flying. His muscles burned and ached as he willed his body to stop in midair.

The creature turned to face Professor Keldon, but the Governor slammed into it before it could charge. It tried to wrap its barbed tentacles around the man, but the Governor used his shield and Ring of Protection to knock the entangling limbs away.

Slipping his wand back into his belt, Russell raised both hands and began chanting. The Dreamer immediately joined him, guiding Russell in his incantation. Tendrils of electricity danced back and forth between his outstretched hands. The small demons only required small Lightning spells. This monster demanded something much larger.

One of Professor Keldon's bolts of electricity slammed into the monster, but Russell's spell wasn't ready. He needed to make it larger. The creature was struggling to entangle the Governor. There was still time to add to his magic.

Arcane Orbs flashed, and a deafening thunderclap echoed across the surface of the bay as Russell finally released his Lightning spell. It was easily as large as any he witnessed Eliana cast in the past. His forearms smoked and blistered, but he welcomed the pain.

Russell's thick, sweltering stream of electricity danced across the night sky. The blast caught the monster directly in the center of all its tentacles and mouths. Fires erupted all across the beast's body as it screamed and writhed under the withering assault. Slowly, Russell's storm of electricity faded until it was just a trickle, but the job was done.

The smoking corpse of the enormous monster splashed into the bay below, slowly sinking beneath the surface.

37

Nathanial

Nathanial knew his Disintegrate spell would work against the warship. It was perfect for dealing with slow or immobile threats. Very little in this world, or any other world for that matter, could resist the intense heat and disruption of a Disintegrate spell.

But the ship never worried Nathanial. In his mind, the small army of demons guarding the vessel was always the true source of danger. As usual, he wasn't wrong. As much as Nathanial tried dissuading Achillion and his little friends from following him out over the water, he was glad they did. Their presence forced the demons to divide their forces. The enemy didn't send many demons at Achillion and his friends. Still, it left less for Nathanial to deal with.

Twin torrents of electricity blasted through the clouds, arcing down from above. A series of tiny golden lights exploded above Nathanial, shattering the deadly streams of lightning into harmless clouds of static. Both demons were skilled casters. It took more Dispels than Nathanial would have liked, but his defenses held.

With their magical attacks failing, Nathanial expected the wind demons to attack him physically. Of all the demons on the battlefield, they were the most dangerous. It wasn't even close. He needed to prepare for their charges, but it was difficult. With all the other demons flying around, there were too many distractions.

Nathanial quickly drew a doorway of shimmering blue light. A host of strange squids, supported by leathery bat wings, rushed him from all directions. They were probably changeling demons. Stepping through the magical doorway, Nathanial disappeared, reappearing a short distance away.

The swarm of flying squids whipped about, searching. It only took them a moment to spot Nathanial and resume their pursuit. Still, the distance created precious time. Raising his hands above his head, Nathanial formed a sphere of swirling magical energy. It started small, but it swelled as he added more and more magic to it.

The flying squids spread out as they approached. Once again, they sought to surround him before attacking, but this time, they were more aggressive. While most flowed around Nathanial, a trio of squids flew directly at him, their barbed tentacles swirling like deadly saws in front of them.

Nathanial's colorful sphere of magic crackled and hissed as the flying squids flew into range. Jagged streams of energy burst forth from the sphere, striking each of the approaching demons. Two of the beams hit their targets cleanly, quickly boring holes through their flesh. Slightly off-target, the third beam carved off several of its victim's tentacles.

A shower of emerald sparks rained down as Nathanial's Shield spell absorbed the impact of the surviving demon's remaining tentacles. The first two, which suffered direct hits, never made it to Nathanial. They exploded into messy clouds of black ichor.

Screeching in anger or fear, the remaining flying squids charged from all directions. Once again, Nathanial quickly drew a door of azure light and stepped through it. His spell was rushed this time, so it didn't move him nearly as far. Still, it carried him outside the deadly cloud of flying squids, and that was far enough.

Several colorful streams of energy exploded from Nathanial's floating sphere of magic, striking nearly half of the squid monsters. Some of them exploded in showers of gore, while others escaped with various wounds. The colorful sphere shrunk as it fired each successive blast of energy. Nathanial knew it wouldn't last much longer, but he was satisfied with the amount of damage it delivered.

Off to the side, a flicker of motion alerted Nathanial to a potential threat. He turned just as one of the wind demons burst from the clouds. It moved so fast, it was a blur. If not for the thin trail of electricity it left in its wake, he would have struggled to spot it against the night sky.

Nathanial only noticed one, but he suspected the other was on the move. The wind demons were acting in unison. They both flew up into the clouds together. They both unleashed their deadly Lightning spells together. If one was charging, so was the other.

Nathanial's Shield flashed brilliant and green as something heavy barreled into him from behind. He tried to cast another quick Portal spell, but the demon wouldn't let go of him. It shook him as it carried him across the night sky, preventing him from using magic to improve his situation. All the while, the other wind demon approached. It would be on him soon.

They baited him! One of the wind demons allowed him to spot it while the other approached from the far side. If he didn't escape, and soon, the two of them would tear him apart. Nathanial's Shield spell was incredibly strong, but it wouldn't survive against the claws of two wind demons. Even his magic had limits.

Reaching into his pouch, Nathanial rested his palm on the Orb of Planes. It immediately flared to life, flooding his vision with a range of options. With all the recent magical activity, the Plane of Magic looked far too dangerous, and Nathanial preferred to avoid the Dreamrealms around Derregain. The weight of misery and depression throughout the city tended to create powerful nightmares.

With only a few wraiths and an apparition nearby, Nathanial opted to step into the Astral Plane. The spirits immediately moved to intercept him, but he recently relearned several spells to protect himself within the Astral Plane. It only took a brief incantation to render himself invisible to the trio of dangerous spirits.

Gazing back into his world, Nathanial watched the wind demons scatter. They didn't understand how he evaded them. They probably assumed he used his wizardry to cast some kind of emergency transport spell.

Nathanial stroked the orb and stepped back into the material world. Both of the wind demons were patrolling the area, one close to the water, and the other up near the clouds. It wouldn't be long before they spotted him, but Nathanial didn't plan on leaving them alive for long.

Chanting, he focused his thoughts with deadly precision. A swirling spot of golden light coalesced in front of him, right between his eyes. He used his sight to target his rapidly intensifying magic until he was confident it would strike true.

One of the wind demons shrieked and charged him, but Nathanial knew it wouldn't reach him in time. Momentarily closing his eyes, he unleashed his burst of thoughts and magic upon the charging demon. There was no sound as the golden beam raced across the night sky.

The demon tried to swerve, but Nathanial's Mindblast spell would not be deterred. It shifted and turned, countering the demon's doomed attempts to dodge it, until it struck the creature in the forehead.

At first, nothing happened, but Nathanial wasn't worried. He knew his enchanting magic was strong enough to fight through the wind demon's defenses. A moment later, the golden beam blasted out the back of the demon's head, spraying the sky with blood and brains.

Once again, Nathanial reached into his pouch and palmed the Orb of Planes. He didn't need to see the second wind demon to know it was bearing down on him. Since his protective spell was still functioning, Nathanial returned to the Astral Plane. Ghosts could pierce his magical veil, but with only wraiths and an apparition present, he was safe there.

Gazing back into the real world, he watched the second wind demon charge through the space he recently occupied. Satisfied it was past him, Nathanial returned to his world. The demon was fleeing to the safety of the ship. It probably witnessed what happened to its companion, and it didn't want to share a similar fate.

Sometimes it was too easy.

Chanting, Nathanial formed a second Mindblast spell. The wind demon was incredibly fast, but there was no outrunning this magic. Without the immediate danger of a charging demon intent on ripping his face off, he found it far easier to cast his spell.

Another golden beam of concentrated thoughts silently streaked across the night sky. In the distance, the wind demon twisted and banked, as if expecting Nathanial's deadly magical attack. None of it mattered, of course. A Mindblast spell couldn't be dodged or evaded. Just like the previous beam, it unerringly struck the head, delivering its energy directly into its victim's mind.

The wind demon shrieked as the remnants of its brain blasted through its forehead. Nathanial smiled. While his Mindblast spell never missed, its magic didn't always work. Strong casters could counter the magic with Dispel spells. Strong minds could sometimes resist it, preventing the magic from fulfilling its deadly purpose. Fortunately, neither of the wind demons was powerful enough to resist.

Spinning slowly, Nathanial surveyed the scene. A few of the flying squids were returning to their sinking ship. He didn't think he needed to deal with those. They were weak. Even if they decided to attack the city, they wouldn't last long.

Achillion and his friends were floating in the air, watching the smoking remains of an enormous monster slowly sink beneath the surface of the bay. Whatever else attacked them, they must have handled it, because there were no other threats around them.

Satisfied the battle was won, Nathanial drifted back toward the docks.

Nathanial took a deep breath as Achillion, Russell, and Professor Keldon landed next to him. The fight was far more taxing than he anticipated. He didn't want the others to know how dangerously depleted his well was. Nathanial didn't think there was any risk. Achillion and the others weren't his enemies, but it was best to be cautious.

"That was fun," said Russell.

"I did what you asked of me, Achillion," said Nathanial. "I trust you're satisfied with the results."

The Governor said nothing. He simply nodded.

Nathanial knew Achillion was angry with him, but would it be so hard for the man to show a little gratitude? The battle wasn't an easy one. No one else could have done what Nathanial did. "Funny, you don't look satisfied."

"I'm glad that warship is finally sinking," said Achillion with a shrug. "Still, I can't help but think about all the fishing we missed out on, and all the people who starved because of it."

"And, somehow, that's my fault?"

"Where have you been all these months?"

Both Russell and Professor Keldon retreated a step. Neither of them seemed interested in interrupting the argument. Nathanial didn't really care what those two thought, but Achillion's opinion mattered to him. "Look, I'm sorry," he said, though not as gently as he might have liked. "The world is much larger than just this city. I was elsewhere, working on matters that required my attention. I'm not sure what you want me to say."

"Whatever, Nate," said Achillion, shaking his head. "Maybe you were off saving the world, I don't know. Either way, we agreed to lead this city together. The way I see it, you ran away, leaving me holding the bag."

"Clearly, you weren't up for the task," mumbled Nate, glancing at the sinking warship in the distance.

Achillion struck in the blink of an eye. Nate never remembered the warrior moving so quickly. The punch landed across his jaw so fast he couldn't even turn to lessen the blow. Raising his Shield spell, or magically transporting out of the way, weren't even possibilities. Achillion caught him off guard. Fortunately, the man didn't put his full force behind the punch.

"You don't get to judge me, or anyone else who's fought for this city!" growled Achillion. "You have no idea what happened here, how hard we fought, or how many died along the way."

Nathanial's fingers tingled as electricity surged between his hands. He wanted to fight back. Achillion struck him! He threw the first punch. Whatever happened next was self-defense.

"Go ahead, try it," said Achillion, his voice surprisingly calm given the circumstances. "After two Mindblasts, a Disintegrate, your Flight spell, plus everything you cast defending yourself from those demons, your power must be waning. Your well is deep, but it isn't endless." He rested his hand on his sword, but he didn't draw it from its scabbard. "Your move, Nate."

Nathanial sighed. Of course, Achillion watched him throughout the battle. The man was more cunning than most gave him credit for. "There has been enough violence for one day. If it's all the same to you, I'd like to conclude our business and go our separate ways."

Russell cleared his throat. "We still have one more spell to settle on. Tell me about those golden, head-exploding beams."

"Mindblast is an enchanting spell," said Nathanial. There was no way he was penning a copy of that spell for Russell, even if the boy was a skilled enchanter. "Do you study that school of magic?"

Russell shook his head.

"Well, then Mindblast is out of the question."

"What about the spell you used to sink the ship," said Russell. "The one that melted a hole in the hull."

The Academy didn't keep spare copies of Disintegrate. It would take him days to write a copy. "I don't think the Disintegrate spell is a good idea. How about a Fireball spell instead?"

"I don't think so, Nate," said Russell, shaking his head. "Besides, one of my friends already knows it. I'm looking to add something new to my Coterie."

Professor Keldon chuckled.

"If I agree to write this for you, the deal is done. No more modifications. No more adding this or that to the deal," said Nathanial. "If I add a scroll of Disintegrate to the already obnoxious list of compensation you're demanding, are we done?"

Russell stared at him for a long moment before nodding "Yeah, I think that'll about do it."

Nathanial hated that kid. He was so damn smug. "What about you, Governor? You're the one who needs to give final approval for this deal. Are you satisfied?"

"I said I'd allow the deal if you dealt with the warship. You did that. There's nothing more to say," said Achillion. "Unlike some people, I keep my promises."

Nathanial looked away. He understood why Achillion was mad, but it didn't make their fractured relationship any easier to deal with. They used to be such great friends. "Very well," said Nathanial with a sigh. "I'll write Russell a scroll of Disintegrate. It should only take me a few days."

38
Saro

He didn't want to believe it, but Saro knew Dimitri was dead. Each El'orin was connected to the Bull. Dimitri's connection was severed at the moment of his death, over an hour ago. It made little sense. With Plaguebringer gone, the sewers were once again safe. Even if something happened, Ghost and Eirini were with him. The three of them should have been able to handle anything they encountered.

"I've finally entered Ghost's thoughts," said Mend.

"What the shek took you so long?"

"If he's close to me, I can do it quickly," said Mend. "The farther away, the longer it takes me to find his thoughts."

Saro doubted her honesty. Mend knew where Ghost was going. It shouldn't have taken her so long to enter his thoughts, but he didn't want to argue about it. "What's he thinking? What happened to them?"

"He's safe. Eirini is with him," said Mend. She spoke slowly, sometimes pausing for a few seconds between words or phrases.

"They were attacked… by Attia, the hunter from the new group. She's the one who killed Claw."

"Yeah, I know who she is." Saro regretted not moving against Attia and her Coterie. They were easy enough to find. A few of them never left that fancy greenhouse the Governor built for them. As much as Saro toyed with the idea of sending an army of street toughs to smash their greenhouse and trash all the plants inside, it wasn't a high priority.

Maybe he needed to rethink that. With all the Bumbles living in the greenhouse, Attia and her shekking friends were hard to get at as long as they stayed there. Fortunately, some of them spent much of their time away from it, making them vulnerable.

Conner worked at the House of Healing. He rarely left the hospital, but now and then, he traveled to the greenhouse to see his friends. It wouldn't be hard to ambush him. All it would take was patience. Killing him would bring the added advantage of pissing off that succubus, Raelyn. Saro owed that bitch pain! She saved the shekking Governor twice now. She needed to suffer.

Then there was Conner's brother, Liam. He spent his days leading several patrols of Bumbles. Most of the time, he kept to Middletown, but it wasn't unheard of for one of his patrols to dip into the Lowlands. Murdering him would be like killing two birds with one stone. A dead rival, and a team of dead Bumbles to go along with it. Who wouldn't want that?

Mend cleared her throat, probably to get his attention.

"I'm listening," said Saro.

"Attia killed Dimitri, and severely wounded Ghost, before they managed to get away. Sorriah is talking with them now. It sounds like she plans to escort them back to the Corners later tonight." Mend closed her eyes, looked down, and sighed. She did that whenever she left someone's mind.

But did Mend really leave Ghost's mind? Saro had no real way of knowing. For all he knew, she was constantly fishing around inside their heads, reading their thoughts. What if she was inside his head right now? She said she'd never read his mind without permission, but he didn't believe her.

Someone cried out in the stairwell, but the sound only lasted a fraction of a second before abruptly cutting off. "Hey, what the shek is going on down there?" shouted Saro. He only let the most loyal members of his gang guard the upper levels of the Corners. Those kids knew not to disturb him.

No one answered, which was strange. Maybe one of them stubbed their toe, turned an ankle, or did some other stupid shit, and they were embarrassed about crying out. Whatever happened, Saro didn't like it. Dimitri just died. Shit wasn't going well. He didn't want to take anything for granted. "Check it out, Mend," he said, gesturing toward the stairwell.

Mend looked at him, shook her head, and rolled her eyes. "Fine, whatever," she mumbled as she made her way across the room.

The door to the stairwell was on the far wall. The only other doors in the spacious room led to sleeping quarters. Saro had all the walls throughout this floor knocked down and rebuilt, turning this floor into a single large gathering area and a series of large personal rooms. Spacious couches, comfortable chairs, and solid tables filled the main room. It was a sanctuary for him and the other members of his Coterie. He rarely let anyone else visit. His trusted gang members were free to roam the rest of the building, but not here.

Mend opened the door and peered down the stairwell. "What the shek is going on down there?" A moment later, she cried out and frantically backed away from the stairs.

"What's gotten into you?" asked Saro. The creature that stepped into the room answered that question, but raised so many more. What the shek was it?

The thing was seven feet tall. Instead of skin, wet, glistening scales covered its body. A giant snake sprouted from its shoulders, replacing its head and neck. Shimmering orange light burned in its eyes, but the objects hanging from its body made it truly terrifying.

Seven miniature dolls hung from the monster's body, each held by a chain looped through a piercing. They weren't ordinary dolls. They were alive! What the actual shek? Saro wanted to believe he was imagining it, but some dolls looked like they were screaming. He even thought he recognized one of them. What kind of monster was he looking at?

It had to be a demon. Did that bitch Raelyn send it after him? It wouldn't surprise Saro. He didn't know much about demons, but he remembered someone telling him that demons could summon others to help them. That must be what happened. Raelyn summoned this disgusting thing and sent it after him!

"Greetings, Saro," hissed the demon. "And I suspect the other one is Mend. Pleased to speak with you."

"What do you want?" asked Saro. The creature was standing in front of the stairwell, the only exit.

The snake monster curled the corners of its mouth into a creepy smile. "To consume your souls, of course. What a silly question."

"Shek this," said Mend as she quickly painted a doorway of shining blue light in front of her. Saro wasn't surprised. He always knew Mend was a coward.

"Not so fast," said the demon, pointing at Mend. A series of tiny golden lights exploded around her. Nothing seemed to happen to her, but the magical doorway she was building suddenly shattered into a sea of useless stars.

"I'm getting out of here," shouted Mend, clearly terrified. She charged the snake monster, probably hoping to slip past it and down the stairwell.

The demon snapped its fingers and the door behind it slammed shut, but it wasn't done. It waved its hands in front of it, and a translucent field of emerald energy appeared behind it, further blocking access to the door.

"Fight or run, make a choice. We can't just stand here," said Saro's El'orin.

With a Shell spell blocking the door, Saro didn't think there was much choice. He reached into his pockets and quickly gathered a fistful of slender blades. Flicking his wrists, he sent a pair of daggers whizzing at the demon. Sadly, neither dagger hit the mark. The demon seemed protected by an invisible barrier, or something like that. Saro guessed it worked like a Shield spell. Maybe, if he hit it with enough daggers, he'd break through.

"Just a second, Saro," said the demon, a teasing tone in its hissing voice. "First, let me deal with this tasty morsel."

Mend was standing ten feet from the demon. If she was doing anything, Saro couldn't tell. Her fear was probably getting the best of her. The demon pointed, and Mend gently rose into the air. She screamed and struggled, but nothing changed. She wasn't able to escape the demon's spell.

Saro tossed another four daggers. He took a little extra time, making sure each throw was as precise as possible. Once again, his daggers were deflected by some kind of invisible barrier. Hopefully, he was draining the demon's magic with each strike.

"No need to struggle. It will all be over soon," cooed the snake demon as Mend gently floated toward it. "Save your screams for later. I simply can't wait to hear you sing."

"Saro, help me!" cried Mend.

The demon snapped its head forward, striking like a viper. As it did, its jaws stretched open, wider than Saro thought possible. Mend's head and shoulders disappeared as the snake demon wrapped its mouth around her. She flailed her arms and legs wildly, but nothing she did seemed to bother the monster.

The demon's serpentine neck pulsed, expanding and contracting in a steady rhythm. Its scales began to glow, painting the room with an eerie yellowish-green light. Gradually, a faint grey mist formed around Mend's body. The mist flowed up her body, curling like lazy smoke until it flowed into the snake's nostrils. Saro thought the mist represented Mend's soul. The demon was inhaling it.

It was consuming her soul!

One of the dolls hanging from the demon's body erupted into flame, quickly burning to ash. A second later, a new doll appeared in its place. It was Mend. Tears raced down her cheeks, and her mouth was wide open as if she were screaming in agony, but there was no sound.

If Saro wasn't terrified before, he was now! There was no way he was getting turned into a doll and stuck on a hook. Without a second thought, he threw another series of daggers at the demon, but once again, they all bounced harmlessly aside, deflected by an invisible barrier.

"Your turn, sweet Saro," said the demon, a wide smile stretching across its lips. "I so look forward to tasting your sorrow, savoring your endless suffering." Mend's bloody remains rested on the ground next to the demon. Her dead body didn't look natural. With the way it was twisted and crumpled, it almost seemed hollow.

Daggers clearly weren't getting the job done, but Saro didn't know what else to do. With a magical barrier blocking the stairwell, he didn't have a clear escape route. Why did he make them seal off all the other stairwells? He should have kept at least one of them active as an emergency exit. How could he have been so stupid?

"The windows," advised his El'orin. *"The fall might kill us, but let's jump. Anything is better than being caught by that thing!"*

Saro didn't have a better idea. Putting his head down, he sprinted toward the closest window. He jumped at the last moment, bringing his forearms forward to protect his face. The glass shattered easily. Sensations of vertigo followed.

But only for a moment.

Saro's felt his fall quickly slow to a crawl. In the next moment, his body was rising. Some kind of invisible force was pulling him back toward the room. He knew the demon was responsible for it. It was doing to him what it did to Mend. Saro struggled to free himself, but he was floating in midair. There was nothing for him to grab or push against.

"Not so fast, Saro," said the demon. "There is no escaping me. I have so many plans for you."

Incomprehensible terror tingled up and down Saro's spine as his body slowly rotated until he was facing the demon. As much as he wanted to look away, he couldn't help but stare at the screaming, crying doll that used to be Mend.

Saro knew the world was a shitty place, filled with poverty, tragedy, and monsters, but nothing prepared him for this. Whatever happened to Mend, it was a fate worse than death. Sadly, he was about to share her fate, and there wasn't a single shekking thing he could do about it.

39
Ssalyssna

Ssalyssna smacked her lips in anticipation as Saro gently glided closer. She couldn't ignore her disappointment. She expected more resistance. Mend didn't even try to fight her. Saro's daggers could have stung her, but they were easily swatted away by a simple Telekinetic Shield.

Simply stated, if she knew it was going to be so easy, she would have done this sooner.

"Let me go, you shekking monster!" shouted Saro.

If Ssalyssna were to release him now, Saro would likely fall to his death. "Sorry, I can't do that. You have a purpose, you see. Several purposes, actually."

"Yeah, what's that?"

"For starters, I wish to wear your skin," said Ssalyssna. "But more than that, I wish to make you suffer."

"What the shek did I ever do to you?" asked Saro. "Raelyn summoned you, didn't she?"

Ssalyssna didn't know what to say. Saro's silly assumptions amused her to no end. "Of course not, you simpleton, but enough talk. It's time to swallow your soul."

Saro wrinkled his nose and spat a glob of thick snot at her, but it never reached her. Like all his daggers, it slammed harmlessly against her protective shield. It was too funny. Even his final act, a silly act of defiance, was wasted. What a sad specimen.

Ssalyssna distended her jaws and wrapped them around Saro's head and shoulders. She slowly siphoned his lifeforce, drinking his memories, his skills, his identity, and eventually gaining access to his skin. Not surprisingly, she found Saro to be an unskilled simpleton. Why did so many people obey him? As far as Ssalyssna was concerned, no one should have ever listened to Saro. Most of his ideas were stupid.

The sounds of sorrowful screams and pitiful begging filled Ssalyssna's ears as she hung the doll of Saro from a chain. Soon, she would be forced to make a difficult choice regarding which souls she kept. She needed both Senator Ominar and Counselor Jurgenson for political reasons. She wanted to keep Selandra, the wizard from the Citadel, and she didn't think she could afford to lose either of her skins from the Academy. Currently, she could keep both Saro and Mend, but if she found another promising soul, she needed to free someone.

Ssalyssna didn't need to make that decision yet, but she already knew the answer. If she absolutely needed to free someone, Selandra was the right choice. Her magic was strong, but Ssalyssna could replicate most of Selandra's spells using the pair of skins she harvested from the Academy.

More importantly, Selandra Mayes was a sincere and accomplished person. Ssalyssna long since tired of teasing and torturing the woman. Selandra survived a skirmish with Cinderhorn and Nesharon, only to succumb to the Queen and her irresistible Desires. Before that, Selandra spent her life teaching and serving the Citadel's children. Sure, she harbored certain sexual proclivities, and a host of sad regrets, but those things weren't worthy of punishment. Selandra's soul deserved salvation from her ceaseless torment. She would be the next one Ssalyssna set free.

Saro's soul, on the other hand, was far more interesting. Ssalyssna was just scratching the surface, and her discoveries already surprised her. She knew he was heartless, but she never imagined to this degree. Closing her eyes, she summoned his skin, wearing it for the first time.

Scattered memories and strange sensations swam through Ssalyssna's consciousness. She immediately felt the presence of Saro's El'orin spirit. It worked! She captured both Saro and his El'orin spirit with a single doll. The possibilities were endless.

Searching through Saro's memories, Ssalyssna was once again confronted by his simple nature. He knew the right words to lead a crowd, and the right gestures to scare those already prone to submission, but beyond that, his skills were pedestrian.

His only true expertise revolved around using small blades. Ssalyssna witnessed that in their brief struggle. With limited martial skills across her other skins, she thought Saro's expertise with blades would serve her well. One of her Academy skins even knew how to craft poisons, turning dangerous blades into potentially deadly ones.

But where Saro lacked in value, his El'orin was absolutely spectacular. Ssalyssna could already feel supernatural speed rushing through her system, but there was something more. She couldn't put her finger on it, but she suspected Saro could manipulate emotions. Searching his thoughts, she easily discovered his secret. He could stoke anger in those around him.

How interesting!

In many ways, Saro was the opposite of Achillion. She didn't think his abilities were anywhere near as expansive, but it was interesting, nonetheless. Sifting through the deeper reaches of

Saro's mind, she found thoughts about the El'ominae spirit, known as the Bull, and memories of the person Saro was before succumbing to its whispers.

Deciding to explore the area, Ssalyssna used Saro's memories to guide her through the various rooms and hallways. There was only one staircase leading up to this floor, which struck her as a strange decision. Had there been another set of stairs, Saro might have escaped. She planned to tease him ceaselessly with this detail. A constant reminder of his staggering stupidity.

Slipping through a series of doors, Ssalyssna navigated a long hallway before reaching Saro's chambers. Scanning Saro's memories, she easily located and bypassed the simple mechanical trap built into the door handle.

Saro's room stank of sexual fluids. Most animals knew not to sleep in their own mess, but apparently not Saro. Ssalyssna resolved to have the room thoroughly cleaned, and soon. In her serpent form, she tasted smells. Ssalyssna had little interest in tasting such scents.

One glance at the ancient helmet on the far table was all Ssalyssna needed to forget Saro's unpleasant stench. The El'ominae spirit lived inside that helmet. Ssalyssna was a soul-sucking demon. While she didn't see spirits quite as clearly as those who practice necromancy, she certainly sensed them. She didn't think it was possible to miss the El'ominae. Its essence sang to her! She could taste its power.

"Greetings, demon," whispered a voice in her head. *"Oh, how I've waited to meet a being such as you. I've been forced to work with pathetic, broken tools for far too long, but you are something much greater. Tell me what you desire, and perhaps together, we can achieve it."*

Ssalyssna slowly approached the ancient helmet. She wasn't surprised it could speak to her. Saro's mind was filled with memories of the El'ominae's whispers. Saro thought of the Bull as a coercive influence. Perhaps she needed to be careful.

"*You have nothing to fear from me, demon,*" said the Bull. "*I recognize true power when I see it. Yes, I coerced Saro and his army of followers, but you are an entirely different beast. Even if I could twist you to my will, there would be no need to. I suspect we both want the same thing.*"

"And what is that?" asked Ssalyssna. She imagined she could conduct the conversation silently, in her thoughts, but she was the only one here. Silence was unnecessary.

"*War and destruction,*" growled the Bull.

Ssalyssna didn't want the same things. While anything was better than the Netherworld, she truly cherished this world. She didn't want to see it burn. "You and I have different aims. I have no desire to harm this world."

"*Neither do I, demon,*" said the Bull. "*I only wish to make this world stronger, but true strength is born from struggle and conflict. Prolonged peace has softened these people. The fires of war will make them strong again.*"

In her estimation, the Bull was only partially right, but Ssalyssna saw little reason to argue with the spirit. Curious, she reached out and placed her hand on the helmet. It tingled, but was otherwise cool to the touch. Plucking it from the table, she returned to the hall. She needed to be in her serpent form to consume the spirit. Best to do that outside the confines of Saro's smelly room.

"*I've told you my wishes. Now it's your turn. What do you desire?*"

Ssalyssna considered ignoring the El'ominae, but she thought it was a fair question. "More than anything else, I want to survive. I wish to free myself from my summoner. I hope to grow in power until I rival even the Ancients. After that, honestly, I don't know. The road I seek to walk is long and twisting. I suspect my dreams and desires will shift along the way."

"*Interesting,*" said the Bull. "*I think I can help you on your journey. Would you like to walk it together?*"

Ssalyssna didn't know what the El'ominae spirit truly had to offer her, but she planned to find out. Shivering, she shook herself free from Saro's skin, once again becoming her serpentine self. She wasn't positive she could consume the El'ominae. She was used to syphoning souls from flesh, not metal, but she expected it would work similarly.

Distending her jaw slightly, she placed the helmet in her mouth and gently bit down. She didn't care for its rusty, coppery taste, but she was willing to put up with it for a few moments. Her neck pulsed and her mouth tingled as she slowly sucked the Bull's soul free from its metal home. There was no struggle. If anything, the spirit seemed eager to succumb to her thirst. How strange. Did it not understand that imprisonment came with endless suffering?

As planned, Ssalyssna released Selandra Mayes from her service. Hopefully, her soul would finally find the peace it deserved. With a piercing now available, Ssalyssna imprisoned the Bull's soul, wrapping it in unbreakable chains.

Ssalyssna listened. She expected to hear the delicious song of the Bull's sorrow, but she heard nothing of the sort. Instead, she heard laughter.

40

Ghost

The moment the Bull died, Ghost knew it. It was like lifting a dark veil. All the irritation, annoyance, and rage he constantly struggled against suddenly melted away. Over time, the weight of the Bull's influence became a part of his life. Eventually, Ghost stopped recognizing it was there, but now that it was gone, it was refreshing to be free of it finally.

Ghost used to be a peaceful boy. He studied necromancy, earth magic, and agriculture at the Academy. Back then, his dream was to sign on with a local farmer. He thought he might find success using animated corpses as a labor force for some of the more difficult farming tasks. Ghost knew his ideas were unconventional, but all he needed to do was find the right farmer to give him a chance. It wouldn't be hard to prove his concept.

The general populace feared necromancers, and Ghost understood why. Life and death were sacred. Most people expected the dead and buried to stay that way, but as far as Ghost was concerned, it was a wasted opportunity. There was no reason animated corpses couldn't dig ditches, push a plow, or even harvest grain.

"Are you absolutely certain the Bull is dead?" asked Sorriah, interrupting Ghost's daydream. "And what about Saro and Mend?"

"I don't know about Saro and Mend," said Ghost, shaking his head. "I'm positive about the Bull though. I don't feel his influence anymore. What about you Eirini?"

"I don't know. I can't tell."

Ghost wasn't surprised. He felt the Bull's presence as an ever present weight of anger, but Eirini was filled with rage before she met the Bull. Beyond that, she just lost her brother. If she wasn't angry before, she certainly was now, and who could blame her?

"Well, we need to find out, don't you think?" said Sorriah, her voice obnoxiously cheerful given the events of the day, "To be safe, I think it would be best if the two of you remained with the Nightcrawlers until we have this all sorted out."

Eirini glanced at Ghost. She looked nervous.

"Is there a room for Eirini, or do you need her to stay with me?" asked Ghost. He preferred they give Eirini her own room, but it wouldn't bother him either way. Now that the Bull was gone, very little bothered him.

"I'm having a proper room prepared for her as we speak," said Sorriah. "Eirini is welcome to stay as long as she likes."

"Thank you. You've been very kind to me," said Eirini softly.

Ghost scratched his recently repaired wrist. The Nightcrawlers' healers did a nice job, but the remnants of the wound itched horribly. Touching it reminded him of how Attia nearly killed him with a single cut. He survived the attack, but what about next time?

Being hunted by Attia wasn't Ghost's only problem. Saro almost burned down Middletown. The Governor wasn't going to let that go unpunished. For all Ghost knew, the Governor killed the Bull. Several situations were spiraling out of control, and it didn't look like things were likely to improve soon. Maybe it was time for a change.

"I hate to ask this of you, Ghost, but do you mind checking on Saro and Mend?" asked Sorriah, her voice sweeter than normal. "You know, using your special spirit form. If the Bull is dead, whoever killed him might still be there. With your spirit form, you'll be safe, but I think it's too dangerous for the rest of us to go with you."

Ghost glared at Sorriah. He wanted to hate her for making the suggestion, but she was right. It was so refreshing to take a moment and think about things before lashing out in anger. "I can, but unless you have some Powerence for me, it will have to wait until tomorrow. Using my spirit form slowly drains my well. Traveling to the Corners and back will be costly."

Sorriah cocked her head to the side. "Fascinating. I didn't know that."

Of course, she didn't know that. Ghost never shared his limitations with her. Mend was the only person who knew. Ghost thought it was pointless to hide a detail like that from a mind reader. "Will tomorrow morning work? I doubt you want to waste valuable resources."

"It's no problem at all," said Sorriah with an impish smile. "Stop by the library and tell Ayaetis you need Powerence. Take as much as you need. When he argues, tell him it's on my authority."

"Okay," said Ghost. "I'll go tonight."

"Actually, please go now. The sooner we know, the better. Besides, I'd like to spend some time with Eirini."

Ghost caught the hidden message beneath Sorriah's words. She didn't want him around while she spoke with Eirini. It didn't surprise or bother him. If Saro was truly gone, Ghost expected Sorriah essentially to adopt Eirini. On a certain level, it made sense. Eirini's powers directly complimented Sorriah's. Those two would work well together.

On the other hand, Ghost didn't see a future for himself with the Nightcrawlers. He wasn't sure he wanted to remain in Derregain, for that matter. Now that he was finally free from the Bull's influence, maybe it was time to pursue his dreams. With Derregain on the verge of starvation, he couldn't think of a better time to put his innovative agricultural plans into action.

"If you would be so kind, please close the door on your way out," said Sorriah.

"Sure, no problem." Ghost didn't even bother reacting to Sorriah's dismissive tone. If anything, he found it funny.

Ghost saw the telltale signs of battle the moment he drifted up through the floor of the main gathering room. Some of Saro's daggers were scattered about, and there was a fairly large bloodstain near the stairwell. He didn't see any corpses, but that didn't surprise him. Someone probably disposed of the bodies.

If Ghost were to guess, the strange creature standing on the far side of the room was responsible. On the outside, it looked like Saro, but a careful study of the Astral Plane told an entirely different story. Ghost didn't know what it was, but he knew it wasn't Saro.

"Is everything alright, Ghost?" said the thing masquerading as Saro. "Mend spoke of an assassin. What the shek happened?"

That didn't sound like Saro. He didn't speak like that. "I don't know. You tell me."

"Don't be like that," said the imposter as he approached. "Is Eirini safe? She's still with Sorriah, isn't she?"

Ghost nodded. He didn't see any harm in sharing that detail.

"We should go see her. It has to shekking suck, losing her brother like that."

"After you," said Ghost, gesturing toward the stairwell.

"You're too shekking slow as a spirit," said the imposter. "Shift back to flesh. We need to move fast."

Ghost chuckled. That was the first time he ever heard Saro use the word flesh. "I don't think so. By the way, don't you think you should collect your daggers?" said Ghost, pointing at the weapons scattered across the floor.

The imposter sighed. "Stop making this difficult."

"Making what difficult?"

The imposter looked around, carefully scanning the room. "You know this is a masquerade, don't you? You know I'm not Saro."

"Yes."

"How did you know?"

"The Astral Plane. The bloodstain. The daggers on the floor. The way you talk," said Ghost. "Take your pick."

"I see," said the imposter. "Most unfortunate."

"I'm guessing you killed Saro. What about Mend? Did you kill her?"

The imposter smiled. "Yes. She's with me now. You should join her. She wants you to."

"No thanks," said Ghost, shaking his head. He didn't know what the imposter meant, but it didn't sound good. "You killed the Bull too, didn't you?"

The imposter nodded.

"So, what happens now?" Ghost didn't think the imposter could hurt him while he remained in his spiritual form. It would have attacked him already if it could.

The imposter reached out, passing a hand through Ghost's spectral body. "Their whispers and memories tell me I can't hurt you when you're a spirit, but perhaps they simply failed to discover your secrets."

Ghost drifted to the left, fading through the wall until he was outside the room, floating five stories above the streets below. He noticed that one of the windows was shattered. Somehow, he missed it when he first scanned the room. "You can add this broken window to the list of reasons I knew you weren't Saro."

The imposter just stared at him, shaking his head.

"I really should thank you," said Ghost. "I didn't realize how much the Bull was influencing me. Now that I'm free, the possibilities are endless."

"Then I propose a truce," said the imposter. "You should join me. With your abilities, the possibilities are indeed endless. I will show you so many mysteries." The imposter's skin shimmered. "I've lived for centuries. I've visited dozens of worlds. I will share it all with you."

Ghost watched, mesmerized, as Saro melted away. The creature that replaced him was a cross between a person and a snake. A glistening membrane covered its scales. Six miniature people hung, chained to its body. A seventh set of chains seemed to contain a swirling sphere of deep red mist. Looking closely, Ghost noticed both Saro and Mend among the tiny people chained to the creature. They looked like they were in incredible pain. All the miniature people appeared to be suffering.

"Now you see me as I am," said the snake monster. "Join me, and I'll release Mend. I promise you won't suffer as severely as the rest of them."

Ghost looked away. He couldn't bear looking at the creature, or its victims. "I think I'm going to pass."

"It's only a matter of time, Ghost," said the creature. "This city shares its secrets with me. I'll find you. It's only a matter of time."

"I don't think I'm staying. It's time for something new," said Ghost as he began slowly descending toward the street. He knew the creature was staring at him, but he did his best to ignore it. Whatever it was offering, he wasn't interested.

Ghost needed to warn Sorriah and Eirini. After that, he planned to take advantage of the Nightcrawlers' hospitality for a few days. Once he was rested, Ghost planned to rob a few of Saro's safe houses. With his ability to pass through walls, it wouldn't be too hard. After gathering all the money he needed, he'd purchase supplies, and journey north until he found a farmer willing to take him on.

It wasn't a great plan. Things were bound to go wrong along the way, but he didn't care. It was his plan, and, for a change, his alone. The Bull and Saro weren't making him do it. As far as Ghost was concerned, that's all that mattered.

41

Raelyn

Raelyn leaned back in her chair. She was on the landing, but she still needed to strain her neck to look Cinderhorn in the eye. She wished the Guardian demon would take a seat, but she didn't want to ask him to. Somehow, she felt beholden to the powerful demon. It was silly. Chariden put her in charge of Derregain. Cinderhorn was there to help her.

"You look terrible," said Cinderhorn.

Raelyn suppressed a yawn. "Sleep has been hard to come by."

"You do too much for this city. Perhaps you should take a step back, at least from the human aspects of things. I suspect everything will work out for them without your intervention."

Cinderhorn often complained about how involved Raelyn was with humanity, but it wasn't like she could easily disengage. She was in a close relationship with the Governor. She was in a playful relationship with Attia, and Conner was essentially running the House of Healing. "Human and demon politics are intertwined. It's far too late to unravel the knot."

"You're the Queen's viceroy over Derregain," said Cinderhorn. "You get to determine how our politics interact with theirs."

"Not after what the Queen made me do to earn this position," said Raelyn, shaking her head. "Need I remind you that I didn't vanquish Lamenica? The Children of the Citadel did it for me."

Cinderhorn sighed. "True. I warned Chariden about that."

Raelyn rose from her chair, making it easier to talk with the enormous Guardian demon. "It's not like that's the first time I've worked with Conner and his friends. They were instrumental in the battle against Plaguebringer. This city would have fallen if not for those kids."

"I heard about their necromancer's special spell."

"Malcolm is his name," said Raelyn. He was on her mind. Their recent argument still bothered her. She couldn't deny his accusations, but at the same time, she felt he was misrepresenting the issues.

"It doesn't matter," said Cinderhorn with a dismissive shrug of his wings. "I only know about it because Daemenos discussed it with me. Conner is bargaining with a useful piece of information, but I question how many buyers will be interested."

"It's a problem, I know," said Raelyn. Anyone who purchased Conner's information would do so to spread it across the Netherworld. Many demons hated Plaguebringer. Some probably hated him enough to pay handsomely to damage him, but the odds of finding such a demon who just happened to have access to rare healing spells were quite low.

"Daemenos is one of the best. If the right buyer exists, he'll find him, but it will take time," said Cinderhorn.

"I already offered to help cover Daemenos' losses," said Raelyn.

"Awfully generous of you. I'm not sure I approve."

"Conner is precious to me," said Raelyn. "Fires below, one of Plaguebringer's flesh demons would have eaten me without his help. I want his first major bargain with the Netherworld to be successful. I think it's important."

"He's only doing this because of his brother," said Cinderhorn. "Do you really think he'll keep bargaining after this?"

"I do, actually," said Raelyn.

"Interesting," mused Cinderhorn. "In that case, maybe I'll offer Daemenos a little extra incentive as well. I kind of like the boy."

"He visited you a few hours ago, didn't he?"

Cinderhorn nodded. "He came to visit his brother, but there really wasn't much for him to do. He spent maybe an hour here. We talked to pass the time."

"I see," said Raelyn. "If Conner is going to be spending time here, I probably need to lighten his duties within the House of Healing, but I don't have time to cover his shifts. For now, my focus needs to be on Derregain's demonic population, not its human one."

"You won't hear any arguments from me," said Cinderhorn. "That's what I've been trying to say."

Raelyn didn't think it was that simple, especially considering she planned to use Attia and her friends to deal with any disobedient or troublesome demons throughout the city. As Raelyn said earlier, everything was too intertwined to be separated. "Speaking of that, have you tracked down the demons who didn't attend my Demonic Court?"

"Some, but not all of them," said Cinderhorn as he used a claw to comb his mane. "It will take me another couple of days to collect the rest of the names."

"Of the names you've uncovered, so far, are any of them easy targets? I'd like to make my first examples as soon as possible."

Cinderhorn shook his head. "If you don't mind, I'd prefer if you waited. Right now, no one is scared. That will change the moment you take action. Let me finish collecting the names. After that, deal with them as you see fit."

Part of her wanted to command the Guardian demon to give her the names, but Raelyn knew she was being foolish. Cinderhorn's logic was sound. Still, her urge to demand obedience, despite his reservations, was undeniable. What was happening to her? "I understand," said Raelyn after a long pause. "That makes sense."

Cinderhorn pursed his lips and peered at her. Raelyn wasn't overly familiar with his expressions and mannerisms. Was he showing concern? "Is something wrong? You don't quite seem yourself."

"I don't know," said Raelyn with a sigh. "Lately, I've been having trouble controlling my emotions. There's just so much anger, but it's more than that. There's this... this... need..." She paused to search for the right words. "I hunger to control everyone around me. Even you."

Cinderhorn's eyes flashed as he curled his lips into a smile. "That's part of your transformation. It rarely happens to a succubus, but there have been a few across the centuries."

Raelyn stepped back, nearly stumbling over the chair behind her. Surely, Cinderhorn was mistaken. She needed him to be wrong. She liked herself as she was. "Are you saying I'm evolving?" she asked, her voice shaky.

"Of course, you are. Soon, you will be a demon of the fifth order."

"What if I don't want it to happen? I never asked for this. I thought most demons work for centuries before evolving."

"And have you not struggled for centuries, perfecting your skills, risking everything, time and time again, to carve out a suitable life for yourself?"

Raelyn looked away. "Of course, I've struggled, but I was never trying to evolve. I just wanted to build a life on my own terms. Is that too much to ask?"

"Yes, it is," said Cinderhorn with a chuckle. "We're demons. We're not meant to live our lives on our own terms."

Raelyn shook her head. "No, there must be some mistake. I don't want to change. I want to remain a member of the fourth order."

"That's not how it works," growled Cinderhorn. "You're one of the most talked about demons in the Netherworld. You're the one who brought down the Citadel, not Chariden. You speak of the humans as if they were the ones who defeated Plaguebringer, but you were the one who stood alone against him until the rest of us finally recognized the danger."

"I don't care," spat Raelyn. "What happens if I refuse?"

"Stop being a child!" roared Cinderhorn. He fanned his wings to their full width, and he stepped forward. "It has already begun. There is nothing you can do to stop it."

Raelyn staggered back. The size and power of the Guardian demon caught her off guard, but the finality of his words scared her more than his sudden advance. There had to be a way to reverse the transformation. What if she resigned her position and stopped appearing on the Netten and Naga show? Maybe that would make it stop.

"When they write the story of how this world fell into the Netherworld, it will start with Chariden, but it won't stay with her," said Cinderhorn, his voice much calmer than before. "When they write the later chapters, the story will shift to you. You're the one making everything happen, not Chariden, and everyone knows it, even her."

"This isn't what I wanted," said Raelyn. "I never wanted to be famous, or important, or anything greater than what I was. I just wanted a place to live, and maybe a chance to make a difference. Is that too much to ask?"

"As I said before, we're demons," said Cinderhorn. "Our lives often fall outside our control. The best we can do is make the most of the situations we're thrust into, and you, my friend, have become the center of it all."

"But what if I'm not ready?" asked Raelyn. She knew she sounded like a child, but she didn't care. In many ways, she was a child compared to Cinderhorn. He was older than her, and far more powerful. "What if I fuck it all up?"

Cinderhorn shrugged, his wings rustling. "I suspect you've already screwed up, more times than I'd care to contemplate. None of us travel in a straight line. The path is always twisting and winding, filled with darkness and danger."

"That's not very reassuring."

"I believe in you, Raelyn," said the Guardian demon. "I researched you for years before I first summoned you, and I must say, you did not disappoint me."

"Stop," said Raelyn, waving her hands. "You don't have to."

"I wasn't finished," snapped Cinderhorn. "When the Queen wanted to punish you, I defied her, setting you free. When she placed a price on your head, I worked with Daemenos, providing what little protection we could. When Chariden refused to recognize your successes, I argued your case. I believed in you the entire time, and I still believe in you now." Cinderhorn crouched, bringing his head level with hers. "It's time to stop worrying about what can't be changed, and start preparing for the inevitable."

"Fine," sighed Raelyn. "What's going to happen to me?"

"It's different for every demon, but I've taken the liberty of reaching out to a pair of demons who experienced similar transformations," said Cinderhorn. "Both of them said their kisses grew stronger."

"Going forward, or will my sway over those I've already kissed grow?"

"They answered that question differently. One noticed her existing control strengthened. The other claimed to experience no change."

Raelyn sighed. "So, we don't know."

"I'm afraid not."

"What else happened to them?"

"Both grew more skilled with their demon magic, although one claimed greater gains than the other. I'm willing to work with you on that, by the way, if you're interested," said Cinderhorn. "Other than that, they both grew physically stronger. I suspect they became more resilient as well, although neither discussed that with me."

Raelyn didn't care about the physical gains her transformation might bring. She was worried about her control over Achillion, Attia, and Russell increasing. Fires below, poor Russell! The boy was fighting so hard to keep a semblance of his autonomy. What would happen if her power over him grew? "Did Chariden ever undergo a similar transformation?" asked Raelyn, trying to stop herself from imagining the worst potential outcomes.

"Oddly enough, no," said Cinderhorn. "Chariden was a demon of the fourth order when she shattered the Gaea spirit and became the Sovereign over this world. As you know, all Sovereign immediately become members of the eighth order."

"Right," said Raelyn with a nod. "What did she gain when she evolved to the eighth order?"

Cinderhorn scratched his mane. "Outside of her substantial physical gains, she gained access to her Desires."

Chariden's Desires were irresistible charms she could direct at nearly anyone. There were limitations, of course, but Raelyn never bothered to research them. She always assumed Chariden gained her Desires after becoming the Sovereign, but it was nice to have that confirmed. "Are they as terrifyingly powerful as I've heard?"

"Yes, and no. They are nearly impossible to resist, that much is true. Even Arronhelm succumbed to one of Chariden's Desires, but they appear useless against demons." Cinderhorn snorted and shook his head. "As I understand it, Chariden was presented with a choice about which ability to gain, and she chose her Desires. She chose poorly, if you ask me."

"Agreed." The last thing Raelyn wanted was outright irresistible control over people. As far as she was concerned, absolute control was nearly useless. She vastly preferred leaving people with as much autonomy as possible. She wanted them to concentrate on her needs first, of course, but she wasn't interested in creating slaves.

"Early on, when humanity was still fighting to hold on to this world, I suspect Chariden's Desires were quite powerful," said Cinderhorn. "As the decades passed, her Desires became less and less useful. In recent times, it's mostly other demons working against her. She faces few, if any, threats from humanity."

Raelyn nodded, but she wasn't worried about Chariden anymore. She was thinking about her transformation, and how it might affect those she held dear to her. No matter what happened, she was determined to control her own destiny.

The Netherworld could reshape her into a more powerful, more terrible version of herself, but she wouldn't let it. Ultimately, Raelyn controlled her own behavior. Even if she constantly needed to struggle against her nature, Raelyn refused to become a monster.

42

Russell

Russell nervously tapped the picnic table as Nathanial Norwitch worked his way between the thick rows of Ganna trees. As much as he hated letting Nathanial see the greenhouse, Russell didn't want to risk making the trade within the Academy.

Malcolm refused to leave the protection of the greenhouse, and no one thought it was a good idea for Fahrilae to set foot in the Academy. Eliana was willing to make the journey, but she wouldn't bring Lord Rumblesnort with her. In the end, it became clear that the only place this could happen was within the greenhouse.

Using the picnic tables was Russell's suggestion. Originally, the transaction was supposed to happen within Professor Keldon's library, but Russell built his Inscription within the library. The last thing he wanted to do was give Nate an opportunity to study his Inscription.

"Well, there he is," said Conner.

Russell was grateful both Conner and Attia could attend. The more of them that were present, the less likely Nathanial would try anything stupid. Liam was the only one not in attendance, and that couldn't be helped.

"He's viewing me from the Astral," said Fahrilae, beneath her breath. "He knows what I am."

"Should I be worried?" asked Malcolm.

"I don't know, but let's hope not," said Fahrilae. "It's like he is simultaneously in both the real world and the Astral Plane. I've never seen anything like it."

"It has to be the Orb of Planes," said Russell. Honestly, he didn't know what powers the Orb provided. Hopefully, Nate couldn't do anything horrible to Fahrilae, or to any of Malcolm's pet spirits, for that matter, but there was nothing to be done about it now.

"A revenant. How interesting," said Nathanial Norwitch as he approached the group. "I must say, I'm impressed. Which one of you is Malcolm?"

"I am," said Malcolm.

"Where did you learn that spell?" asked Nathanial. "The Academy certainly didn't provide it, and with what I've heard about the Hidden Tower's recent moves against you, they didn't give you a copy. Did you find it in Semilae?"

"It's not something I'm willing to discuss," said Malcolm.

"A pity."

Professor Keldon cleared his throat. "Have you brought everything? If so, I think we should proceed."

Nathanial smiled in a fashion Russell could only associate with condescension. "I'm paying a fortune for this spell. I intend to take a few minutes to savor the moment. Besides, I want to learn about this fine group of adventurers. According to the Governor, they saved the city."

Russell wished Achillion was there, but apparently, with everything going on throughout the city, it wasn't possible. Still, he felt relatively safe and secure, despite Nathanial's formidable power. He didn't think anyone, not even Nathanial, was a match for an ancient ghost, augmented by a luck-manipulating spirit. Fahrilae and Lord Rumblesnort Bunny-Fur were an incredible pairing.

"So, that's Malcolm, and I already know Russell. That must make you Conner. Isn't there supposed to be another boy? Liam is his name, right?"

"My brother is recovering from wounds he recently sustained defending the city," said Conner, his tone measured.

"I'm sorry to hear that. Give him my regards," said Nathanial before smiling and pointing at Lord Rumblesnort Bunny-Fur. "And you have an El'orin cat. How marvelous!"

Eliana snaked her hand around Rumblesnort, who was sitting on the table, and pulled him tight against her body. He didn't seem to mind. If anything, he seemed out of sorts. Russell wasn't sure, but Rumblesnort appeared scared of Nate. His tail wasn't quite bushed, but his ears were back, and his hackles were up.

"Did you need to remove someone's El'orin? Arronhelm had me do that for a member of his Coterie once. Silver was her name, I believe. I put her El'orin inside a parrot."

Russell tapped the table and cleared his throat. Nathanial ignored him, so Russell did it again. When the annoying man finally turned to face him, Russell pointed at Professor Keldon. "Maybe this isn't a conversation we should be having right now?"

"Oh, sorry," said Nathanial.

"I'm not an idiot, you know," said Professor Keldon. "It's not like I'm unaware there are fundamental differences between us. I don't understand them, of course, but that is neither here nor there." The professor momentarily looked down at his hands before taking a deep breath. "Can we please just get on with the transaction?"

Nathanial sighed. "Very well," he said, as he set an ornately carved wooden box on the edge of the table. Reaching into one of the pockets of his robes, he produced a key, setting it on top of the box. "Please make sure everything is there."

Russell took a moment to study Nathanial's robe. It was black and covered in elaborate runes. While he wasn't skilled enough to decipher any of them, the sheer volume of runes surprised him. Russell's armored robe deepened his well. Conner's armored robe strengthened his spells. Both robes carried more runes than Malcolm's simple armor robe. Nathanial's robe displayed more runes than any of theirs, and it wasn't even close.

"Let me see," said Professor Keldon. He slid the box across the table until it was in front of him before opening it. "Water and earth elementals, and a Disintegrate spell. That should cover the scrolls. And here are the rings." The professor hummed softly as he rummaged around in the box. "Excellent. I believe everything is here."

"I've held up my end of the bargain," said Nathanial Norwitch. "Now it is your turn. Give me my spell."

"Are you sure you're okay with this, Ellie?" said Russell, but they already discussed it. He knew the answer. He was just asking out of kindness.

She nodded and placed a tiny glowing gem in his hand.

Russell smiled at Rumblesnort. "Are you willing to help me, buddy?"

Lord Rumblesnort Bunny-Fur glanced at Nathanial before climbing from Eliana's arms. He approached Russell, gently pressing his muzzle against Russell's nose. The cat licked a few times before biting.

Russell suppressed a yelp. "You'll help, but you're not happy about it, huh?"

Lord Rumblesnort Bunny-Fur nodded.

"Simply fascinating," breathed Nathanial. "Can the cat actually help him?"

"It's not something we're willing discuss," said Malcolm sternly.

Russell pushed all the distractions away. A few words were exchanged, but he was past the point of hearing them. His Portal spell required his complete concentration. Standing up, he spread his hands to his side and began to recite the first set of phrases. Immediately, Russell heard the Dreamer chanting along with him, showing him the proper pronunciation and rhythm.

He fanned his fingers and painted his first lines. Each of Russ's fingers painted a different beam in the air, each a slightly different hue of blue. Russell gently rotated his hands and bent his fingers in such a way as to make his magical lines twist around each other. It required tremendous concentration. He was grateful the Dreamer was reciting the words for him. It allowed him to focus on drawing his magical doorway.

Lord Rumblesnort Bunny-Fur interrupted his throaty purr to meow softly. Despite Russell's intense focus, all the chanting, and the words of the Dreamer, he heard the cat clearly. Whatever Rumblesnort did, Russell was grateful for it. Normally, his skin was burning by the time he reached this part of the spell.

Swirling energy built within Russell's body. It raced through his arms, flew out his fingers, and flowed into the Elestone. This was the first time he cast a spell into an Elestone. He didn't know what to expect, but he found the process easier than building a Portal large enough to transport people.

"Is it done?" said Nathanial. "I must say, that was most impressive. That seems to be a very complicated piece of magic. How was the cat involved?"

"Stop asking about the cat," growled Malcolm.

"But it's a fair question," said Nathanial. "I mean, is a cat required? Can I cast this spell without a cat?"

Russell picked up the Elestone and held it out for Nathanial. "Stop being shekking difficult. You know you don't need a damn cat to cast this spell. For that matter, you already pointed out that Rumblesnort isn't an ordinary cat."

"Yes, but he obviously helped you."

"Of course, he helped me!" snapped Russell. "I got knocked out for a week the first time I tried to cast this spell. The second time I tried, I pulled it off, but I nearly burned to death. I'm not some grand Archmage who's studied magic all his life. I'm just a shekking kid! Sometimes I need a little help!"

Nathanial Norwitch regarded him for a long moment before plucking the Elestone from his hands. "Very well. It seems our business has concluded, although I have half a mind to reclaim that box of scrolls and rings. As far as I'm concerned, you've exploited the Academy. You charged me far too much for this spell. Five rings are too many. Three would have been more appropriate."

"I wouldn't advise trying to reclaim that box," said Fahrilae. "I don't think it will end well for you."

Nathanial glared at Fahrilae, but said nothing. Russell couldn't imagine Nathanial was actually considering violence. He was terribly outnumbered.

"Just go, Nathanial," said Professor Keldon. "You accepted our terms. There is nothing more to be said."

"Very well," said Nathanial with a sigh. "I'm sure the Academy will survive for a year without magical rings to bribe its students with."

With the moment of tension gone, Russell flopped down in his chair, exhausted. Casting his Portal spell was never easy, even with Rumblesnort's help. "Have a nice night. It wasn't a pleasure doing business with you," he called to Nathanial as the man turned and stomped off.

"What an asshole," said Malcolm after Nathanial was well out of earshot.

"Sexist asshole," added Attia.

"What do you mean?" asked the professor.

"He went out of his way to identify all the boys, but he didn't even bother acknowledging me or Eliana."

Russell hadn't noticed, but it wouldn't surprise him if it were true. "I'm just happy it's over. Something about Nathanial scares me. I hope we never need to deal with him again."

"Agreed," said Professor Keldon as he retrieved a trio of rings from the ornate wooden box and set them on the table in front of him. "These are Rings of Power. If I'm reading the notations correctly, the one on the left is slightly stronger than the other two."

"Russell and I are receiving spells as well," said Eliana. "You take that one, Conner."

"Are you sure?"

"Of course, she is," said Russell.

"Okay, thanks," mumbled Conner, as he retrieved the ring.

Russell waited for Eliana to choose one of the remaining two before grabbing the third. He knew they were essentially the same, but giving her the first pick still seemed like the right thing to do.

"Here are your elemental spells," said the professor, as he handed Eliana a pair of scrolls. "And for you, Russell, Disintegrate," he said, handing Russell a tightly bound roll of parchment.

Russell wanted to read the scroll now, but he didn't think it would be appropriate. There were still another two rings to distribute, and it was rare that all of his friends were gathered together. Then again, Liam wasn't there. They weren't all together.

"This Ring of Protection is for you, Attia," said the professor, as he handed her a golden ring. "And finally, this ring is for Liam. Conner, I think you should hold on to it."

Conner took a deep breath. He looked at each of his friends for a moment before speaking. "Liam will be back with us before you know it."

"It's okay, Conner," said Eliana softly. "We understand."

"I'm not sure how I'm going to do it, but I'm going to," continued Conner, ignoring her. "Nothing will stop me."

Attia placed her hand on Conner's shoulder. "This isn't something you have to do alone, Conner. If you need help, we're here for you."

"I know," said Conner, looking away. "But this is something that I want to do on my own. I hope you can understand that."

"You won't catch me throwing any stones," said Malcolm.

Russell didn't like what he was hearing. He knew Malcolm was preparing to do some truly horrible things, but that didn't bother him. Ever since the Other possessed Malcolm, he was destined to walk a dark path.

But Conner always seemed different to him. Then again, Conner spent most of his time in the House of Healing, working with Raelyn. Russell knew Conner was studying demonology. They all knew it.

As much as Russell adored and respected Raelyn, he knew she was a succubus. She was a demon, specifically designed to coerce, enthrall, and corrupt. Was she needlessly dragging Conner along a dark and dangerous path? He didn't want to believe it, but anything was possible.

"I look forward to the day he comes back to us," said Attia, breaking the silence that suddenly smothered the group like a blanket.

"To Liam," said Eliana, though her heart didn't seem in it.

"Yes," said Russell. He added as much enthusiasm to his voice as he could muster. He didn't like the thought of Conner making dark deals to save his brother, but ultimately, it was his choice. If Conner wanted to make sacrifices, Russell planned to support him every step of the way. They weren't children anymore. They were each growing in their own directions, walking their own paths. There was no sense in fighting it. "To Liam, and his safe return."

Epilogue
Kostanus

Kostanus crouched off to the side, observing the gathering. The talons turned and ran the moment the Lurker died. They had already broken through the city's defenses. They could have done considerable damage if they pressed the assault, but perhaps seeing their God die was too much for them.

Countless people perished during the battle. The city's streets and walls were in shambles. Most of their skiffs and boats were sitting at the bottom of the swamp. And all the while, the storms raged on, flooding the region with more water than the swamp seemed prepared to deal with.

But still, they won!

In truth, Gunther won the battle. The rest of them just survived long enough to see it happen. Kostanus didn't have the right vantage point to see Gunther fight the Lurker, but he saw the flashes of blue light. In Gunther's final hour of need, whatever created those Portals for him returned. Kostanus believed it was the spirit of Arronhelm. Maybe it was a silly notion, but he didn't care.

"As we reflect on all we've been through," bellowed Chancellor Falstaff. "Losing the Citadel, the constant attacks as we fled through the swamps, the struggle to build a new home for ourselves, and now this." He paused, letting the echoes of his magically amplified voice reverberate across the water. "The Lurker and his armies, showing up on our very doorstep, laying siege on our home."

Kostanus was grateful for the rainy, overcast day. The main assembly hall collapsed during the battle, forcing the chancellor to host his gathering outside. The rain was unpleasant, but a few hours beneath the withering sun would have been downright miserable.

"Yet we're still here," continued Chancellor Falstaff. "Hosts of demons and orcs and even an ancient God tried to destroy us, yet we still stand!" Falstaff sent a cascade of electricity racing through the air. The crowd responded with bellows and cheers. "Today marks a new day! Yes, we need to rebuild, but our civilization has never been stronger. We are more than ready for this challenge."

Kostanus thought the chancellor was going to address the shimmering turquoise glow in the waters, but perhaps it was best not to. The Lurker's body disappeared overnight, leaving a strange glow in its place. Despite the currents, the turquoise light never left the area. Had it simply been discoloration in the water, like blood, the currents would have carried it downriver, but the magical light remained in the region.

Pathmaker Norinae believed it was the essence of the Lurker. She thought it was some kind of ancient magic and hoped it would bring tremendous vibrance and growth to the region. Kostanus wanted to believe her, but what if she was wrong? The Lurker didn't seem like a helpful creature. What if the strange energy was some kind of terrible curse that it left behind after its passing?

"But our victory came at a terrible price," shouted the chancellor. "Too many brave men and women died defending our home, and in time, we will honor each and every one of them, but today we need to pay our respects to the greatest among us." Once again, Chancellor Falstaff paused to let his voice echo across the water. "Today, we honor Gunther."

Kostanus shook his head and picked up his bulging backpack from the ground next to him. The last thing he wanted to listen to was Falstaff talk about Gunther. The two of them never got along. As far as Kostanus was concerned, Falstaff had no business talking about Gunther.

"Most of you didn't know Gunther like I did. He was difficult and uncompromising, yet honorable. One couldn't help but admire—"

A small bubble of silence sprung up around Kostanus, protecting him from the dishonest blather of Chancellor Falstaff. Kostanus understood what was going on. Gunther died in battle, but he managed to take the Lurker with him. In doing so, he saved their civilization. The chancellor needed to celebrate and elevate Gunther's feats. In short, he was turning Gunther into a martyr.

It needed to happen, but it was the last thing Gunther would have wanted. The least Kostanus could do was avoid listening to the speech. He was happy with his memories of Gunther. He didn't need the man to be any better or worse than the person he was.

Tossing his backpack over his shoulders, Kostanus left the gathering. A few people waved to him as he passed, but he didn't take the time to acknowledge them. He made up his mind earlier this morning, and wasn't interested in anyone challenging his decision.

He left a long note for Norinae, explaining his plans to her and the others. He knew they would have tried to convince him to stay, but he needed to live his life as he saw fit. While he enjoyed the time he spent with this group, other challenges and adventures awaited him. He hoped to make it this far south again someday, hopefully with all the ingredients necessary to produce several scrolls of Breath of Battle, but there were no promises.

There never were.

Countless mysteries waited for him to the north. He wanted to see what became of the Citadel. He wondered if it was still standing, or if the orcs let it crumble under the weight of this season's torrential rains.

More than that, he wanted to revisit the Theleram. He wanted to understand what happened to Attia and the others. There were signs of battle, but no bodies. He knew in his bones that they didn't die in that library, but if not, what happened to them?

One thing was certain. He wasn't going to find the answers to his questions deep in the bowels of this sweltering, stinking swamp.

About the Author

A classical pianist and marginal triathlete, Jeff Konkol is permitted to live in the sprawling home of four very large cats. He published his first table top RPG, *Of Gods and Men,* in the early 90s, and has been running games within that setting ever since. He recently returned to writing with the hope of sharing those stories with a wider audience.

Other Titles by J.R. Konkol

REBIRTH OF THE FALLEN SERIES

Citadel of the Fallen

Gathering of the Fallen

Flight of the Fallen

The Crumbling City

The Sundered City

The Fallen City

Crumbling Alliances – Coming Soon

THE FELINITY CHRONICLES

The Guardian's Gambit

Note from JR Konkol

Word-of-mouth is crucial for any author to succeed. If you enjoyed *Crumbling Alliances*, please leave a review online—anywhere you are able. Even if it's just a sentence or two. It would make all the difference and would be very much appreciated.

Thanks!
JR Konkol

We hope you enjoyed reading this title from:

www.blackrosewriting.com

Subscribe to our mailing list – *The Rosevine* – and receive **FREE** books, daily deals, and stay current with news about upcoming releases and our hottest authors.
Scan the QR code below to sign up.

Already a subscriber? Please accept a sincere thank you for being a fan of Black Rose Writing authors.

View other Black Rose Writing titles at www.blackrosewriting.com/books and use promo code **PRINT** to receive a **20% discount** when purchasing.